Both Sides the Border

G. A. Henty

Contents

BOTH SIDES THE BORDER

BY

G. A. Henty

Preface.

The four opening years of the fifteenth century were among the most stirring in the history of England. Owen Glendower carried fire and slaughter among the Welsh marches, captured most of the strong places held by the English, and foiled three invasions, led by the king himself. The northern borders were invaded by Douglas; who, after devastating a large portion of Northumberland, Cumberland, and Durham, was defeated and taken prisoner at the battle of Homildon, by the Earl of Northumberland, and his son Hotspur. Then followed the strange and unnatural coalition between the Percys, Douglas of Scotland, Glendower of Wales, and Sir Edmund Mortimer--a coalition that would assuredly have overthrown the king, erected the young Earl of March as a puppet monarch under the tutelage of the Percys, and secured the independence of Wales, had the royal forces arrived one day later at Shrewsbury, and so allowed the confederate armies to unite.

King Henry's victory there, entailing the death of Hotspur and the capture of Douglas, put an end to this formidable insurrection; for, although the Earl of Northumberland twice subsequently raised the banner of revolt, these risings were easily crushed; while Glendower's power waned, and order, never again to be broken, was at length restored in Wales. The continual state of unrest and chronic warfare, between the inhabitants of both sides of the border, was full of adventures as stirring and romantic as that in which the hero of the story took part.

G. A. Henty.

Chapter 1: A Border Hold.

A lad was standing on the little lookout turret, on the top of a border fortalice. The place was evidently built solely with an eye to defence, comfort being an altogether secondary consideration. It was a square building, of rough stone, the walls broken only by narrow loopholes; and the door, which was ten feet above the ground, was reached by broad wooden steps, which could be hauled up in case of necessity; and were, in fact, raised every night.

The building was some forty feet square. The upper floor was divided into several chambers, which were the sleeping places of its lord and master, his family, and the women of the household. The floor below, onto which the door from without opened, was undivided save by two rows of stone pillars that supported the beams of the floor above. In one corner the floor, some fifteen feet square, was raised somewhat above the general level. This was set aside for the use of the master and the family. The rest of the apartment was used as the living and sleeping room of the followers, and hinds, of the fortalice.

The basement--which, although on a level with the ground outside, could be approached only by a trapdoor and ladder from the room above--was the storeroom, and contained sacks of barley and oatmeal, sides of bacon, firewood, sacks of beans, and trusses of hay for the use of the horses and cattle, should the place have to stand a short siege. In the centre was a well.

The roof of the house was flat, and paved with square blocks of stone; a parapet three feet high surrounded it. In the centre was the lookout tower, rising twelve feet above it; and over the door another turret, projecting some eighteen inches beyond the wall of the house, slits being cut in the stone floor through which missiles could be dropped, or boiling lead poured, upon any trying to assault the entrance. Outside was a courtyard, extending round the house. It was some ten yards across, and surrounded by a wall twelve feet high, with a square turret at each corner.

Everything was roughly constructed, although massive and solid. With the exception of the door, and the steps leading to it, no wood had been used in the construction. The very beams were of rough stone, the floors were of the same material. It was clearly the object of the builders to erect a fortress that could defy fire, and could only be destroyed at the cost of enormous labour.

This was indeed a prime necessity, for the hold stood in the wild country between the upper waters of the Coquet and the Reed river. Harbottle and Longpikes rose but a few miles away, and the whole country was broken up by deep ravines and valleys, fells and crags. From the edge of the moorland, a hundred yards from the outer wall, the ground dropped sharply down into the valley, where the two villages of Yardhope lay on a little burn running into the Coquet.

In other directions the moor extended for a distance of nearly a mile. On this two or three score of cattle, and a dozen shaggy little horses, were engaged in an effort to keep life together, upon the rough herbage that grew among the heather and blocks of stones, scattered everywhere.

Presently the lad caught sight of the flash of the sun, which had but just risen behind him, on a spearhead at the western edge of the moor. He ran down at once, from his post, to the principal room.

"They are coming, Mother," he exclaimed. "I have just seen the sun glint on a spearhead."

"I trust that they are all there," she said, and then turned to two women by the fire, and bade them put on more wood and get the pots boiling.

"Go up again, Oswald; and, as soon as you can make out your father's figure, bring me down news. I have not closed an eye for the last two nights, for 'tis a more dangerous enterprise than usual on which they have gone."

"Father always comes home all right, Mother," the boy said confidently, "and they have a strong band this time. They were to have been joined by Thomas Gray and his following, and Forster of Currick, and John Liddel, and Percy Hope of Bilderton. They must have full sixty spears. The Bairds are like to pay heavily for their last raid hither."

Dame Forster did not reply, and Oswald ran up again to the lookout. By this time the party for whom he was watching had reached the moor. It consisted of twelve or fourteen horsemen, all clad in dark armour, carrying very long spears and mounted on small, but wiry, horses. They were driving before them a knot of some forty or fifty cattle, and three of them led horses carrying heavy burdens. Oswald's quick eye noticed that four of the horsemen were not carrying their spears.

"They are three short of their number," he said to himself, "and those four must all be sorely wounded. Well, it might have been worse."

Oswald had been brought up to regard forays and attacks as ordinary incidents of life. Watch and ward were always kept in the little fortalice, especially when the nights were dark and misty, for there was never any saying when a party of Scottish borderers might make an attack; for the truces, so often concluded between the border wardens, had but slight effect on the prickers, as the small chieftains on both sides were called, who maintained a constant state of warfare against each other.

The Scotch forays were more frequent than those from the English side of the border; not because the people were more warlike, but because they were poorer, and depended more entirely upon plunder for their subsistence. There was but little difference of race between the peoples on the opposite side of the border. Both were largely of mixed Danish and Anglo-Saxon blood; for, when William the Conqueror carried fire and sword through Northumbria, great numbers of the inhabitants moved north, and settled in the district beyond the reach of the Norman arms.

On the English side of the border the population were, in time, leavened by Norman blood; as the estates were granted by William to his barons. These often married the heiresses of the dispossessed families, while their followers found wives among the native population.

The frequent wars with the Scots, in which every man capable of bearing arms in the Northern Counties had to take part; and the incessant border warfare, maintained a most martial spirit among the population, who considered retaliation for injuries received to be a natural and lawful act. This was, to some extent, heightened by the fact that the terms of many of the truces specifically permitted those who had suffered losses on either side to pursue their plunderers across the border. These raids were not accompanied by bloodshed, except when resistance was made; for between the people, descended as they were from a common stock, there was no active animosity, and at ordinary times there was free and friendly intercourse between them.

There were, however, many exceptions to the rule that unresisting persons were not injured. Between many families on opposite sides of the border there existed blood feuds, arising from the fact that members of one or the other had been killed in forays; and in these cases bitter and bloody reprisals were made, on either side. The very border line was ill defined, and people on one side frequently settled on the other, as is shown by the fact that several of the treaties contained provisions that those who had so moved might change their nationality, and be accounted as Scotch or Englishmen, as the case might be.

Between the Forsters and the Bairds such a feud had existed for three generations. It had begun in a raid by the latter. The Forster of that time had repulsed the attack, and had with his own hand killed one of the Bairds. Six months later he was surprised and killed on his own hearthstone, at a time when his son and most of his retainers were away on a raid. From that time the animosity between the two families had been unceasing, and several lives had been lost on both sides. The Bairds with a large party had, three months before, carried fire and sword through the district bordering on the main road, as far as Elsdon on the east, and Alwinton on the north. News of their coming had, however, preceded them. The villagers of Yardhope had just time to take refuge at Forster's hold, and had repulsed the determined attacks made upon it; until Sir Robert Umfraville brought a strong party to their assistance, and drove the Bairds back towards the frontier.

The present raid, from which the party was returning, had been organized partly to recoup those who took part in it for the loss of their cattle on that occasion, and partly to take vengeance upon the Bairds. As was the custom on both sides of the border, these expeditions were generally composed of members of half a dozen families, with their followers; the one who was, at once, most energetic and best acquainted with the intricacies of the country, and the paths across fells and moors, being chosen as leader.

Presently, Oswald Forster saw one of the party wave his hand; and at his order four or five of the horsemen rode out, and began to drive the scattered cattle and horses towards the house. Oswald at once ran down.

"Father is all right, Mother. He has just given orders to the men, and they are driving all the animals in, so I suppose that the Bairds must be in pursuit. I had better tell the men to get on their armour."

Without waiting for an answer, he told six men, who were eating their breakfast at the farther end of the room, to make an end of their meal, and get on their steel caps and breast and back pieces, and take their places in the turret over the gate into the yard. In a few minutes the animals began to pour in, first those of the homestead, then the captured herd, weary and exhausted with their long and hurried journey; then came the master, with his followers.

Mary Forster and her son stood at the top of the steps, ready to greet him. The gate into the yard was on the opposite side to that of the doorway of the fortalice, in order that assailants who had carried it should have to pass round under the fire of the archers in the turrets, before they could attack the building itself.

She gave a little cry as her husband came up. His left arm was in a sling, his helmet was cleft through, and a bandage showed beneath it.

"Do not be afraid, wife," he said cheerily. "We have had hotter work than we expected; but, so far as I am concerned, there is no great harm done. I am sorry to say that we have lost Long Hal, and Rob Finch, and Smedley. Two or three others are sorely wounded, and I fancy few have got off altogether scatheless.

"All went well, until we stopped to wait for daybreak, three miles from Allan Baird's place. Some shepherd must have got sight of us as we halted, for we found him and his men up and ready. They had not had time, however, to drive in the cattle; and seeing that we should like enough have the Bairds swarming down upon us, before we could take Allan's place, we contented ourselves with gathering the cattle and driving them off. There were about two hundred of them.

"We went fast, but in two hours we saw the Bairds coming in pursuit; and as it was clear that they would overtake us, hampered as we were with the cattle, we stood and made defence. There was not much difference in numbers, for the Bairds had not had time to gather in all their strength. The fight was a stiff one. On our side Percy Hope was killed, and John Liddel so sorely wounded that there is no hope of his life. We had sixteen men killed outright, and few of us but are more or less scarred. On their side Allan Baird was killed; and John was smitten down, but how sorely wounded I cannot say for certain, for they put him on a horse, and took him away at once. They left twenty behind them on the ground dead; and the rest, finding that we were better men than they, rode off again.

"William Baird himself had not come up. His hold was too far for the news to have reached him, as we knew well enough; but doubtless he came up, with his following, a few hours after we had beaten his kinsmen. But we have ridden too fast for him to overtake us. We struck off north as soon as we crossed the border, travelled all night by paths by which they will find it difficult to follow or track us, especially as we broke up into four parties, and each chose their own way.

"I have driven all our cattle in, in case they should make straight here, after losing our track. Of course, there were many who fought against us who know us all well; but even were it other than the Bairds we had despoiled, they would hardly follow us so far across the border to fetch their cattle.

"As for the Bairds, the most notorious of the Scottish raiders, for them to claim the right of following would be beyond all bearing. Why, I don't believe there was a head of cattle among the whole herd that had not been born, and bred, on this side of the border. It is we who have been fetching back stolen goods."

By this time, he and his men had entered the house, and those who had gone through the fray scatheless were, assisted by the women, removing the armour from their wounded comrades. Those who had been forced to relinquish their spears were first attended to.

There was no thought of sending for a leech. Every man and woman within fifty miles of the border was accustomed to the treatment of wounds, and in every hold was a store of bandages, styptics, and unguents ready for instant use. Most of the men were very sorely wounded; and had they been of less hardy frame, and less inured to hardships, could not have supported the long ride. John Forster, before taking off his own armour, saw that their wounds were first attended to by his wife and her women.

"I think they will all do," he said, "and that they will live to strike another blow at the Bairds, yet.

"Now, Oswald, unbuckle my harness. Your mother will bandage up my arm and head, and Elspeth shall bring up a full tankard from below, for each of us. A draught of beer will do as much good as all the salves and medicaments.

"Do you take the first drink, Jock Samlen, and then go up to the watchtower. I see the men have been posted in the wall turrets. One of them shall relieve you, shortly."

As soon as the wounds were dressed, bowls of porridge were served round;

then one of the men who had remained at home was posted at the lookout; and, after the cattle had been seen to, all who had been on the road stretched themselves on some rushes at one end of the room, and were, in a few minutes, sound asleep.

"I wonder whether we shall ever have peace in the land, Oswald," his mother said with a sigh; as, having seen that the women had all in readiness for the preparation of the midday meal, she sat down on a low stool, by his side.

"I don't see how we ever can have, Mother, until either we conquer Scotland, or the Scotch shall be our masters. It is not our fault. They are ever raiding and plundering, and heed not the orders of Douglas, or the other Lords of the Marches."

"We are almost as bad as they are, Oswald."

"Nay, Mother, we do but try to take back our own; as father well said, the cattle that were brought in are all English, that have been taken from us by the Bairds; and we do but pay them back in their own coin. It makes but little difference whether we are at war or peace. These reiving caterans are ever on the move. It was but last week that Adam Gordon and his bands wasted Tynedale, as far as Bellingham; and carried off, they say, two thousand head of cattle, and slew many of the people. If we did not cross the border sometimes, and give them a lesson, they would become so bold that there would be no limit to their raids."

"That is all true enough, Oswald, but it is hard that we should always require to be on the watch, and that no one within forty miles of the border can, at any time, go to sleep with the surety that he will not, ere morning, hear the raiders knocking at his gate."

"Methinks that it would be dull, were there nought to do but to look after the cattle," Oswald replied.

It seemed to him, bred up as he had been amid constant forays and excitements, that the state of things was a normal one; and that it was natural that a man should need to have his spear ever ready at hand, and to give or take hard blows.

"Besides," he went on, "though we carry off each others' cattle, and fetch them home again, we are not bad friends while the truces hold, save in the case of those who have blood feuds. It was but last week that Allan Armstrong and his two sisters were staying here with us; and I promised that, ere long, I would ride across the border and spend a week with them."

"Yes, but that makes it all the worse. Adam Armstrong married my sister Elizabeth, whom he first met at Goddington fair; and, indeed, there are few families, on either side of the border, who have not both English and Scotch blood in their veins. It is natural we should be friends, seeing how often we have held Berwick, Roxburgh, and Dumfries; and how often, in times of peace, Scotchmen come across the border to trade at the fairs. Why should it not be so, when we speak the same tongue and, save for the border line, are one people? Though, indeed, it is different in Kirkcudbright and Wigtown, where they are Galwegians, and their tongue is scarce understood by the border Scots. 'Tis strange that those on one side of the border, and those on the other, cannot keep the peace towards each other."

"But save when the kingdoms are at war, Mother, we do keep the peace, except in the matter of cattle lifting; and bear no enmity towards each other, save when blood is shed. In wartime each must, of course, fight for his nation and as his lord orders him. We have wasted Scotland again and again, from end to end; and they have swept the Northern Counties well nigh as often.

"I have heard father say that, eight times in the last hundred years, this hold has been levelled to the ground. It only escaped, last time, because he built it so strongly of stone that they could not fire it; and it would have taken them almost as long, to pick it to pieces, as it took him to build it."

"Yes, that was when you were an infant, Oswald. When we heard the Scotch army was marching this way, we took refuge with all the cattle and horses among the Pikes; having first carried out and burnt all the forage and stores, and leaving nothing that they could set fire to. Your father has often laughed at the thought of how angry they must have been, when they found that there was no mischief that they could do; for, short of a long stay, which they never make, there was no way in which they could damage it. Ours was the only house that escaped scot free, for thirty miles round.

"But indeed, 'tis generally but parties of pillagers who trouble this part of the country, even when they invade England. There is richer booty, by far, to be gathered in Cumberland and Durham; for here we have nought but our cattle and horses, and of these they have as many on their side of the border. It is the plunder of the towns that chiefly attracts them, and while they go past here empty handed, they always carry great trains of booty on their backward way."

"Still, it would be dull work if there were no fighting, Mother."

"There is no fighting in Southern England, Oswald, save for those who go across the sea to fight the French; and yet, I suppose they find life less dull than we do. They have more to do. Here there is little tillage, the country is poor; and who would care to break up the land and to raise crops, when any night your ricks might be in flames, and your granaries plundered? Thus there is nought for us to do but to keep cattle, which need but little care and attention, and which can be driven off to the fells when the Scots make a great raid. But in the south, as I have heard, there is always much for farmers to attend to; and those who find life dull can always enter the service of some warlike lord, and follow him across the sea."

Oswald shook his head. The quiet pursuits of a farmer seemed to him to be but a poor substitute for the excitement of border war.

"It may be as you say, Mother; but for my part, I would rather enter the service of the Percys, and gain honour under their banner, than remain here day after day, merely giving aid in driving the cattle in and out, and wondering when the Bairds are coming this way, again."

His mother shook her head. Her father and two brothers had both been slain, the last time a Scottish army had crossed the border; and although she naturally did not regard constant troubles in the same light in which a southern woman would have viewed them, she still longed for peace and quiet; and was in constant fear that sooner or later the feud with the Bairds, who were a powerful family, would cost her husband his life.

Against open force she had little fear. The hold could resist an attack for days, and long ere it yielded, help would arrive; but although the watch was vigilant, and every precaution taken, it might be captured by a sudden night attack. William Baird had, she knew, sworn a great oath that Yardhope Hold should one day be destroyed; and the Forsters wiped out, root and branch. And the death of his cousin Allan, in the last raid, would surely fan the fire of his hatred against them.

"One never can say what may happen," she said, after a pause; "but if at any time evil should befall us, and you escape, remember that your uncle Alwyn is in Percy's service; and you cannot do better than go to him, and place yourself under his protection, and act as he may advise you. I like not the thought that you should become a man-at-arms; and yet methinks that it is no more dangerous than that of a householder on the fells. At least, in a strong castle a man can sleep without fear;

whereas none can say as much, here."

"If aught should happen to my father and you, Mother, you may be sure that I should share in it. The Bairds would spare no one, if they captured the hold. And although Father will not, as yet, take me with him on his forays, I should do my share of fighting, if the hold were attacked."

"I am sure that you would, Oswald; and were it captured I have no doubt that, as you say, you would share our fate. I speak not with any thought that it is likely things will turn out as I say; but they may do so, and therefore I give you my advice, to seek out your uncle. As to a capture of our hold, of that I have generally but little fear; but the fact that your father has been wounded, and three of his men killed, and that another Baird has fallen, has brought the possibility that it may happen more closely to my mind, this morning, than usual.

"Now, my boy, you had best spend an hour in cleaning up your father's armour and arms. The steel cap must go to the armourer at Alwinton, for repair; but you can get some of the dints out of his breast and back pieces, and can give them a fresh coat of black paint;" for the borderers usually darkened their armour so that, in their raids, their presence should not be betrayed by the glint of sun or moon upon them.

Oswald at once took up the armour, and went down the steps into the court-yard, so that the sound of his hammer should not disturb the sleepers. As, with slight but often repeated blows, he got out the dents that had been made in the fray, he thought over what his mother had been saying. To him also the death of three of the men, who had for years been his companions, came as a shock. It was seldom, indeed, that the forays for cattle lifting had such serious consequences. As a rule they were altogether bloodless; and it was only because of the long feud with the Bairds, and the fact that some warning of the coming of the party had, in spite of their precaution, reached Allan Baird; that on the present occasion such serious results had ensued.

Had it not been for this, the cattle would have been driven off without resistance, for Allan Baird's own household would not have ventured to attack so strong a party. No attempt would have been made to assault his hold; for he had often heard his father say that, even in the case of a blood feud, he held that houses should not be attacked, and their occupants slain. If both parties met under arms the matter was different; but that, in spite of the slaying of his own father by them, he would not kill even a Baird on his hearthstone.

Still, a Baird had been killed, and assuredly William Baird would not be deterred by any similar scruples. His pitiless ferocity was notorious, and even his own countrymen cried out against some of his deeds, and the Earl of Douglas had several times threatened to hand him over to the English authorities; but the Bairds were powerful, and could, with their allies, place four or five hundred men in the field; and, in the difficult country in which they lived, could have given a great deal of trouble, even to Douglas. Therefore nothing had come of his threats, and the Bairds had continued to be the terror of that part of the English border that was the most convenient for their operations.

Oswald was now past sixteen, and promised to be as big a man as his father, who was a fine specimen of the hardy Northumbrian race--tall, strong, and sinewy. He had felt hurt when his father had refused to allow him to take part in the foray.

"Time enough, lad, time enough," he had said, when the lad had made his petition to do so. "You are not strong enough, yet, to hold your own against one of the Bairds' moss troopers, should it come to fighting. In another couple of years it will be time enough to think of your going on such an excursion as this. You are clever with your arms, I will freely admit; as you ought to be, seeing that you practise for two hours a day with the men. But strength counts as well as skill, and you want both when you ride against the Bairds; besides, at present you have still much to learn about the paths through the fells, and across the morasses. If you are ever to become a leader, you must know them well enough to traverse them on the darkest night, or through the thickest mist."

"I think that I do know most of them, Father."

"Yes, I think you do, on this side of the border; but you must learn those on the other side, as well. They are, indeed, of even greater importance in case of pursuit, or for crossing the border unobserved. Hitherto, I have forbidden you to cross the line, but in future Mat Wilson shall go with you. He knows the Scotch passes and defiles, better than any in the band; and so that you don't go near the Bairds' country, you can traverse them safely, so long as the truce lasts."

For years, indeed, Oswald, on one of the hardy little horses, had ridden over the country in company with one or other of the men; and had become familiar with every morass, moor, fell, and pass, down to the old Roman wall to the south, and as far north as Wooler, being frequently absent for three or four days at a time. He had several times ridden into Scotland, to visit the Armstrongs and other friends of the family; but he had always travelled by the roads, and knew nothing of the hill paths on that side. His life had, in fact, been far from dull, for they had many friends and connections in the villages at the foot of the Cheviots, and he was frequently away from home.

His journeys were generally performed on horseback, but his father encouraged him to take long tramps on foot, in order that he might strengthen his muscles; and would, not infrequently, give him leave to pay visits on condition that he travelled on foot, instead of in the saddle.

Constant exercise in climbing, riding, and with his weapons; and at wrestling and other sports, including the bow, had hardened every muscle of his frame, and he was capable of standing any fatigues; and although his father said that he could not hold his own against men, he knew that the lad could do so against any but exceptionally powerful ones; and believed that, when the time came, he would, like himself, be frequently chosen as leader in border forays. He could already draw the strongest bow to the arrowhead, and send a shaft with a strength that would suffice to pierce the light armour worn by the Scotch borderers. It was by the bow that the English gained the majority of their victories over their northern neighbours; who did not take to the weapon, and were unable to stand for a moment against the English archers, who not only loved it as a sport, but were compelled by many ordinances to practise with it from their childhood.

Of other education he had none, but in this respect he was no worse off than the majority of the knights and barons of the time, who were well content to trust to monkish scribes to draw up such documents as were required, and to affix their seal to them. He himself had once, some six years before, expressed a wish to be sent for a year to the care of the monks at Rothbury, whose superior was a distant connection of his father, in order to be taught to read and write; but John Forster had scoffed at the idea.

"You have to learn to be a man, lad," he had said, "and the monks will never teach you that. I do not know one letter from another, nor did my father, or any of my forebears, and we were no worse for it. On the marches, unless a man means to become a monk, he has to learn to make his sword guard his head, to send an arrow straight to the mark, to know every foot of the passes, and to be prepared, at the order of his lord, to defend his country against the Scots.

"These are vastly more important matters than reading and writing; which are, so far as I can see, of no use to any fair man, whose word is his bond, and who deals with honest men. I can reckon up, if I sell so many cattle, how much has to be paid, and more of learning than that I want not. Nor do you, and every hour spent on it would be as good as wasted. As to the monks, Heaven forfend that you should ever become one. They are good men, I doubt not, and I suppose that it is necessary that some should take to it; but that a man who has the full possession of his limbs should mew himself up, for life, between four walls, passing his time in vigils and saying masses, in reading books and distributing alms, seems to me to be a sort of madness."

"I certainly do not wish to become a monk, Father, but I thought that I should like to learn to read and write."

"And when you have learnt it, what then, Oswald? Books are expensive play-things, and no scrap of writing has ever been inside the walls of Yardhope Hold, since it was first built here, as far as I know. As to writing, it would be of still less use. If a man has a message to send, he can send it by a hired man, if it suits him not to ride himself. Besides, if he had written it, the person he sent it to would not be able to read it, and would have to go to some scribe for an interpretation of its contents.

"No, no, my lad, you have plenty to learn before you come to be a man, without bothering your head with this monkish stuff. I doubt if Hotspur, himself, can do more than sign his name to a parchment; and what is good enough for the Percys, is surely good enough for you."

The idea had, in fact, been put into Oswald's head by his mother. At that time the feud with the Bairds had burned very hotly, and it would have lessened her anxieties had the boy been bestowed, for a time, in a convent. Oswald himself felt no disappointment at his father's refusal to a petition that he would never have made, had not his mother dilated to him, on several occasions, upon the great advantage of learning.

No thought of repeating the request had ever entered his mind. His father had thought more of it, and had several times expressed grave regret, to his wife, over such an extraordinary wish having occurred to their son.

"The boy has nothing of a milksop about him," he said; "and is, for his age, full of spirit and courage. How so strange an idea could have occurred to him is more than I can imagine. I should as soon expect to see an owlet, in a sparrow hawk's nest, as a monk hatched in Yardhope Hold."

His wife discreetly kept silence as to the fact that she, herself, had first put the idea in the boy's head; for although Mary Forster was mistress inside of the hold, in all other matters John was masterful, and would brook no meddling, even by her. The subject, therefore, of Oswald's learning to read and write, was never renewed.

Chapter 2: Across The Border.

Amost vigilant watch was kept up, for the next week, at Yardhope Hold. At night, three or four of the troopers were posted four or five miles from the hold, on the roads by which an enemy was likely to come; having under them the fleetest horses on the moor. When a week passed there was some slight relaxation in the watch, for it was evident that the Bairds intended to bide their time for a stroke, knowing well that they would not be likely to be able to effect a surprise, at present. The outlying posts were, therefore, no longer maintained; but the dogs of the hold, fully a dozen in number, were chained nightly in a circle three or four hundred yards outside it; and their barking would, at once, apprise the watchers in the turrets on the walls of the approach of any body of armed men.

Two days later, Oswald started for his promised visit to the Armstrongs. It was not considered necessary that he should be accompanied by any of the troopers, for Hiniltie lay but a few miles across the frontier. In high spirits he galloped away and, riding through Yardhope, was soon at Alwinton; and thence took the track through Kidland Lee, passed round the head of the Usmay brook, along the foot of Maiden Cross Hill, and crossed the frontier at Windy Guile. Here he stood on the crest of the Cheviots and, descending, passed along at the foot of Windburgh Hill; and by noon entered the tiny hamlet of Hiniltie, above which, perched on one of the spurs of the hill, stood the Armstrongs' hold. It was smaller than that of Yardhope, and had no surrounding wall; but, like it, was built for defence against a sudden attack.

Adam Armstrong was on good terms with his neighbours across the border. Although other members of his family were frequently engaged in forays, it was seldom, indeed, that he buckled on armour, and only when there was a general call to arms. He was, however, on bad terms with the Bairds, partly because his wife was a sister of Forster's, partly because of frays that had arisen between his herdsmen and those of the Bairds, for his cattle wandered far and wide on the mountain slopes to the south, and sometimes passed the ill-defined line, beyond which the Bairds regarded the country as their own. Jedburgh was but ten miles away, Hawick but six or seven, and any stay after the sun rose would speedily have brought strong bodies of men from these towns, as well as from his still nearer neighbours, at Chester, Abbotrule, and Hobkirk.

Oswald's approach was seen, and two of his cousins--Allan, who was a lad of about the same age, and Janet, a year younger--ran out from the house to meet him.

"We have been expecting you for the last ten days," the former exclaimed, "and had well nigh given you up."

"I hold you to be a laggard," the girl added, "and unless you can duly excuse yourself, shall have naught to say to you."

"My excuse is a good one, Janet. My father made a foray, a fortnight since, into the Bairds' country, to rescue some of the cattle they had driven off from our neighbours, some days before. There was a sharp fight, and Allan Baird was killed; and since then we have been expecting a return visit from them, and have been sleeping with our arms beside us. Doubtless they will come someday, but as it is evident they don't mean to come at present, my father let me leave."

"In that case we must forgive you," the girl said. "Some rumours of the fray have reached us, and my father shook his head gravely, when he heard that another Baird had been killed by the Forsters."

"It was not only us," Oswald replied. "There were some of the Liddels, and the Hopes, and other families, engaged. My father was chosen as chief; but this time it was not our quarrel, but theirs, for we had lost no cattle, and my father only joined because they had aided us last time, and he could not hold back now. Of course, he was chosen as chief because he knows the country so well."

"Well, come in, Oswald. It is poor hospitality to keep you talking here, outside the door."

A boy had already taken charge of Oswald's horse and, after unstrapping his valise, had led it to a stable that formed the basement of the house.

"Well, laddie, how fares it with you, at home?" Adam Armstrong said, heartily, as they mounted the steps to the main entrance. "We have heard of your wild doings with the Bairds. 'Tis a pity that these feuds should go on, from father to son, ever getting more and more bitter. But there, we can no more change a borderer's nature than you can stop the tide in the Solway. I hear that it was well nigh a pitched battle."

"There was hard fighting," Oswald replied. "Three of our troopers, and eight or ten of the others were killed. My father was twice wounded, one of the Hopes was killed, and a Liddel severely wounded. But from what they say, the Bairds suffered more. Had they not done so, there would have been a hot pursuit; but as far as we know there was none."

"The Bairds will bide their time," Armstrong said gravely. "They are dour men, and will take their turn, though they wait ten years for it."

"At any rate they won't catch us sleeping, Uncle; and come they however strong they may, they will find it hard work to capture the Hold."

"Ay, ay, lad, but I don't think they will try to knock their heads against your wall. They are more like to sweep down on a sudden, and your watchman will need keen eyes to make them out before they are thundering at the gate, or climbing up the wall. However, your father knows his danger, and it is of no use talking more of it. What is done is done."

"And how is your mother, Oswald?" Mistress Armstrong asked.

"She is well, Aunt, and bade me give her love to you."

"Truly I wonder she keeps her health, with all these troubles and anxieties. We had hoped that, after the meeting last March of the Commissioners on both sides, when the Lords of the Marches plighted their faith to each other, and agreed to surrender all prisoners without ransom, and to forgive all offenders, we should have had peace on the border. As you know, there were but three exceptions named; namely Adam Warden, William Baird, and Adam French, whom the Scotch Commissioners bound themselves to arrest, and to hand over to the English Commissioners, to be tried as being notorious truce breakers, doing infinite mischief to the dwellers on the English side of the border. And yet nothing has come of it, and these men still continue to make their raids, without check or hindrance, either by the Earl of March or Douglas."

"There are faults on both sides, wife," her husband said.

"I do not deny it, gudeman; but I have often heard you say these three men are the pests of the border; and that, were it not for them, things might go on reasonably enough, for no one counts a few head of cattle lifted, now and again. It is bad enough that, every two or three years, armies should march across the border, one way or the other; but surely we might live peaceably, between times. Did not I nearly lose you at Otterburn, and had you laid up on my hands, for well-nigh six months?"

"Ay, that was a sore day, for both sides."

"Will you tell me about it, Uncle?" Oswald asked. "My father cares not much to talk of it; and though I know that he fought there, he has never told me the story of the battle."

"We are just going to sit down to dinner, now," Adam Armstrong said, "and the story is a long one; but after we have done, I will tell you of it. Your father need not feel so sore about it; for, since the days of the Bruce, you have had as many victories to count as we have."

After dinner, however, Armstrong had to settle a dispute between two of his tenants, as to grazing rights; and it was not until evening that he told his story.

"In 1388 there were all sorts of troubles in England, and France naturally took advantage of them, and recommenced hostilities, and we prepared to share in the game. Word was sent round privately, and every man was bidden to gather, in Jedburgh forest. I tell you, lad, I went with a heavy heart, for although men of our name have the reputation of being as quarrelsome fellows as any that dwell on the border, I am an exception, and love peace and quiet; moreover, the children were but young, and I saw that the fight would be a heavy business, and I did not like leaving them, and their mother. However, there was no help for it, and we gathered there, over 40,000 strong. The main body marched away into Cumberland; but Douglas, March, and Moray, with 300 spears and 2000 footmen, including many an Armstrong, entered Northumberland.

"We marched without turning to the right or left, or staying to attack town, castle, or house, till we crossed the river Tyne and entered Durham. Then we began the war; burning, ravaging, and slaying. I liked it not, for although when it comes to fighting I am ready, if needs be, to bear my part, I care not to attack peaceful people. It is true that your kings have, over and over again, laid waste half Scotland; killing, slaying, and hanging; but it does not seem to me any satisfaction, because some twenty of my ancestors have been murdered, to slay twenty people who were not born until long afterwards, and whose forbears, for aught I know, may have had no hand in the slaughter of mine.

"However, having laden ourselves with plunder from Durham, we sat down for three days before Newcastle, where we had some sharp skirmishes with Sir Henry and his brother, Sir Ralph Percy; and in one of these captured Sir Henry's pennant.

"Then we marched away to Otterburn, after receiving warning from Percy that he intended to win his pennant back again, before we left Northumberland. We attacked Otterburn Castle, but failed to carry it, for it was strong and well defended. There was a council that night, and most of the leaders were in favour of retiring at once to Scotland, with the abundance of spoil that we had gained. But Douglas persuaded them to remain two or three days, and to capture the castle, and not to go off as if afraid of Percy's threats. So we waited all the next day; and at night the Percys, with 600 spears and 8000 infantry, came up. Our leaders had not been idle, for they had examined the ground carefully, and arranged how the battle should be fought, if we were attacked.

"Having heard nothing of the English, all day, we lay down to sleep, not expecting to hear aught of them until the morning. It was a moonlight night, and being in August, there was but a short darkness between the twilights; and the English, arriving, at once made an attack, falling first on the servants' huts, which they took for those of the chiefs. This gave us time to form up in good order, as we had lain down each in his proper position.

"A portion of the force went down to skirmish with the English in front, but the greater portion marched along the mountain side, and fell suddenly upon the English flank. At first there was great confusion; but the English, being more numerous, soon recovered their order and pushed us back, though not without much loss on both sides.

"Douglas shouted his battle cry, advanced his banner, fighting most bravely; as did Sir Patrick Hepburn, but for whose bravery the Douglas banner would have been taken, for the Percys, hearing the cry of 'a Douglas! a Douglas!' pressed to that part of the field, and bore us backwards. I was in the midst of it, with ten of my kinsmen; and though we all fought as became men, we were pressed back, and began to think that the day would be lost.

"Then the young earl, furious at seeing disaster threaten him, dashed into the midst of the English ranks, swinging his battle-axe and, for a time, cutting a way for himself. But one man's strength and courage can go for but little in such a fray. Some of his knights and squires had followed him, but in the darkness it was but few who perceived his advance.

"Presently three knights met him, and all their spears pierced him, and he was borne from his horse, mortally wounded. Happily the English were unaware that it was Douglas who had fallen. Had they known it, their courage would have been mightily raised, and the day would assuredly have been lost. We, too, were ignorant that Douglas had fallen, and still fought on.

"In other parts of the field March and Moray were holding their own bravely. Sir Ralph Percy, who had, like Douglas, charged almost alone into Moray's ranks, was sorely wounded and, being surrounded, surrendered to Sir John Maxwell. Elsewhere many captures were made by both parties; but as the fight went on the advantage turned to our side; for we had rested all the day before, and began the battle fresh, after some hours of sleep; while the English had marched eight leagues, and were weary when they began the fight.

"Sir James Lindsay and Sir Walter Sinclair, with some other knights who had followed Douglas, found him still alive. With his last words he ordered them to raise his banner, and to shout 'Douglas!' so that friends and foes should think that he was of their party. These instructions they followed. We and others pressed forwards, on hearing the shout; and soon, a large party being collected, resumed the battle at this point. Moray and March both bore their arrays in the direction where they believed Douglas to be battling, and so, together, we pressed upon the English so hardly that they retreated, and for five miles we pursued them very hotly. Very many prisoners were taken, but all of quality were at once put to ransom, and allowed to depart on giving their knightly word of payment within fifteen days.

"It was a great victory, and in truth none of us well knew how it had come about, for the English had fought as well and valiantly as we did ourselves; but it is ill for wearied men to fight against fresh ones. Never was I more surprised than when we found that the battle, which for a time had gone mightily against us, was yet won in the end. Methinks that it was, to a great extent, due to the fact that each Englishman fought for himself; while we, having on the previous day received the strictest orders to fight each man under his leader, to hold together, and to obey orders in all respects, kept in our companies; and so, in the end, gained the day against a foe as brave, and much more numerous, than ourselves."

"Thank you, Uncle Armstrong. I have often wondered how it was that the Percys, being three to one against you, were yet defeated; fighting on their own ground, as it were. 'Tis long, indeed, since we suffered so great a reverse."

"That is true enough, Oswald. In the days of Wallace and Bruce, we Scots often won battles with long odds against us; but that was because we fought on foot, and the English for the most part on horseback--a method good enough on an open plain, but ill fitted for a land of morass and hill, like Scotland. Since the English also took to fighting on foot, the chances have been equal; and we have repulsed invasions not so much by force, as by falling back, and so wasting the country that the English had but the choice of retreating or starving.

"There is reason, indeed, why, when equal forces are arrayed against each other, the chances should also be equal; for we are come of the same stock, and the men of the northern marches of England, and those of Scotland, are alike hardy and accustomed to war. Were we but a united people, as you English are, methinks that there would never have been such constant wars between us; for English kings would not have cared to have invaded a country where they would find but little spoil, and have hard work to take it. But our nobles have always been ready to turn traitors. They are mostly of Norman blood and Norman name, and no small part of them have estates in England, as well as in Scotland. Hence it is that our worst enemies have always been in our midst.

"And now it is time for bed, or you will be heavy in the morning; and I know that you intend starting at dawn, with the dogs, and have promised to bring in some hares for dinner."

Not only Oswald and Allan, but Janet also was afoot early; and, after taking a basin of porridge, started for the hills, accompanied by four dogs. They carried with them bows and arrows, in case the dogs should drive the hares within shot.

Six hours later they returned, carrying with them five hares and a brace of birds. These had both fallen to Oswald's bow, being shot while on the ground; for

in those days the idea that it was unsportsmanlike to shoot game, except when flying, was unknown.

For a week they went out every day, sometimes with the dogs, but more often
with hawks; which were trained to fly, not only at birds in their flight, but at hares,
on whose heads they alighted, pecking them and beating them so fiercely with their
wings, that they gave time for the party on foot to run up, and despatch the quarry
with an arrow.

Once or twice they accompanied Adam Armstrong, when he rode to some of
the towns in the neighbourhood, and spent the day with friends of the Armstrongs
there. For a fortnight, the time passed very pleasantly to the English lad; but, at the
end of that time, Adam Armstrong returned from a visit to Jedburgh with a grave
face.

"I have news," he said, "that your King Richard has been deposed; that Henry,
the Duke of Lancaster, having landed in Yorkshire, was joined by Percy and the
Earl of Westmoreland, and has been proclaimed king. This will cause great troubles
in England, for surely there must be many there who will not tamely see a king
dethroned by treasonable practices; and another, having no just title to the crown,
promoted to his place.

"Such a thing is contrary to all reason and justice. A king has the same right to
his crown as a noble to his estates, and none may justly take them away, save for
treasonable practices; and a king cannot commit treason against himself. Therefore
it is like that there will be much trouble in England, and I fear that there is no
chance of the truce that concludes, at the end of this month, being continued.

"The fact that the two great northern lords of England are both, with their
forces, in the south will further encourage trouble; and the peace that, with small
intermissions, has continued since the battle of Otterburn, is like to be broken.
Therefore, my lad, I think it best that you should cut short your visit, by a week,
and you shall return and finish it when matters have settled down.

"Here in Scotland we are not without troubles. Ill blood has arisen between
March and Douglas, owing to the Duke of Ramsay breaking his promise to marry
the Earl of March's daughter, and taking Douglas's girl to wife. This, too, has sorely
angered one more powerful than either Douglas or March--I mean, of course, Albany, who really exercises the kingly power.

"But troubles in Scotland will in no way prevent war from breaking out with England. On the contrary, the quarrel between the two great lords of our marches will cause them to loose their hold of the border men, and I foresee that we shall have frays and forays among ourselves again, as in the worst times of old. Therefore, it were best that you went home. While these things are going on, the private friendship between so many families on either side of the border must be suspended, and all intercourse; for maybe every man on either side will be called to arms, and assuredly it will not be safe for one of either nation to set foot across the border, save armed, and with a strong clump of spears at his back."

"I shall be sorry, indeed, to go," Oswald said, "but I see that if troubles do, as you fear, break out at the conclusion of the peace, a fortnight hence--"

"They may not wait for that," Adam Armstrong interrupted him. "A truce is only a truce so long as there are those strong enough to enforce it, and with Douglas and March at variance on our side, and Northumberland and Westmoreland absent on yours, there are none to see that the truce is not broken; and from what I hear, it may not be many days before we see the smoke of burning houses rising, upon either side of the border."

"The more reason for my going home," Oswald said. "My father is not likely to be last in a fray, and assuredly he would not like me to be away across the border when swords are drawn. I am very sorry, but I see that there is no help for it; and tomorrow, at daybreak, I will start for home."

That evening was the dullest Oswald had spent, during his visit. The prospect that the two nations might soon be engaged in another desperate struggle saddened the young cousins, who felt that a long time might elapse before they again met; and that in the meantime their fathers, and possibly themselves, might be fighting in opposite ranks. Although the breaches of the truces caused, as a rule, but little bloodshed, being in fact but cattle lifting expeditions, it was very different in time of war, when wholesale massacres took place on both sides, towns and villages were burned down, and the whole of the inhabitants put to the sword. Ten years had sufficed to soften the memory of these events, especially among young people, but each had heard numberless stories of wrong and slaughter, and felt that, when war once again broke out in earnest, there was little hope that there would be any change in the manner in which it would be conducted.

Oswald rode rapidly, until he had crossed the border. The truce would not expire for another thirteen days, but the raiders might be at work at any moment; for assuredly there would be no chance of complaints being made, on the eve of re-commencement of general hostilities. He met no one on the road, until he reached the first hamlet on the English side. Here he stopped to give his horse half an hour's rest, and a feed. As he dismounted, two or three of the villagers came up.

"Have you heard aught, lad, of any gatherings on the other side of the border?"

"None from where I came; but there was a talk that notices had been sent, through the southern Scottish marches, for all to be in readiness to gather to the banner without delay, when the summons was received."

"That is what we have heard," a man said. "We have made everything in readiness to drive off our cattle to the fells; the beacons are all prepared for lighting, from Berwick down to Carlisle; and assuredly the Scotch will find little, near the border, to carry back with them.

"You are the son of stout John Forster of Yardhope Keep, are you not? I saw you riding by his side, two months since, at Alwinton fair."

"Yes, I was there with him."

"He will have hot work, if a Scotch army marches into Tynedale. The Bairds will be sure to muster strongly, and they won't forgive the last raid on them; and whichever way they go, you may be sure that your father's hold will receive a visit."

"It was but a return raid," Oswald said. "The Bairds had been down our way, but a short time before, and lifted all the cattle and horses that they could lay hands on, for miles round."

"That is true enough. We all know the thieving loons. But men remember the injuries they have suffered, better than those they have inflicted; and they will count Allan Baird's death as more than a set-off for a score of their own forays."

"If we have only the Bairds to settle with, we can hold our walls against them," Oswald said; "but if the whole of the Scotch army come our way, we must do as you are doing, drive the cattle to the hills, and leave them to do what harm they can to the stone walls, which they will find it hard work to damage."

"Aye, I have heard that they are stronger than ordinary; and so they need be, seeing that you have a blood feud with the Bairds. Well, they are not like to have much time to waste over it, for our sheriff has already sent word here, as to the places where we are to gather when the beacon fires are lighted; and you may be sure that the Percys will lose no time in marching against them, with all their array; and the Scots are like to find, as they have found before, that it is an easier thing to cross the border than it is to get back."

Late that evening, Oswald returned home. After the first greetings, his father said:

"It is high time that you were back, Oswald. Rumour is busy, all along the border; but for myself, though I doubt not that their moss troopers will be on the move, as soon as the truce ends, I think there will not be any invasion in force, for some little time. The great lords of the Scotch marches are ill friends with each other; and, until the quarrel between Douglas and Dunbar is patched up, neither will venture to march his forces into England. It may be months, yet, before we see their pennons flying on English soil.

"My brother Alwyn has been over here, for a day or two, since you were away. The Percys are down south, so he was free to ride over here. He wants us to send you to him, without loss of time. He says that there is a vacancy in Percy's household, owing to one of his esquires being made a knight, and a page has been promoted to an esquireship. He said that he spoke to Hotspur, before he went south, anent the matter; and asked him to enroll you, not exactly as a page, but as one who, from his knowledge of the border, would be a safe and trusty messenger to send, in case of need. As he has served the Percys for thirty years, and for ten has been the captain of their men-at-arms; and has never asked for aught, either for himself or his relations, Percy gave him a favourable answer; and said that if, on his return, he would present you to him, and he found that you were a lad of manners that would be suitable for a member of his household, he would grant his request; partly, too, because my father and myself had always been stanch men, and ready at all times to join his banner, when summoned, and to fight doughtily. So there seems a good chance of preferment for you.

"Your mother is willing that you should go. She says, and truly enough, that if you stay here it will be but to engage, as I and my forebears have done, in constant feuds with the Scots; harrying and being harried, never knowing, when we lie down to rest, but that we may be woke up by the battle shout of the Bairds; and leaving behind us, when we die, no more than we took from our fathers.

"I know not how your own thoughts may run in the matter, Oswald, but methinks that there is much in what she says; though, for myself, I wish for nothing better than what I am accustomed to. Percy would have knighted me had I wished it, years ago; but plain Jock Forster I was born, and so will I die when my time comes; for it would alter my condition in no way, save that as Jock Forster I can lead a raid across the border, but as Sir John Forster it would be hardly seemly for me to do so, save when there is open war between the countries.

"It is different, in your case; You are young, and can fit yourself to another mode of life; and can win for yourself, with your sword, a better fortune than you will inherit from me. Besides, lad, I am like enough, unless a Baird spear finishes me sooner, to live another thirty years yet; and it is always sure to lead to trouble, if there are two cocks in one farmyard. You would have your notions as to how matters should be done, and I should have mine; and so, for many reasons, it is right that you should go out into the world. If matters go well with you, all the better; if not, you will always be welcome back here, and will be master when I am gone.

"What say you?"

"It comes suddenly upon me, Father; but, as I have always thought that I should like to see something of the world beyond our own dales, I would gladly, for a time at least, accept my uncle's offer; which is a rare one, and far beyond my hopes. I should be sorry to leave you and my mother but, save for that it seems to me, as to you, that it would be best for me to go out into the world, for a time."

"Then that is settled, and tomorrow you shall ride to Alnwick and see, at any rate, if aught comes of the matter.

"Do not cry, Wife. It is your counsel that I am acting upon, and you have told me you are sure that it is best that he should go. It is not as if he were taking service with a southern lord. He will be but a day's ride away from us, and doubtless will be able to come over, at times, and stay a day or two with us; and once a year, when times are peaceable, you shall ride behind me, on a pillion, to see how things go with him at the Percys' castle. At any rate it will be better, by far, than if he had carried out that silly fancy of his, for putting himself in the hands of the monks and learning to read and write; which would, perchance, have ended in his shaving his crown and taking to a cowl, and there would have been an end of the Forsters of Yardhope.

"Now, put that cold joint upon the table, again. Doubtless the lad has a wolf's appetite."

There was no time lost. The next day was spent in looking out his clothes and packing his valise, by his mother; while he rode round the country, to say goodbye to some of his friends. The next morning, at daybreak, he started; and, at nightfall, rode into the castle of Alnwick, and inquired for Alwyn Forster. The two men-at-arms, who had regarded his appearance, on his shaggy border horse, with scarce concealed contempt; at once answered, civilly, that the captain would be found in his room, in the north turret. They then pointed out to him the stables, where he could bestow his horse; and, having seen some hay placed before it, and a feed of barley, to which the animal was but little accustomed, Oswald made his way up the turret, to the room in which his uncle lodged.

The stately castle, and the beauty, as well as the strength, of the Percys' great stronghold, had in no small degree surprised, and almost awed the lad, accustomed only to the rough border holds. It was situated on rising ground, on the river Aln; and consisted of a great keep, which dated back to the times of the Saxons; and three courts, each of which were, indeed, separate fortresses, the embattled gates being furnished with portcullises and strong towers. Within the circuit of its walls, it contained some five acres of ground, with sixteen towers, the outer wall being surrounded by a moat.

The Percys were descended from a Danish chief, who was one of the conquerors of Normandy, and settled there. The Percy of the time came over with William the Norman, and obtained from him the gift of large possessions in the south of England, and in Yorkshire; and, marrying a great Saxon heiress, added to his wide lands in the north.

One of the Percys, in the reign of Henry the Second, made a journey to Jerusalem, and died in the Holy Land. None of his four sons survived him. His eldest daughter Maud married the Earl of Warwick; but, dying childless, her sister Agnes became sole heir to the broad lands of the Percys. She married the son of the Duke of Brabant, the condition of her marriage being that he should either take the arms of the Percys, instead of his own; or continue to bear his own arms, and take the name of Percy. He chose the latter alternative. Their son was one of the barons who forced King John to grant the Magna Carta.

The Percys always distinguished themselves, in the wars against the Scot; and received, at various times, grants of territory in that country; one of them being made Earl of Carrick, when Robert the Bruce raised the standard of revolt against England.

Upon the other hand, they not unfrequently took a share in risings against the Kings of England; and their estates were confiscated, for a time, by their taking a leading part in the action against Piers Gaveston, the royal favourite.

It was in the reign of Henry the Second that the Percy of the time obtained, by purchase, the Barony of Alnwick; which from that date became the chief seat of the family. The present earl was the first of the rank, having been created by Richard the Second. He was one of the most powerful nobles in England, and it was at his invitation that Henry of Lancaster had come over from France, and had been placed on the throne by the Percys, and some other of the northern nobles; and, as a reward for his service, the earl was created High Constable of England.

Chapter 3: At Alnwick.

Y ou are rarely changed, Oswald," his uncle said, as the lad entered his apartment. "'Tis three years since I last saw you, and you have shot up nigh a head, since then. I should not have known you, had I met you in the street; but as I was expecting you, it is easy to recall your features. I made sure that you would come; for, although your father was at first averse to my offer, I soon found that your mother was on my side, and I know that, in the long run, my brother generally gives in to her wishes; and I was sure that, as you were a lad of spirit, you would be glad to try a flight from home.

"You are growing up mightily like your father, and promise to be as big and as strong as we both are. Your eyes speak of a bold disposition, and my brother tells me that you are already well practised with your arms.

"You understand that it is Sir Henry, whom they call Hotspur, that you are to serve. As to the earl, he is too great a personage for me to ask a favour from, but Sir Henry is different. I taught him the first use of his arms, and many a bout have I had with him. He treats me as a comrade, rather than as the captain of his father's men-at-arms, here; and when I spoke to him about you, he said at once:

"'Bring him here, and we will see what we can do for him. If he is a fellow of parts and discretion, I doubt not that we can make him useful. You say he knows every inch of our side of the border, and something of the Scottish side of it, his mother's sister being married to one of the Armstrongs. There is like to be trouble before long. You know the purpose for which I am going away; and the Scots are sure to take advantage of changes in England, and a youth who can ride, and knows the border, and can, if needs be, strike a blow in self defence, will not have to stay idle in the castle long. His father is a stout withstander of the Scots, and the earl would have given him knighthood, if he would have taken it; and maybe, in the future, the son will win that honour. He is too old for a page, and I should say too little versed in our ways for such a post; but I promise you that, when he is old enough, he shall be one of my esquires.'

"So you may soon have an opportunity of showing Hotspur what you are made of. And now, I doubt not that you are hungry. I will send down to the buttery, for a couple of tankards and a pasty. I had my supper two hours ago, but I doubt not that I can keep you company in another."

He went to the window, and called out, "John Horn!"

The name was repeated below, and in two minutes a servant came up. The captain gave him directions, and they shortly sat down to a substantial meal.

"The first thing to do, lad, will be to get you garments more suitable to the Percys' castle than those you have on; they are good enough to put on under armour, or when you ride in a foray; but here, one who would ride in the train of the Percys must make a brave show. It is curfew, now; but tomorrow, early, we will sally into the town, where we shall find a good choice of garments, for men of all conditions. You hold yourself well, and you have something of your mother's softness of speech; and will, I think, make a good impression on Sir Henry, when suitably clad.

"You see, there are many sons of knights, of good repute and standing, who would be glad, indeed, that their sons should obtain a post in Hotspur's personal following; and who might grumble, were they passed over in favour of one who, by his appearance, was of lower condition than themselves.

"John Forster is well known, on the border, as a valiant fighter, and a leading man in Coquetdale. It is known, too, that he might have been knighted, had he chosen; and doubtless there are many who, having heard that his hold is one of the strongest on the border, give him credit for having far wider possessions than that bit of moor round the hold, and grazing rights for miles beyond it. If, then, you make a brave show, none will question the choice that Hotspur may make; but were you to appear in that garb you have on, they might well deem that your father is, after all, but a moss trooper.

"He told me that you had, once, a fancy to learn to read and write. What put that idea into your head? I do not say that it was not a good one, but at least it was a strange one, for a lad brought up as you have been."

"I think, Uncle, that it was rather my mother's idea than my own; she thought that it might conduce to my advancement, should I ever leave the hold and go out into the world."

"She was quite right, Oswald; and 'tis a pity that you did not go, for a couple of years, to a monastery. It is a good thing to be able to read an order, or to write one, for many of the lords and knights can do no more than make a shift to sign their names. As for books I say nothing, for I see not what manner of good they are; but father Ernulf, who is chaplain here, tells me that one who gives his mind to it can, in a year, learn enough to write down, not in a clerkly hand, but in one that can be understood, any letter or order his lord may wish sent, or to read for him any that he receives.

"In most matters, doubtless, an order by word of mouth is just as good as one writ on vellum; but there are times when a messenger could not be trusted to deliver one accurately, as he receives it; or it might have to be passed on, from hand to hand. Otherwise, a spoken message is the best; for if a messenger be killed on the way, none are the wiser as to the errand on which he is going; while, if a parchment is found on him, the first priest or monk can translate its purport.

"The chaplain has two younger priests with him; and, should you be willing, I doubt not that one of these would give you instruction, for an hour or two of a day. The Percys may not be back for another month or two, and if you apply yourself to it honestly, you might learn something by that time."

"I should like it very much, Uncle."

"Then, so it shall be, lad. For two or three hours a day you must practise in arms--I have some rare swordsmen among my fellows--but for the rest of the time, you will be your own master. I will speak with father Ernulf, in the morning, after we have seen to the matter of your garments."

A straw pallet was brought up to the chamber; and, after chatting for half an hour about his visit to the Armstrongs, Oswald took off his riding boots and jerkin, the total amount of disrobing usual at that time on the border, and was soon asleep.

"I am afraid, Uncle," he said in the morning, "that the furnishment of the purse my father gave me, at starting, will not go far towards what you may consider necessary for my outfit."

"That need not trouble you at all, lad. I told your father I should take all charges upon myself, having no children of my own, and no way to spend my money; therefore I can afford well to do as I like towards you. Once the war begins, you will fill your purse yourself; for although the peoples of the towns and villages suffer by the Scotch incursions, we men-at-arms profit by a war. We have nought that they can take from us, but our lives, while we take our share of the booty, and have the ransom of any knights or gentlemen we may make prisoners."

Accordingly they went into Alnwick, and Alwyn Forster bought for his nephew several suits of clothes, suitable for a young gentleman of good family; together with armour, of much more modern fashion than that to which Oswald was accustomed. When they returned to the castle, the lad was told to put on one of these suits, at once.

"Make your old ones up in a bundle," his uncle said. "There may be occasions when you may find such clothes useful; though here, assuredly, they are out of place. Now, I will go with you to Father Ernulf."

The priest's abode was in what was called the Abbots' Tower, which was the one nearest to the large monastery, outside the walls.

"I told you, father," the captain said, "that belike my nephew would join me here, as I was going to present him to Sir Henry Percy. The good knight will not be back again, mayhap, for some weeks; and the lad has a fancy to learn to read and write, and I thought you might put him in the way of his attaining such knowledge."

"He looks as if the sword will suit his hand better than the pen," the priest said, with a smile, as his eye glanced over the lad's active figure. "But surely, if he is so inclined, I shall be glad to further his wishes. There is a monk at the monastery who, although a good scholar, is fitted rather for the army than the Church. He was one of our teachers, but in sooth had but little patience with the blunders of the children; but I am sure that he would gladly give his aid to a lad like this, and would bear with him, if he really did his best. I have nought to do at present, and will go down with him, at once, and talk to Friar Roger.

"If the latter would rather have nought to do with it, one of my juniors shall undertake the task; but I am sure that the friar would make a better instructor, if he would take it in hand.

"He is a stout man-at-arms--for, as you know, when the Scots cross the border, the abbot always sends a party of his stoutest monks to fight in Percy's ranks; as is but right, seeing that the Scots plunder a monastery as readily as a village. Friar Roger was the senior in command, under the sub-prior, of the monks who fought at Otterburn, and all say that none fought more stoutly, and the monks were the last to fall back on that unfortunate day. They say that he incurred many penances for his unchurchly language, during the fight; but that the abbot remitted them, on account of the valour that he had shown."

Accordingly, the priest went off with Oswald to the monastery, while Alwyn Forster remained, to attend to his duties as captain of the men-at-arms. On his saying that he wished to see the friar Roger, the priest was shown into a waiting room, where the monk soon joined them.

He was a tall, powerful man, standing much over six feet in height, and of proportionate width of shoulders. He carried his head erect, and looked more like a man-at-arms, in disguise, than a monk. He bent his head to the priest, and then said in a hearty tone:

"Well, Father Ernulf, what would you with me, today? You have no news of the Scots having crossed the border, and I fear that there is no chance, at present, of my donning a cuirass over my gown?"

"None at present, brother, though it may well be so, before long. I hope that we shall soon have the earl and his son back again, for the Scots are sure to take advantage of their absence, now that the truce is expired.

"No, I want you on other business. This young gentleman is the nephew of Alwyn Forster, whom you know."

"Right well, Father; a good fellow, and a stout fighter."

"He is about to enter Sir Henry's household," the priest went on; "but, seeing that the knight is still away, and may be absent for some weeks yet, the young man is anxious to learn to read and write--

"Not from any idea of entering the Church," he broke off, with a smile, at the expression of surprise on the monk's face; "but that it may be useful to him in procuring advancement.

"I have, therefore, brought him to you; thinking that you would make a far better teacher, for a lad like him, than your brothers in the school. I thought perhaps that, if I spoke to the abbot, he might release you from your attendance at some of the services, for such a purpose."

"That is a consideration," the monk laughed.

"Well, young sir, I tell you fairly that among my gifts is not that of patience with fools. If you are disposed to work right heartily, as I suppose you must be, or you would not make such a request, I on my part will do my best to teach you; but you must not mind if, sometimes, you get a rough buffet to assist your memory."

"I should doubt whether a buffet, from you, would not be more likely to confuse my memory than to assist it," Oswald said, with a smile; "but at any rate, I am ready to take my chance, and can promise to do my best to avoid taxing your patience, to that point."

"That will do, Father," the monk said. "He is a lad of spirit, and it is a pleasure to train one of that kind. As to the puny boys they send to be made monks because, forsooth, they are likely to grow up too weak for any other calling, I have no patience with them; and I get into sore disgrace, with the abbot, for my shortness of temper."

"I am afraid, from what I hear," the priest said, shaking his head, but unable to repress a smile, "that you are often in disgrace, Brother Roger."

"I fear that it is so, and were it not that I am useful, in teaching the lay brothers and the younger monks the use of the carnal weapons, I know that, before this, I should have been bundled out, neck and crop. 'Tis hard, Father, for a man of my inches to be shut up, here, when there is so much fighting to be done, abroad."

"There is good work to be done, everywhere," the priest said gravely. "Many of us may have made a mistake in choosing our vocations; but, if so, we must make the best we can of what is before us."

"What time will you come?" the monk asked Oswald.

"My uncle said that he would suit my hours to yours; but that, if it was all the same to you, I should practise in arms from six o'clock till eight, and again for an hour or two in the evening; so that I could come to you either in the morning or afternoon."

"Come at both, if you will," the monk said. "If the good father can get me off the services, from eight till six, you can be with me all that time, save at the dinner hour. You have but a short time to learn in, and must give yourself heartily to it.

"There is the chapel bell ringing, now, and I must be off. The abbot will not be present at this service, Father; and if you will, you can see him now. I doubt not that he will grant your request, for I know that I anger him, every time I am in chapel. I am fond of music, and I have a voice like a bull; and, do what I will, it will come out in spite of me; and he says that my roaring destroys the effect of the whole choir."

So saying, he strode away.

"Do you wait outside the gates, my son," the priest said. "I shall be only a few minutes with the abbot; who, as Friar Roger says, will, I doubt not, be glad enough to grant him leave to abstain from attendance at the services."

In a short time, indeed, he rejoined Oswald at the gate.

"That matter was managed, easily enough," he said. "The abbot has, himself, a somewhat warlike disposition, which is not to be wondered at, seeing that he comes from a family ever ready to draw the sword; and he has, therefore, a liking for Friar Roger, in spite of his contumacies, breaches of regulations, and quarrels with the other monks. He is obliged to continually punish him, with sentences of seclusion, penance, and fasting; but methinks it goes against the grain. He said, at once, that he was delighted to hear that he had voluntarily undertaken some work that would keep him out of trouble, and that he willingly, and indeed gladly, absolved him from attendance in chapel, during the hours that he was occupied with you.

"'He is not without his uses,' he said. 'He is in special charge of the garden, and looks after the lay brothers employed in it. I will put someone else in charge, while he is busy, though I doubt if any will get as much work out of the lay brothers as he does; and indeed, he himself labours harder than any of them. With any other, I should say that tucking his gown round his waist, and labouring with might and main was unseemly; but as it works off some of his superabundant energy, I do not interfere with him.'"

"How ever did he become a monk, Father?"

"It seems that he was a somewhat sickly child, and his father sent him to the monastery to be taught, with a view to entering the Church. He was quick and bright in his parts, but as his health improved he grew restless, and at fifteen refused to follow the vocation marked out for him, and returned home; where, as I have heard, he took part in various daring forays across the border. When he was five-and-twenty, he was wounded well-nigh to death in one of these, and he took it as a judgment upon him, for deserting the Church; so he returned here, and became a lay brother. He was a very long time, before he recovered his full strength, and before he did so he became a monk, and I believe has bitterly regretted the fact, ever since.

"Some day, I am afraid, he will break the bounds altogether, throw away his gown, assume a breast plate and steel cap, and become an unfrocked monk. I believe he fights hard against his inclinations, but they are too strong for him. If war breaks out I fear that, some day, he will be missing.

"He will, of course, go down south, where he will be unknown; and where, when the hair on his tonsure has grown, he can well pass as a man-at-arms, and take service with some warlike lord. I trust that it may not be so, but he will assuredly make a far better man-at-arms than he will ever make a good monk."

The next morning, after practising for two hours with sword and pike, Oswald went down, at eight o'clock, to the monastery, and was conducted to friar Roger's cell. The latter at once began his instruction, handing him a piece of blackened board, and a bit of chalk.

"Now," he said, "you must learn to read and write, together. There are twenty-six letters, and of each there is a big one and a little one. The big ones are only used at the beginning of a sentence--that is where, if you were talking, you would stop to take breath and begin afresh--and also at the first letter of the names of people, and places.

"The first letter is 'A'. There it is, in that horn book, you see. It looks like two men, or two trees, leaning against each other for support; with a line, which might be their hands, in the middle.

"Now, make a letter like that, on your board. The little 'a' is a small circle with an upright, with a tail to it; you might fancy it a fish, with its tail turned up.

"Now, write each of those, twelve times."

So he continued with the first six letters.

"That will be as much as you will remember, at first," he said. "Now we will begin spelling with those letters, and you will see how they are used. You see, it is a mixture of the sounds of the two: 'b a' makes ba, and 'b e' be, 'c a' ca, 'da' da, 'd e' de, and so on. Now, we will work it out."

Oswald was intelligent, and anxious to learn. He had been accustomed, when riding, to notice every irregularity of ground, every rock and bush that might serve as a guide, if lost in a fog, and he very quickly took in the instruction given him; and, by the time the convent bell rung to dinner, he had made a considerable progress with the variations that could be formed with the six letters that he had learned; and the friar expressed himself as highly satisfied with him.

"You have learned as much, in one morning, as many of the boys who attend schools would learn in a month," he said. "If you go on like this, I will warrant that, if Percy delays his return for two months, you will know as much as many who have been two years at the work. I have always said that it is a mistake to teach children young; their minds do not take in what you say to them. You may beat it into them, but they only get it by rote; and painfully, because they don't understand how one thing leads to another, and it is their memory only, and not their minds, that are at work."

The next day came news that the Scotch had crossed the border, and there was great excitement in the castle; but it was soon learned that the invasion was not on a great scale, neither the Douglases nor the Earl of March having taken part in it.

"There is no fear of our being attacked, here," Alwyn Forster said to Oswald. "The sheriffs of the county will call out their levies, and will soon make head against them. At the same time, we shall make preparations against any chance of their coming hither."

This was done. Vast quantities of arrows were prepared, stones collected and carried up to the points on the wall most exposed to attack; and orders sent out, by the governor of the castle in the Percys' absence, to the people for many miles round, that on the approach of the Scots all were to retire to refuge, the women and children taking to the hills, while the men capable of bearing arms were to hasten to the defence of the castle.

For a time, the Scots carried all before them, wasting and devastating the country. Oswald heard that they had captured, without resistance, his father's hold. He rejoiced at the news, for he feared that, not knowing the strength of the invading force, resistance might have been attempted; in which case all in the hold might have been put to the sword. He had no doubt, now, that his father and mother had retired with their followers to the hills, as they had always determined to do, in case of an invasion by a force too strong to resist.

Had the Percys been at home, they might have held out, confident that the

Scotch would be attacked before they could effect its capture; but as all the northern lords, with their retainers, were away in the south, it would be some time before a force could be collected that could make head against the Scots.

A portion of the Scottish army laid siege to the castle of Wark, on the Tweed. This castle had always played a conspicuous part in the border wars. It had been besieged and captured by David of Scotland, in the reign of Stephen; and two or three years later was again besieged, but this time repulsed all attacks. David, after his defeat at the battle of the Standard, resumed the siege. It again repulsed all attacks, but at last was reduced to an extremity by famine, and capitulated.

The castle was demolished by the Scots, but was rebuilt by Henry the Second. In 1215 it was again besieged, this time by King John, who resented the defection of the northern barons; and it was captured, and again destroyed. In 1318 it was captured and destroyed by Robert Bruce. In 1341 it was besieged by David Bruce, but held out until relieved by King Edward, himself. In 1383 it was again besieged by the Scots, and part of its fortifications demolished. On the present occasion it was again captured, and razed to the ground.

Another portion of the Scottish army, plundering and burning, advanced along the valley of the Coquet. As they approached, the inhabitants of the district round Alnwick began to pour into the castle; but orders were issued that all the fighting men should join the force of Sir Robert Umfraville, the sheriff of the district, who was gathering a force to give the Scots battle.

"I fear that there is small chance of the Scots making their way hither," Oswald's instructor said, in lugubrious tones. "Sir Robert is a stout fighter, and the Scots, laden as they must be with booty, and having hitherto met with no resistance, will be careless and like to be taken by surprise. Methinks the abbot ought to send off a contingent, to aid Sir Robert."

Oswald laughed.

"I suppose he wants to keep them for more urgent work, and thinks that the Church should only fight when in desperate straits. However, Father, you may have an opportunity yet; for we cannot regard it as certain that Sir Robert will defeat the Scots."

Three days later, however, the news arrived that Sir Robert had attacked the Scots, at Fulhetlaw, and utterly defeated them; taking prisoner Sir Richard Rutherford and his five sons, together with Sir William Stewart, John Turnbull, a noted border reiver, and many others; and that those who had escaped were in full flight for the border.

The Scotch incursion had made no change in Oswald's work. He continued to study hard with the monk. As a rule, he fully satisfied his teacher; but at times, when he failed to name the letters required to make up a certain sound, the latter lost all patience with him; and, more than once, with difficulty restrained himself from striking him. Spelling in those days, however, had by no means crystallized itself into any definite form, and there was so large a latitude allowed that, if the letters used gave an approximate sound to the word, it was deemed sufficient.

The consequence was that Oswald's education progressed at a speed that would, in these more rigid days, be deemed impossible. He was intensely interested in the work, and even his martial exercises were, for the time, secondary to it in his thoughts. He felt so deeply grateful to his instructor that, even if he had struck him, he would have cared but little. In those days rough knocks were readily given, and the idea that there was anything objectionable, in a boy being struck, had never been entertained by anyone. Wives were beaten not uncommonly, servants frequently; and from the highest to the lowest, corporal punishment was regarded as the only way to ensure the carrying out of orders.

Oswald was slower in learning to write down the letters than he was to read them. His hands were so accustomed to the rein, the bow, and the sword that they bungled over the work of forming letters. Nevertheless, by the time the Percys returned, three months and a half after his arrival at the castle, he could both read and write short and simple words; and as these formed a large proportion of English speech, at the time, he had made a considerable step in the path of learning, and the monk was highly pleased with his pupil.

"I shall not be able to come tomorrow, Father," he said to the monk, one day. "The earl and Sir Henry will be back tonight, and my uncle says that I must keep near him, tomorrow; so that, if opportunity offers, he may present me to the knight."

"I feared it would come to that," the monk said. "I wish they had all stopped away, another three or four months; then you would have got over your difficulty of piecing together syllables, so as to make up a long word. 'Tis a thousand pities that you should stop altogether, just when you are getting on so well."

"I will come as often as I can, Father, if you will let me."

"No, no, lad. I know what it is, when the family are at home. It will be, 'Here, Oswald, ride with such a message;' or Hotspur, himself, may be going out with a train, and you will have to accompany him. There will always be something.

"Indeed, save but for your teaching, it is high time that the Percys were back again; for there has already been a great deal of hot work, on the border, and report says that the Scots are mustering strongly, and that there is going to be a great raid into Cumberland; so you will be busy, and so shall I. The lay brothers have made but a poor hand of it, while I have been busy. I went down in the evening, yesterday, to see them drill; and it was as much as I could do to prevent myself from falling upon them, and giving them a lesson of a different sort.

"As it was, I gave it to their instructor heartily, and was had up before the abbot on his complaint, this morning; and am to eat Lenten fare for the next ten days, which accords but ill either with my liking or needs."

In the evening, the courtyard was ablaze with torches as, amid the cheers of the garrison, the Earl of Northumberland and his son rode in, with a strong body of men-at-arms. The greater portion of the following with which they had met Henry of Lancaster on his landing, and escorted him to London, had long since returned to their homes; being released from service, when it was seen that no opposition was to be looked for from the adherents of Richard. The followings of the various nobles and knights of the northern counties had left the main body on the way home, and Northumberland had brought with him, to Alnwick, only the men-at-arms who formed the regular force retained under his standard.

Oswald was greatly struck with the splendid appearance, and appointments, of the earl and the knights who attended him, and with the martial array of his followers. Hitherto, he had seen but the roughest side of war; the arms and armour carried not for show, but for use, and valued for their strength, without any reference to their appearance. On the border there was not the smallest attempt at uniformity in appearance, polished armour was regarded with disfavour, and that worn was of the roughest nature, the local armourer's only object being to furnish breast and back pieces that would resist the strongest spear thrust. Of missiles they made little account, for the Scots had but few archers, and their bows were so inferior in strength, to those carried by the English archers, that armour strong enough to resist a spear thrust was amply sufficient to keep out a Scottish arrow.

There was not, even in the array of the Earl of Northumberland's men-at-arms, any approach to the uniformity that now prevails among bodies of soldiers. The helmets, breast and back pieces, were, however, of similar form, as the men engaged for continued service were furnished with armour by the earl; but there was a great variety in the garments worn under them, these being of all colours, according to the fancy of their wearers. All, however, carried spears of the same length, while some had swords, and others heavy axes at their girdles. The helmets and armour were all brightly polished, and as the lights of the torches flashed from them and from the spearheads; Oswald, for the first time, witnessed something of the pomp of war.

His uncle, as captain of the men-at-arms left in the castle, was invited to the banquet held after the arrival of the force. Oswald, therefore, was free to wander about among the soldiers, listening to their talk of what they had seen in London, and of the entertainments there in honour of the new king; exciting, thereby, no small amount of envy among those who had been left behind in garrison.

Oswald already knew that the earl had been appointed Constable of England, for life, and now heard that the lordship of the Isle of Man had since been conferred on him.

Chapter 4: An Unequal Joust.

Y ou must don your best costume tomorrow, Oswald," his uncle said, when he returned from the banquet. "Sir Henry Percy's first question, after asking as to the health of the garrison, was:

"'Has this nephew of yours, of whom you were speaking to me, come yet?'

"I told him that you had been here well-nigh four months, that you had been practising in arms with my best swordsmen, who spoke highly of you, and that the whole of your spare time had been spent at the monastery, where you had been studying to acquire the art of reading and writing, thinking that such knowledge must be useful to you in his service. I told him that brother Roger had reported that you had shown marvellous sharpness there, and could already read from a missal, barring only some of the long words.

"'Oh, he had the fighting monk for his master!' Sir Henry said, laughing. 'Truly he must have been a good pupil, if he has come out of it without having his head broken, a dozen times. The friar is a thorn in the abbot's flesh, and more than once I have had to beg him off, or he would have been sent to the monastery of Saint John, which is a place of punishment for refractory monks. But in truth he is an honest fellow, though he has mistaken his vocation. He is a valiant man-at-arms, and the abbot's contingent would be of small value, without him.

"'Well, I will see your nephew in the morning. His perseverance in learning, and his quickness in acquiring it, show him to be a youth of good parts, and intelligent; but until I see him, I cannot say what I will make of him.'"

Accordingly, the next morning the lad accompanied his uncle to Sir Henry's private apartment, and found the knight alone. Sir Henry, Lord Percy, was now about forty years old. He had received the order of knighthood at the coronation of Richard the Second, when his father was created earl; and, nine years later, he was made governor of Berwick and Warden of the Marches; in which office he displayed such activity in following up and punishing raiders, that the Scots gave him the name of Hotspur. He was then sent to Calais, where he showed great valour. Two years later he was made Knight of the Garter, and was then appointed to command a fleet, sent out to repel a threatened invasion by the French. Here he gained so great a success that he came to be regarded as one of the first captains of the age.

At Otterburn, his impetuosity cost him his freedom; for, pressing forward into the midst of the Scotch army, he and his brother Ralph were taken prisoners, and carried into Scotland. He had just been appointed, by King Henry, sheriff of Northumberland, and governor of Berwick and Roxburgh, and received other marks of royal favour.

Although of no remarkable height, his broad shoulders and long, sinewy arms testified to his remarkable personal strength. His face was pleasant and open, and showed but small sign of his impetuous and fiery disposition.

"So this is the young springal," he said, with a smile; as, with a quick glance, he took in every detail of Oswald's figure and appearance. "By my troth, you have not overpraised him. He bears himself well, and is like to be a stout fighter, when he comes to his full strength. Indeed, as the son of John Forster of Yardhope, and as your nephew, good Alwyn, he could scarce be otherwise; although I have not heard that either his father, or you, ever showed any disposition for letters."

"No indeed, Sir Henry; nor have we, as far as I have ever seen, been any the worse for our lack of knowledge on that head. But with the lad here, it is different. Under your good patronage he may well hope to attain, by good conduct and valour, a promotion where book learning may be of use to him; and therefore, when he expressed a desire to learn, I did my best to favour his design."

"And you did well, Alwyn. And since he has gained so much, in so short a time, it were a pity he should not follow it up; and he shall, if it likes him, so long as he is in this castle, have two hours every morning in which he can visit the fighting monk, until he can read and write freely.

"Now, young sir, the question is, how can we best employ you? You are too old for a lady's bower, but not old enough, yet, for an esquire."

"Nor could I aspire to such a position, my lord, until I have proved myself worthy of it. My uncle told me that he had suggested that I might be useful as a bearer of messages, and orders; and as I know every foot of the border, from near Berwick to Cumberland, methinks that I might serve you in that way. I ride lightly, know every morass and swamp, and every road through the fells; and have at times, when there was peace, crossed the Cheviots by several of the passes, to pay visits to my mother's sister, who is married to one of the Armstrongs, near Jedburgh. If your lordship will deign to employ me in such service, I can promise to do so safely, and to justify my uncle's recommendation; and shall be ready, at all times, to risk my life in carrying out your orders."

"Well spoken, lad. I like the tone of your voice, and your manner of speech. They are such as will do no discredit to my household, and I hereby appoint you to it; further matters I will discuss with your uncle."

Oswald expressed his thanks in suitable terms, and then, bowing deeply, retired.

"A very proper lad, Alwyn. I would have done much for you, old friend, and would have taken him in some capacity, whatever he might have turned out; but, frankly, I doubted whether John Forster, valiant moss trooper as he is, would have been like to have had a son whom I could enroll in my household, where the pages and esquires are all sons of knights and men of quality. It is true that his father might have been a knight, had he chosen, since the earl offered him that honour after Otterburn; for three times he charged, at the head of a handful of his own men, right into the heart of the Scottish army, to try and rescue me; but he has always kept aloof in his own hold, going his own way and fighting for his own hand; and never once, that I can recall, has he paid a visit to us here, or at our other seats. I feared that under such a training as he would be likely to have, the lad would have been but a rough diamond. However, from his appearance and bearing, he might well have come of a noble family."

"'Tis his mother's doing, methinks, Sir Henry. She is of gentle birth. Her father was Sir Walter Gillespie. He was killed by the Scots, when she was but a girl, or methinks he would scarcely have given her in marriage to my brother John. She went with a sister to live with an old aunt, who let the girls have their way, without murmur; and seeing that they had no dowry, for their father was but a poor knight, there were not many claimants for their hands; and when she chose John Forster, and her sister Adam Armstrong, she did not say them nay. She has made a good wife to him, though she must have had many an anxious hour, and doubtless it is her influence that has made the lad what he is."

"How think you I had best bestow him, among the pages or the esquires?"

"I should say, Sir Henry, as you are good enough to ask my opinion, that it were best among the esquires. It would be like putting a hunting dog among a lady's pets, to put him with the pages. Moreover, boys think more of birth than men do. The latter judge by merit, and when they see that the lad has something in him, would take to him; whereas were he with the pages there might be quarrels, and he might fall into disgrace."

"I think that you are right, Alwyn. He might get a buffet or two, from the esquires, but he will be none the worse for that; while with the pages it might be bickering, and ill will. He shall take his chance with the squires. Bring him to me at twelve o'clock, and I will myself present him to them, with such words as may gain their goodwill, and make the way as easy as may be for him."

Accordingly, at twelve o'clock, Oswald went to Hotspur's room, and was taken by him to the hall where the esquires, six in number, had just finished a meal. They varied in age from eighteen to forty. They all rose, as their lord entered.

"I wish to present to you this young gentleman, my friends. He is the son of John Forster of Yardhope, whose name is familiar to you all, as one of the most valiant of the defenders of the border against the Scottish incursions. None distinguished themselves more at the battle of Otterburn, where he performed feats of prodigious valour, in his endeavours to rescue me and my brother from the hands of the Scots. The earl my father offered him knighthood, but he said bluntly that he preferred remaining, like his father, plain John Forster of Yardhope. The lad's mother is a daughter of Sir Walter Gillespie, and he is nephew of Alwyn, captain of the men-at-arms here.

"He knows every foot of the border, its morasses, fells, and passes; and will prove a valuable messenger, when I have occasion to send orders to the border knights and yeomen. I have attached him to my household. You will find him intelligent, and active. He comes of a fighting stock; and will, I foresee, do no discredit to them in the future. I hesitated whether I should place him with the pages or with you, and have decided that, with your goodwill, he will be far more comfortable in your society, if you consent to receive him."

"We will do so willingly, on such recommendation," the senior of the esquires said; "as well as for the sake of his brave uncle, whom we all respect and like, and of his valiant father. The addition of young blood to our party will, indeed, not be unwelcome; and while, perchance, he may learn something from us, he will assuredly be able to tell us much that is new of the doings on the border, of which nothing but vague reports have reached our ears."

"Thanks, Allonby," Hotspur said. "I expected nothing less from you. He will, of course, practise at arms regularly, when not occupied in carrying messages; and you will be surprised to hear that he will go for two hours daily to the monastery, where he has, for the last three months, been learning reading and writing at the hands of Brother Roger, the fighting monk. It is his own desire, and a laudable one; and when I say that he has succeeded in giving Brother Roger satisfaction, you may well imagine that he must have made great progress."

A smile ran round the faces of the esquires, for Brother Roger's pugnacious instincts were widely known.

"Truly, Sir Henry, if brother Roger did not lose patience with him, it would be hard, indeed, if we could not get on with him; and in truth, this desire to improve himself speaks well for the lad's disposition."

When Hotspur left, Allonby said, "Take a seat, Master Oswald. But first, have you dined?"

"I took my meal an hour since, with my uncle," Oswald replied.

"Ay, I remember that your uncle sticks to the old hours. Tell us, were you with your father in that foray he headed, to carry off some cattle that had been lifted by the Bairds? We heard a report of it, last night."

"I was not with him, to my great disappointment; for he said that another year must pass, before I should be fit to hold my own in a fray. The affair was a somewhat hot one. Three of my father's men were killed, and some ten or twelve of those under other leaders; and my father and several of the band were wounded, some very sorely. It happened thus."

And he then told the details of the affair.

"It might well have been worse," Allonby said, "for, had the Bairds had time to assemble, it would have gone hardly with your father's party; especially as there is, as I have heard, a blood feud between him and them."

"They have scored the last success," Oswald said, "seeing that they accompanied Sir Richard Rutherford in his raid, nigh two months ago; and, as I hear, while the rest came on harrying and plundering Croquetdale, the Bairds and their gathering remained at our hold, which they found deserted, for indeed my father could not hope to defend it successfully, against so large a force; and there they employed themselves in demolishing the outer wall, and much of the hold itself; and would have completed their task, had it not been for the defeat inflicted upon the rest of the Scots by Sir Robert Umfraville, when they were forced to hasten back across the border. My father sent me a message afterwards, saying that he and my mother, with their followers, had been forced to take to the fells; and that, on their return, they found the place well-nigh destroyed; but that he was going to set to work to rebuild it as before, and that he hoped, some time, to demolish the Bairds' hold in like fashion. It will be some time before the place is restored; for, my father's means being limited, he and his retainers would have to turn masons; but as the materials were there, he doubted not that, in time, they would make a good job of it."

"Truly, it is a hard life on the border," the squire said, "and it is wonderful that any can be found willing to live within reach of the Scotch raiders. I myself have done a fair share of fighting, under our lord's banner; but to pass my life, never knowing whether I may not awake to find the house assailed, would be worse than the hardest service against an open foe.

"Now, Master Oswald, we will go down to the courtyard, and see what your instructors have done for you, in the matter of arms. With whom have you been practising, since you came here?"

"Principally with Godfrey Harpent, Dick Bamborough, and William Anell; but I have had a turn with a great many of the other men-at-arms."

"The three men you name are all stout fellows, and good swordsmen. As a borderer, I suppose that you have practised with the lance?"

"We call it by no such knightly term. With us it is a spear, and nought else; but all borderers carry it, both for fighting and for pricking up cattle; and from the time that I could sit a horse I have always practised for a while, every day, with some of my father's troopers, or with himself, using blunt weapons whitened with chalk, so as to show where the hits fell. Although in a charge upon footmen, our border spearmen would couch their weapons and ride straight at their foe; in skirmishes, where each can single out an enemy, and there is a series of single combats, they do not so fight, but circle round each other, trusting to the agility of their horses to avoid a thrust, and to deliver one when there is an opening. Our spears are nothing like so heavy as the knightly lances, and we thrust with them as with the point of a sword."

"But in that way you can hardly penetrate armour," one of the other esquires said.

"No, it is only in a downright charge that we try to do so. When we are fighting as I speak of, we thrust at the face, at the armpit, the joints of the armour, which in truth seldom fits closely, or below the breastplate. The Scotch use even less armour than do our borderers, their breast pieces being smaller, and they seldom wear back pieces. It is a question chiefly of the activity of the horses, as of the skill of their riders, and our little moor horses are as active as young goats; and although neither horse nor rider can stand a charge of a heavily-armed knight or squire, methinks that if one of our troopers brought him to a stand, he would get the better of him, save if the knight took to mace or battle-axe."

"Have you your horse with you, Oswald?"

"Yes, it is in the stable. I have gone out with it, every morning, as soon as the castle gates were opened, and have ridden for a couple of hours before I began my exercises."

"Do you take him in hand first, Marsden," Allonby said to one of the younger esquires, a young man of two or three and twenty.

Light steel caps with cheeks, gorgets, shoulder and arm pieces, and padded leathern jerkins were put on; and then, with blunted swords, they took their places facing each other. The squire took up a position of easy confidence. He was a good swordsman, and good-naturedly determined to treat the lad easily, and to play with him for a time before scoring his first hit.

He soon, however, found that the game was not to be conducted on the lines that he had laid down. Oswald, after waiting for a minute or two, finding his opponent did not take the offensive, did so himself; and for a time Marsden had all his work to do, to defend himself. Several times, indeed, it was with the greatest difficulty that he guarded his head. The activity of his assailant almost bewildered him, as he continually shifted his position, and with cat-like springs leapt in and dealt a blow, leaping back again before his opponent's arm had time to fall.

Finding at last that, quick as he might be, Marsden's blade always met his own, Oswald relaxed his efforts, as he was growing fatigued; and as he did so Marsden took the offensive, pressing him backwards, foot by foot. Every time, however, that he found himself approaching a barrier, or other obstacle, that would prevent his further retreat, Oswald, with a couple of springs, managed to shift his ground. When he saw that Marsden was growing breathless from his exertions, he again took the offensive, and at last landed a blow fairly on his opponent's helm.

"By my faith," the squire said, with a laugh that had nevertheless a little mortification in it, "I would as soon fight with a wildcat; and yet your breath scarce comes fast, while I have not as much left in me as would fill an eggshell."

"It was an excellent display," Allonby said.

"Truly, lad, your activity is wonderful, and you might well puzzle the oldest swordsman, by such tactics. Marsden did exceedingly well, too. Many times I thought that your sword would have gone home, but up to the last, his guard was always ready in time. As for yourself, we had scarce the opportunity of seeing how your sword would guard your head, for you trusted always to your legs, rather than your arms.

"Well, lad, you will do. Your arm is like iron, or it would have tired long before, with that sword, which is a little over heavy for you. As to your wind, you would tire out the stoutest swordsman in the Percys' train. I do not say that, in the press of a battle, where your activity would count for little, a good man-at-arms would not get the better of you; but in a single combat, with plenty of room, it would be a good man, indeed, who would tackle you; especially were he clad in armour, and you fighting without it. His only chance would be to get in one downright blow, that would break down your guard. As Marsden says, you fight like a wildcat, rather than as a man-at-arms; but as the time may come when you will ride in heavy armour, and so lose the advantage of your agility, you had best continue to practise regularly with us, and the men-at-arms, and learn to fight in the fashion that would be needed, were you engaged in a pitched battle when on horseback, and in armour."

"I shall be glad, indeed, to do so," Oswald said modestly. "I know that I am very ignorant of real swordsmanship, and the men-at-arms have me quite at their mercy, when they insist upon my not shifting my ground. At home, I have only practised with my father's troopers, and we always fight on foot, and with stout sticks instead of swords, and without defences save our head pieces; but fighting in knightly fashion I knew nothing of, until I came here."

"You will soon acquire that, lad. With your strength of arm, length of wind, quickness of eye, and activity, you will make a famous swordsman, in time.

"Ah! Here is Sir Henry."

"Have you been trying the lad's metal?" Hotspur asked, as he saw Oswald in the act of taking off his steel cap. Marsden had already done so.

"That have we, Sir Henry, and find it as of proof. Marsden here, who is no mean blade, has taken him in hand; and the lad has more than held his own against him, not so much by swordsmanship as by activity, and wind. It was a curious contest. Marsden compared Oswald to a wildcat, and the comparison was not an ill one; for, indeed, his springs and leaps were so rapid and sudden that it was difficult to follow him, and the fight was like one between such an animal, and a hound. Marsden defended himself well against all his attacks, until his breath failed him, and he was dealt a downright blow on his helm, on which I see it has made a shrewd dent. As for his blows, they fell upon air, for the lad was ever out of reach before the ripostes came. In his own style of fighting, I would wager on him against any man-at-arms in the castle."

"I am glad to hear it," Hotspur said. "I shall feel the less scruple, in sending him on missions which are not without danger. He will need training, to fit him for combat in the ranks. No doubt he has had no opportunity for such teaching, and would go down before a heavy-armed man, with a lance, like a blade of grass before a millstone."

"He thinks not, Sir Henry, at least not in a single combat, for by his accounts his horse is as nimble as himself; but of course, in charges he and his horse would be rolled over, as you say."

"He thinks not? Oh, well, we will try him! I have an hour to spare.

"Do you put on a suit of full armour, Sinclair, and we will ride out to the course beyond the castle.

"What will you put on, lad?"

"I will put on only breast piece and steel cap; but I only said I should have a chance against a lance, Sir Henry. I do not pretend that I could stand against any man-at-arms, armed with sword and mace; but only that I thought that, with my horse, I could evade the shock of a fully-accoutred man, and then harass and maybe wound him with my spear."

"Well, we will try, lad. Put on what you will, and get your horse saddled. It will be rare amusement to see so unequal a course. We shall be ready in a quarter of an hour."

Oswald went up to his uncle, and told him what was proposed. Alwyn, who had witnessed his exercises with the rough riders of his father, smiled grimly.

"If you can evade his first charge, which I doubt not that you can, you will have him at your mercy, with your light spear against his lance, and your moor horse against his charger; but put on the heaviest of your two steel caps, and strong shoulder pieces. 'Tis like enough that, in his temper, he may throw away his lance and betake him to his sword. I will demand that he carries neither mace nor battle-axe, and that you should only carry sword and spear. Your horse's nimbleness may keep you out of harm, which is as much as you can expect, or hope for. Put on a light breast plate, too, for in spite of the wooden shield to his lance head, he may hurt you sorely if he does chance to strike you."

Oswald saw that his horse was carefully saddled. He procured from his uncle a piece of cloth; and, removing the spearhead, wrapped this round the head of the shaft, until it formed a ball the size of his fist. This he whitened thickly with chalk. In a few minutes Sinclair, who was the heaviest and strongest of the esquires, rode out into the courtyard in full armour. Sir Henry, with his own esquires, and several of the gentlemen of the earl's household, came down; and Hotspur laughed at the contrast presented by the two combatants: the one a mass of steel, with shield and lance, on a warhorse fully caparisoned; the other a slight, active-looking figure, with but little defensive armour, on a rough pony which had scarce an ounce of superfluous flesh.

"Now, gentlemen," he said, "we may be engaged in warfare with the Scots, before long; and you will here have an opportunity of seeing the nature of border fighting. The combat may seem to you ridiculously unequal, but I know the moss trooper, and I can tell you that, in a single combat like this, activity goes far to counterbalance weight and armour. You remember how Robert Bruce, before Bannockburn, mounted on but a pony, struck down Sir Robert Bohun, a good knight and a powerful one."

As the party went out, through the gates, to the tilting ground outside the walls, the men-at-arms, seeing that something unusual was going to take place, crowded up to the battlements, looking down on the ground.

"Now, gentlemen," Percy said, "you will take your places at opposite ends of the field; and when I drop my scarf, you will charge. It is understood that you need not necessarily ride straight at each other; but that it is free, to each of you, to do the best he can to overthrow his opponent."

As he gave the signal, the two riders dashed at full speed at each other; and, for a moment, the spectators thought that Oswald was going to be mad enough to meet his opponent in full course. When, however, the horses were within a length of each other, the rough pony swerved aside with a spring like that of a deer; and, wheeling round instantly, Oswald followed his opponent. The latter tried to wheel his charger, but as he did so, Oswald's spear struck him in the vizor, leaving a white mark on each side of the slit; and then he too wheeled his horse, maintaining his position on the left hand, but somewhat in rear, of his opponent; who was, thereby, wholly unable to use his lance, while Oswald marked the junction of gorget and helmet with several white circles. Furious at finding himself incapable of either defending himself, or of striking a blow, the squire threw away his lance, and drew his sword. Hotspur shouted, at the top of his voice:

"A breach of the rules! A breach of the rules! The combat is at an end."

But his words were unheard, in the helmet. Making his horse wheel round on his hind legs, Sinclair rode at Oswald with uplifted sword. The latter again couched his spear under his arm and, touching his horse with his spur, the animal sprung forward; and before the sword could fall, the point of the spear caught the squire under the armpit, and hurled him sideways from his saddle.

Hotspur and those round him ran forward. Sinclair lay without moving, stunned by the force with which he had fallen. Oswald had already leapt from his horse, and raised Sinclair's head, and began to unlace the fastenings of his helmet. Hotspur's face was flushed with anger.

"Do not upbraid him, my lord, I pray you," Oswald said. "He could scarce have avoided breaking the conditions, helpless as he felt himself; and he could not have heard your voice, which would be lost in his helmet. I pray you, be not angered with him."

Hotspur's face cleared.

"At your request I will not, lad," he said; "and, indeed, he has been punished sufficiently."

By the time that the helmet was removed, one of the soldiers from the battlements ran out from the castle, with a ewer of water. This was dashed into the squire's face. He presently opened his eyes. A heavy fall was thought but little of in those days; and as Sinclair was raised to his feet, and looked round in bewilderment at those who were standing round him, Hotspur said good temperedly:

"Well, Master Sinclair, the lad has given us all a lesson that may be useful to us. I would scarce have believed it, if I had not seen it; that a stout soldier, in full armour, should have been worsted by a lad on a rough pony; but I see now that the advantage is all on the latter's side, in a combat like this, with plenty of room to wheel his horse.

"Why, he would have slain you a dozen times, Sinclair. Look at your vizor. That white mark is equal on both sides of the slit, and had there been a spear head on the shaft, it would have pierced you to the brain. Every joint of your armour, behind, is whitened; and that thrust, that brought you from your horse, would have spitted you through and through.

"Now, let there be no ill feeling over this. It is an experiment, and a useful one; and had I, myself, been in your place, I do not know that I could have done aught more than you did."

Sinclair was hot tempered, but of a generous disposition, and he held out his hand to Oswald, frankly.

"It was a fair fight," he said, "and you worsted me, altogether. No one bears malice for a fair fall, in a joust."

"The conditions were not at all even," Oswald said. "On a pony like mine, unless you had caught me in full career, it was impossible that the matter could have turned out otherwise."

"I often wondered," Hotspur said, as they walked towards the gate, "that our chivalry should have been so often worsted by the rough Scottish troopers; but now I understand it. The Scotch always choose broken ground, and always scatter before we get near them; and, circling round, fall upon our chivalry when their weight and array are of no use to them. Happily, such a misadventure has never happened to myself; but it might well do so. The Scotch, too, have no regard for the laws of chivalry; and once behind will spear the horse, as indeed happened to me, at Otterburn. 'Tis a lesson in war one may well take to heart; and when I next fight the Scots, I will order that on no account, whatever, are the mounted men to break their ranks; but, whatever happens, are to move in a solid body, in which case they could defy any attacks upon them by light-armed horse, however numerous."

At the gate of the castle, Alwyn Forster met them.

"You have given me a more useful addition to my following than I dreamt of, Alwyn," Hotspur said. "Did you see the conflict?"

"I watched it from the wall, Sir Henry. I felt sure how the matter would end. The lad is quick and sharp at border exercises. I have seen him work with his father's troopers. There were not many of them who could hold their own against him, and in fighting in their own way, I would back the moss troopers against the best horsemen in Europe. They are always accustomed to fight each man for himself, and though a score of men-at-arms would ride through a hundred of them, if they met the charge; in single combat their activity, and the nimbleness of their horses, would render them more than a match for a fully-caparisoned knight."

"So it seems," Hotspur said; "and yet, if Sinclair had but known that the lad was about to swerve in his course, which indeed he ought to have known--for it would have been madness to meet his charge--he too should have changed his course to his left, when a couple of lengths away; for he might be sure that the lad would turn that way, so as to get on his left hand, and in that case he would have ridden over him like a thunderbolt."

"Yes, Sir Henry, but Oswald would have had his eye on knee and bridle; and the moment the horse changed his direction, he would have been round the other way, like an arrow from a bow; and would have planted himself, as he did, in the squire's rear."

"Perhaps so," Hotspur said thoughtfully. "At any rate, Alwyn, the boy has given us all a lesson, and you have done me good service, by presenting him to me."

Chapter 5: A Mission.

For the next three or four months, Oswald was but little at the castle; Percy utilizing his services, in the manner most agreeable to him, by sending him on errands to various knights and gentlemen, in different parts of Northumberland, and to the fortified places held by the English across the Border. A fortnight after his contest with Sinclair, Sir Henry formally appointed him one of his esquires.

"You are young," he said, "for such a post; but as you have shown that you are well able to take care of yourself in arms, and as I perceive you to be shrewd and worthy of confidence, your age matters but little. As my messenger, you will be more useful travelling as one of my esquires, than as one without settled rank; and I can not only send written communications by you, but can charge you to speak fully in my name, and with my authority."

Oswald was not slow in finding out the advantages that the position gave him. On the first errands on which he had been sent, he had been treated as but an ordinary messenger, had been placed at dinner below the salt, and herded with the men-at-arms. As an esquire of Lord Percy, he was treated with all courtesy, was introduced to the ladies of the family, sat at the high table, and was regarded as being in the confidence of his lord. His youth excited some little surprise, but acted in his favour, because it was evident that Percy would not have nominated him as one of his esquires, had he not shown particular merit. In his journeys, he often passed near Yardhope, where the rebuilding of the wall and keep was being pushed on with much vigour; the inhabitants of the villages in the valley lending their assistance to restore the fortalice, which they regarded as a place of refuge, in case of sudden invasion by the Scots. His parents were both greatly pleased at his promotion, especially his mother, who had always been anxious that he should not settle down to the adventurous, and dangerous, life led by his father.

"By our Lady," John Forster said, "though it be but six months since you first left us, you have changed rarely. I speak not of your fine garments, but you have grown and widened out, and are fast springing from a boy into a man; and it is no small thing that Percy should have thought so well of you as to make you one of his esquires, already."

"It was from no merit of mine, Father, but because he thought that, as his messenger, I should be able to speak in his name with more authority than had I been merely the bearer of a letter from him."

"'Tis not only that," his father replied. "I received a letter but two days since from my brother Alwyn, written by the hand of a monk of his acquaintance, telling me that Lord Percy was mightily pleased with you; not only because you had set yourself to read and write, but from the way in which you had defeated one of his esquires in a bout at arms. Alwyn said that he doubted not that you would win knightly spurs, as soon as you came to full manhood. So it is clear that merit had something to do with your advancement, though this may be also due, to some extent, to the cause you assign for it. The monk who wrote the letter added, on his own account, that he had been your preceptor; and that, though he had often rated you soundly, you had made wonderful progress."

"The monk is a good teacher," Oswald laughed; "but he would have made a better man-at-arms than he will ever make a monk. I believe it pleased him more that I worsted Sinclair--which indeed was a small thing to do, seeing that he had no idea of fighting, save of charging straight at a foe--than at the progress I made at my books. He commands the contingent that the monastery sends, when Percy takes the field to repel an invasion; and, could he have his own will, would gladly exchange a monk's robes for the harness of a man-at-arms. I would wish for no stouter companion in the fray."

The speed with which he had performed his journeys, and the intelligence which he showed in carrying out his missions and reporting on their issue, earned for the lad an increasing amount of liking and confidence, on the part of his lord. It was not only that he delivered the replies to Hotspur's messages accurately; but his remarks, upon the personal manner and bearing of those to whom he was sent, were of still greater value to Percy. Naturally, all had promised to have their contingent of fighting men ready, in case of serious invasion by the Scots; but Oswald was able to gather, from their manner, whether the promises would surely be fulfilled; or whether, in case of trouble, the knights were more likely to keep their array for the defence of their own castles than to join Percy in any general movement.

One day, when Oswald had been engaged six months at this work, which had taken him several times into Cumberland and Westmoreland, as well as the north, Lord Percy summoned him to his private apartment.

"Hitherto you have done well, Oswald, and I feel now that I can trust you with a mission of far higher importance than those you have hitherto performed. 'Tis not without its dangers, but I know that you will like it none the less for that reason. You are young, indeed, for business of such importance; but it seems to me that, of those around me, you would be best fitted to carry it out. Your manner of speech has changed much, since you came here; but doubtless you can fall at will into the border dialect, which differs little from that on the other side; and you can pass, well enough, as coming from Jedburgh, or any other place across the border.

"All the world knows, lad, that George, Earl of March and Dunbar, was mightily offended at Rothesay breaking off the match with his daughter, and marrying the child of his rival Douglas; but now I am going to tell you what the world does not know, and which is a secret that would cost many a life, were it to be blabbed abroad, and which I should not tell you, had I not a perfect confidence in your discretion. The anger of March--as he is mostly called on this side of the border, while in Scotland they more often call him Earl of Dunbar--goes beyond mere displeasure with the Douglas, and sullen resentment against Rothesay. He has sent a confidential messenger to me, intimating that he is ready to acknowledge our king as his sovereign, and place himself and his forces at his disposal.

"I see you are surprised, as is indeed but natural; but the Marches have ever been rather for England than for Scotland, although they have never gone so far as to throw off their allegiance to the Scottish throne. It is not for us to consider whether March is acting treacherously, to James of Scotland; but whether he is acting in good faith, towards us.

"It was easy for him to send a messenger to me, since Scotland trades with England, and a ship bound for London might well touch at one of our ports on the way down; but the presence of an Englishman, at Dunbar, would not be so readily explained. His messenger especially enjoined on me not to send any communication in writing, even by the most trustworthy hand; since an accident might precipitate matters, and drive him to take up arms, before we were in a position to give him aid. Therefore, in the first place, I wish you to journey to Dunbar, to see the earl, and deliver to him the message I shall give you, and endeavour to inform yourself how far he is to be trusted. Say what he will, I can scarce bring myself to believe that he will really throw off his allegiance to Scotland; save in the event of a great English army marching north, when doubtless he would do what most Scotch nobles have always done, namely, hasten to give in his submission, and make the best terms he can, for himself. 'Tis a business which I like not, although it is my duty to accept a proposal that, if made in good faith, would be of vast value to the king.

"You must, after seeing the earl, return here with all speed, to bear me any message March may give you, and to report your impressions as to his sincerity, and good faith. 'Tis a month since I received his message. Since then, I have communicated with the king, and have received his authority to arrange terms with March, to guarantee him in the possession of his lordships, to hand over to him certain tracts of the Douglas country which he bargained for, and to assure him of our support. But he must be told that the king urges him to delay, at present, from taking any open steps; as, in the first place, he is bound by the truce just arranged, for the next two years; and in the second because, having no just cause of quarrel with Scotland, and being at present but newly seated on the throne, he would have difficulty in raising an army for the invasion of that country. The king is ready to engage himself not to renew the truce, and to collect an army, in readiness to act in concert with him, as soon as it is terminated.

"The earl has sent, by his messenger, a ring; which, on being presented at Dunbar, will gain for the person who carries it immediate access to him; and I shall also give you my signet, in token that you are come from me. You will carry, also, a slip of paper that can be easily concealed, saying that you have my full authority to speak in my name. You yourself can explain to him that I have selected you for the mission because of your knowledge of border speech, and because a youth of your age can pass unobserved, where a man might excite attention and remark, and possibly be detained, until he could render a satisfactory account of himself.

"Here are the conditions, set down upon paper. Take it, and commit them to heart, and then tear the paper into shreds, and burn them. As far as Roxburgh you can, of course, ride as my squire; but beyond, you must travel in disguise. This you had better procure here, and take with you; for although the Governor of Roxburgh is a trusty knight, it were best that no soul should know that you go on a mission to March; and I shall simply give you a letter to him, stating that you are engaged in a venture in my service, and that your horse and armour are to be kept for you, until your return."

Thanking Lord Percy for the honour done him, in selecting him for the mission, and promising him to carry it out, to the best of his power, Oswald retired and, making his way up to an inner room, set about learning the contents of the paper given him, which was, indeed, a copy of the royal letter to Percy. When he had thoroughly mastered all the details, and could repeat every word, he followed Sir Henry's instructions, tore the letter up, and carefully burned every fragment. Then he went out into the town, and bought garments suited for travelling unnoticed in Scotland, the dress being almost identical on both sides of the border, save for the lowland Scotch bonnet.

On his return, he found that Lord Percy had sent for him during his absence, and he at once went to his apartments.

"I have been thinking over this matter further," Sir Henry said. "The abbot came in, just as you left me; and, among other things, he mentioned that friar Roger had again fallen into disgrace, having gone so far as to strike the sub-prior on the cheek, almost breaking the jaw of that worthy man; and that, finding discipline and punishment of no avail with him, he was about to expel him, in disgrace, from the community. He said that he had only retained him so long on account of my goodwill for the fellow, and from the fact that he would, as I had often urged, be most valuable as leader of the abbot's forces, in case of troubles with the Scots, but that his last offence has passed all bearing.

"For the time I could say nothing, for discipline must be maintained, in a monastery as well as in the castle; but after the abbot had left me, and I was walking up and down in vexation over the affair--for I like the rascal, in spite of his ways, and there is no one else who could so well lead the contingent of the monastery--a thought occurred to me. I like not your going altogether alone, for the times are lawless, and you might meet trouble on the road; and yet I did not see whom I could send with you. Now it seems to me that this stout knave would make an excellent companion for you.

"In the first place, you like him, and he likes you; secondly, a monk travelling north on a mission, say from the abbot to the prior of a monastery near Dunbar, could pass anywhere unheeded; and in the third place, although as a peaceful man he could carry no military arms, he might yet take with him a staff, with which I warrant me he would be a match for two or three ordinary men; and lastly, I may be able to convince the abbot that he can thus get rid of him from the monastery, for some time, and avoid the scandals he occasions, and yet hold him available on his return for military service.

"What say you, lad?"

"I should like it much, Sir Henry. I could wish for no stouter companion; and although he may be quarrelsome with his fellows, it is, methinks, solely because the discipline of the monastery frets him, and he longs for a more active life; but I believe that he could be fully trusted to behave himself discreetly, were he engaged in outdoor work, and there can be no doubt that he is a stout man-at-arms, in all ways."

"I should not trust him, in any way, with the object of your mission. If I obtain the abbot's consent, I shall simply send for him, rate him soundly for his conduct, but telling him I make all allowances for his natural unfitness for his vocation; and that I have, as a matter of grace, obtained from the abbot permission to use his services for a while, and to suspend his sentence upon him, until it be seen how he comports himself; and, with that view, I am about to send him as your companion, on a commission with which I have intrusted you, to the town of Dunbar. I shall hint that, if he behaves to my satisfaction, I may persuade the abbot to allow him to remain in my service, until the time comes when he may be useful to the convent for military work; he still undertaking to drill the lay brothers, and keep the abbot's contingent in good order; and that, when the troubles are at an end, I will obtain for him full absolution from his vows, so that he may leave the monastery without the disgrace of being expelled, and may then take service with me, or with another, as a man-at-arms.

"I wish you to be frank with me. If you would rather go alone, matters shall remain as they are."

"I would much rather that he went with me, my lord. From the many conversations that I have had with him, I am sure that he is shrewd and clever, and that, once beyond the walls of the monastery and free to use his weapon, he would be full of resource. There is doubtless much lawlessness on both sides of the border, and although I should seem but little worth robbing, two travel more pleasantly than one; and the monk has taken such pains with me, and has been so kind, that there is no one with whom I would travel, with greater pleasure."

"Then I will go across to the monastery, at once, and see the abbot; and I doubt not that he will grant my request, for, much and often as brother Roger has given him cause for anger, I know that he has a sort of kindness for him, and will gladly avoid the necessity for punishing and disgracing him. If all is arranged, the monk shall come over here, and see you."

An hour later, Brother Roger came in to the captain's quarters.

"So you have been in trouble again, Brother Roger," Alwyn Forster said with a laugh, as he held out his hand to him.

"That have I, and an hour ago I was lying in a prison cell, cursing my hot temper; and with, as it seemed, the certainty of being publicly unfrocked, and turned out like a mangy dog from a pack. It was not, mind you, that the thought of being unfrocked was altogether disagreeable; for I own that I am grievously ill fitted for my vocation, and that fasts and vigils are altogether hateful to me; but it would not be a pleasant thing to go out into the world as one who had been kicked out, and though I might get employment as a man-at-arms, I could never hope for any promotion, however well I might behave. However, half an hour ago the cell door was opened, and I was taken before the abbot, whom I found closeted with Hotspur.

"The latter rated me soundly, but said that, for the sake of Otterburn, he had spoken for me to the abbot; and that as he would, for the present, be able to make use of me in work that would be more to my liking, the abbot had consented to reconsider his decision, and would lend me to him for a time, in hopes that my good conduct would, in the end, induce him to overlook my offences; and that, in that case, he might even be induced to take steps, of a less painful description than public disgrace, for freeing me of my gown.

"I naturally replied that I was grateful for his lordship's intercession; and that, outside monkish offices, there was nothing I would not do to merit his kindness. He told me that I was to report myself to your nephew, who would inform me of the nature of the service upon which I was, at first, to be employed."

"It is to undertake a journey with me," Oswald said. "I am going on a mission for our lord, to Dunbar. The object of my mission is one that concerns me only, but it is one of some importance; and as the roads are lonely, since March and Douglas quarrelled, and order is but badly kept on the other side of the border, he thought that I should be all the better for a companion. Assuredly, I could wish for none better than yourself, for in the first place you have proved a true friend to me; in the second, you have so much knowledge, that we shall not lack subjects for conversation upon the journey; and lastly, should I get into any trouble, I could reckon upon you as a match for two or three border robbers."

"Nothing could be more to my taste," the monk said joyfully. "I did not feel quite sure, before, whether I was glad or sorry that my expulsion was put off, for I always thought that it would come to that some day; but now that I learn for what service Hotspur intends me, I feel as if I could shout for joy.

"Get me a flagon of beer, good Alwyn. I have drunk but water for the last twenty-four hours, and was in too great haste, to learn what was before me, even to pay a visit to brother Anselm, the cellarer, who is a stanch friend of mine.

"And do I go as a man-at-arms, Master Oswald? For, as your mission is clearly of a private character, disguise may be needful."

"No, Roger, you will go in your own capacity, as a monk, journeying on a mission from the abbot to the head of some religious community, near Dunbar. I doubt not that Lord Percy will obtain a letter from the abbot, and though it may be that there will be no need to deliver it, still it may help us on the way. As you are going with me, I shall attire myself as a young lay servitor of the convent."

"I would that it had been otherwise," the monk said, with a sigh. "I should have travelled far more lightly, in the heaviest mail harness, than in this monk's robe. Besides, how can I carry arms, for use in case of necessity?"

"You can carry a staff," Oswald said, laughing; "and being so big a man, you will assuredly require a long and heavy one; and, even if it is heavily shod with iron, no one need object."

"That is not so bad, Master Oswald. A seven-foot staff, of the thickness of my wrist; with an iron shoe, weighing a pound or two, is a carnal weapon not to be despised. As you doubtless know, our bishops, when they ride in the field, always carry a mace instead of a sword, so that they may not shed blood; though I say not that the cracking of a man's skull is to be accomplished, without some loss thereof. However, if a bishop may lawfully crack a man's head, as an eggshell, I see not that blame can attach to me, a humble and most unworthy son of the church, if some slight harm should come to any man, from the use of so peaceful an instrument as a staff. And how about yourself, young master?"

"I can carry a sword," Oswald replied. "In times like these, no man travels unarmed; and as I go as a servitor, and an assistant to your reverence, there will be nothing unseemly in my carrying a weapon, to defend you from the attack of foes."

"You can surely take a dagger, too. A dagger is a meet companion to a sword, and is sometimes mighty useful, in a close fight. And, mark me, take a smaller dagger also, that can be concealed under your coat. I myself will assuredly do the same. There are many instances in which a trifle of that kind might come in useful, such as for shooting the lock of a door, or working out iron bars."

"I will do so," Oswald said, "though I hope there will be no occasion, such as you say, for its use."

"When do we start, Master Oswald?"

"Tomorrow, at daybreak. We shall ride as far as Roxburgh. I shall go on my own horse, which, though as good an animal as was ever saddled, has but a poor appearance. You had best purchase a palfrey, as fat and sleek as may be found, but with strength enough to carry your weight. I shall be amply provided with money; and if you find a bargain, let me know, and I will give you the means. Mind, buy nothing that looks like a warhorse, but something in keeping with your appearance."

That evening, Oswald had another interview with Percy, and received his final instructions, and a bag of money.

"Be careful with it, lad," he said; "not so much because of the use that it may be to you, but because, were you seized and searched by robbers, and others, the sight of the gold might awake suspicions that you were not what you seemed, and might lead to a long detention. Keep your eye on Brother Roger, and see that he does not indulge too much in the wine cups, and that he comports himself rather in keeping with his attire, than with his natural disposition; and if you have any difficulty in restraining him, or if he does not obey your orders, send him back, at once. Will you see him again this evening?"

"He is waiting for me in my apartment, now, my lord, having come for the money for the purchase of a palfrey, which I bade him get."

"Send him to me, when you get there."

When the monk appeared before Hotspur, the latter said, "See here, monk, I have saved you from punishment, and become, as it were, your surety. See that you do not discredit me. You will remember that, although my young esquire may ask your advice, and benefit by your experience, he is your leader; and his orders, when he gives them, are to be obeyed as promptly as if it were I myself who spoke, to one of my men-at-arms. He is my representative in the matter, and is obeying my orders, as you will obey his. The mission is one of importance, and if it fails from any fault of yours, you had better drown yourself in the first river you come to, than return to Northumberland."

"I think that you can trust me, my lord," the monk said, calmly. "I am a very poor monk, but methinks that I am not a bad soldier; and although I go in the dress of the one, I shall really go as the other. I know that my duty, as a soldier, will be to obey. Even as regards my potations, which I own are sometimes deeper than they should be, methinks that, as a soldier, I shall be much less thirsty than I was as a monk. If the enterprise should fail from any default of mine, your lordship may be sure that I shall bear your advice in mind."

"I doubt not that you will do well, Roger. I should not have sent you with my esquire, on such a business, had I not believed that you would prove yourself worthy of my confidence. I know that a man may be a good soldier, and even a wise counsellor, though he may be a very bad monk."

The next morning the pair rode out from the castle, at daybreak. Roger was dressed in the usual monkish attire of the time, a long loose gown with a cape, and a head covering resembling a small turban. He rode a compactly built little horse, which seemed scarce capable of carrying his weight, but ambled along with him as if it scarcely felt it. Oswald was dressed as a lay servitor, in tightly-fitting high hose, short jerkin girt in by a band at the waist, and going half-way down to the knee. He rode his own moorland horse, and carried on his arm a basket with provisions for a day's march. He wore a small cloth cap, which fell down to his neck behind. His uncle accompanied him to the gate, which was, by his orders, opened to give them egress.

"Goodbye, lad," he said. "I know not, and do not wish to know, the object of your journey. It is enough for me that it is a confidential mission for Hotspur, and I am proud that you should have been chosen for it, and I feel convinced that you will prove you have merited our lord's confidence.

"Goodbye, friend Roger! Don't let your love of fisticuffs and hard knocks carry you away, but try and bear yourself as if you were still in the monastery, with the abbot keeping his eye upon you."

Brother Roger laughed.

"You make a cold shiver run down my back, Alwyn. I was feeling as if I had just got out of a cold cellar, into the sunshine, and could shout with very lightness of heart. I am not in the least disposed to quarrel with anyone, so let your mind be easy as to my doings. I shall be discretion itself; and even if I am called upon to strike, will do so as gently as may be, putting only such strength into the blow as will prevent an opponent from troubling us further."

So, with a wave of the hand, they rode on.

"I had better strap that staff beside your saddle, and under your knee," Oswald said, when they had ridden a short distance. "You carry it as if it were a spear, and I have seen already three or four people smile, as we passed them."

Roger reluctantly allowed Oswald to fasten the staff beside him.

"One wants something in one's hands," he said. "On foot it does not matter so much, but now I am on horseback again, I feel that I ought to have a spear in hand, and a sword dangling at my side."

"You must remember that you are still a monk, Roger, although enlarged for a season. Some day, perhaps, you will be able to gratify your desires in that way. You had best moderate the speed of your horse, for although he ambles along merrily, at present, he can never carry that great carcase of yours, at this pace, through our journey."

"I should like one good gallop," Roger sighed, as he pulled at the rein, and the horse proceeded at a pace better suited to the appearance of its rider.

"A nice figure you would look, with your robes streaming behind you," Oswald laughed. "There would soon be a story going through the country, of a mad monk.

"Now, we take this turning to the right, and here leave the main north road, for we are bound, in the first place, to Roxburgh."

"I thought that it must be that, or Berwick, though I asked no questions."

"We shall not travel like this beyond Roxburgh, but shall journey forward on foot."

"I supposed that we should come to that, Master Oswald, for otherwise you would not have told me to provide myself with a staff."

They journeyed pleasantly along. Whenever they approached any town or large village, Oswald reined back his horse a little, so that its head was on a level with Roger's stirrup. They slept that night at Kirknewton, where they put up at a small hostelry. Oswald had intended going to the monastery there, but Roger begged so earnestly that they should put up elsewhere, that he yielded to him.

"I should have no end of questions asked, as to our journey across the border, and its object," Roger said; "and it always goes against my conscience to have to lie, unless upon pressing occasions."

"And, moreover," Oswald said, with a laugh, "you might be expected to get up to join the community at prayers, at midnight; and they might give you a monk's bed, instead of a more comfortable one in the guest chambers."

"There may be something in that," Roger admitted, "and I have so often to sleep on a stone bench, for the punishment of my offences, that I own to a weakness for a soft bed, when I can get one."

However, Oswald was pleased to see that his follower behaved, at their resting place, with more discretion than he could have hoped for; although he somewhat surprised his host, by the heartiness of his appetite; but, on the other hand, he was moderate in his potations, and talked but little, retiring to a bed of thick rushes, at curfew.

"In truth, I was afraid to trust myself," he said to Oswald, as they lay down side by side. "Never have I felt so free, since Otterburn--never, indeed, since that unfortunate day when I was wounded, and conceived the fatal idea of becoming a monk. Two or three times, the impulse to troll out a trooper's song was so strong in me, that I had to clap my hand over my mouth, to keep it in."

"'Tis well you did, Roger, for assuredly if you had so committed yourself, on the first day of starting, I must have sent you back to Alnwick, feeling that it would not be safe for you to proceed with me farther. When we get upon the Cheviots, tomorrow, you may lift your voice as you choose; but it were best that you confined yourself to a Latin canticle, even there, for the habit of breaking into songs of the other kind might grow upon you."

"I will do so," Roger said, seriously. "Some of the canticles have plenty of ring and go, and the words matter not, seeing that I do not understand them."

The next morning they resumed their journey, crossed the Cheviots, which were here comparatively low hills; and, after four hours' riding, arrived at Roxburgh.

"Why do we come here?" Roger asked. "It would surely have been much shorter had we travelled through Berwick, and along the coast road."

"Much shorter, Roger; but Sir Henry thought it better that we should go inland to Haddington, and thence east to Dunbar; as, thus entering the town, it would seem that we came from Edinburgh, or from some western monastery; whereas, did we journey by the coast road, it might be guessed that we had come from England."

As before, they put up at a hostelry; and Oswald then proceeded, on foot, to the governor's house. Some soldiers were loitering at the door.

"What do you want, lad?" one of them asked, as he came up.

"I have a letter, which I am charged to deliver into the governor's own hands."

"A complaint, I suppose, from some worthy prior, who has lost some of his beeves?"

"Maybe the governor will inform you, if you ask him," Oswald replied.

"I shall pull your ear for you, when you come out, young jackanapes," the soldier said, hotly.

"That danger I must even risk. Business first, and pleasure afterwards."

And while the other soldiers burst into a fit of laughter, at the astonishment of their comrade at what he deemed the insolence of this young servitor of a monastery, he quietly entered. The guard at the door, who had heard the colloquy, led him into the governor's room.

"A messenger with a letter desires speech with you, Sir Philip," he said.

"Bid him enter," the knight said, briefly.

Oswald entered, and bowed deeply. He waited until the door closed behind the attendant, and then said:

"I am the bearer of a letter, sir, from Lord Percy to you."

The knight looked at him in surprise.

"Hotspur has chosen a strange messenger," he muttered to himself, as he took the missive Oswald held out to him, cut the silk that bound it with a dagger, and read its contents. As he laid it down, he rose to his feet.

"Excuse my want of courtesy," he said. "Lord Percy tells me that you are one of his esquires--no slight recommendation--and that you are intrusted with somewhat important a mission, on his part, to Dunbar, a still higher recommendation--for assuredly he would not have selected you for such a purpose, had you not stood high in his regard. But, indeed, at first I took you for what you seemed, as the bearer of a complaint from some abbot; for in truth, such complaints are not uncommon, for whenever a bullock is lost, they put it down to my men.

"Where are your horses that Percy speaks of? You will, I hope, take up your abode here, as long as you stay in the town."

"Thank you, Sir Philip; but I shall go forward in the morning. I have already put up at the Golden Rose. It would attract attention, were I to come here, and it were best that I remain as I am; and indeed, I have brought no clothes with me, save those I stand in."

"Well, perhaps, as you do not wish to attract attention, it were best so; and I pray you inform Lord Percy of the reason why you declined my entertainment."

"I shall be glad, Sir Philip, if you will send down a couple of your men to fetch the horses up to your stables; as I shall start, as soon as the gates are open, tomorrow morning."

"I will do so, at once."

And the governor rang a handbell on the table.

"Send two of the men up here," he said, as an attendant entered.

A minute later a door opened, and two soldiers came in, and saluted. One of them, to Oswald's amusement, was the man with whom he had exchanged words, below.

"You will accompany this gentleman to the Golden Rose, and bring back two horses, which he will hand over to you, and place them in the stables with mine.

"Are you sure, Master Forster, that there is nothing more that I can do for you?"

"Nothing, whatever, I thank you, sir; and I am greatly obliged by your courtesy, and with your permission I will take my leave. I hope to return here in the course of a week, or ten days."

So saying, Oswald shook hands with the governor and went downstairs, followed by the soldiers, who had not yet recovered from their surprise at seeing Oswald seated, and evidently on familiar terms with their lord. Oswald said nothing to them, until he arrived at the Golden Rose. Then he led the way to the stables, and handed the horses over to them.

"I suppose that that pulling of the ear will be deferred, for a time?" he said, with a smile, to the soldier who had made the remark.

The man sheepishly took hold of the bridle.

"I could not tell, sir--" he began.

"Of course you could not," Oswald interrupted. "Still, it may be a lesson, to you, that it is just as well not to make fun of people, until you are quite sure who they are. There, I bear no malice; get yourselves a stoup of wine, in payment for your services."

"I thought that there was something out of the way about him," the other man said, as they walked up the street with the two horses; "or he would never have turned upon you, as he did. It is evident that he is someone of consequence, and is here on some secret business or other, with Sir Philip. It is well that he did not bear malice, for you would have got it hot, from the governor, had he reported what you said to him."

Chapter 6: At Dunbar.

The journey passed without any incident of importance, but Oswald had reason to congratulate himself on having taken the monk with him. On one occasion, as they were passing over a wild heath, a party of eight or ten men, on rough ponies, rode up. They were armed with spears and swords. They reined up with exclamations of disappointment as Roger, who had rolled up his robe round his waist, for convenience of walking, let it fall round him.

"You have played us a scurvy trick, monk," the leader said, angrily. "Who was to guess it was a monk, who was thus striding along?"

"You would find it difficult to walk, yourself, with this robe dangling about your heels," Roger said.

"Whither are you bound, and whence are you going?"

"We are travelling to Dunbar, being sent to the convent of Saint Magnus there, and come from Roxburgh."

"'Tis a shame that so stalwart a fellow as you are should be leading a drone's life, in a convent; when every true Scotsman is sharpening his spear, in readiness for what may come when the truce with England expires."

"I am glad to hear that you are so well employed," Roger replied; "but methinks that, in days like these, it is sometimes useful to have a few men of thews and sinews, even in a religious house; for there are those who sometimes fail in the respect they owe to the Church."

"That is true enough," the men laughed. "Well, go thy way. There is naught to be gained from a travelling monk."

"Naught, good friend, save occasionally hard blows, when the monk happens to be of my strength and stature, and carries a staff like this."

"'Tis a goodly weapon, in sooth, and you look as if you knew how to wield it."

"Even a monk may know that, seeing that a staff is not a carnal weapon."

And rolling up his sleeves, Roger took the staff in the middle with both hands, in the manner of a quarterstaff, and made it play round his head; with a speed, and vigour, that showed that he was a complete master of the exercise.

"Enough, enough!" the man said, while exclamations of admiration broke from the others. "Truly from such a champion, strong enough to wield a weapon that resembles a weaver's beam, rather than a quarterstaff, there would be more hard knocks than silver to be gained; but it is all the more pity that such skill and strength should be thrown away, in a convent. Perhaps it is as well that you are wearing a monk's gown, for methinks that, eight to one as we are, some of us might have got broken heads, before we gained the few pence in your pocket.

"Come on, men. Better luck next time. It is clear that this man is not the one we are charged to capture."

And, with his followers, he rode off across the moor.

"I do not think that they are what they seem," Oswald said, as they resumed their journey. "The man's speech was not that of a border raider, and his followers would hardly have sat their horses so silently, and obeyed his orders so promptly, had they been merely thieving caterans; besides, you marked that he said you were not the man they were watching for."

"Whom think you that they are, then, Master Oswald?"

"I think it possible that they may be a party of Douglas's followers, led by a knight. It may be that Douglas has received some hint of March's being in communication with England; and that he has sent a party to seize, and search, any traveller who looked like a messenger from the south. Of course, this may be only fancy. Still, I am right glad that you were wearing your monkish robe; for, had I been alone, I might have been cross-questioned so shrewdly as to my purpose in travelling, that I might have been held on suspicion, and means employed to get the truth out of me."

At the small town where they stopped, next night, they learned that many complaints had been made, by travellers from the south, of how they had been stopped by a party of armed men on the border, closely questioned, and searched, and in some cases robbed. This had been going on for some weeks, and the sheriff of the county had twice collected an armed force, and ridden in search of the robbers, but altogether without success. It was believed that they were strangers to the district, and the description given of them had not agreed with those of any noted bad characters, in the neighbourhood.

"Certainly, Master Oswald," the monk said, "all this seems to support your idea. Money and valuables are soon found; but by what these men say of the way in which the clothes and belongings of these travellers were searched, it would seem to show that money was not the object of the band, but rather the discovery of correspondence, and that money was only taken as a cloak."

"I have no doubt that they were there to intercept someone, Roger, though it may not have been Percy's messengers; still, we are well rid of them, and I hope that we shall meet no more, on our way."

The hope was fulfilled, and they reached Dunbar without further interruption. Here they deemed it better to separate. The monk went to a convent, and gave out there that he was on the way to Edinburgh, being on a journey thither to see his aged father, who was in his last sickness. Oswald went to a shop, and bought clothes suited for the son of a trader in a fair position; and, changing his things at the inn where he had put up, made his way to the castle.

"I would have speech with the earl," he said, to the warder at the gate. "I have his orders to wait upon him."

"What is your name and condition?"

"That matters not. I am here by the earl's orders. He sent me a ring, by which it might be known that I am authorized to have access to him."

On seeing the ring, the warder at once called to one of the servitors, and bade him conduct Oswald to the earl's apartment.

"Whom shall I say?" he asked, when he reached the door.

"Give this ring to him, and say that the bearer awaits admittance to him."

The man entered the room and then, opening the door again, motioned to Oswald to enter. The earl, a tall and powerfully-built man, looked with a keen scrutiny at him.

"From whom come you, young sir?"

"From the holder of that ring, my Lord Earl," Oswald said, presenting the ring that Percy had given him. "My name is Oswald Forster, and I have the honour to be one of Lord Percy's esquires."

"Come you alone?" the earl asked.

"I came with a companion, a monk. I was in the disguise of a young servitor of his convent. We came on foot from Roxburgh."

He then unscrewed the handle of a dagger Percy had given him, for the purpose, and pulled out a small roll of paper, which he handed to the earl. It contained only the following words:

"Do not intrust undue confidence in the bearer. The matters you wot of are in good train; of them my messenger knows nothing."

"This was so writ by Sir Henry Percy," said Oswald, "in order that, if I were detained and searched on the way, and this paper found on me, I might not be forced, by torture, to say aught of my message."

"But this signet ring would have shown to whom you were coming."

"It was concealed in my staff, my lord, and could not have been discovered, had not that been split open. Had it been so, I should have admitted that Lord Percy had indeed committed the signet and the writing to me to carry, and had bid me travel as the servitor of a monk on his journey north; but that, more than that these were to be delivered to you, I knew nothing. Lord Percy selected me as his messenger partly because, from my youth, I should not be likely to be suspected of being a messenger between two great lords; and in the second place because, if arrested, and these matters found on me, the statement in the letter would be readily believed. It would not be supposed that important state secrets would be committed to a lad, like myself."

The earl made no reply, for a time, but sat with his eyes fixed on Oswald's face, as if he were reading him thoroughly.

"Then you do know the matters in question?"

"I do, my lord. I am the bearer of a further communication to you."

"Say on, then."

"Lord Percy bids me say that, on the receipt of your message to him, he forwarded it by one of his knights to the king at Westminster; and that the matter was discussed, by his majesty, with two or three of his most trusted councillors. After full consideration, the king has accepted your offer, and will grant all its conditions. He sent, my lord, also a document with his royal seal attached, engaging to observe all the conditions of the compact. This document Lord Percy holds, to be given to you on a convenient occasion; but he deemed it of so important a nature that it would be too hazardous to send it to you. The king, in a letter to Lord Percy, begged him to tell you that, so long as the truce continued, he could not collect an army to support you; but that, as the time for its termination approached, he would begin to do so, and would be in readiness to take the field, in the north, immediately you move in the matter."

The earl sat for some time, in thought.

"Do you know the conditions of the compact?" he asked, suddenly.

Oswald had expected this question, and felt sure that the earl, who was, when not inflamed by anger, a cool and cautious man, would highly disapprove of Hotspur's frankness; and might possibly detain him, if he knew that he possessed so important a secret. He therefore replied:

"As to such grave matters, it was not necessary that I should know more than I have said to you, my Lord Earl. As it is no secret that you and the Douglases have personal enmity, I deemed that the compact referred to our king giving you aid, should you need it against the Douglases."

The answer was apparently satisfactory. The earl asked no further questions, on this head.

"Were there other reasons than those you have stated why he chose you as his messenger?"

"Another reason he gave me, my lord, was that, as I came of a family who reside within a few miles of the border, and had relatives on this side whom I sometimes visited, my language was similar to that spoken in Roxburghshire; so that I could therefore pass as a Lowland Scot, without difficulty. No one, in fact, at the various places at which we have stopped, has taken me for aught but a countryman; though the monk with me was often taxed with being an Englishman, though belonging to a monastery at Roxburgh."

Again the earl was silent for some time.

"I must think over the message that I shall give you, for Percy," he said. "I like not the delay, though I see that there is good reason for it. As one of Hotspur's esquires, I would fain treat you with all courtesy, and lodge you here; but this might cause question as to who you are, and it were, therefore, better that you should lodge in the town. Have you put up anywhere?"

"I rested for an hour at the sign of the Lion, my lord; engaging a room there, in order to effect a change in my clothes. I left by the back entrance, in order that the change should not be observed."

"It were best that you fetched those you travelled in away, or rather that you returned unnoticed; and, as it is getting dark now, this can doubtless be managed; and, when you sally out, place that cloak over your shoulders to hide your dress as a servitor, and go to the other inn, the Falcon. Say, there, that you are staying for a few days in Dunbar, having come here on business with me; and that I bade you go there, so that I might know where to send for you, if necessary. You can pass for what you seem, a young trader who has come from Edinburgh to arrange, on the part of your father, a cloth merchant there, for a supply of stuffs for the clothing of my retainers."

Oswald carried out his instructions, walked about until it was quite dark, then entered the inn, made his way unobserved to the chamber where he had left his clothes, put these on, made the others up into a bundle, and then went downstairs again and paid his bill; saying, as he did so, that he had found the friends he came to see, and that they had room to take him in. After leaving the house he threw the cloak, which he had carried on his arm, over his shoulders; and put on the cap that belonged to his other dress, and then went to the Falcon Inn, and repeating to the landlord the statement the earl had made, was at once shown to a chamber, with some deference.

"Will your worship have supper here, or in the room below?"

"I will come down," he said. "It is dull work, sitting alone."

Having ordered his supper, with a flask of wine, Oswald again donned his attire as a trader, and went downstairs. Just as he entered the room, in which several persons were sitting, a soldier came in from the outer door. He looked round the room.

"I have a message, from the earl, for the person who was with him, this afternoon."

Oswald at once rose, and went across to him.

"The earl bade me tell you," the soldier said, in a low voice, "that his present furnisher is Robert Micklethwaite, and that his place of business is near the castle gate, at Edinburgh."

"Please thank the earl for the information," Oswald replied, and then returned to his seat.

He had indeed, while dressing, been wondering what name he should give. It was like enough that, in Dunbar, many might know the names of the principal traders in Edinburgh; and that, were he to give an unknown one, he might be questioned as to his place of business. The message, therefore, relieved him of this difficulty.

After he had finished his supper, which was an excellent one, he beckoned to the landlord.

"I am a stranger here, landlord," he said. "I pray you to drink a cup with me, and tell me the news of the place.

"You may know the name of Micklethwaite," he went on, as the landlord sat down, "and that he comes, or sends regularly, to arrange for the supply of cloth, its quality and price, required for the earl's retainers."

"Master Micklethwaite always puts up here, when he visits Dunbar," the landlord said. "I must have misunderstood him, for one day, when he was talking with me, he said that it was a trouble to him that he had no sons."

"Nor has he," Oswald said; "luckily for me, who am but a nephew."

"He is a good customer," the landlord went on, "and good company, too; but he cares not for French wines, and does not trouble my cellarer, much."

"He is a careful man," Oswald said, with a smile; "and though he is a good trencherman, he does not waste his money on such matters. However, he lets me have a freer hand than he uses himself; and asks not, when I return, for a close account of my outgoings.

"What do they say, here, as to the chances of another war with England?"

"I fear the worst," the landlord replied. "These wars are ruin to us, and we have had the English at the gates of Dunbar over many times, already; and the town sacked, and burnt over our heads, more than once. Though I do not say that it might not have been worse, for our earls have ever stood aloof, as much as possible, and have often inclined towards the English side. Still, even then it is bad enough, for the whole country, from Berwick, has often been wasted to check the progress of the armies, and our trade well-nigh ruined. A pest on all wars, say I!"

"And which way, think you, that the present earl's leanings would go?"

"I think not about it, one way or the other. My business is to sell food and liquor, the earl's to take part in affairs of state. In days like these, it is quite enough for each man to attend to his own business, without troubling about that of other people; more especially when that other is a powerful noble, who thinks little enough of slitting a tongue that wags too freely.

"No, no, lad; John Sanderson is no fool, and knows better than to open his mouth, touching the affairs of great nobles. I know not how it may be with you, and the burghers of Edinburgh, but here we are content to cool our own porridge, and let others take their food hot or cold, as they choose."

"I was not wishing you to give me so much your own ideas, as the common talk of the town; but I see that my question was indiscreet, and I ask your pardon."

"I know you meant no harm, lad, and that your question was just one that any young man of your age might ask, without thinking that there was harm in it, or that the answering of it might lead to harm. I can tell you that, whatever folk may think here in Dunbar, they say naught about it to their nearest neighbour. We can talk of war with England, that is too common a thing for there to be harm in it; and as no one knows aught, one man's opinion is as good as another's; but the talk is general, and assuredly no man asks his neighbour what this great lord will do, or how matters will go. There is no harm in two gossips wondering whether, if the English come, the town will hold out till help comes, or whether they will batter down the walls first.

"It is a kind of riddle, you see, and all the more that no one knows who may be by the king's side, when the storm breaks. A generation back, men might make a fair guess; but now it were beyond the wisest head to say and, for my part, I leave the thinking to those whom it concerns. You from Edinburgh ought to know more than we do, for in great cities men can talk more freely, seeing that no one lord has the place in his hands, and that the citizens have rights, and hold to them.

"The general thought is that we shall have war, directly the truce is over. Among us who live by peaceful trade, we still hope for peace; for we see not what good comes of war, save to those who make raids in England, and as often as not these get more hard knocks than plunder; but to the quiet trader it means loss, and may well mean ruin, if the English army again marches through Scotland. We can discover no reason why the two countries should not live peaceably together, each going about its own business. I have heard it said, before now, that it would be a good thing for both countries if the border districts on both sides were stripped altogether of their people, and allowed to lie desolate.

"Ay, it would be a rare thing, that. It is thieving loons, on both sides of the border, that keep up the ill feeling; and the loss would not be great, seeing that there are plenty of waste tracts where the people might be bestowed, and pass their time more profitably, in raising crops and cattle, than in destroying or carrying off those of their neighbours. However, young sir, that is not like to be, in our time."

"I am afraid not, Sanderson, and we must needs make the best we can of things, as they stand. I think that 'twould be well, if the English do come north again and capture Edinburgh, and ruin trade for years, to cross the seas to France, and take service there."

"Scarce spoken like a peaceful trader," the landlord laughed; "but I doubt not you would make a good soldier, and that a sword would suit your hand to the full as well as a yard measure.

"Well, it makes not so much difference, to me. Men must eat and drink, and though my wine would be drunk up without payment, and I should have to run the risk of being killed on the walls, if the English came; I should know that, in a short time, men would come and go as before, and that they will drink good wine if they have money to pay for it, and in six months my trade would be as brisk as ever; but men seem to think that, this time, it will be the Scots who will invade England, for the English barons have had enough of wars in France, and will be slow in furnishing their quota when called on; and that we shall carry fire and sword through the northern counties."

"That we may do, though Northumberland and Hotspur will doubtless have something to say to it. I fear it will be as it has been, many a time before. Our armies will march back with their plunder, the news of the damage done will inflame all England, and then a great army will march north. The nobles will hasten to make terms for themselves, and the harm and damage will fall upon quiet people, who had nought whatever to do with the invasion."

"True enough, young sir, true enough, though it is a shame that it should be said. Had the cities a voice in the matter of peace and war, you may be right sure that we should hear no more of invasions and troubles, from this side of the Border.

I say not that there would be peace, for the claims of the English kings to author-ity in Scotland, although we have not heard so much of them since Bannockburn, are but in abeyance; and the first time that there is really peace, between them and France, you may be sure that we shall hear of them again, and then the towns as well as the country would join, heartily, in repelling an invasion."

"They never did so in the past time, Sanderson. They generally opened their gates at once, or if they closed them, it was because there was a strong garrison, un-der some knight or noble who, and not the townspeople, had the say in the matter. Now, methinks I will to bed, for I have had a long day's travel."

The next day passed without any message from the earl, but on the following morning one of the retainers from the castle came in, with the message that the earl desired the presence of Mr. Micklethwaite.

Oswald went up, at once. The earl was, as before, alone.

"I have been thinking, Master Forster, that it would be safer, both for you and for me, were you to tarry here for a while. You came through safely, it is true, but you might not have such good fortune on your return; and even though I sent no written answer, it would be enough, were Percy's signet found upon you, to ensure your imprisonment, and perhaps death. At any rate, they would have the means of wringing from you the mission of which you were in charge; while I could send equally well a message by sea, as I did before."

"I see that there might be some slight danger, my Lord Earl," Oswald said qui-etly; "but I, as well as another, might take passage down by ship touching at Ber-wick, or other port."

The earl's brow clouded.

"'Tis a matter to be thought over," he said, moodily. "A ship might be captured, seeing that there are often French freebooting vessels on the coast. And what were your orders from Lord Percy?"

"That I was to return, immediately I had conveyed his message to you."

"I would gladly hasten your departure," the earl said, after a moment's pause, "but you see, great issues hang upon this affair. However, I will think the matter over again, and will see how it can be best managed."

After leaving the castle, Oswald went to the convent where the monk was lodged, and asked for speech with Brother Roger. In a minute or two the latter came out.

"Are we off, young master?" he asked. "In truth, it is as bad here as at Alnwick; and, after a taste of liberty, I am longing to be out again; and indeed, I have had some trouble in accounting for my stay here, instead of continuing my journey to see my aged father."

"If it depended upon me, I would say that we would start forthwith; but what I have somewhat feared, all along, has come to pass. I was the bearer of a certain message of much importance, from Hotspur to the earl, and I fear that the latter will detain me. He thinks that I know more than I have said, which indeed is true, and likes not that one who is so entirely cognisant of his secret counsels, and intentions, should go free. He put it down to the fact that I might be captured, on my way back, and forced to confess the whole details of the mission with which I am charged. It is possible that this is so, but it is more likely that he dislikes that anyone should know secrets that concern his safety; and although he has not said as much, at present, I believe that it is his intention to hold me here as prisoner; though doubtless with due courtesy, as befits Percy's messenger and esquire; until affairs come to a head, which may not be for a year or two, yet."

"Is there a guard over you, at present?"

"Not that I know of, Roger, but it may be that the inn is watched. At any rate, he would try to overtake me, did I attempt to leave without his permission."

"Then, Master Oswald, I should say let us be off, at once."

"But how, Roger? On foot we should be speedily overtaken, and if not watched at present, doubtless I shall be, after my interview with the earl this morning. Were I to try and buy horses, I might be arrested at once. However, I have been thinking that the best plan would be for you to go round to the port, and to bargain for a passage for us to Edinburgh. Then we would slip on board quietly, half an hour before she sailed.

"Methinks it were as well that you did not go in your robes. I will purchase a dress suitable to a cattle drover, for you, and a similar one for myself. I will bring yours for you here, in an hour's time, if you will wait a hundred yards from the gate for me. Then you can go to some quiet spot and change your garments, and then go down to the port. I will be standing at the door of my inn, and as you pass say, without checking your pace, the hour at which a boat sails, today or tomorrow; and then do you be near the hotel, again, an hour before that time.

"Do not speak to me as I come out, but keep a short distance behind me; and if you see that I am followed by anyone, you must do your best to rid me of him. You had better bring your present garments along with you. They may be useful."

Roger assented joyously. The thought that, at any rate for a time, he was to get rid of his robes filled him with joy; and the possibility that there might be danger in the enterprise only added to his pleasure.

Feeling the need for great care, Oswald walked for some little time before entering a shop, passing through several quiet streets; and, when assured that he was not followed, he went into the booth of a clothier.

"I have occasion for two suits of clothes, such as would be worn by cattle drovers," he said. "I am about to travel and, having money about me, can best do so safely in such a garment. I want one suit to fit me, and another for a companion, who is a big stout man, a good deal above the ordinary height."

"'Tis a wise precaution, your honour, for the roads are by no means safe, at present. I can fit you, with ease, and will pick out the largest clothes I have in stock, for your companion."

The purchase was soon made. It consisted of a rough smock of blue cloth, reaching to the knees, and girded in by a strap at the waist; and breeches of the same material, reaching below the knees, with strips of gray cloth to be wound round and round the leg, from the knee to the ankle. In addition, Oswald bought two pairs of rough sandals, and two lowland bonnets. Each suit was done up, at his request, in a separate parcel; and then, retracing his steps, he joined Roger and handed his clothes to him.

"I will go outside the gates and change my things," Roger said, "and then go down to the port. I will then come to your hotel, as you said. If no ship sails until tomorrow, I have only to put my robe on over these garments, and return to the convent. If there is one sailing this evening, I shall not go back there again; but will be on the lookout for you, half an hour before the boat leaves the port."

"The nearer the time of sailing, the better, Roger; for if I am watched, and there is any trouble with the man who follows me, the sooner we are on board before any alarm is raised, the better. But I should hardly think a boat would start, in the evening."

"I don't know, Master Oswald. I was down at the port, yesterday, and the tide was high at three o'clock; and methinks that a boat would put out an hour or two before low tide, so as to take the water with it as far as New Berwick, and there catch the flood flowing into the Firth. In that case, the boat would put out at six, or maybe seven o'clock."

"I would that it had been two hours later, Roger. After dark, it were easy enough to silence a man without attracting much attention; but in broad daylight, it would not be so easily done."

"Not if we went straight from the inn to the port, Master, but there is no need for you to take that route."

"You are right, Roger. Indeed, it would be better not to do so, for were they to have an idea that we had escaped by water, the earl might send a fast boat after us. Therefore, when I come out I will turn off and go, by unfrequented streets and lanes, in the opposite direction. In that way you will be better able to see if I am followed, and may find some quiet place, where you can give a man a clout on the head that will rid us of him."

"Will you come out, Master Oswald, in your present attire, or in your disguise?"

"I will wear this cloak and headgear, and will put these leggings over the others, so that I shall have but to take them off and fling them aside, and to throw off my cloak and cap and put on this bonnet, all of which will not take a minute and can be done in a doorway or passage without attracting observation. I should be afraid to go out, in the drover's attire. The servants at the inn know me, now; and moreover, a man of such condition would not think of going to the Falcon. Were I to be noticed, coming out, it might be thought that I had entered it for some evil purpose."

"I shall be on hand, master. I had thought of not returning to the monastery, but I must do so, for I have left my staff there, and it will be as suitable for a drover as a monk. I shall go to the harbour, as soon as I have seen you; and if it is this evening a boat sails, I shall go back at once and bid them farewell, saying that a ship is sailing for Leith, and that I have taken passage in her."

Oswald returned to the inn and, half an hour later, went down to the doorway, where he stood as if idly watching the flow of traffic. A quarter of an hour later, he saw Roger approaching. He looked the character that he had assumed, to the life. He had dirtied his hands and face, and smudged his smock with stains of mud. He strolled along, with a free step and head erect. He did not look at Oswald as he passed, but said, "Boat sails at seven, tonight."

Oswald stood for some time longer. A short distance down the street, he observed two of the earl's retainers. They were standing, apparently looking at the goods in a mercer's window. After a time, they moved on a short distance, passed the inn, and stopped again to look in another shop, twenty or thirty yards away.

Then Oswald left the door. The landlord was standing in the passage, and beckoned to him to enter his private room.

"Young sir," he said, "I know not whether you have done anything that has displeased the earl, nor is it any business of mine; but you are a fair-spoken young gentlemen, and I would not that any ill came to you. I like not to meddle in the earl's affairs, for he would think nothing of ordering my house to be burnt over my head. However, I may warn you that he is making inquiries about you. One of his retainers has been here, two hours ago, with a confidential message from the earl, to inquire whether you had said anything about leaving, and to bid me send a message to him, secretly, should you do so."

"I thank you warmly, my good host," Oswald replied. "I have had no quarrel with the earl, but we have differed as to the value of the goods he requires. He would fain have them at last year's prices; but wool has gone up, and we could not sell them, save at a loss. It may be that he thinks I shall go away, and that if he finds I am about to do so he will send for me, and agree to my terms, which indeed are so low that they leave but little profit. However, it were well that you should let me know how much I owe you, and I will pay that, at once. Do not make up the account, but tell me roundly there or thereabouts; and then, should I leave suddenly, you can say truly that I had not asked for my bill, and that you were altogether ignorant of my intention of leaving."

"There can be no occasion for that," the host said. "You can pay me the next time you come, should you decide to leave suddenly."

"Nay, I would rather settle obligations, for if I do not do business with the earl, it may be some time before I return."

The landlord made rapid calculations, and named a sum, which Oswald at once handed to him, with warm thanks for the warning he had given him.

"I may stay here three or four days longer," he said meaningly, "as the earl may, at the last moment, come to an agreement as to the price of the goods. I should be sorry to return to my uncle without getting an order, for the earl has, for years, been one of our best customers."

The landlord nodded.

"I understand," he said. "It would be as well, perhaps, that you should say as much in the hearing of one of the drawers; so that, if questioned, I shall have a witness who can bear me out."

Chapter 7: Back To Hotspur.

It was still broad daylight when, at half-past six, Oswald left the inn and sauntered, at a leisurely pace, down the street. His eye at once fell on Roger's tall figure, and he also saw two retainers of the earl, loitering about. They were not the same men he had seen in the morning, but doubtless had relieved those on watch.

He took the first turning off the main street and, after passing through several lanes, found himself at the foot of the town wall. A narrow lane ran between it and a row of small houses. No one was about, and he thought that Roger would take advantage of the loneliness of the spot, to endeavour to rid him of his followers, whose footsteps he could hear some distance behind him. Presently, he glanced carelessly round. The men were some thirty or forty yards behind him; and coming up with them, at a rapid step, was Roger. A minute later, he heard a voice raised in anger.

"Where are you going, fellow? There is plenty of room to pass, without pushing between us. You want teaching manners."

Roger gave a loud laugh.

"Who is going to teach me?" he said.

"I will!" one of the men said, angrily placing his hand upon his sword hilt.

As he did so, he was levelled to the ground by a tremendous blow from Roger's staff. With a shout, the other soldier drew his sword; but, before he could guard himself, the staff again descended, and he fell senseless beside his comrade.

Roger at once knelt beside them, tore off strips of their garments and, rolling them up, pressed them into their mouths; and, with string which he had brought for the purpose, tied them in their place. Then, taking out a few pieces of cord he tied their hands behind them, and their ankles together; dragged them into a dark entry, and left them lying there.

The whole transaction had occupied but two or three minutes, and had attracted no attention, whatever. The soldiers' shout might have been heard; but there was no clashing of weapons, and a shout was too unimportant a matter for anyone within hearing to take any trouble about.

Oswald, seeing that Roger needed no assistance, had occupied himself with stripping off the outer pair of leggings; and had made these, with his cloak and cap, into a bundle; and, pressing the drover's cap down over his eyes, was ready by the time Roger came up to him.

"It was splendidly managed, Roger."

"It did well enough," the other said, carelessly. "It may be an hour before anyone stumbles over them; and, long before that, we shall be at sea."

They made their way back through quiet lanes until near the port, and then boldly went down to the side of a small craft.

"You are just in time, my men," the skipper said. "In another five minutes, we should be throwing off the ropes and hoisting sails. Now that you have come, we shall do so, at once. The tide is just right for us, and we have nothing further to stop for."

The boat was a large fishing smack, and had put into Dunbar but that afternoon, with the intention of disposing of the catch. Two others had, however, come in still earlier. The market being glutted, the skipper had determined to take his catch, which was a heavy one, on to Leith; and had agreed, for a very small sum, to carry the two drovers to that port.

Oswald and Roger aided in getting up the sails, and in a few minutes the smack was at sea. The wind was from the southwest, and the boat ran rapidly up the coast.

"The earl will be in a nice way, when he finds that you have gone," Roger said, as he stood in the stern to watch the rapidly receding towers of Dunbar. "There will be a hot hue and cry for you. The earl is not accustomed to be thwarted, and they say that he is a mighty hot-tempered man. I have no doubt that, as soon as his fellows bring him word of what has happened to them, and he finds that you have quitted the inn, he will send parties of horse out to scour the roads to Berwick and Haddington; and to search the country, far and near."

"He is welcome to do that," Oswald said. "My fear is that he will send down to the port, to inquire if any craft put out about the hour at which his men were attacked. But even if he does so, there is no great chance of our being overtaken. We are travelling fast, and in another hour it will be dark; and long before daybreak we shall reach Leith, having both wind and tide in our favour, all the way."

They kept an anxious watch, as long as there was light enough for them to make out if a vessel left Dunbar. Both fancied that they could see a sail, just as twilight was falling, but neither could be sure that it was not the effect of imagination. They were already ten miles away, and as the tide had now begun to make along the shore, it was certain that for some time, at least, a ship, however fast she might be, would gain but little upon them, until she had fairly entered the Firth. There would be no moon and, even should she overtake them, she might well pass them in the dark.

When they lay down, they agreed that they would keep awake in turns; and that, if they made out a ship apparently pursuing them, they would offer the skipper the full value for his boat, and betake themselves to it, and row for shore.

"The greatest danger," Roger said, "would be of their passing us, unseen; and then lying-to near the entrance of the port, and overhauling us as we came in."

"That is a danger that we cannot guard against. Can you swim, Roger?"

"It is years since I have done so," the monk replied, "but I used to do so, in the old days."

"There is an empty cask here, by my side," Oswald went on. "If we are challenged, the best plan would be to lower it down, quietly, into the water; and to hold on by it. The boat would certainly go some distance, before she had lost her way and brought up; and we should be out of sight of both ships, before they came together."

"That is a good idea. If we hear a hail, I will at once cut a good length of rope, and twist it round a barrel for us to hold on by. But I don't think there is any chance of our being overhauled."

"I agree with you in that respect; still, it is just as well to have our plans prepared, in case it should happen."

They kept a vigilant watch through the night, without catching sight of any craft proceeding in the same direction as themselves.

It was still dark when the helmsman hailed the skipper: "I see the lights of

Leith ahead," and later they passed the beacon fire that marked the entrance to the port. Five minutes later Oswald and his companion, after paying the sum agreed on, stepped on shore.

"That danger is over. I did not think that there was any real cause for fear. I should like to see the earl, as his bands of horsemen ride in, today, with the news that they can hear nothing of us."

"I should like to hit him just such a clout, with my staff, as I gave his two retainers," Roger said. "Earl as he is, it was scandalous, and contrary to all usages, to arrest a messenger; especially when that messenger is an esquire of one of equal rank to himself, and his message, as I suppose, a friendly one."

"I don't so much blame him. He had no means of judging my discretion; and the consequences, to him and others, had I fallen into the hands of Douglas, or those of a marauding leader, might have been serious, indeed. I doubt not that, had I been content to stay with him, he would have treated me with all honour. I might even have done so, and have got him to send another messenger to Percy; but the latter bade me to return at once, and moreover said that he had another mission, as soon as I had carried the present one to a successful termination."

"And have you done so, Master Oswald?"

"Yes, I think so, Roger. I was to ascertain the earl's real intentions regarding certain matters, and I think that he means honestly to adhere to an offer he made. The very fear that he has shown, lest his intentions should be betrayed, seems to prove that he is most anxious that naught should occur to interfere with his plans."

"The Earls of Dunbar have ever been a treacherous race," Roger said earnestly, "and ready to betray their own countrymen, in order to curry favour with England, and continue in possession of their estates. However, as we have benefited from it, we need not grumble, if the Scots are contented.

"Now, Master Oswald, what are we to do next?"

"I should say that we had better find a corner to lie down, until daybreak. I don't think that either of us have slept. Then we will go into a tavern and breakfast, and afterwards go on to Edinburgh. I should like to see the town and castle, and the chance may never come again to me.

"Then, tomorrow morning, we will start in earnest. We shall have plenty of opportunities to talk over our plans, so let us lose no time, now, in looking for a bed."

Fortunately, they soon came upon some fishing nets, carelessly piled under the lee of a stack of timber. Here they threw themselves down, and were soon fast asleep.

When they woke, the sun was well up. Fishermen were preparing to get up sail; and those who had, like themselves, come in during the night, were commencing to unload their cargoes.

"Look there!" Oswald exclaimed, as he pointed to a vessel, from whose masthead floated a flag with the arms of the Earl of March. "She is just entering the port. They did chase us after all, you see, but they did not gain on our fishing boat."

"Well, methinks that we had better be off, at once," Roger said. "They will soon learn which boat has come from Dunbar, and find out from the men what were the disguises worn by us. So we had best lose no time in getting out of Leith."

"They would never dare to seize us, here," Oswald said.

"I don't know that. If they have strict orders to bring us back, they would not feel much hesitation in seizing us, wherever they found us; knowing well enough that the burghers of Leith would not concern themselves greatly about the capture of two drovers, who would probably be charged with all sorts of crime. Were it one of their own citizens, it would be different; but it is scarce likely that the burghers would care to quarrel, with a powerful noble, for the sake of two strangers of low degree. The gates will be open before this, and we shall be safer in Edinburgh than we are here."

Accordingly, they postponed their breakfast and, passing through the town without a pause, issued out by the south gate, and walked briskly to Edinburgh. As soon as they arrived, they found a small tavern, and partook of a hearty meal. Listening while they ate to the conversation going on around them, they found that the young Duke of Rothesay was, at present, staying at the castle.

"Men say that the disputes between him and his uncle, the Duke of Albany, have of late grown hotter."

"That might well be," another said. "Rothesay is a man, now. He has shown himself a brave soldier, and it is not likely that he would support, with patience, the haughtiness and overbearing manner of Albany. It was an evil day for Scotland when our good king, who was then but prince, lamed himself for life; and so was forced, on his accession, to leave the conduct of affairs to Albany, then Earl of Fife. The king, as all men know, is just and good, and has at heart the welfare of his subjects; but his accident has rendered him unfit to take part in public affairs, and he loves peace and quiet as much as Albany loves intrigues, and dark and devious ways. 'Tis a sore pity that the king cannot make up his mind to throw himself into the arms of Douglas, and call upon the nobility to join in expelling Albany from his councils; and to give the charge of affairs into the hands of Rothesay, or even to bestow upon him the kingly dignity, while he himself retires to the peaceful life he loves."

"That would have been better done," the other said, "before the young duke married; for many of the nobles, who would have otherwise supported him, would hold aloof, seeing that the accession of Rothesay would be but handing over the real power of the state from Albany to Douglas. Men say that the feud between March and Douglas grows hotter and hotter, and that the boldness with which March upbraided the king, for the breaking off by Rothesay of his marriage with Elizabeth of Dunbar, has so angered him, Rothesay, and Albany, who had aided in bringing about the match with Elizabeth Douglas, that 'tis like that March will, ere long, be arraigned for his conduct, and the threats that he uttered in his passion."

"Well, gossips, it matters little to us," an elderly man said. "Whether king or prince or duke is master, we have to pay; and assuredly, were Rothesay king, our taxes would not abate; seeing that he is extravagant and reckless, though I say not that he has not many good qualities. But these benefit, in no way, men like ourselves; while the taxation to support extravagance touches us all."

There was a murmur of assent from the little group who were talking, who struck Oswald as being farmers, who had come in from the country to sell cattle to the butchers of the town. They were interrupted in their talk by the landlord, who came across to them.

"My good friends," he said, "I pray you talk not so loudly concerning princes and nobles. It is true that we are a royal city, and that the burghers of Edinburgh have their rights and their liberties; nevertheless, it were dangerous to talk loud concerning nobles. We are quiet people all, and none here wear the cognizance of Douglas or Albany. Still, it would do me much harm, were it reported that there had been talk here concerning such powerful nobles; and though the Douglas might care little what was said of him, methinks that there are others--I name no names--who would spare neither great nor small who incurred their resentment."

"I knew not that we were talking loudly, John Ker; and methinks that none, save the two men at the near table, have heard our words; and they look honest fellows enough. Still, what you say is right, and while we may talk of these things by our firesides, 'tis best to keep a silent tongue, while abroad."

"You need not disquiet yourself about us," Roger broke in. "We have no communion with lords or princes; and, so that we can drive our herds safely down into Cumberland, we care not whether one noble or another has the king's ear. We have but just returned, from England."

"Well, man, I may put you in the way of getting a job, if you want one," the eldest of the party said. "I myself have a small farm, near Lavingston, and but breed cattle for the Edinburgh market; but I have a brother, at Lanark, who buys cattle up in the north; and, when there is peace between the countries, sends the droves down to Carlisle, and makes a good profit on their sales. I saw him but two hours ago, and he told me that he was daily expecting a lot of cattle from the north; and that he intended to send them on, without delay, to Carlisle. If you say to him that you have seen me, and that I recommended you to call on him, and see if he wanted any drovers to aid in taking them down; I doubt not he will take you on, unless he has already engaged men."

"I thank you for the offer," Roger said, "but our home lies near Roxburgh, and we intend to abide there for a time; for the roads are by no means safe, at present. Douglas is thinking more of his quarrel with Dunbar than of keeping down border freebooters. We escaped them this time; but we heard of their taking heavy toll from some herds that followed us, and of their killing two or three drovers who offered objection; so we have determined to abide at home, for a time, to see how matters go."

After taking a brief view of the town they started, in the afternoon, to walk to Dalkeith, where they slept; and, leaving there at daybreak, crossed a lofty range of hills, and came down into Lauderdale. They had no fear of any interruption such as they had experienced before--as, had Douglas news of negotiations going on between March and England, he would not think it necessary to watch the road between Edinburgh and the border--and late in the evening they arrived at Ancrum, on the Teviot, having done fully fifty miles, since starting.

Ten miles in the morning took them to Roxburgh. Here they put up at a small tavern, and Oswald donned the servitor's suit that he had brought with him from Dunbar; while Roger, to his great disgust, resumed his monk's gown, which he put on over the drover's suit.

Oswald then went to the governor's. His former acquaintance happened to be at the door, and endeavoured to atone for his former rudeness, by at once ushering him to the governor's room.

"Welcome back, Master Forster!" the latter said. "Your mission, whatever it was, is speedily terminated. From what you said, I had not looked for you for another fortnight."

"If I had not come when I did," Oswald said, "my absence might have been prolonged, for months. However, all has gone well, and I purpose starting at once for Alnwick, and would fain reach Wooler by nightfall."

"That you can do, easily enough. I will order the horses to be saddled, at once."

"I thank you, Sir Philip. I will mount here in the courtyard. I care not, now, what notice may be taken of me; seeing that there is but some ten miles to be ridden, to the frontier."

"Nor, I warrant me, will you meet with interference on the road," the knight said. "I have not heard of anyone being stopped for toll, for the past year, between this and the border."

A quarter of an hour later they left Roxburgh; and, travelling at an easy pace, arrived at Wooler before sunset; and on the following evening entered Alnwick. They could have reached it earlier, but Oswald thought it as well not to enter the castle until after dark, as he did not wish to be noticed in his present attire.

Fastening the horses to hooks in the courtyard, Oswald ran up to his apartment, which was next to that of his uncle.

"Welcome back, Oswald!" the latter said, as he opened his door on hearing his footsteps. "I had thought that you would be longer away."

"I am back sooner than I expected, Uncle. Will you order supper to be brought up here, for Roger and myself? We are both hard set; though, indeed, we had a meal of bread and cheese, at noon, at a wayside tavern."

"Brother Roger has behaved well?"

"Excellently. He has cracked but two sconces since we left, and these were on my behalf. He will sleep on some rushes in my room, tonight. He hates the thought of returning to the monastery, and has begged me, most earnestly, to ask Percy to continue him in his employment."

As soon as Oswald had donned his ordinary attire, he went to Lord Percy's quarters.

"You are back sooner than I had expected, Oswald," Hotspur said, as he entered. "Nothing has gone wrong, I hope?"

"Nothing, my lord, but I was forced to leave Dunbar, after but three days' stay there; for the earl was so fearful that I might be detected, on my way back, that he would have retained me with him until the time for action came; sending down another messenger, by sea, to you. As your orders were to return with all speed, I gave him the slip, and made my way back as quickly as possible."

"And March?"

"I think that the earl is in earnest in his professions, my lord; and that you can rely upon him for such aid as he can render. But, from what I heard in Edinburgh--"

"In Edinburgh!" Hotspur said, in surprise; "what took you there?"

"I will tell you, my lord; but the point is that men said openly, there, that there was a report that he would be attainted, and deprived of his land, for treasonable words spoken by him to the king, the Duke of Albany, and the Duke of Rothesay. If this is so, he will have to fly; for assuredly he has, at present, no force gathered that could resist those of the king and Douglas."

"Give me an account of what has happened," Hotspur said, frowning. "I feared that March's impetuous temper would lead him into trouble, before we were in a position to march to his assistance; and I heard rumours of a stormy scene between him and Rothesay, when he learned that he had been fooled; but I knew not that the king, himself, was present."

Oswald related the story of his journey, and the interruption on the moor; and the reports, that he had afterwards heard, of the stoppage of all travellers coming from the south, by the same band.

"The leader was evidently above the rank of an ordinary marauder, and his followers obeyed him as men-at-arms would obey an officer; and it seemed to me, my lord, that Douglas must have heard a vague report that the earl was in communication with England; and sought to intercept some messenger, on whom he might find a letter, or from whom he could extract proofs of the earl's treachery."

"'Tis like enough," Hotspur said. "When a man is so rash as to upbraid the king, and still more Albany, he must needs fall under suspicion. Now, go on with your story."

When Oswald had brought his narration to an end, Percy said:

"You have done very well, Oswald, and have deserved the confidence that I placed in you. You have shown much circumspection, and you did well in escaping from Dunbar, as you did. The mad monk, too, seems to have behaved well. I doubted your wisdom in taking him, but he has certainly proved a useful fellow."

"I would petition, my lord, that you should continue him in your service; and that, should you employ me upon another mission, you will again allow me to take him with me. He is a shrewd fellow, as well as a stout one, and I could wish for no better companion; though I own that, since he put on his gown again at Roxburgh, and rode hither, his spirits have greatly failed him."

"I will arrange that with the abbot," Hotspur said; "but tell him that, while he is here, he must continue to wear his robe. His face is too well known for him to pass as a man-at-arms, without being recognized by half the garrison. The Lord Abbot would well object to one of his monks turning into a swaggering man-at-arms, at his very door.

"At any rate, I shall tell the abbot that, if he will consent quietly to the monk's unfrocking himself, until he can obtain for him release from his vows; I will scud him away to one of the other castles, whence I can fetch him, if you need him to accompany you on any errand, and where he can form part of the regular garrison. But the knave must be informed that it were best that he say nought about his former profession, and that he comport himself as quietly as is in his nature.

"I will give him a small command, as soon as may be; for although a very bad monk, he has proved himself to be a good soldier."

"I thank you greatly, my lord," Oswald said; "and will talk seriously to the monk, who will be delighted when he hears that the abbot will take steps to allow him to lay aside his gown."

Roger was, indeed, delighted when he heard the news; and still more so when, three days later, Oswald informed him that Hotspur had obtained, from the abbot, what was practically a release from his vows. The good abbot said that he felt that harm, rather than good, would ensue from keeping the monk a member of the monastery.

"He infects the lay brothers, with his talk," he said. "He is a good instructor in arms, but he teaches not as one who feels that it is a dire necessity to carry arms, but as one who delights in it. Moreover, he causes scandals by his drinking bouts, and does not add to the harmony of the place. At a time like this, when the Scots may, at any moment, fall across the border, such a fellow may do good service to his country; and it is surely better that a man should be a good soldier, than that he should be a bad monk. Therefore I will let him go, my lord; but keep him away from here. It would be a grave scandal, were he to be brawling in the town where he is known. Therefore, I pray you, take him elsewhere. I have striven long to make him a worthy member of his order, but I feel that it is beyond me; and it would be best, therefore, that he should go his own way. He may come to be a worthy soldier, and so justify me in allowing him to unfrock himself.

"As he is abiding in your castle, I pray you bid him present himself here, to-morrow. I would fain speak to him, and give him such advice, concerning his future conduct, as may be of benefit to him."

When Roger returned from the monastery, the next day, he wore a much more serious face than usual.

"The abbot has done me more good, by his talk this morning," he said to Oswald, "than by all the lectures and penances he has ever imposed on me. In truth, he is a good man, and I had half a mind to say that I would return to the convent, and do my best to comport myself mildly and becomingly.

"But I felt that it would not do, Oswald. The thing is too strong for me and, however I might strive, I know that when the temptation came I should break out again; and so, I held my peace."

"What did he say to you, Roger?"

"He said many things, but the gist of it was that there were as good men outside the walls of a monastery as there were within it, and that a soldier has as many opportunities--indeed many more opportunities--of showing himself a good man as a monk has. In battle, he said, a soldier must act as such, and fight stoutly against the enemy, and take life as well as risk his own; but after the fight is over he should show himself merciful, and if he cannot follow out the precept to love his enemies, he should at least be compassionate and kind to them. But above all, he should never oppress the helpless, should comport himself honourably and kindly to women and children, and, if necessary, draw sword in their defence against those who would ill use them. And, though the spoils of war were honourable and necessary, when captured in fair fight, yet the oppression and robbery of the poor were deadly crimes.

"'Comport yourself always, Roger, as if, though a soldier in arms, you were still a monk at heart. You are brave and strong, and may rise to some honour; but, whether or no, you may bear yourself as if you were of gentle blood, and wore knightly spurs. Not all who are so are honourable and merciful, as they have vowed to be. Remember, I shall hear of you from time to time, through my Lord Percy; and that it will gladden me to have a good account of you, and to feel that I have not done wrong in letting you go forth, from this house of rest, to take part in the turmoil and strife of the world.'

"He said more than this, but this is the pith of it. I knelt down, and swore that I would strive, to the utmost in my power, to do as he bade me; and he put his hands on my head, and bade me go in peace; and I tell you, I mean to prove to him that his words have not been in vain."

Two days later, Oswald started with Roger, and rode to Warkworth Castle, some ten miles away; bearing an order to the governor to add Roger to the strength of the garrison, telling him that he had shown himself to be a brave soldier, and a skilful one, and that he could place confidence in him, and appoint him to any sub-command that might become vacant.

On the way, they entered a wood. Here Roger took off his monastic garb, and clad himself in armour such as was worn by the garrison of Alnwick. The monk's clothes were made up into a bundle, and left in the wood, Oswald saying:

"I will carry them back with me, on my return, Roger. It may be that they may come in useful, yet, if you and I travel together again in the Percys' service."

A month passed, and then the Earl of March came, by sea, to Alnwick. Douglas and the regent had marched against him with an overwhelming force; and, as they were both personal enemies, he knew that his fate would be sealed if he fell into their hands, and he had therefore been driven to declare himself, openly, as a vassal of the English king.

On the day after his arrival he happened to be in Hotspur's room, when Oswald entered.

"Ah! ah!" he said, "This is your messenger, Percy.

"You left me with scant notice, sir."

And he smiled.

"I was forced to do so, my lord earl; for, in truth, I was not sure that you would not prevent me from following my lord's orders, to return after seeing you."

"You were right. In the first place, I was not sure that you were a true messenger; and in the second place, I feared that you might, on return, fall into the hands of the Douglases; who would speedily find means to wring from you an account of your mission. Therefore, I thought that it were best that you should tarry a while with me, at Dunbar.

"The young fellow has a good head, Lord Percy, and is as hard to hold as a wildcat. I put the matter of watching him into the hands of two or three of my men, whose wits I have tried more than once, and know them to be among the most trustworthy of my followers. This lad, however, outwitted them. How, they have never been able to explain; but my fellows were found, trussed up like fowls for roasting, in an alley into which they had been thrown; having, as they declared, been knocked down by a giant fellow, who sprung from they knew not where, just as they were about to lay hands upon your messenger. After they had vanished, none had seen him pass the walls, and we judged that he must have started in a craft that sailed up the Forth. Fearing that, if they landed, he might speedily fall into the hands of Douglas, I sent a vessel in chase; but they missed him, and indeed, from that time to this I knew not, save by your letter to me, whether he had reached here safely."

After a short stay, the Earl of March was about to return to Dunbar; when he heard that the king, himself, was coming north with an army for the invasion of Scotland, and would then confer with him, and consider the terms on which he proposed to transfer his allegiance to him. A month later the king arrived at Alnwick, and there George Dunbar, Earl of March, entered into an agreement with him; in which he renounced all fealty to the King of Scotland, in consideration for which he was granted an estate in Lincolnshire, and other revenues. It was also agreed that the subjects of the King of England should support the earl, in time of necessity; and should be supported by him, and received into his fortresses.

He was not, now, in a position to render any very efficient aid to the king; for Robert Maitland, his nephew, to whom he had committed the castle of Dunbar, had been summoned by Douglas, who had marched there with a strong force, by order of the king, and had surrendered the stronghold to him. However, he brought Dunbar's wife and family, and a considerable force of his retainers, safely across the border.

He and Percy, together, then made a raid into the Douglas territory; and penetrated as far as Haddington, and collected much spoil from the country round. Douglas, however, came suddenly upon them in great force, and they were obliged to retreat hastily across the frontier again, abandoning their baggage and booty.

The king's invasion was no more satisfactory. The Earl of March was unable to place Dunbar in his hands; and, as the Scots declined battle in the open, he laid siege to Edinburgh, but without success. Dunbar being closed to him, he was unable to obtain provisions, and was forced to fall back to England, having accomplished nothing.

During his invasion, he had shown much more leniency than had been the custom with his predecessors. He had taken what was necessary to support the army, but had abstained from wasting the country, destroying villages and towns, and slaughtering the country people; and, so far from embittering the animosity between the two nations, he had produced a better state of feeling; and a truce was, in consequence, concluded for a year, at Kelso, by special commissioners from both kings, on the 21st of December, 1400.

Chapter 8: Ludlow Castle.

Oswald Forster had not been present when, in June, 1400, the king arrived at Alnwick. A few days after the coming of the Earl of March, Hotspur received a letter from Sir Edmund Mortimer, the brother of his wife; asking him to send a body of men-at-arms, under an experienced captain who could aid him to drill newly-raised levies; for that one Owen Glendower had taken up arms against the Lord Grey de Ruthyn, and that turbulent men were flocking to his standard, and it was feared that serious trouble might ensue. Percy was in a position to send but few men, for with war with the Scotch imminent, he could not weaken himself by sending off a large force. However, he sent for Alwyn Forster.

"I need twenty picked men, for the service of Sir Edmund Mortimer, Alwyn. I would send more, were it not for the position of affairs here. What say you to taking the command of them?"

"I would gladly do so, my lord, if it be that there is a chance of something more lively than drilling hinds, and turning them into men-at-arms, which has been my business for years now, without a chance of striking a blow in earnest."

"I think that there will be a certainty of fighting, Alwyn. The Welshmen are growing troublesome again, and Sir Edmund thinks that there may be tough work, on the Welsh marches, and has written to me for aid.

"With the king coming hither, there is a chance that the Earl of March, and myself, will open the war by harrying the Douglas's lands. I can spare no great force, but even twenty tried men-at-arms would, no doubt, be welcome. As the king is going to march into Scotland, there is no fear that there will be any serious invasion by the Scots, and therefore you can be spared for a while. I think not that any of my knights would care to go in command of so small an array, but I thought that you might like to take it."

"I shall be right glad to do so, my lord."

"I shall send your nephew with you. He is a shrewd and gallant young fellow, and I know he would far rather be taking part in active service, against the Welsh, than spending his time in idleness, here. He has been too long used to a life on horseback to rest contented to be cooped up in a castle. Besides, there will be a good opportunity of distinguishing himself, and of learning something of a warfare even wilder, and more savage, than that in these northern marches."

"I should like much to have him with me, my lord. Methinks that he has the making of a right good knight; and, young as he is, I am sure that his head is better than mine, and I should not be too proud to take counsel of him, if needs be."

"That is settled then, Alwyn. Choose your men, and set off tomorrow morning. Ralph Peyton, your lieutenant, shall take the command of the garrison until you return."

Oswald was delighted when his uncle told him of the mission with which he was charged, and that he himself was to accompany him.

"You are to have the choice of the men-at-arms, Uncle?"

"Yes, Oswald. I know what you are going to say. You would like to have that mad monk of yours, as one of them."

"That should I, Uncle. You have no stouter man-at-arms in all your band, and he has proved that he can be discreet when he chooses, and did me good service in my last expedition."

"Very well, lad, we will take him. I will send one of the men over, at once, for him to join us on the road tomorrow. I shall choose young and active fellows, of whom we have plenty. I have never fought against the Welsh; but they are light footed, and agile, and their country is full of hills and swamps. The older men would do as good service here, were the castle besieged in our absence; of which, however, there is but slight chance; but for work against the Welsh, they would be of little use."

Hotspur himself spoke to Oswald, that evening.

"Here is a missive to give to Sir Edmund Mortimer. I have commended you to him, telling him that, though young, there is not one of my squires in whom I could more implicitly trust; and that you had carried out a delicate mission for me, with rare discretion and courage. Your uncle, as an old retainer, and a good fighter, and the captain of my garrison, goes in command of the men-at-arms, and in regular fighting one could need no better officer; but in such warfare as that against the Welsh is like to be, yours will be the better head to plan, and as my squire you will represent me. I have specially commended you to him, as one always to be depended upon."

"I am greatly beholden to your lordship," Oswald said, "and will try to justify the commendations that you have given me."

At daybreak on the following morning, the little party rode out from the castle. Oswald with his uncle rode in front; the former in the highest spirits, while the sturdy old soldier was himself scarce less pleased, at this change from the monotony of life in garrison.

"Years seem to have fallen off my shoulders, lad," he said, "and I feel as young as I did when I fought at Otterburn."

"That was a bad business, Uncle; and I trust that no such misfortune as that will befall us, this time."

"I hope not, indeed, Oswald. It was a sore fight, and we are scarce likely to have a pitched battle with these Welsh carls. They fight not much in our fashion, as I have heard; but dash down from their hills, and carry fire and sword through a district, and are off again before a force can be gathered to strike a blow. Then there are marches to and fro among their hills, but it is like chasing a will-o'-the-wisp; and like enough, just when you think you have got them cooped up, and prepare to strike a heavy blow, they are a hundred miles away, plundering and ravaging on our side of the frontier. They are half-wild men, short in stature, and no match for us when it comes to hand-to-hand fighting; but broad in the shoulder, tireless, and active as our shaggy ponies, and well-nigh as untamable. 'Tis fighting in which there is little glory, and many hard knocks to be obtained; but it is a good school for war. It teaches a man to be ever watchful and on his guard, prepared to meet sudden attacks, patient under difficulties; and, what is harder, to be able to go without eating or drinking for a long time, for they say that you might as well expect to find corn and ale on the crest of the Grampians, as you would on the Welsh hills."

"The prospect doesn't look very pleasant, Uncle," Oswald laughed. "However, their hills can scarcely be more barren than ours, nor can they be quicker on the stroke than the border raiders; and for such work, we of the northern marches have proved far more useful than the beefy men of the south."

"No doubt, no doubt; and maybe that, for that reason, Sir Edmund prayed Hotspur to send a detachment to his aid; for he would know that we are accustomed to a country as rough, and to a foe as active as he has now to meet.

"I wonder what has stirred up the Welsh now, knowing as they do that, although they may gain successes at first, it always ends in the harrying of their lands, and the burning of their castles and villages. They have been quiet for some years. But they are always like a swarm of bees. They will work, quietly enough, till they take offence at something; then they will pour out in a fury, attacking all they come across, and caring nothing about death, so that they can but prick an enemy with their stings. Maybe it is the report that the king is engaging in another Scotch war, and they think that it is a good time to gather spoil from their neighbours. They used to be mightily given to warring among themselves, but of late I have heard but little of this.

"It is a hundred years, now, since they were really troublesome, and rose under Morgan ap Madoc; and Edward the Second had himself to reduce them to submission, and build strong castles at Conway, Beaumaris, and other places. There have been one or two partial risings, since then, but nothing of much consequence. It may well be that the present generation, who have not themselves felt the power of English arms, may have decided to make another stroke for independence; and if so, it will need more than Mortimer's force, or that of the other border barons, to bring them to reason; and as for our little detachment, it will be but a drop in the ocean. However, it may be that this is a mere quarrel, between Mortimer and some of his neighbours.

"I have heard somewhat of the Welshman Owen Glendower, who lives in those parts. He has a grievance against Lord Grey of Ruthyn; who, as he says, unjustly seized a small estate of his. I know that he petitioned Parliament for redress, but that his petition was lately refused."

"'Tis strange that such a man should have known enough of English law to have made a petition to our parliament."

"Yes; but he is no common man. He went to England and studied at our universities, and even lived in the inns of court, and learned the laws of this country.

Then, strangely enough, he became an esquire in the household of King Richard, and did good service to him; and when the court was broken up, on Richard being dethroned, he went away to his estate in Wales. Since then I have not heard of him, save as to this dispute with Lord Grey and his petition to Parliament thereon; but men who were at Richard's court have told me that he was a courteous gentleman, of excellent parts and, it was said, of much learning."

"Such a man might be a formidable enemy," Oswald said; "and if he has been robbed by Lord Grey, he might well head an insurrection, to recover his estates from that noble."

In the course of their ride they were joined by Roger, who warmly thanked Alwyn for having selected him as one of his band. The other soldiers received him heartily, for the fighting monk had been a familiar personage at Alnwick, and his mighty strength and jovial disposition rendered him very popular among the soldiers of the garrison. There had been general satisfaction among them, when it was known that he had laid aside his monk's gown, and had become one of the Percys' men-at-arms; and there had been many expressions of regret that he had been sent off, instead of forming one of the garrison of Alnwick. Two or three of them addressed him, as usual, as monk, but he said:

"Look here, comrades, I have been a monk, and a bad one, and the less said about it the better. I am no longer a monk, but a man-at-arms; and as I am not proud of my doings as a monk, I have given up the title, as I have given up the garb. Therefore I give fair notice that whosoever, in future, shall address me as monk, will feel the weight of my arm. My name is Roger, and as Roger let me be called, henceforth."

So saying, he fell into his place in the line, when the cavalcade continued their way.

The journey was a long one. Oswald had been well supplied with funds, and seldom found difficulty in obtaining lodgings for the party. The sight of an esquire, with a small troop of men-at-arms wearing the Percy cognizance, excited no curiosity as they rode south; but when they turned westward it was otherwise, and at their halting places Oswald and his uncle, who dined apart from the others, were always questioned as to their destination.

But when it was known that they were travelling to the castle of Mortimer, whose sister was the wife of their lord, none were surprised; for rumours were already current of troubles on the Welsh border; and when they entered Shropshire they heard that Owen Glendower, with a considerable force, had fallen suddenly upon the retainers of Lord Grey de Ruthyn, had killed many, and had reoccupied the estates of which he had been deprived by that nobleman.

On the fifteenth day after leaving Alnwick they arrived at Ludlow Castle, of which Mortimer was the lord. Oswald was at once conducted to the hall where the knight was sitting.

"I am bearer of a message from Sir Henry Percy," he said; "he has sent hither a party of twenty men-at-arms, under the command of the captain of his garrison, at Alnwick."

"I had hoped for more," the knight said, taking the missive and opening it; "but I can understand that, now the king is marching against Scotland, Percy cannot spare troops to despatch so long a distance. I trust that he and my sister, his wife, and the earl are in good health?"

"I left them so, sir."

The knight read Hotspur's letter.

"He speaks in terms of high commendation of you, young sir," he said, as he laid the letter down on the table. "Such commendation is rarely bestowed on one so young. I marvelled somewhat, when you entered, that Sir Henry Percy should have sent so young a squire; but from what he says, I doubt not that his choice is a good one; and indeed, it is plain that your muscles have had rare exercise, and that you can stand fatigue and hardship better than many older men. It is like that you will have your share, for the whole border seems to be unsettled. You have heard that this Glendower has boldly attacked, and driven out, Lord Grey's retainers from the estates he had taken.

"As to the rights of that matter, I have nought to say. Lord Grey manages the affairs with the Welsh in his own county of Denbighshire, and along the north; and I keep their eastern border, and I meddle not with his affairs, nor he with mine. I know that this Glendower is a supporter of King Richard, of whom there are many tales current; some saying that he escaped from Pomfret, and is still alive, though I doubt not that the report that he died there is true. We know that there is, in Scotland, a man whom it pleases Albany to put forward as Richard; but this, methinks, is but a device to trouble our king. Whether this Glendower believes in this man, or not, I know not; but certain it is that he would embrace any opportunity to prove his hostility to Henry, whom he professes to regard as a usurper. Whether it is on account of his holding such opinions, and foolishly giving expression to them, that Lord Grey thought fit to seize his estates I know not; nor, indeed, do I care. Now, however, that the man has taken up arms, and by force has dispossessed Lord Grey, the matter touches all of us who are responsible for the keeping of peace in the Welsh marches.

"Were it only a quarrel between Lord Grey and this man, it would matter but little; but, from all I hear, he exercises a strange influence over his countrymen, who deem that he has mysterious powers, and can call up spirits to aid him. For myself, I have never known an instance where necromancy or spirits have availed, in any way, against stout arms and good armour; but such is not, assuredly, the opinion of the unlearned, either in this country or in Wales. But these mountaineers are altogether without learning, and are full of superstitions. Even with us, a man more learned than the commonalty is deemed, by them, to dabble in the black art; and it may well be that this reputation Glendower has obtained is altogether due to the fact that he has much knowledge, whereas the people have none. However that may be, there is no doubt that the Welsh people are mostly ignorant; and that, at the call of this Glendower, men from all parts are hastening to join his banner. Even on this side of the border there are complaints that the Welsh servants are leaving, not openly and after a due termination of service, but making off at night, and without a word of warning.

"All this would seem to show that there is trouble on hand, and it behoves us to be watchful, and to hold ourselves in readiness; lest at any time they should, as in the days of old, cross the border, and carry fire and sword through Shropshire and Hereford. The royal castles in Wales could, doubtless, hold out against all attacks; but the garrisons would have to remain pent up within their walls, until succour reached them. Fortunately, most of them are situated near the sea, and could be relieved without the troops having to march through places where a heavily armed man can scarce make his way, and where these active and half-clad Welshmen can harass them, night and day, without ever giving them a chance of coming to close quarters.

"A messenger from Lord Grey arrived here, yesterday. Indeed, since the attack on his retainers, we have been in constant communication. At first he made light of the matter, and said that he should like to have the Welshman hanging from the battlements of his castle; but, during the last week, his messages have been less hopeful. Glendower had disappeared from the neighbourhood altogether, leaving a sort of proclamation to Lord Grey affixed to the door of his house; saying that, next time he heard of him, no mercy would be shown, and every man would be slain. He now says that rumours reach him of large gatherings, and that there are bonfires, nightly, on the hilltops. He doubts not that the troubles will soon be suppressed, but admits that much blood may have to be spilt, ere it is done.

"I can bear testimony to the bonfires, for from the top of the keep a dozen can be seen, any night, blazing among the hills."

"Of course, sir, your messenger, asking Lord Percy to send a body of men-at-arms here, was despatched before Glendower's attack on Lord Grey?"

"Certainly; but it is three months, now, since Parliament refused Glendower's appeal for justice against Lord Grey; and rumours have been busy, ever since. Some said that he was travelling through the valleys, accompanied by some of the harpers, who have always taken a leading part in stirring up the Welsh to insurrection. Some avow that he has retired to a fortress, and was there weaving designs for the overthrow of Lord Grey, and even of the whole of the English castles. Some say that he claims to be a descendant of Llewellyn, and the rightful king of Wales.

"There is some foundation for this, for I have talked to some of the better class of Welsh; who have, like Glendower, studied in our universities. The Welsh are, above all things, fond of long pedigrees, and can trace, or pretend to trace, the lineage of all their principal families up to Noah; and some of them admit that there is some ground for the claim Glendower is said to have made.

"Still, all these rumours make me feel uneasy. As we have had many years of quiet here, it has not been necessary to keep up more than a sufficient number of men-at-arms for the defence of this castle. I might have increased the force, for the people of these parts bear a deep animosity against the Welsh, and dread them greatly; as they may well do, from the many wrongs and outrages they have suffered at their hands. One reason why I have not taken on many men, since the talk of coming troubles began, is that, close to the border as we are, many have connections with the Welsh by business or marriage; and these, if enrolled in the garrison, might serve as spies, and give warning of any movement we might undertake. I had hoped that Percy could have spared me a hundred good men-at-arms. I would rather have had his men than others, because they have been trained in border warfare, by the constant troubles in Scotland; and would, moreover, come to me with a better heart than others, since Sir Henry's wife is my sister, and it is, therefore, almost a family quarrel upon which they have entered.

"Had I known, when I wrote, that the king was on his way north, I should have taken steps to raise my strength elsewhere, as of course Percy would have occasion to use every lance he could muster. Lord Grey has sent off a messenger to the king, begging him to denounce this fellow as an outlaw; and should he be troublesome, he himself may, after he has done with the Scots, send hither a force; for although we may hope, with the aid of the levies of the border counties, to drive back the Welsh in whatever force they may come, 'tis another thing to march into the mountains. The matter has been tried, again and again, and has always taxed the power of England to the utmost.

"'Tis of no use lamenting over spilt milk but, for my part, I regret that Parliament did not give a fair hearing to Glendower's complaint against Lord Grey. The refusal to do so was a high-handed one. It has driven this man to desperation, and has enlisted the sympathies of all Welshmen who have English neighbours; for they cannot but say, among themselves, 'If he is to be plundered and despoiled, and his complaints refused a hearing, what is to prevent our being similarly despoiled? 'Tis surely better to take up the sword, at once, and begin again the fight for our independence.'

"As it is, it may cost thousands of lives, immense efforts, and vast trouble before things are placed on their former footing.

"Doubtless, the captain of the men-at-arms you have brought is a good soldier, since Percy says that he is captain of his garrison at Alnwick!"

"He bears a high reputation in Northumberland, Sir Edmund. I may say that he is my uncle, and 'tis from his recommendation that Lord Percy, in the first place, took me into his household."

"I will go down and speak with him," the knight said. "I gave orders, as soon as I heard who had arrived, that proper entertainment should be given to all; yet it is but right that I should, myself, go down to thank them for having come so far; and to welcome their captain, whose experience will be of no small use to my own men, who have never been engaged in border war. Some have fought in France, but under conditions so different that their experience will aid them but little; save, indeed, if the Welsh grow so strong and so bold that they venture to attack this castle."

Percy's men, when the knight descended, had indeed sat down to supper with the retainers of the castle, while Alwyn was being entertained by the captain of his men-at-arms. All rose to their feet when Sir Edmund entered, but he waved his hand to them, to be seated.

"Finish your meal," he said, "and afterwards, if you will muster in the court-yard, I will inspect you, and see what stout Northumberland men Lord Percy has sent me."

He then went up to the top of the keep with Oswald, pointed out the distant hills, and told him what valleys and villages lay among them, and the direction in which such roads as there were ran. By the time they had descended, Percy's men were drawn up in the courtyard.

"This is my uncle, Captain Alwyn Forster," Oswald said, "of whom Lord Percy has written to you."

"I am glad to see so stout a soldier here," the knight said, holding out his hand to Alwyn; "and I am grateful to Lord Percy for sending, in answer to my request, one in whom he has such perfect confidence; and I specially thank you for having willingly relinquished so important a post, to head so small a following."

"I was glad to come, Sir Edmund, for I had rested so long, at Alnwick, that I longed for some brisk action, and fell gladly into my lord's view, when he requested me to come hither. I can answer for my men, for they are all picked, by myself, from among the stoutest of Sir Henry's following."

"That I can well believe," the knight said, as he looked at the twenty troopers. "Tall, strong men all; and as brave as they are strong, I doubt not. I shall be glad to have so stout a band to ride behind me, if these Welshmen break out.

"You are all accustomed to border warfare, but this differs a good deal from that in Northumberland. While the northern forays are mostly made by horsemen, it is rare that your Welshman adventures himself on horseback. But they are as active as your wild ponies, and as swift; and, if the trouble increases, they will give you plenty to do.

"I learn from your lord's letter that you will be, as usual, under pay from him while you are with me. I shall pay you as much more. 'Tis meet that, if you render me service, I should see that you are comfortable, and well contented."

There was a murmur of satisfaction among the men and, after recommending them to the care of the captain of the garrison, and bidding Alwyn speak in the name of his men, fearlessly, for anything that should be lacking, Sir Edmund left the courtyard.

The seneschal of the castle, Sir John Wyncliffe, requested Oswald to follow him. He first showed him the chamber, in one of the turrets, that he was to occupy; and then took him down to the hall, where two other knights, four esquires, and two or three pages were assembled, in readiness for the supper.

Mortimer, with his wife and two daughters, presently came down and took his place at the head of the table; at which the others sat down, in order of their rank. As a guest, Oswald was placed among the knights. Before sitting down, Sir Edmund presented him to his wife and daughters.

"This is one of Sir Henry Percy's esquires," he said, "and can give you more news of Sir Percy's wife; of whom, beyond saying that she sends her greetings to you all, Hotspur tells us nothing."

"Have you been long a member of Sir Henry Percy's household?"

"But a year, my lady."

"Hotspur speaks of him in very high terms, and says that he has rendered him great services, and that he has the highest confidence in him."

"To what family do you belong, sir?" the dame asked. "From my husband's sister, who was staying here some months since, I learned much of your northern families."

"I am the son of John Forster of Yardhope, who has the reputation of being as hard a fighter as any on the border. He is not a knight, though of fair estates; for, although Earl Percy offered him knighthood, for his services at the battle of Otterburn, he said that he preferred remaining plain John Forster, as his fathers had been before him. My mother was a daughter of Sir Walter Gillespie, and my uncle is captain of the garrison of Alnwick; and it was for his goodwill towards him, and my father, that Sir Henry appointed me one of his esquires, thinking, moreover, that I might be more useful than some, because I know every foot of the border, having relations on the Scottish side of it."

They now sat down to supper. After it was over, Sir Edmund took Oswald with him to his wife's bower.

"There," he said, "you can talk at your ease, and tell us how my sister, your mistress, is, and the children."

"Did you not say, Sir Edmund," his wife asked, "that it was the captain of his men-at-arms that Sir Hotspur sent hither, in command of the band?"

"That is so, dame."

"Then, surely, he should have been at our table."

"I asked him," Sir Edmund replied, "but he said that he would rather, with my permission, lodge with John Baldry; who is, like himself, a stout soldier, but who likes better his own society than that of the high table. He said that, except upon rare and special occasions, he always has been accustomed to take his meals alone, or with some comrades whom he could take to his room. As this is also John Baldry's habit, he prayed me to allow him to accept his invitation to share his room."

"What he says about his habits is true, my lady. I can well understand my uncle cares not for company where it would not be seemly for him to raise his voice, or to enter into a hot argument, on some point of arms."

"What were the services of which Sir Henry speaks?"

"It was a mission with which he charged me, and which involved some danger."

"By the way," Dame Mortimer said, "my sister-in-law wrote to me, some time since, telling us of a strange conflict that was held between one of the squires, and another who had been newly appointed; and who, on one of the mountain ponies, worsted his opponent, although the latter was much older, and moreover clad in full armour, and riding a heavy warhorse. Was it you who were the victor on that occasion?"

"I can scarce be said to have been the victor, my lady. It was, indeed, hardly a combat. But I maintained that one accustomed to the exercises in use among our border men, and mounted on one of our ponies, accustomed to move with great rapidity, and to turn and twist at the slightest movement of the rider's knee, would be a match for a heavy-armed knight in single combat; although a number would have no chance, against the charge of a handful of mailed knights; and Sir Henry put it to the proof, at once."

Chapter 9: The Welsh Rising.

For a time the garrison at the castle had but little to do. Lord Grey had taken no steps to recover the estates from which his retainers had been so unceremoniously ejected. He had, indeed, marched a strong force through them; but the Welsh had entirely withdrawn, and it would be necessary to keep so large a force unemployed, were he to reoccupy the land, that he abstained from taking any decisive action, prior to the return of the messenger whom he had despatched to inform the king of the forcible measures that Glendower had taken to recover the estate. It would have been no trifling step to take, to carry his arms into Wales, and so bring on a fresh struggle after so many years of peace; and he would not move in the matter, until he had the royal authority.

Henry lost no time in replying. Glendower had been an open supporter of Richard, and had retired from court rather than own his successor as king. He had made his complaints against Lord Grey before Parliament, and his appeal had been rejected by an overwhelming majority. His attack upon Lord Grey was, therefore, viewed in the light of an insult to the royal power; and, a fortnight after Oswald and his party arrived at Sir Edmund's, a messenger arrived with a royal order, to all barons holding castles on the border, to proclaim Owen Glendower an outlaw, and to take all measures necessary to capture him.

Sir Edmund shook his head, as he read the proclamation, copies of which were to be fixed to the castle gate, and in other conspicuous places.

"Lord Grey has stirred up a fire that it will be difficult to extinguish. It were as wise to kick over a hive of bees, when naked to the waist, as to set Wales in a ferment again. Had this proclamation been sent to me, only, I would have taken it upon myself to hold it over until I had, myself, made a journey north to see the king, and to submit to him my views on the subject; and to point out how dire might be the consequences, to the inhabitants of our marches, and how great would be the effort required, if Glendower should be supported by the whole of his countrymen, as I believe he will be. However, as it has been sent to all the keepers of the marches this cannot be done; and I shall, at once, send orders to the sheriffs of Shropshire, and Hereford, to warn the militia that they may be called out at any moment, and must hold themselves in preparedness, having every man his arms and accoutrements in good condition, and fit for service, according to the law. I shall also issue orders to my own tenants to be ready to take up arms, and to drive their herds away, and bring their wives and families into the castle, as soon as the beacon fire is lighted on the summit of the keep."

This was said to Oswald, to whom Sir Edmund had taken a strong liking, and to whom he spoke more freely than he might have done to his own knights and officers, as being in Earl Percy's service, and having no personal interest in the matters in debate.

"You yourself have heard the tales that have been brought in to me, showing how greatly the people have been stirred by the belief in Glendower's powers of necromancy; how blue flames have been seen to issue from every window and loophole of his house; how red clouds, of various strange shapes, hover over it; and mysterious sounds are heard throughout the night. For myself, I believe not these tales, though I would not take upon myself to say they are false, since everyone knows that there are men who have dealings with the powers of darkness. Still, I should have, myself, to see these things, before I gave credence to them. That, however, makes no difference in the matter; true or not, they seem to be believed by the Welsh, and cannot but increase his power.

"Well, we shall soon hear what reply he makes to the proclamation, of which he will certainly hear, within a few hours of its posting."

The answer, indeed, was not long in coming; for, within a week, a copy of the reply sent by Glendower to the king appeared, side by side with every proclamation put up, none knowing who were daring enough to affix them. In this, Glendower no longer spoke of his grievance against Lord Grey; but declared that, with the will of the people, he had assumed the sovereignty of Wales, to which he was legally entitled, by his descent from her kings. He called upon every Welshman in England to resort, at once, to his standard.

"The die is cast, now," Sir Edmund said, as he read the paper affixed to the castle gate. "It is no longer a question whether Glendower is wrongfully treated by Lord Grey; it is a matter touching the safety of the realm, and the honour of our lord the king. There is, I have now learned, some foundation for Owen's claim to be the representative of the kings of Wales, through his mother, Elinor. She was the eldest daughter of Elinor the Red, who was daughter and heiress of Catharine, one of the daughters of Llewellyn, the last Prince of Wales. For aught I know, there may be others who have a better claim than he; but at least he has royal blood in his veins.

"At present, that matters little. He has usurped the title of King of Wales, and is evidently a most ambitious and dangerous fellow; and none can doubt that this scheme has not just sprung from his brain, but has long been prepared, and that his quarrel with Lord Grey has but hastened the outbreak.

"I shall myself ride to Ruthyn, and consult with Lord Grey as to the measures to be taken. It may be that our forces may be sufficient to crush the movement, ere it gains strength; though I greatly doubt it. Still, it would be well that we should act in concert.

"Sir John Burgon and Sir Philip Haverstone, do you take half a dozen men-at-arms, and ride through the country, bidding all the tenants assemble here, next Saturday, in their arms and harness, that I myself may inspect them. You may tell them that a third of their number must be in readiness tonight, and must ride hither by morning. The others must, on an alarm being given, gather in strong houses, selected by themselves as the most defensible in their district, with their wives and families, so as to repel any attack the Welsh may make; leaving behind them the boys and old men, to drive out their flocks and herds, either towards the nearest castle, or to Hereford or Shrewsbury, as may be nearest to them."

When the knights had left, messengers were sent out to all the owners of castles in Radnor, Hereford, and Shropshire; bidding them assemble, in four days' time, at Ludlow. On the day of the meeting, nearly three hundred tenants and vassals presented themselves. To them Sir Edmund, having first inspected them and their arms, explained the situation. Then, each man was asked how many he could bring into the field, in accordance with the terms of his holding, and it was found the total amounted to nigh eight hundred men.

"I know not when the affair is likely to begin; and will, therefore, call only for a quarter of your force. Send your sons and unmarried men. At the end of a month they can return to you and, if needs be, you can send as many more in their places. It may be that I shall not require these; but, possibly, every man may have to come out; but you must bear in mind it is not for the defence of this town and castle that men are required, for the garrison and burghers can hold out against any attack, but to save your homesteads from destruction."

The news had created a deep sensation. Although none of those present had experienced the horrors of border warfare, there was not one but had heard, from their fathers, tales of burning, massacre, and wholesale destruction by the Welsh forays. But so long a time had passed, since the last serious insurrection, that the news that Wales might shortly be in arms, again, came as a terrible blow to them. All agreed to send in their proportion of men, at once, and to see that the rest were all ready to assemble, immediately the summons came.

The next day some forty knights, owners of the castles thickly scattered through the border counties, assembled in Ludlow Castle. There was a long consultation. Arrangements were made for the despatch of messengers, by those nearest to the frontier, with news of any Welsh raid. Points were fixed upon where each should assemble, with what force he could gather; thence to march to any threatened place, or to assemble at Ludlow Castle, Mortimer being the warden of the marches along that line of the border.

On the following day Sir Edmund rode, with two of his knights, to hold council with Lord Grey, at Ruthyn. The distance was considerable, and he was absent six days from his castle. Before he returned, an event happened that showed Glendower was in earnest, and intended to maintain his pretensions by the sword.

At daybreak, on the third day after Mortimer had left, a messenger arrived at the castle; with news that a large body of Welsh had, the evening before, entered Radnor by the road across the hills from Llanidloes, and were marching towards Knighton, burning the villages as they went, and slaying all who fell into their hands.

The horn was at once sounded, and Sir John Wyncliffe and the other knights hastily assembled in the courtyard. Here, after a short consultation, it was determined that a mounted party should be, at once, despatched to endeavour to harass the advance of the Welsh; the troop consisting of Alwyn's men-at-arms, twenty men of the garrison, and fifty mounted men who formed part of the new levy. Four hundred footmen were to follow, at once.

Sir John Wyncliffe at first thought of taking the command himself, but it was pointed out to him that his presence would be required, in Ludlow, to marshal the forces that would speedily arrive from all the country round. Sir John Burgon, therefore, a valiant knight, who had greatly distinguished himself against the French, was unanimously chosen by his companions as leader of the whole party; while with him rode Sir Philip Haverstone, and Sir William Bastow.

"This reminds one of one's doings at home, Oswald," his uncle said, as he formed up his little troop. "I trust the Welsh will not retreat, until we have had a taste of their quality; but I doubt much if they will prove as formidable foes as the Scotch borderers."

For a considerable portion of the distance, the roads led through forests, which at that time covered the greater part of the country. Oswald, at the invitation of the knights, rode with them at the head of the cavalcade. The way was beguiled by anecdotes, that had been passed down from mouth to mouth, of the last Welsh war.

They reached Knighton by nine o'clock. The enemy had not, as yet, come within sight of the town; but, throughout the night, the sky to the west had been red with the flames of the burning villages and homesteads.

The male inhabitants were all under arms. Many had already sent their wives and children, in waggons, towards Ludlow; but, as the town had a strong wall, the men were determined upon making a stout defence.

They crowded round the newly arrived troops, with loud cheers; which were raised, again and again, when they heard that, by midday, four hundred footmen would arrive to their assistance. It had been arranged that Sir Philip Haverstone should remain in the town, to take charge of the defence; and that the mounted men should, under Sir John Burgon, endeavour to check the Welsh plundering parties in the open. Sir William Bastow was to remain, to assist Haverstone in the defence of the town. There was no great fear of this falling; as, before the day was out, four or five thousand men would be assembled at Ludlow, and would be able to march to its relief. These matters being arranged, Sir John Burgon led his little troop out of the town.

The accounts of the Welsh forces were very conflicting, but the balance of opinion was that there were not less than four or five thousand of them. Beyond the fact that they were skirting the hills, and advancing towards Knighton, the terrified fugitives could say nothing, save of their own experiences. It was evident, however, that the Welsh force was not keeping together; but, after crossing the border, had broken up and scattered over the country, burning and slaying. Some of the bands had approached to within five miles of the town; and they might, not improbably, come in contact with fresh bands of the enemy, crossing the hills near the source of the Severn. As soon as they had sallied from the castle, and left the town behind them, Sir John halted his party.

"Now, men," he said, "there is one thing that you should remember--these Welshmen are not to be despised. Doubtless you will be able to ride over them, but do not think that, when you have done so, you have defeated them. They will throw themselves down on the ground, leap up as you pass over them, stab your horses from below, seize your legs and try to drag you from your saddles, leap up on to the crupper behind you, and stab you to the heart. This is what makes them so dangerous a foe to horsemen, and at Crecy they did terrible execution among the French chivalry.

"Therefore be careful, and wary. Spit all you see on the ground, with your lances; and hold your swords ever in readiness, to strike them down as they rise up beside you. Keep in as close order as you can, for thus you will make it more difficult for them to rise from the ground, as you pass over."

He then formed his troop into two lines. In the centre of the front line he placed the twenty men-at-arms from the castle, with fifteen of the tenants on either hand. Oswald's troop formed the centre of the second line, with ten of the tenants on either flank. Another of the knights was in command in this line. They were to ride some fifty paces behind the first, to cut down all who rose to their feet after the first line had passed; and if the resistance were strong, and the first line brought to a stand, they were to ride up and reinforce them.

They had ridden some three miles, when they saw a column of smoke rise, half a mile away. The pace was quickened, and they had gone but a short distance when some panic-stricken men came running down the road.

"How many Welshmen have attacked your village?" Sir John asked.

"Hundreds of them, Sir Knight," one of the men panted out; "at least, so it seemed to me; but indeed, we were this side of the village when they rushed into it; and, seeing that nought could be done to resist them, we fled at once."

When within three hundred yards of the village they entered open ground, and at once formed up in the order the knight had directed. Oswald took his place by the side of his uncle, a couple of lengths in advance of their own troop.

Scarce a word was spoken in the ranks. Here and there dead bodies were scattered over the ground, showing that the pursuit of the fugitives had been maintained thus far. From the village the wild shouts of the triumphant Welsh sounded plainly; but mingled with these came, occasionally, a cry of pain, that seemed to show that either the work of slaughter was not yet completed, or that some of the villagers still held one of the houses, and were defending themselves until the last.

Every face was set and stern. The tenants knew that, at any moment, similar scenes might be enacted in their own villages; while the men-at-arms were eager to get at the foe, and take vengeance for the murders they had perpetrated.

"Be sure you keep your ranks," Sir John said; "remember that any who straggle may be attacked by a score of these wild men, and slain before others can come to their help. Ride forward in perfect silence, till we are within striking distance."

At a gallop, the troop swept down upon the village. As they reached the first houses, they saw that the road was full of wild figures. Some were emerging from the houses, laden with such spoil as could be gathered there, chiefly garments; others, with torches, were setting fire to the thatched roofs; while, in the middle of the village, a number were attacking a house somewhat larger and more massively built than the rest.

Sir John raised his sword, with the shout of "A Mortimer! A Mortimer!"

The shout was re-echoed by his followers, and a moment later they dashed into the midst of the Welsh. At first they swept all before them; but speedily the mountaineers, running out from the houses, gathered thickly on each side of the road and, as the first line passed, closed in behind it; and, running even more swiftly than the charging horses, strove to leap up behind. Some struck at the horses with their swords, hamstringing several of them, and slaying their riders as they fell.

"Ride, ride!" the knight in command of the second line shouted, and at even greater speed than before his followers rode hotly forward; and came, ere long, on the struggling mass, for the first line were now endeavouring to turn, so as to face their assailants.

With a great shout, the second line fell upon them, the war cries of "A Percy! A Percy!" being mingled with those of "A Mortimer!" Their approach had been unnoticed by the Welsh, and their onslaught was irresistible. The Welsh were hurled to the ground by the impetus of the charge, and the two lines joined hands.

"Forward again!" Sir John shouted, and the troop, dashing forward, were soon hotly engaged with the enemy, who were in strong force at the point where they were attacking the house. The orders of their commander were now impossible to follow. It was a fierce melee, where each fought for himself.

"Face round!" Oswald shouted. "Now, men, lay about you.

"A Percy! A Percy!"

The active little horses swung round instantly, and faced the crowd surging up against them. This was the style of fighting to which the border men were accustomed. Active as the Welsh were, the border ponies were as quick in their movements, wheeling and turning hither and thither, but keeping ever within a short distance of each other. The troopers hewed down the foe with their heavy swords; and, being partly protected by their armour, they possessed a great advantage over their opponents.

Oswald and his uncle fought slightly in advance of the others, lending a helping hand to each other, when the pressure was greatest. On one occasion a Welshman seized Alwyn's leg, while he was engaged with a foeman on the other side, and strove to throw him from his horse. Oswald wheeled his pony, and with a sweeping blow rid his uncle of his foe; but, at the same moment, a man leapt up behind him, while two others assailed him in front.

The Welshman's sinewy arms prevented him from again raising his sword, and he would have been slain by those in front, had he not, at the moment, slipped his right foot from his stirrup and thrown himself from his horse, his leg sweeping off the man who held him behind, and hurled him to the ground beneath him.

The Welshman's grasp instantly relaxed; but, as Oswald tried to rise, a blow fell upon his helmet, and four Welshmen threw themselves upon him. He threw his arms around two of them, and rolled over and over with them, thereby frustrating the efforts of their companions to strike or stab him, through some unguarded point in his armour; when suddenly there was a mighty shout, two tremendous blows were struck in quick succession, then there was a shout, "Hold them still, Master Oswald, hold them still!"

Oswald tightened his grasp on his assailants, who were now striving to rise. There was another crashing blow, and then his last opponent slipped from his grasp, and fled.

"Thanks, Roger," he said, as he leapt to his feet, "you were but just in time; another minute, and those fellows would have got their knives into me."

"I have had my eye upon you, master, all the time; and while doing a little on my own account, have kept myself in readiness to come to your aid, if need be."

Roger was fighting with a heavy mace, and the number of men lying round, with their skulls crushed in, showed with what terrible effect he had been using it. Oswald again leapt on to his horse, which had been too well trained to leave his master's side; and had indeed in no small degree aided him, by kicking furiously at the Welsh, as they strove to aid their comrades on the ground.

By this time the combat was well-nigh over. The protection afforded by Alwyn's band, against any attack on their rear, had enabled Sir John's men-at-arms and the tenants to clear the street in front of them; but the Welsh, though unable to hold their own in open fight, had now betaken themselves to their bows and arrows, and from behind every house shot fast.

The door of the house that had still resisted had been thrown open, and eight men had come out, followed by some twenty women and children.

"Do each of you leap up behind one of us!" Sir John shouted.

"Help the women up, men, then right-about, and ride out of the village. It is getting too hot for us, here."

The order was quickly obeyed and, placing the horses carrying a double burden in the centre, the troop rode out in a compact body. The Welsh poured out into the road behind them.

"Level your spears!" Alwyn shouted to his men; who had, by his orders, fallen in in the rear of the others.

The long spears were levelled and, with a shout, the twenty men rode down on their pursuers, bursting their way through them as if they had been but a crowd of lay figures; then, wheeling, they returned again, none venturing to try to hinder them, and rejoined the main body.

"Well done, indeed!" Sir John Burgon exclaimed, "and in knightly fashion. Verily, those long border spears of yours are right good weapons, when so stoutly used."

Once outside the village, the troop rode quietly on to the spot at which they had first charged. Then the villagers dismounted.

"You made a stout defence, men," Sir John said. "It was well that you had time to gain that house."

"It was agreed that all should take to it, Sir Knight," one of the men said; "but the attack was so sudden that only we, and these women, had time to reach it before they were on us; and, had it not been for your arrival, they must soon have mastered us, for they were bringing up a tree to burst in the door; and as none of us had time to catch up our bows and arrows, we had no way of hindering them. Still, methinks many would have fallen, before they forced their way in."

The men now fell in again. Their numbers were counted. The losses were by far the heaviest in the front line. Five of the castle men-at-arms, and fourteen of the levy were killed. Several others had gashes from the long knives and light axes of the Welsh. Five of the tenants in the second line had fallen, but none of Alwyn's band, although most of the latter had received wounds, more or less serious, in their combat with the Welsh.

"The loss is heavy," Sir John said, "but it is as nought to that inflicted upon the Welsh. I did not count them, as we rode back, but assuredly over a hundred have fallen, not counting those who were slain in that last charge of yours, Alwyn. Truly your men have fought gallantly, as was shown by the pile of dead, where your men-at-arms defended our rear.

"The Welsh will be moving, ere long. Half the village is already burning, and you may be sure that there is nothing left to sack, in the other houses. If they come this way we must fall back, for in the forest we shall be no match for them. If they move across the open country, we may get an opportunity of charging them, again."

He told two of his men to dismount, and to crawl cautiously along, one on each side of the burning village; and to bring back news, the moment the Welsh began to leave it. In twenty minutes both returned, saying that the enemy were streaming out at the other end of the village, laden with plunder of all kinds. There seemed to be no order or discipline among them, each trooping along at his pleasure.

"Good!" the knight said. "We will give them another lesson, and this time on more favourable terms than the last."

The troops formed into column, and galloped at a canter through the burning village. At the other end they came upon a number of stragglers, who were at once killed. Then they emerged into the fields beyond, and formed line. The plain was dotted with men, the nearest but a hundred yards away, the farthest nearly half a mile.

In a single line the horsemen swept along. The rearmost Welshmen turned round at the tramp of the horses, and at once, throwing to the ground the bundles that they carried, took to their heels with shouts of warning. As these were heard, the alarm spread among the rest, who, believing that their foes had ridden away through the forest, were taken completely by surprise.

A panic seized them. Leaders in vain shouted orders, their voices were unheard among the cries of the men. Some, indeed, gathered together as they ran; but the greater portion fled in various directions, to escape the line of spears vengefully following them.

Those unable to avoid the charge stood at bay, like wild animals. First shooting their arrows, they drew their short axes or their knives, as the horsemen came within a short distance of them. Few had a chance of striking, most of them falling, pierced through and through by the spears. Those who, by swiftness of eye, escaped this fate, sprung at the horses like wildcats, clinging to the saddles, while they strove to bury their knives in the riders' bodies.

Their back pieces now served the troopers in good stead, as did their superior personal strength. Some beat their assailants down on to the pommel of their saddles, and throttled or stabbed them; while in many cases, where they were hard pressed, the sword of a comrade rid them from their foes.

So the line held on its way, until they reached the head of the body of fugitives. Then in obedience to the shout of Sir John Burgon they turned, broke up into small bodies, and scoured the plain, cutting down the flying foe; and did not draw bridle, until what remained of the enemy had gained the shelter of the wood. Then, at the sound of their leader's trumpet, they gathered around him in the centre of the plain.

Two or three had fallen from the Welsh arrows, and not a few had received ugly slashes from their knives; but, with these exceptions, all had come scatheless through the fray. At least two hundred dead Welshmen were scattered on the plain.

"You have done your work well, men," Sir John said, "and taught them a lesson that they will not forget. Now, let us ride back to Knighton, and see how matters go there."

On arriving at the little town, they found that all was quiet, and that no bodies of Welsh had approached the town. The party of horse were again sent out, in various directions, the smoke serving them as a guide. The villages were found to be entirely deserted; but, pushing farther on, many fugitives came out from hiding places.

Their reports were all of the same character. The Welsh were in full retreat for their own country.

By the time the troops returned with the news to Knighton, the footmen from Ludlow had marched in, and were being entertained by the inhabitants; who, now that the danger had passed, had returned.

"Retired have they, Sir John?" his two fellow knights said, as he arrived with his following. "It was but a raid for plunder, then, and not an invasion. Doubtless, Glendower merely wished to warm their blood, and to engage them so far in his enterprise that they could no longer draw back. They must have carried off some hundreds of cattle and sheep, to say nothing of other plunder; and, had it not been for our having the news soon enough to get here before they retired, they would have got off scatheless. As it is, they have learned that even a well-planned foray cannot be carried out with impunity; but the loss of three hundred lives will not affect them greatly, when it is clear that they have murdered twice that number, as well as enriched themselves with plunder."

"I think not that we shall hear of them, again," Sir John said. "Glendower has shown us, without doubt, what are his intentions; and he may now wait to see what comes of last night's work. I expect that he will keep among the hills, where he can fight to better advantage; for horsemen are of little use, where there are mountains and forests."

After a consultation between the knights, it was agreed that two hundred of the footmen were to remain, for two or three days, at Knighton; in case the retreat of the Welsh might be a feigned one, intended to lull the inhabitants into a state of security, and then to make a sudden night attack upon the walls. The whole force remained until the next morning, and then, leaving Sir Philip Haverstone in command of the party remaining at Knighton, the rest, horse and foot, marched back to Ludlow.

"Your band have indeed distinguished themselves, Oswald," Sir John had said, on the previous evening, as they talked on the events of the day. "Truly they are as stout men as I have ever seen fighting. And you have escaped without a wound, though I marked that your armour and clothes were covered with mire, as if you had been rolling in the road."

"That is just what I have been doing, Sir John. One of them leaped on to the horse behind me, and pinioned my arms; while two or three others made at me, with axes and staves. The clasp of the fellow was like an iron band and, seeing that my only chance was to rid myself of him, I slung my leg over my horse, and we came down together, he undermost. Whether the fall killed him or not, I cannot say, but his arms relaxed. Half a dozen sprang on me, and in another minute I should have been killed, had not that big trooper of mine come to my aid, and with a mighty mace dashed out their brains, well-nigh before they knew that they were attacked."

"A stout fellow, indeed," Sir John said, "and one I should like to have to ride behind me, on the day of battle. I had marked him before, and thought that I had never seen a more stalwart knave; though methinks that he would look better, did he not crop his hair so wondrously short."

Oswald laughed.

"He does it not to beautify himself, Sir John, but to hide the fact that the hair on his crown is but of six weeks' growth."

And then he related the circumstances under which Roger came to be a member of his troop.

"By my faith, he has done well!" Sir John said. "A man with such sinews as that is lost in a cloister. He is a merry fellow, too. I have often marked him at the castle, and his laugh is a veritable roar, that would sound strange echoing along the galleries of a monastery. The abbot did well to let him go, for such a fellow might well disturb the peace and quiet of a whole convent.

"You say that he has skill in war?"

"Yes, Sir John. He has been the instructor in arms of the lay brothers, and of some of the monks, too; and he led the contingent of the abbey at Otterburn; and, although the day went against the English, he and his followers greatly distinguished themselves."

"If you would part with him, I would better his condition, Master Oswald; for, on my recommendation, Sir Edmund would, I am sure, make him captain of a company."

"I should be sorry, indeed, to part with him, Sir John, and the more so since he has saved my life today; but, even were I willing, I feel sure he would not leave me, as we have gone through some adventures together, and he believes that it is to me that he owes his escape from the convent."

"What were these adventures, Oswald?"

"It was a matter touching the Earl of March--not Sir Edmund's nephew, now in the care of the king, but the Scottish earl, George, Earl of Dunbar, also bearing the title of Earl of March. Now that he has taken the oath to King Henry, there is no reason why I should not speak of it."

And he then gave them an account of his visit to Dunbar, and of his escape.

"And why did the earl wish to keep you?"

"Maybe, sir, that he had not then made up his mind, and thought that affairs might yet have been accommodated between himself, Douglas, and the Scottish king."

"Perhaps that was so," Sir John agreed. "He is a crafty, as well as a bold man. However, you were well out of Dunbar, and you and your monk managed the affair well. Think you that the earl is to be trusted?"

"I should say so. These great Scottish nobles deem themselves well-nigh the king's equal, and carry on their wars against each other as independent lords. His castle of Dunbar is in the hands of his bitterest enemy, and Douglas will come into no small portion of his estates. Without the aid of England he could not hope to recover them, and his interests, therefore, are wholly bound up with ours."

"'Tis strange that there should be two Earls of March, of different families and names; and, now that Dunbar has become a vassal of the king, it will make the matter stranger. However, at present no mistakes can arise, seeing that the one is an able warrior, and the other a mere boy. But in the future, were the two Earls of March at the same time at the court of our king, mistakes might well be made, and strange complications take place.

"Doubtless you are aware that Sir Edmund's nephew is, by right of birth, King of England. He was, you know, sprung from the Duke of Clarence, the elder brother of the Duke of Lancaster. The duke died without male issue, and his rights fell to Edmund Mortimer, Earl of March, the husband of his daughter Philippa. From their marriage was born the Roger Mortimer who was lord lieutenant of Ireland, during a part of King Richard's reign, and was killed in the wars of that country. He left two sons, of whom the elder was but eight or nine years old, when Richard was dethroned; and he and his brother are now living at Windsor, and are well treated there by the king.

"Had my lord's nephew attained the age of manhood, at the deposition of Richard, many would doubtless have supported his right to the throne; but for a child of eight to rule this realm, and keep in check the turbulence of the great lords, would be so absurd that no one even mentioned his name; and Henry, of course, ascended the throne as if by right of conquest."

"I have heard something of this before, Sir John; but as the Percys were among the chief supporters of Henry, the fact that there was one who had greater rights to the throne was never talked of, at Alnwick; although, by Percy's marriage with Sir Edmund's sister, he became uncle of the young Earl of March."

"I can understand that, and indeed Sir Edmund himself has never, in the most intimate conversation with us, expressed any opinion that the young earl would, if he had his rights, be King of England."

Chapter 10: A Breach Of Duty.

Two or three hours after the return of the force to Ludlow, Sir Edmund Mortimer returned, having ridden almost without a halt, since be received the news of the Welsh incursion. His knights met him in the courtyard.

"Well, my friends, I hear you have sent the Welsh back again, as fast as they came."

"We cannot say that, Sir Edmund," Sir John Wyncliffe replied. "Sir John Burgon went out, with ninety horse; and, coming upon a party of five or six hundred of them, killed half their number, and put the rest to flight; but their main body left of their own free will, and without any urging. 'Tis a pity that they were so hurried, for in another twenty-four hours we should have had some four thousand men on the march against them, besides those who first went on."

"Have they done much damage?"

"There is scarce a house left standing, between the hills on this side of Llanidloes, and Knighton. From what we can gather, they must have slain three or four hundred, at least. At first the total was put much higher; but, as soon as they retired, many fugitives made their way into Knighton; having slipped away in the darkness, when their villages were attacked, and concealed themselves in the woods, or among the rocks."

"There has been fighting up in the north, too," Sir Edmund said. "When I got to Ruthyn, I found that Lord Grey was away; but I talked over matters with his knights. I was to have left on the morning of the fifth day after leaving here, but at night Glendower's men raided almost up to the gates of the castle. Their plans were well laid; for, just at midnight, an alarm was given by a sentry on the walls. Everyone ran to arms, the instant the warder's horn was sounded; but when I reached the top of the walls, fires were bursting out in twenty places. It was not long before the knights rode out, with a hundred and fifty men-at-arms, but the Welsh were already gone. It seems that they had laid an ambuscade round every village and, on the signal being given, fell at once upon the sleeping inhabitants, put all to the sword, fired the houses; and in ten minutes from the first alarm made off, driving horses, cattle, and sheep before them.

"I was with the party, and we rode hard and fast, but we came up with none of them. Each party must have gone its own way, striking off into the hills. As soon as we returned to the castle I started, with my four men-at-arms, and we have lost no time on the road; especially after the rumour reached us that there had been a Welsh raid here, also.

"Now, Sir John Burgon, will you give me an account of the doings of your party?"

The knight reported their proceedings, after leaving Ludlow, and concluded:

"It is like that the story would not have so run, Sir Edmund, had it not been for the bravery shown by the northern men, under the young squire Oswald and his captain, Alwyn. So furiously did the Welsh assail us, in rear, that we should have suffered heavily, indeed, even if we had not met with a grave disaster; had it not been that this band covered our rear, while we charged forward, fighting so stoutly that the spot where they posted themselves was thickly covered with dead. I found time to look round, now and then, for they made but a poor resistance to our advance. Never did I see stronger fighting.

"I have questioned the men. All say that none fought more bravely than young Oswald, and his uncle gives him warm praise. The lad, however, would have lost his life, had it not been for that stout fellow, who stands half a head above his comrades, and is a very giant in strength. Oswald, himself, told me how it came about," and he repeated the account of the incident.

"It was a quick thought, to throw himself and the fellow who held him off the horse; though it would not have availed him, much, had not this stout man-at-arms been at hand. Still, in no case could he have defended himself, single handed, against five of these knaves; though doubtless he would have given a good account of some of them, had not his arms been held.

"Alwyn said that, three times during the fray, the young esquire saved his life, by cutting down men who were attacking him from behind, while he was occupied by other opponents in front."

"He will make a valiant knight, some day, Sir John. Sir Henry Percy would not have written so strongly about him, had he not good reason for feeling that he would not do discredit to his recommendation.

"Well, Sir Knights, you have all merited my thanks, for the manner in which you have discharged your duties, during my absence.

"Of course, you were perfectly right, Wyncliffe, in remaining here; until, at any rate, the knights brought in their following from the country round. It was important to save Knighton, but vastly more so to prevent their overspreading the whole country; which might, for aught we can tell, have been Glendower's object; and it is as well that Haverstone and Bastow should have remained at Knighton.

"Now, as I have not broken my fast, and have ridden since midnight without a stop, I will breakfast; and we can then talk over the plans to be pursued, for there is no disguising the fact that the Welsh are up in arms, and that we have long and heavy work before us.

"However, it is a matter too serious for us to undertake by ourselves, but is for the king himself to take in hand. A raid can be punished by a counter-raid; but now that Glendower has declared himself sovereign of Wales, and that everything points to the fact that the men of his nation are all ready to support him, it is a matter that touches his majesty very closely; and I doubt not that, as soon as he has finished this war with the Scots, he will march hither, at the head of his army.

"However, I shall send out a summons to the tenants of all my nephew's estates, in Herefordshire, and order them to hold themselves in readiness, should Glendower venture to invade us. But I think not that he will do so. He knows that these counties bristle with castles, in which the people could find refuge; and that, if he undertook to besiege them, he would speedily lose the best part of his army.

"None of his people have experience of war, and to besiege a strong place needs machines of all kinds, and of these Glendower has none, nor is it likely that he can construct them. Besides, while marching out he would be exposed to an attack, by the garrisons of these castles sallying out in his rear. Therefore, I think not that he will be foolish enough to undertake any great enterprises; though he may make raids, and carry off booty and cattle, as he has now done.

"Moreover, I cannot keep the vassals in the field longer than their feudal obligations compel them to stay, unless I pay and feed them; which might be done readily enough, for two or three months. But the war may last for years, and I must reserve my means, and strength, till they are urgently needed.

"Lord Grey will doubtless be of my opinion, but is sure to do what he can to capture Glendower; as he will consider him, not only as an enemy of the king, but as a personal foe. However, powerful as he is, I think not that he will venture, alone, to lead an army into the Welsh hills; until he receives assistance from the king."

Two days later, news came that the king, as soon as he heard of Glendower's proclamation, had sent orders to Lord Grey and Lord Talbot, to punish him.

"They will reach Chester, two days hence," Sir Edmund said. "After the raid they made here, I would gladly take some small share in punishing this rebel.

"You, Sir John Burgon, have had a full share of honour, by your defeat of him, the other day; therefore, I will send Sir William Bastow.

"Do you, Sir William, take thirty of the best mounted men of the garrison, together with Lord Percy's troop, and ride to Chester. I will give you a letter to Lord Talbot, saying that, being anxious to aid in the punishment of the rebel who has just raided my marches, I have sent you in all haste, with fifty stout men, to aid him in striking a blow; and, if possible, in effecting Glendower's capture, before he can do further harm to the king's loyal subjects."

Half an hour later, the troop mounted. Oswald was in high spirits, for Sir Edmund had spoken a few words to him, when telling him of the service to which he had appointed him.

"I am sending your troop with Sir William Bastow," he said, "chiefly in order that I may give you another opportunity of distinguishing yourself; and also because I am sure that Percy would be glad that his men should take part in an enterprise in which there may be honour, and credit. Lastly, because I would that my party should do me credit; and the fighting, the other day, showed me that your followers better understand warfare, of this kind, than do mine."

The troop arrived at Chester the second day after leaving, and rested their horses for twenty-four hours. On the arrival of the Earl of Talbot, and Lord Grey, Sir William Bastow called, at the inn where they put up, and delivered the letter from Sir Edmund Mortimer.

"'Tis well done of Sir Edmund," the Earl of Talbot said; "and although Ruthyn lies beyond his government of the marches, he is defending his own command, by aiding Lord Grey and myself against this presumptuous traitor. I will gladly take your clump of spears with me, among whom are, I see, a small party of Lord Percy's men-at-arms.

"I hear that Sir Edmund's men inflicted a sharp blow upon the Welsh, near Knighton. I met his messenger, bearing his report to the king, as we came along; and he gave me the particulars, from which it seems that the fight was, for a time, a hard one, and that the Welshmen fought, as they used to do, with much bravery."

"They did, my lord. I was not with the party that defeated them, having been left at Knighton to aid in the defence there, should the Welsh attack the town; but Sir John Burgon, who commanded, said that, in the village, they fought as if they cared not for their lives; though they made scarce any defence, when he fell upon them as they retired, in disorder. The success he gained he attributes, in no small degree, to Percy's little troop; led by their captain, a stout soldier who commands the garrison of Alnwick, and by a young squire of Sir Henry Percy, who, though but a lad, fought with extreme bravery.

"He is with me now. Sir Henry places great trust in him, and wrote most warmly, concerning him, to Sir Edmund Mortimer."

"We are just going to supper, sir," the earl said. "I hope that you will join us. And I pray you, tell me where this young squire is lodging, that I may send for him, at once; as I would fain learn, from his lips, some closer account of the fighting, which may be of utility to us, in our adventure."

Oswald arrived just as supper was brought in, and was introduced to the earl, and Lord Grey, by Sir William Bastow.

"Sit down with us, young sir," the earl said, kindly. "You are an esquire, I hear, of my good friend Sir Henry Percy. As you eat, I pray you tell me about this fight with the Welsh. Sir Edmund himself was not in command, I hear."

"No, my lord, he was away at the time, having ridden to Ruthyn, to hold council with Lord Grey."

"Ah! I had not heard that he had been there," Earl Grey said.

"He arrived the day before the Welsh raid on your estate, sir. Finding that you were absent, he intended to return home the next morning; but the matter delayed him, for a day, as he rode out with your knights to punish the marauders; who, however, made off before they could be overtaken."

"When you see him, I pray you give him my thanks, for so doing; and now, tell us what happened."

"Sir William Bastow can better inform you, sir, of what took place until we rode away from Knighton; where he remained, with Sir Philip Haverstone, to take command of the townspeople, in case the Welsh should arrive before strong aid should come."

Sir William then related the measures that had been decided upon, and the steps taken to call out the levies; and how he and his brother knights had ridden to Knighton, with the intent to hinder, as far as possible, the Welsh advance; until the footmen could reach the town, to be followed, shortly afterwards, by the troops that would come in from the castles of Radnor.

Oswald then continued the story, and gave an account of the fight in the village, and the manner in which the Welsh were attacked, while retiring with their booty, and completely routed.

"Their tactics have in nowise changed, then," the earl said, "since the days of Griffith and Llewellyn. Against a direct charge they were unable to stand; but they attacked, with fury, whenever there was an opportunity of fighting under circumstances when our weight and discipline gave us little advantage. I hear, from Sir William Bastow, that your little band covered the rear of Sir John Burgon's troop, and succeeded in keeping them at bay, until he had broken the resistance in front, and carried off a small party of villagers who were still defending themselves."

"That was so, my lord. Our men were all accustomed to border warfare; and had for the most part, before entering Percy's service, been often engaged in border forays; and had taken to soldiering after their own homes had been burnt, and their cattle driven off, by Scottish raiders. Therefore they were accustomed to fight each for himself, instead of in close order. Their horses, too, bred on the moors, are far more active and nimble than are the heavier horses of the south; and enter heart and soul into a fray, kicking and plunging and striking with their forelegs at any who approach to assail their riders. Thus it was that they were able to hold the Welsh carles at bay, far better than men otherwise trained and mounted would have been. Another thing is, that in these Border conflicts each man is accustomed to keep his eye on his neighbour; and, if he sees him hard pressed, to give him aid.

Therefore it is not surprising that, while the men slew many of the Welsh, they themselves escaped with but a few cuts from blows and hatchets."

"But you yourself were unhorsed, Sir William tells me, and were in great peril. How did that come about?"

"Both my unhorsing, sir, and my rescue, were the result of what I just said, our habit of keeping an eye on our neighbours. A Welshman was on the point of attacking Captain Alwyn, when he was engaged with two others in front. I struck the man down but, as I did so, a Welshman sprang on to my horse, behind, and pinned my arms to my side; while four others rushed at me."

He then related how he had thrown himself and his assailant off his horse, and had been saved by Roger.

"It was a good device, and quickly carried into effect," Earl Talbot said; "though it was well that the man-at-arms next to you was watching you, just as you had watched his captain; else it must have gone hard with you. It is evident that, if you continue as you have begun, you will turn out a right valiant knight.

"Your narrative is useful, and I see that, when we fall in with the Welsh, it will be necessary to have a picked body of men-at-arms, whose duty shall be to cover the rear of the main attack; for it seems that this is the real point of danger. Should we come into conflict with them, I will assign to you a body of men-at-arms, who with Percy's men shall, under your command, fulfil that duty. This would at once be of signal benefit to us, and will give you another opportunity of distinguishing yourself, and winning your spurs when the time comes."

"I thank you greatly, my lord, and trust that I may so bear myself as to merit your approbation."

The next morning the force mounted, at daybreak. It consisted of two hundred horse, that the earl had brought with him; and which was to be joined, at Chirk, by a hundred and fifty of Lord Grey's men from Ruthyn, orders having been already sent on for them to hold themselves in readiness. This was to be done quietly, and without stir, as word would be sure to be sent to Glendower, were it to be known in the town that preparations had been made for an expedition. They were to start from the castle at ten o'clock at night, when the town would be wrapped in sleep, and would arrive at Chirk before daybreak.

On arriving at the castle, it was found that the troops from Ruthyn had duly come in. They were received by the seneschal of William Beauchamp, Lord of Abergavenny. Chirk Castle had passed through many hands, having been several times granted to royal favourites; being a fine building, standing on a lofty eminence, which afforded a view of no less than seventeen counties. It was square and massive, with five flanking towers, and its vast strength was calculated to defy the utmost efforts of the Welsh to capture it. It was but a short distance thence to the valley of the Dee, in which was the estate of Glendower, extending for some eight miles north, into what is now the neighbourhood of Llangollen.

As one of the detachments had arrived before daybreak, and the other two hours after dark, it was improbable that their advent had been noticed; and, at the request of the knight who commanded the troop from Ruthyn, the gates of the castle had been kept closed all day, no one being allowed to enter or leave.

At daybreak the next morning, the whole force sallied out. Three-quarters of an hour later, they dashed down into the valley at a point about half a mile distant from Glendower's dwelling.

This was a very large and stately building. Near it stood a guest house and a church, and all the appurtenances of a man of high rank. It was called Sycharth. Here Glendower maintained an almost princely hospitality; for, in addition to this estate, he possessed others in South Wales.

More especially bards were welcomed here. Some resided for months; others, who simply paused on their rambles through the country, remained but for a few days; but all were received with marked honour by Glendower, who was well aware of the important services that they could render him. Indeed, it was on them that he relied, to no small extent, to arouse the feelings of the populace; and his hospitality was well repaid by the songs they sung, in hall and cottage, in his praise; and by their prophecies that he was destined to restore the ancient glories of the country.

The house was surrounded by a moat and wall, but had otherwise no defensive works; as, for a hundred years, the English and Welsh had dwelt peaceably, side by side. Many of the castles were, indeed, held by Welshmen, and there were few garrisons but had a considerable proportion of Welsh in their ranks.

It was singular that Glendower should, after his defiance of the king, and the raids that had lately been made, have continued to dwell in a spot so open to attack, and within striking distance of the three great castles of Ruthyn, Chirk, and Holt. Certain it is that he kept no garrison that would suffice to offer a stout defence against a strong band, although the precaution was taken of keeping a watchman, night and day, in one of the turrets. The sound of his horn was heard by the horsemen, as soon as they began to descend the hill.

"A pest on the knave!" Lord Grey exclaimed. "He will slip through our fingers, yet."

It was scarce a minute later when a mounted man was seen to dash out, at full speed, from the other side of the building. He was evidently well mounted; and although the pursuit was hotly kept up, for two miles, he gained the forest while they were still a quarter of a mile behind him, and was lost to view; for although they beat the wood for some distance, they could find no traces of him.

When passing by the house, a detachment of a hundred men were ordered to surround it, and to suffer none to enter or leave it. On the return of the pursuing party the house was entered, and ransacked from end to end. The male retainers found in it were ruthlessly killed. The furniture, which showed at once the good taste and wealth of the owner, was smashed into pieces, the hangings torn down, and the whole place dismantled. Only two female attendants were found, and these were suffered, by Earl Talbot's orders, to go free.

"This is evidently the ladies' bower, when they happen to be here," Lord Grey said; as, an hour later, he entered a room in one of the turrets, which had been already plundered by the soldiers. "'Tis a pity that we did not find one or two of Glendower's daughters here. They would have been invaluable as hostages.

"We were too hasty, Talbot. We should have closely questioned some of the men, or those two women, and should have found means to learn whether they were staying here. It may be that it was so, and that they are, even now, concealed in some secret hiding place, hard by."

He at once called up several of his men, and set them to search every room in the turret, for some sign of an entrance to a secret chamber; but although the walls were all tapped, and the floors examined, stone by stone, no clue was found to such an entrance, if it existed.

The house, which was built entirely of stone, offered no facilities for destroying it by fire. The doors were all hewn down; the gates in the wall taken off their hinges, and thrown into the moat, being too massive to be destroyed by the arms of the soldiers. The outlying buildings were all burned down, the vineyard rooted up, and the water turned out of the fish pond. Then, greatly vexed at their failure to seize Glendower himself, the two nobles rode back to Chirk; leaving a hundred men, of whom the band from Ludlow formed part, under two of Earl Talbot's knights, to retain possession of the house, until it should be decided whether it should be levelled stone by stone; or left standing, to go, with the estate, to whomsoever the king might assign it.

By Lord Grey's advice, sentries were posted outside the walls, from nightfall till daybreak, to prevent any risk of surprise by Glendower, whose spies might take him word that the main body of the assailants had left. One of the great halls had been left untouched, to serve for the use of the garrison; and as an abundance of victuals were found in the house, and the cellar was well stocked with wines, it was but a short time before the garrison made themselves thoroughly comfortable.

As soon as it became dark, twenty men were placed on watch. Oswald, with his party, were to take the third watch, at midnight; and Mortimer's men-at-arms the second. The captain of each band was to place the men, at such points as he might select. Alwyn talked the matter over with his nephew.

"It seems to me," the former said, "that there is but a small chance of anyone trying to leave the castle; and at any rate, if they did so, it would scarcely be over the wall, for a splash in the moat would at once betray them. Moreover, I love not killing in cold blood, and should any poor fellows be stowed away somewhere, I should be willing enough to let them go free."

"I agree with you altogether, Alwyn," Oswald, who had not heard the talk between Grey and Talbot, concerning Glendower's daughters, replied heartily. "I would have gladly saved the men who were killed today. It is one thing to slay in battle, but to slaughter unresisting men goes altogether against my grain."

"Then as we are agreed on that, Oswald, I should say that we had best place the greater portion of our men well away from the wall. We can leave two at the gate, and set two others to march round and round the moat. I should say we had best plant the others, in pairs, a quarter of a mile round the house. It is vastly more important to prevent Glendower from recapturing his house, by surprise, than it is to take prisoners two or three fellows making their escape."

"I agree with you, Alwyn."

Accordingly, when they filed out from the gate, four were posted as Alwyn had suggested. The rest were disposed, in pairs, in a circle at a distance round the house.

"I will keep watch with Roger," Oswald said. "'Tis some time since I have had an opportunity for a talk with him. I will take the next post, if you like. The wood comes closer to the house, there, than at any other point; and there are patches, behind which an enemy might creep up. My eyes and ears are both good; and as for Roger, if he lifts that mighty voice of his in tones of alarm, it will reach the ears of all the others, and be the signal for them to run back to the gate, at the top of their speed."

"Very well, Oswald. I shall walk round the ground, and see that all are vigilant. We know not where Glendower's men were lying. It may hap they were twenty miles away, but even so he would have had plenty of time to have brought them up, by now. I don't think there is much chance of any of our men being surprised; most of them having, in their time, been so used to midnight rides across moor and hill, and so accustomed to see in the dark that, crafty as the Welshmen may be, I do not think there is a chance of their getting within a hundred yards of any of our posts, without being seen; especially as the moon is still half full."

"Do you think that there is any chance of our being disturbed, Master Oswald?" Roger said, as they took up their post under a low, stunted tree.

"I do not think so. If Glendower's spies have told him that the main body, of those who surprised him this morning, have returned to Chirk; he may be sure that enough have been left, to hold the place successfully against him and his wild followers, till assistance can reach us; and he would have nothing to gain by recapturing his house, for he could not hold it long against the force assembled at Chirk. Besides, he must know, well enough, that if he is to fight successfully, it must be in the woods. Whether he has studied the black art, or no, there is little doubt that he has turned his attention greatly to military matters, and that he is a foe who is not to be despised. He is playing a deep game, and will give us a deal of trouble, unless I am greatly mistaken, before we have done with him."

"I hear all sorts of strange stories of his powers, Master Oswald."

"Yes; but you see, Roger, the spirits who, as they say, serve him, cannot be of much use; or they would have warned him of the coming of Talbot, and we should not have taken him unawares, this morning."

"That is true enough," Roger said, in a tone of relief. "For my part, I am not greatly alarmed at spirits. The good abbot used to threaten me that I should be carried off by them, unless I mended my ways; but I always slept soundly enough, and never saw aught to frighten me. They used to say that the spirits of some of the dead monks used to walk in the convent garden, but though my cell looked down upon it, and I have often stood there by the hour, never did I see anything to frighten me.

"If the Welsh do come, what are we to do, master--fight them?"

"By no means, Roger. Our duty is to watch, and not to fight. You must lift up your voice, and shout as loud as you can, and then we must run to the gate. There we can make a fight, till the rest join us. But, whatever you do, do not shout until I tell you. A false alarm would raise the whole garrison; and, if naught came of it, would make us a laughing stock."

While they were talking, both were keeping a close lookout on the ground in front of them, and also to the right and left, for the watches were two hundred yards apart, and they had to make sure that no party of the enemy slipped unseen between them. Suddenly Roger plucked Oswald's sleeve, and said in a whisper:

"Unless my eyes deceive me, master, I saw two dark figures flit from that clump of bushes, some forty yards away, to those next to them. There they go again!"

"I see them, Roger. It may be that they are spies, who have crept up close. Let us give chase to them."

"Shall I shout, master?"

"No, no. This is not an attack. Stoop as low as you can or, if they look back, they will see that great figure of yours, and be off like hares. Run as softly as you can."

Stooping low, they set off at a run and, being certain that the figures were making straight for the forest, they did not pause to get another glimpse of them, but ran straight on. They had gone some seventy or eighty yards, when they heard a stifled exclamation; and then, without further attempt at concealment, two figures rose from a bush twenty yards ahead, and fled for the forest. There was no more occasion for stooping and, at the top of their speed, Oswald and Roger pursued the fugitives.

These ran fast, but Oswald, who had outpaced his heavier companion, came up to them when within fifty yards of the edge of the forest; and, passing them, drew his sword and faced them.

"Surrender," he said, "or I will cut you down."

Instead of the fierce spring that he had anticipated, the two figures stopped suddenly, exchanged a word in Welsh, and then dropped their cloaks. To Oswald's astonishment, two young women stood before him. They evidently belonged to the upper class. Both were richly dressed. They wore heavy gold chains round their necks, and bracelets of the same metal; set, as Oswald noticed by the reflection of the moon, with jewels. They had also brooches, and their girdles were held in with massive gold clasps.

By this time Roger had come up, and stood staring with astonishment.

"Take these, good fellows," the girl said in English, as she began to unfasten her necklace. "Take these, and let us go. They will make you rich."

"I am an esquire of Sir Henry Percy," Oswald said, "and I rob not women. By your appearance, I should judge you to be daughters of Glendower."

"It would be useless to deny it," one of the girls said, proudly.

"Why do you come spying here?" Oswald said. "Surely, among your father's warriors, others better suited for such work might have been found."

"We were not spying," the girl replied. "We have lain hidden all day, and were but making our escape."

"How can that be, madam? We had a guard all round the castle, and know that none can have escaped."

"Being an esquire, you are a gentleman, sir, and will not disclose what I am about to tell you; though, indeed, now that our father's house is in your hands, it boots not much whether the secret is known. There is a secret passage from the castle that opens into these bushes, and it was through that that we issued out; having been in hiding all day, in the secret chamber from which it leads.

"Well, sir, we are your prisoners; and shall, I suppose, be sent to London, there to be held until our father is in the usurper's hands, which will not be, believe me, for years yet."

Oswald was silent. The two girls, some seventeen or eighteen years of age, both possessed singular beauty they had inherited from their father; and bore themselves with an air of fearlessness that won his admiration. He was still but a lad and, thinking of the years these fair girls might pass in a prison, he felt a deep pity for them. He drew Roger aside.

"What think you, Roger? Must we send these fair young girls to prison?"

"In faith, I know not, master. Having been shut up many a time in a cell, I have a sort of fellow feeling for prisoners; and indeed, two fairer maidens I have never seen. Our orders were to look after Welshmen, and see that they did not attack us. No word was said of Welsh women. And besides, they were running away, and not thinking of attacking us."

"That is all very well, Roger, but I cannot deceive myself. There is no doubt that it is our duty to take these two maidens prisoners, but my heart aches at the thought that they might pass years of their lives in a prison. They are not responsible for their father's misdeeds and ambition, and it may be that, if they are restored, Glendower may be induced to treat those who fall into his hands mercifully. None but ourselves know of this, and no one need ever know.

"I will risk it, anyhow," he said after a short pause. "I know that I am not doing my duty in letting them go; and that, were it ever known, I should lose all chance of further advancement, if indeed I did not lose my life. However, it need never be known, and my conscience would sorely trouble me, whenever I thought of them shut up in one of King Henry's prisons."

He turned to the girls again.

"Think you, ladies," he asked, "that were you in the king's hands, your father would make terms and submit himself?"

"Certainly not," the one who had spoken before said. "He has other children--sons and daughters--and he would not dream of abandoning his rights, and betraying his country, to obtain the liberty of two of us."

"In that case, then, your imprisonment would in no degree stop this war, or bring about a renewal of peace between the two countries?"

"Certainly not; and as for us, we would strangle ourselves in prison, did we think that any thought of us would turn our father from his noble purpose."

"Then in that case," Oswald said quietly, "it is clear that your captivity would do nought to bring about peace, or to allay the troubles that have now begun. Therefore I will take on me to let you go, though in so doing I may be failing somewhat in my duty. Only promise me that, in the future, you will use what influence you may possess with your father, to obtain kind treatment for prisoners who may fall into his hands."

The expression of haughty defiance, that they had hitherto worn, faded from the girls' faces.

"We shall never forget your kindness, sir," one said, in a low voice. "We thank you, with all our hearts; not so much for our own sake, as for our father's. He has been cruelly ill used. He has much to trouble him, and although I know that our captivity would not turn him from his purpose, it could not but greatly grieve and trouble him, and he has already troubles enough on his shoulders.

"Will you accept one of these jewels, as a token only of our gratitude for your kindness, shown this night to us?"

"Thanks, lady, but no gift will I take. I am failing in my duty, but at least it shall not be said that I received aught for doing so."

"Then at least--" the girl began, turning to Roger.

"No, lady," the man-at-arms said. "I am neither knight nor esquire, but a simple soldier; but I take no presents for saving two maidens from capture and captivity. I have been a monk all my life, though now a man-at-arms. Never before have I had an opportunity of doing aught of kindness for a woman, and I am glad that the chance has fallen in my way."

"May I ask the name of one who has done us such kindness?" the girl said, turning to Oswald.

"It were best not, lady. It is a service that might cost me my head, were it to be bruited about. 'Tis best, then, that even you should not know it. I doubt not that you would preserve the secret; but you would perhaps mention it to your father, and it were best that it were known to none."

The girls were silent for a minute.

"Sir," the elder said, after exchanging a word or two with her sister, "we would ask a boon of you. The successes in a war are not always on one side. My sister and I will think often of one who has so greatly befriended us; and were you, by any accident of war, to fall into the Welsh hands, and should evil befall you, it would be a deep grief to us. We pray you then, sir, to accept this little gold necklet. Its value is small, indeed, but it was given to me when a child by my father. My name and his are engraved on the clasp. Should you, at any time of stress, send this to my father; right sure am I that, on recognizing it, he would treat as dear friends those who have done so much for his daughters. I pray you to accept it, and to wear it always round your neck or wrist; and if it should never prove useful to you, it will at least recall us to your thoughts."

"I cannot be so churlish, lady, as to refuse your token so offered; and though I hope that it will not be needful to use it as you say--for, indeed, I expect to return very shortly to my lord in Northumberland--it will be a pleasant remembrance of the service that a good fortune has enabled me to render, to two fair maidens. Be assured that I shall ever keep your necklet, for the sake of the givers.

"And now, farewell! We must be back at our post, for the captain of the guard will be going his round, and we might be missed."

"We shall never forget you, sir. May the blessing of God fall on you, for your kind deed!"

"May all good fortune attend you!" Oswald answered; and then, with Roger, he made his way back to his post; while the girls hurried on, and entered the forest.

Chapter 11: Bad News.

T his has been a strange adventure, Roger."

"A very strange one, master. Lord Grey would tear his hair, if he knew that those two pretty birds had been hiding in the cage all day, and he never knew it. However, I see not that it can do us harm. Nay, more, there is a probability that it may even benefit us, for if it should happen, by ill fortune, we should ever fall into the hands of the Welsh, and they should abstain from cutting our throats then and there, perchance these young ladies would repay the service we have rendered them, by taking us under their protection."

"It may be so, indeed, Roger, though I hope that I shall never hear more of tonight's adventure. We may reason as we will, but there is no doubt that, although we had no instructions touching the capture of women, we have failed in our duty."

"That will in no way trouble me, Master Oswald. When I was a monk, I failed in my duty scores of times, and am no whit the worse for it; rather the better, indeed, since it is owing to my failures that I am now a free man-at-arms, instead of being mewed up for life in a convent. I shall not sleep one wink less, for having saved two of the prettiest girls I ever saw from having been shut up, for years, in a prison."

"I am afraid your sense of duty is not strong, Roger."

"I am afraid not, master, saving in the matter of doing my duty in face of an enemy."

"You mean, Roger, that you will do your duty when it so pleases you, and not otherwise."

"I expect that is the way with a good many of us," Roger laughed. "I wonder whether Lord Grey had any idea that Glendower's daughters were in the house when we arrived there?"

"I know not, but I remember now that they had men searching, for some time, for signs of secret passages. Whether it was from any idea that Glendower's daughters might be hidden away, I know not."

"Truly it might have been," Roger said, "for I saw, among the spoil that was carried off when the others rode for Chirk, some silks and stuffs that looked like feminine garments.

"There is somebody coming across from the next post," he broke off. "Doubtless it is the captain. You would not tell him what we have done?"

"Certainly not, Roger. My uncle is an old soldier, and though he would not, for my sake, say anything about it, I think not that he would approve of what has been done. 'Tis best, at any rate, to keep it entirely to ourselves."

"All quiet here, as elsewhere?" Alwyn asked as he came up.

"All quiet, Uncle."

"'Tis well; for although methinks that we could hold the place against the Welshmen, we could hardly hope that some of our posts would not be cut off, before they could reach the house. It is well to keep watch, but the more I think of it, the more I feel that Glendower will scarce attack us. He could not hold the place, did he gain it; and it might well be that, after we were turned out again, the place would be destroyed, seeing that it would need two or three hundred men to be shut up here, in garrison."

After waiting half an hour, Alwyn again made the round of the posts, and then went in to rouse the party that were to relieve them. As soon as these issued out, the sentries were called in, and stretched themselves for three hours' sleep.

Before day dawned, a messenger rode in from Chirk, bearing Earl Talbot's orders for the evacuation of the house, as there could be no advantage in retaining it; and, were it empty, Glendower might return there, and afford them another opportunity for capturing him.

On the following day the party broke up. Lord Grey rode with his men to Ruthyn, and the forty men-at-arms from Ludlow returned to that town; where, a few days later, the news arrived that Glendower, with a large following, had established himself on the rugged height of Corwen, and was engaged in strengthening the ancient fortifications on its summit.

For a time there was quiet on the border, and then came the startling news that

Glendower had suddenly surprised, plundered, and burnt to the ground the town of Ruthyn, where a fair was being held at the time. Then, having obtained great booty, and greatly injured his enemy Lord Grey, he again retired. It was evident that no local force of sufficient strength could be found to pursue Glendower into his fastnesses on the ranges of Berwyn and Snowdon, and nothing was done until, three months later, the king, on his return from Scotland, marched into Wales with the levies of Warwickshire, Leicestershire, and eight other adjacent counties, while orders were issued to the people of Shrewsbury, and other towns on the eastern border, to hold themselves in readiness to repel any movement of the Welsh in that direction.

The king, however, accomplished nothing. Glendower, with his following, took refuge among the forests of Snowdon; and the English army marched along the north coast, putting to the sword a few bands of peasantry, who ventured to oppose them; crossed to the Isle of Anglesey and, entering the Franciscan monastery of Llanfaes, slew some of the monks and carried the rest to England, and established a community of English monks in the convent. This was done because the Franciscans had been supporters of the late king, and were believed to have given aid and encouragement to Glendower.

The Welsh expedition was, therefore, no more successful than the Scotch had been.

For a time, matters settled down. Glendower was occupied in strengthening his position. So much had his reputation spread, that large numbers of Welshmen who had settled in England now sold their property, gave up their positions and abandoned their careers, and made their way across the border to join him. Still, for some months no operations were undertaken, on either side; and, a week after the return of the king and his forces, Sir Edmund Mortimer said to Oswald:

"I will no longer keep you and your following from your lord's side. I have largely strengthened my garrison, and twenty men, however valiant, are no longer of importance. As you know, I should not have asked Percy to aid me, had I not thought that, perchance, he might have come himself, bringing with him two or three hundred men; and that my sister might have accompanied him. Maybe, if matters go on quietly on the northern marches, he may be able to do so yet; but I fear that the Scotch will take advantage of the troubles here, and may, for aught

I know, have entered into communication with Glendower, so that they may together harass the kingdom. I have written several times to him, telling him what good service you and his men have rendered; and that I would I had five hundred such good fighters with me, in which case I would undertake, single handed, to bring this fellow to reason.

"I have written a letter which I will hand you to deliver, saying that, as at present things are quiet and Glendower is in hiding among the mountains, I have sent you back to him; not without the hope that, should greater events take place, he himself will come hither, for a while, to give me the benefit of his knowledge of border warfare, even if he comes accompanied only by my sister and a dozen spears. I may tell you that, some two months since, he wrote saying that he should be glad to have you, and the captain of his garrison of Alnwick, back again; and I then wrote to him, saying that while the king was in Wales I would hold you, seeing that Glendower might make a great foray here, while the king was hunting for him in the north; but that, as soon as he left with his army, I would send you home."

Alwyn and the men were all well pleased when they heard that they were to return; for, since the raid on Glendower's house, their life had been a dull one, to which even the fact that they were receiving pay from Sir Edmund, as well as from Percy, was insufficient to reconcile them; and it was with light hearts that they started, on the following morning, for the north, arriving at Alnwick ten days after leaving. Sir Hotspur came down into the courtyard, as they rode into the castle.

"Welcome back, Oswald; and you, my trusty Alwyn!

"I thank you all, my men, for the manner in which you have borne yourselves, and that you have shown the men of the west how stoutly we Northumbrians can hold our own, in the day of battle. I am glad, indeed, to find that all that went have returned home; some bearing scars, indeed, but none disabled. I will instruct your captain to grant all of you a month's leave, to pay a visit to your families.

"You must sup with us tonight, Alwyn, and give us a full account of your doings, and also your frank opinion as to the state of things in the west, and the probability of long trouble with this strange Welshman, who has so boldly taken up arms, and defied the strength of England."

It was nearly a year since the party had left Alnwick, and Oswald had, in that time, greatly increased in height and strength. He was now eighteen, and as he was nearly six feet in height, and his figure had filled out greatly since he had left his home, he might well have passed as three or four years older than his real age. That evening, Alwyn gave a full account of their fray with the Welsh.

"These men fight stoutly, Alwyn," Percy said, when he had concluded his story.

"Right stoutly, Sir Henry, and were their discipline equal to their bravery, they would be formidable opponents, indeed; but as it is, they are quite unable to stand against men-at-arms in a set battle. In this respect they are by no means equal to the Scotch, but for surprises, or irregular fighting, I could wish to see no better men."

"It is an unfortunate affair," Percy said. "It seemed that we had finished with Wales, at Llewellyn's death, and that the two nations had become one. In London, and many other places, they were settled among us. Numbers of them studied at our universities, and in Shropshire, Radnor, Flint, and other border counties I have heard that most of the labouring men were Welsh, and have come to speak our language; and indeed, they form no small portion of the garrisons of the castles; so much so that I fear that, should the Welsh really ravage the border counties, 'tis like that not a few of the castles will fall into their hands by the treachery of their fellow countrymen in the garrisons.

"Sir Edmund speaks very highly of you, Oswald, not only for your behaviour in the fight, which was reported to him by Sir James Burgon, a knight well fitted to judge in such matters, but as an inmate of his castle. He said that, from your conversation, he has conceived a high opinion of you.

"At present things are somewhat quiet here, and it were well that you should, like your uncle, take a holiday for a time, and visit your father and mother. They have sent over, several times, for news of you."

The next morning Oswald mounted and rode off, attended by Roger, who had asked Oswald to take him with him, as he had no relations he cared to visit. Alwyn was going for a few days only, and indeed, would probably have declined to take a holiday at all, had not Oswald earnestly begged him to go with him.

"'Tis two years since you have been there," Oswald said.

"That is so, Oswald, but I have often been longer without seeing my brother; and, in truth, of late I have had so little to do, with but twenty men to look after, that I long for regular work and drill again. Still, it were best that I went with you.

There are turbulent times on hand, both on this border, in Wales, and maybe in France. I may get myself killed, and your father's house may be harried again by the Bairds, and he may not succeed in getting off scatheless, as he did last time; and I should blame myself, afterwards, if I had not seen him, and shaken his hand, when I had an opportunity such as the present."

Oswald had seen so much, during the two years that had passed since he first left the hold that, as he rode towards it, it seemed strange that everything should be going on as if it was but the day before that he had ridden away--the only difference being that the hold looked strangely small, and of little account, after the many strong castles he had seen.

As soon as they reached the moor, within sight of the hold, a horseman was seen to leave it, and ride at a gallop towards them.

"That is ever the way," Oswald said; "we like to know, when a visitor is seen, whether he comes as friend or foe."

As the moss trooper rode up, and was about to put the customary question, he recognized Oswald; and, wheeling his pony without a word, dashed off at full gallop, waving his spear and shouting, as he approached the hold.

They rode at a canter after him and, as they reached the entrance, his father and mother appeared at the door at the top of the steps. The latter ran down the steps and, as Oswald leapt from his horse, threw her arms round his neck.

"Thank God you are back again, my boy!" she cried; "though as yet, I can hardly believe that this tall fellow is my Oswald. But otherwise you are in no way changed."

"I think, Mother, that you are looking better than when I saw you last."

"I am well, dear," she said. "We have had a quiet year, and no cause for anxiety, and things have gone well with us; and it has been pleasant, indeed, for us to have received such good news of your doings, and to know that you stood so well with Hotspur."

Oswald now ran up the steps to greet his father, who was already talking with Alwyn, who had slipped off his horse and run to speak to his brother, while Oswald was occupied with his mother.

"Well, lad," John Forster said, laying his hand upon his shoulder, and looking him up and down, "you have grown well nigh into manhood. I always said that you would over top me, and though methinks that I have still three inches of advantage, you have yet time to grow up to look down on me.

"Well, you have done credit to us, boy, and your monkish reading and writing has not harmed you, as I was afraid it would. Alwyn tells me that no man of Percy's troop did better than you, in that fight with the Welsh; save, mayhap, that big man-at-arms down there, who, he tells me, cracked the skulls of four Welshmen who were trying to stab you, besides those he disposed of on his own account."

"I owe him my life, indeed, Father. He is a man after your own heart, strong and brave and hearty, even jovial when occasion offers. He can troll out a border lay with the best, and can yet read and write as well as an abbot. His name is Roger."

"Come up, Roger," John Forster shouted, "and give me a grip of your hand. You have saved my son's life, as he tells me; and, so long as you live, there will be a nook by the fire, here, and a hearty welcome, when you are tired of soldiering."

"In truth, you are a mighty man," he went on, after he and Roger had exchanged a grip that would have well nigh broken the bones of an ordinary man. "I have been looked upon as one able to strike as hard a blow as any on the border; but assuredly, you would strike a heavier one. Why, man, you must be five or six inches bigger, round the chest, than I am."

"You have been an active man from your youth," Roger replied, "ever on horseback and about, while I spent years with nought to do but eat and drink, and build up my frame, in a monastery."

"Oswald told us, in his letters, that you had been a monk; but had, with the consent of the abbot, unfrocked yourself."

"It was so," Roger replied, with a laugh. "Methinks that it was a happy day for the abbot, as well as for myself, when I laid aside my gown; for I fear that I gave him more trouble than all the rest of his convent. Besides, it was as if a wolf's cub had been brought up among a litter of ladies' lapdogs--it was sure to be an ill time for both."

"And for how long are you at home with us, brother Alwyn?" John Forster asked, presently.

"I am here for a week only, John; but Oswald has leave for a month, seeing that, at present, there is no great chance of Hotspur needing his services. The Scotch are quiet since the king returned, I hear."

"Ay, they are as quiet as is their nature to be, but 'tis not likely to last long. I went not with the army, but I hear that Henry behaved so gently that the Scotch feel that it would be almost an act of ingratitude to meddle with us, for a time. However, that will not last long. Next spring they will doubtless be storming down over the hills again."

The holiday passed delightfully to Oswald. Roger enjoyed it even more. It was so long since the latter had been permitted the freedom of riding at will, over mountain and moor, that he was like a schoolboy enjoying an altogether unwonted holiday. He and Oswald scoured the country, sometimes returning late in the afternoon, but often staying for the night at the houses of one or other of Oswald's friends. Once they crossed the border, and rode to the Armstrongs', where they stopped for a couple of days, bringing Allan and Janet back with them; for Roxburgh was still held by the English, and unless when hostilities were actively going on, the people of the border, save the marauders, who were always ready to seize any opportunity that offered of carrying off booty, were on friendly terms, and maintained frequent intercourse with each other.

Alwyn had returned to Alnwick when his leave was up. He had spent his time quietly at the hold. He and his brother had discussed many plans by which its defences could be strengthened, but arrived at the same conclusion: that it could defend itself, at present, against any small party, but must yield, however much its defences were increased, at the approach of an invading army; since, even with the assistance of the inhabitants of the surrounding districts, it could not maintain itself until an army was gathered, and the invaders driven out.

Occasionally an afternoon was devoted to sports on the moor; and, on one occasion, John Forster sent messengers down to Yardhope, and other villages on the Coquet, and to the holds of his neighbours; inviting them to come to a gathering, at which there would be prizes for riding, wrestling, running, shooting, and feats of arms on horseback and foot, and at which all comers would be entertained.

The result was a gathering such as had not taken place, in that part of the country, for years. Over a thousand people assembled, comprising women as well as men. The sports began early, and the various events were all eagerly contested. Ralph Gray won the horse race, a horse which he had brought from the south being far superior, in speed, to any of the smaller border horses; although, had the trial been for endurance, it would have had but small chance with them. The shooting was close, one of Percy Hope's men winning at last. The quarterstaff prize was awarded to Long Hackett, one of John Forster's retainers. At wrestling Roger bore off the palm. Some of his opponents were, in the opinion of lookers on, more skilled at the sport; but his weight and strength more than counterbalanced this, and one after another tried, in vain, to throw him to the ground; succumbing, themselves, as soon as he put out his strength, and theirs began to be exhausted; when, drawing them up to him with irresistible strength, he laid them quietly on the ground.

Oswald himself carried off the palm in a mile foot race.

At one o'clock the sports were concluded. While they had been going on, a score of men were attending to the great joints roasting over bonfires, six bullocks having been slaughtered the day before. Ducks, geese, and chickens innumerable were also cooking; while, for the table in the hold, at which the principal guests sat down, were trout, game, and venison pasties. Here wine was provided, while outside a long row of barrels of beer were broached, for the commonalty.

Dinner over, there was singing and dancing. Alwyn had engaged, and sent from Alnwick, a score of musicians. These were divided into five parties, stationed at some little distance apart, and round these the younger portion of the gathering soon grouped themselves; while the elders listened to border lays sung by wandering minstrels. The days were shortening fast and, as many of those present had twenty miles to ride, by six o'clock the amusements came to an end, and the gathering scattered in all directions, delighted with the day's proceedings; which, although they would have been thought of but small account in the southern counties, were rare, indeed, in a district so thinly populated, and so frequently engaged in turmoil and strife.

Except in the running match, Oswald had engaged in none of the contests, he being fully occupied in aiding his mother in welcoming the guests, and seeing to their comfort; while his father, assisted by his friends, Hope, Gray, and Liddel, superintended the arrangements for the sports, and acted as judges. In the afternoon, Oswald and his cousins had joined heartily in the dances, and enjoyed the day to the full as much as their visitors.

Gatherings of this kind were not uncommon. Shooting, wrestling, and sword-playing for the men, and dancing on the green for the young people, took place at most of the village fairs; but the gathering at Yardhope was long talked about, as a special occasion, from the hospitality in which all were included, and the number of the heads of the border families who were present, and took part in the proceedings.

Oswald's mother had been the prime mover in the matter. She was proud of her son, and thought that it was a good occasion to present him to the countryside, as one who was now arriving at manhood, and was likely, in time, to make a figure on the border. John Forster had at first declared that it was wholly unnecessary, and that such a thing had never taken place in his time, or in his father's before him.

"That may be, husband," she said, "but Oswald has been away from us for two years, and it may be as much more before he returns. He is like to become a knight, before long--Alwyn said that the lad was sure to win his spurs--and it would be well that he should not slip out of the memory of folks here. Besides, we have his cousins, and it is well that they should carry back news that, in spite of the troublous times, we can yet be merry on suitable occasions.

"The cost will not be very great. The meat can scarcely be counted, seeing that we have as many cattle on the moor as can pick up a living there. Moreover, our neighbours all gave us a helping hand, to repair the hold after it was sacked last year, and 'tis but right that we should hold some sort of gathering, and this will do for the two purposes."

The last argument had more weight with John Forster than the former ones. Once having consented, he took as much interest in it as did his wife; and dug up the pot in which he stowed away any sums that remained, at the end of each year, over and above the expenses of the hold; and provided all that was required, without stinting.

Three days after the gathering, the Armstrongs returned home, and Oswald rode with Roger to Alnwick. The next three months passed quietly and uneventfully. Snow was lying deep on the Cheviots, and until spring there was little chance of the Scotch making a foray.

Oswald worked hard in the hall, where the knights kept themselves in exercise, practised with the young squires, and superintended the drilling and practice of the men-at-arms, of whom the number at the castle had been much increased; for none doubted that in the spring the Scots would, after Henry's invasion, pay a return visit to England, and that the northern counties would need a very strong force to hold them in check.

He was, several times, sent by Percy with messages to the governors of Roxburgh and Jedburgh, and to other commanders; calling upon them to be vigilant, and to send in lists of arms and stores required, so that all should be in good order to make a stout resistance, when the need came.

When he had received no special orders to return with speed to Alnwick, Oswald generally found time to pay a visit of a few hours to the Armstrongs. On these excursions Roger and another man-at-arms always rode with him, for it would not have been becoming for a squire, and messenger of Hotspur, to ride without such escort.

Alwyn had picked out, for Roger's use, one of the strongest horses in the castle. It was not a showy animal, having a big ugly head, and being vicious in temper; therefore, after some trial, it had been handed over to the men-at-arms, instead of being retained for the service of the knights. It had, at first, tried its best to establish a mastership over the trooper; but it soon found that its efforts were as nothing against the strength of its rider, and that it might as well try to shake off its saddle as to rid itself of the trooper, the grip of whose knees almost stopped its breathing. Oswald, too, was very well mounted, Sir Edmund Mortimer having presented him with one of the best horses in the stable, upon his leaving him.

Upon nearing Hiniltie one day, just as the new year had begun, Oswald was alarmed at seeing smoke wreaths ascending from the knoll behind the village upon which the Armstrongs' hold stood. Galloping on, he soon saw that his first impressions were correct, and that his uncle's tower was on fire. He found the village in confusion.

"What has happened?" he asked, reining in his horse for a moment.

"The hold was suddenly attacked, two hours ago," a man said. "A party of reivers rode through here. None had seen them coming, and there was no time for us to take our women and children, and hurry to the shelter of the hold. Adam Armstrong is away at Roxburgh. Young Allan, with what few men there were at the hold, had but just time to shut the gates; but these were hewed down, in a short time, by the troopers. There was a stout fight as they entered. Allan was cut down and left for dead, and the troopers were all killed. Dame Armstrong was slain, and her daughters carried off by the reivers; and these, as soon as they had sacked the house, set it alight and galloped off. Most of the men here were away in the fields, or with the flocks in the valleys, and we were too few to hinder them, and could but shut ourselves up in the houses, until they had gone."

Oswald had dropped his reins, in speechless dismay.

"It is terrible," he said, at last. "Aunt killed, Janet and Jessie carried away, and Allan wounded, perhaps to death!"

"Whence came these villains?" he asked suddenly. "From beyond the Cheviots? It can hardly be so, for this part is under the governor of Roxburgh, and no English raiders would dare to meddle with any here. Besides, my uncle has always been on good terms with them, holding himself aloof from all quarrels, and having friends and relations on both sides of the border."

"We believe that it was the Bairds," a man said. "There has long been a standing quarrel between them and the Armstrongs, partly about stolen cattle, but more, methinks, because of the relationship between the Armstrongs and your people"-- for Oswald's visits to his uncle had made his face familiar to the villagers--"and they say that the Bairds have sworn that they will never rest, until they have slain the last of the Forsters."

"Where is Allan Armstrong?"

"They have carried him down to the last house in the village. The priest and Meg Margetson, who knows more of wounds and simples than anyone here, are with him."

"Has his mother's body been recovered?"

The man shook his head.

"The hold was on fire, from roof to cellar, before they left," he said. "I and others ran up there, directly they had galloped away. The house was like a furnace. And indeed, we knew not of her death until a boy, who had seen her slain, and had dropped from a window and hidden himself till they had gone, came out and told us. He, and two or three others, are the only ones left alive of those in the hold, when we arrived and saved young Allan; and indeed, whether he lives now, or not, I know not. The priest said, when we carried him in, that his state was almost beyond hope."

Oswald galloped on to the end of the village, leapt from his horse, and threw the reins to Roger, who had been muttering words that he certainly would not have found in the missals, or the books, of the monastery.

"Is there nothing to be done, Master Oswald?"

"Not at present. We must wait till my uncle returns."

Then he entered the house. He had met the priest frequently, during his stay with the Armstrongs; as he entered the room, he was standing by a pallet on which Allan was laid, while a very old woman was attending to a decoction that was boiling over the fire.

"Is there any hope, father?"

"I know not," the priest replied, shaking his head sorrowfully. "We have stanched the wounds, but his head is well nigh cleft open. I have some skill in wounds, for they are common enough in this unfortunate country, and I should say that there was no hope; but Meg here, who is noted through the country round for her knowledge in these matters, thinks that it is possible he may yet recover. She is now making a poultice of herbs that she will lay on the wound; or rather on the wounds, for he has no less than four."

"I think that he will live, young master," the old woman said in a quavering, high-pitched voice. "'Tis hard to kill an Armstrong. They have ever been a hardy race and, save the lad's father, have ever been prone to the giving and taking of blows. I watched by his grandfather's bed, when he was in as sore a strait as this; but he came round, and was none the worse for it, though the blow would have killed any man with a softer skull.

"A curse upon the Bairds, I say. They have ever been a race of thieves and raiders, and it is their doings that have brought trouble on the border, as long as I can remember."

"Has any gone to bear the news to Adam Armstrong, father?"

"Yes. I sent off a messenger on horseback, as soon as they had gone. Adam left early, and the man will meet him on his way back."

Half an hour later, indeed, Adam Armstrong rode in. Oswald met him outside. His face was set and hard, and Oswald would scarce have recognized the kindly, genial man who had always received him so heartily.

"There are hopes that he will live," Oswald said.

There was a slight change in the expression of Armstrong's face.

"'Tis well," he said, "that one should be saved, to take revenge for this foul business. All the others are gone."

"I hope we may rescue my cousins."

"We might as well try to rescue a young lamb, that had been carried off by an eagle," he said bitterly. "Even could an archer send a shaft through the bird's breast-bone, the lamb would be bleeding and injured, beyond all hope, ere it touched the ground. We may revenge, Oswald, but I have no hope of rescue."

Then he went into the house, without further word.

Chapter 12: A Dangerous Mission.

Half an hour later, Adam Armstrong came out of the cottage where his son was lying. His mood had changed. He had gathered hope from Meg Margetson's confident assurances that there was ground for it.

"Now, let us talk of what had best be done, Oswald," he said, as he led the way into the next cottage, where the woman at once turned her children out, and cleared a room for him.

"What force could you gather, Uncle?"

"In my grandfather's time," he said, "two hundred Armstrongs, and their followers, could gather in case of need; but the family was grievously thinned, in the days when Edward carried fire and sword through Scotland; and for the last fifty years Roxburgh and these parts have been mostly under English rule, and in that time we have never gathered as a family. Still, all my kin would, I know, take up this quarrel; and I should say that, in twelve hours, we could gather fifty or sixty stout fighting men.

"But the Bairds would be expecting us, and can put, with the families allied to them and their retainers, nigh three hundred men under arms. Their hold is so strong a one that it took fifteen hundred Englishmen, under Umfraville, three weeks to capture it. It was destroyed then, but it is stronger now than ever.

"Could we get aid from Roxburgh, think you?"

"I fear not, Uncle. I know that the governor has strict orders not to give Douglas any pretext for invading us, and to hold his garrison together; since the earl may, at any moment, endeavour to capture the town before help could arrive. And even were he to send four or five hundred men, the Bairds could hold out for a fortnight, at least; and long before this Douglas would be down, with an army, to his rescue.

"I have been talking it over with my trusty companion, here, and he agrees with me that, unless a body of men-at-arms that would avail to capture the fortal-ice by a sudden assault can be raised, we must trust to guile rather than force; and I propose that he and I shall, at once, start for the hold and see how matters stand, and where the prisoners are confined, and what hope there is of getting them free. I propose to send my other man to Yardhope, to tell my father what has happened, and to ask him to warn his friends to be ready to cross the border, and to join any force you can gather for an attack on the Bairds. It is true that stringent orders have been issued that there is to be no raiding in Scotland, but my father would not heed that for a moment. The attack that has been made upon you, the killing of his wife's sister, the wounding of Allan, and carrying off of his nieces would be deemed, by him, a grievance sufficient to justify his disregarding all orders. Besides which, he has the old grievance against the Bairds, which is all the more bitter since they led the Scots to attack Yardhope. I can guarantee that, when he gets word from you as to the day and place, he will meet you there with at least a hundred spears. It is true that, with this force and that which you can bring, he could not hope to capture the Bairds' hold; but together you could carry sword and fire through his district, before he could gather a force to meet you in the field."

"I fear that would not do, Oswald. William Baird would be capable of hanging the girls from the battlements, when the first fire was lit."

Oswald was silent. From the tales he had heard of the ferocity of these dreaded marauders, he felt that it was more than probable that his uncle was right.

"It seems to me," he said, after a pause, "that it were best for you to send two men to Parton; which is, as I have heard, though I have never been there, ten miles south of the Bairds'. Let them give the name of Johnstone; and, at the tavern where they put up, say they expect a relative of the same name. As soon as I can find out how the affair had best be managed, I will give them instructions as to the plans I propose. One will carry them to you, and the other to my father. Will Parton be a good place for you to join forces?"

"As well as any other, Oswald. Your plan seems to me a good one. At any rate, I can think of nothing better. My brain is deadened by this terrible misfortune. Had I my own will, I would ride straight to the Bairds' hold and challenge him and his brothers and sons to meet me, one after another, in fair combat; and should be well contented if I could slay one or two of them, before being myself killed."

"I can quite understand that, Uncle. But your death would be, in no way, an advantage to the girls; nay, would rather render them more helpless, therefore I pray you to let me carry things out as I have planned."

His uncle nodded.

"I shall send out a dozen runners to my friends," he said, "and beg them to be here tomorrow morning, early. Then, when I have talked matters over with them, I shall ride to Roxburgh and lay the matter before the governor. I know that I shall get no help from him; but at least, when he hears of a gathering here, he will know that 'tis with no evil intention against the English."

Ten minutes later, Oswald's messenger started for Yardhope, with a full account of the step he was taking, and of the arrangements that had been made. This done, he had a long talk with Roger.

"Now, Roger," he said, "this will be the most dangerous business in which we have been concerned; and I should not venture to undertake it, did I not know that I could rely, absolutely, upon you."

"I will do my best, master, and will adventure my life all the more willingly, since it is in the service of Allan and Janet Armstrong. They were always pleasant and friendly with me, at Yardhope, and I like them for themselves, as well as because they are your cousins. Now, master, what is to be done?"

"Have you your gown with you, Roger?"

"No, master. I know you always told me to take it with me, thinking that it might come in useful, and I carried it under my saddle all the time we were in Wales; but, seeing that this was but a ride to Jedburgh and back, I thought that there would be no occasion for it."

"That is unfortunate, Roger, for it is upon this that we must depend to get an entry into the Bairds' hold."

"Well, master, I can doubtless get some rough cloth of the colour, at Jedburgh; and indeed, there is a small monastery about three miles hence on the road, and it may be that, if Adam Armstrong will go with us and say wherefore it is wanted, the prior will let him have one."

"I will see him at once. No time must be lost. While he is away, you must shave your head again."

Roger's face fell.

"'Tis hard, master, after it has grown so well to match the rest. Still, for so good a purpose I must even give in."

On hearing what was wanted, Armstrong mounted and rode off at once and, while he was away, one of the villagers shaved the top of Roger's head again. In an hour, Armstrong brought back a monk's gown.

"He was loath to let me have it even, for such a purpose, though I told him that you were once a monk of the order. Finally he said that his conscience would not allow him to lend it, but that he would sell it to me for six pennies, which I gladly gave him."

"It is dark now," Oswald said, "and I know not the road. Can you give me some man to put me on the way? We will not make straight for the Bairds', but will strike the road from Glasgow, some ten or twelve miles north of his place, so that we can come down from that direction. Then our guide, after taking us on to the road, had best take charge of the horses and lead them to Parton, there to remain with them until your messenger, and the one from Yardhope, arrive. It would be as well to have the horses there, for we cannot know what need we may have of them."

"That I will arrange at once, Oswald. Is there aught else?"

"Yes, Uncle, I must leave my armour and clothes here, and borrow others that will pass as a disguise."

"How would you go, Oswald?"

"In truth, it is a difficult matter. That of a minstrel would be the best passport, but I know nought of harp or other instrument. I might go as a vendor of philters and charms, a sort of half-witted chap, whose mother concocted such things."

"They would never let you into the Bairds' castle, Oswald."

"Then I must be a rough man-at-arms, one who had been in the service of the Earl of March; and who, when he turned traitor and went over to the English, found himself without employment; and asked nothing better than to enter the service of someone who will give him bread and meat, in return for any services that he can render, whether in hunting up any cattle among the hills, or striking a shrewd blow in the service of his employer, if needs be."

"That must do, if we can think of nothing better, Oswald. I will speedily bring you the things you require, as they will be found in every house in the village; and some, alas! will be needed no more by those who wore them."

"They must be of good size, Uncle."

"Ay, ay, lad. There must have been some tall fellows, among those they slew today."

Half an hour later, Roger and Oswald mounted. His uncle sent two of his men with them, saying that it would look strange were one man to come, with two horses, to Parton; but that two, saying that their masters would follow, would seem a more probable tale.

"They will, if they can, find some quiet farmhouse a mile out of the village, and there get lodgings for themselves and beasts. You can arrange with them to take up their station on the road, so that you can, if needs be, find them."

It was with a sigh that Roger flung himself into the saddle. It was not the horse on which he had ridden there, but a strong, shaggy pony.

"He does not look much," one of the men said, "but there is no better horse, of the sort, in the country. He has both speed and bottom, and can carry you up or down hill, and is as sure-footed as a goat."

Roger had assented to the change, for his own horse was as unlike one that a monk would have bestrode as could be well imagined. He had obtained a stout staff, to which the village smith had added two or three iron rings at each end, rendering it a formidable weapon, indeed, in such hands.

"It reminds me of our start for Dunbar, master," he said. "One might have a worse weapon than this;" and he swung it round his head, in quarterstaff fashion; "still, I prefer a mace."

"That staff will do just as well, Roger. A man would need a hard skull, indeed, to require more than one blow from such a weapon."

Now that Adam Armstrong had done all that there was to do, he went again to the cottage where Allan lay. He had paid several visits there, in the afternoon; but there was nought for him to do, and no comfort to be gained from the white face of the insensible lad. Meg assured him, however, that he was going on as well as could be expected.

"He is in a torpor, at present," she said; "and may so lie for two or three days; but so long as there is no fever he will, I hope, know you when he opens his eyes. There is nought to do but to keep wet cloths round his head, and to put on a fresh poultice over the wound, every hour."

Now Armstrong took his place by his son's pallet. For a time, the work of making preparations for Oswald's departure, and of sending off messages to his friends, had prevented his thoughts from dwelling upon his loss. Throughout the night, the picture of his home, as he had left it when he rode out that morning; and the thought that it was now an empty shell, his wife dead, his daughters carried off, and his son lying between life and death, came to him with full force, and well nigh broke him down.

In the meantime, the little party were making across the hills, and before morning they came upon the northern road, fifteen miles from the Bairds' hold. Here Oswald and Roger dismounted. It was arranged that the men should return with the horses into the hills, and should there rest until late in the afternoon, and then mount and ride for Parton. One or other of them was to come down, at seven o'clock each evening, to the road half a mile from the village; and was there to watch till nine. If no one came along, they were then to return to their lodging.

"I feel stiff in the legs, master," Roger said; "a fifty-mile ride, up and down the hills, is no joke after a hard day's work."

"They will soon come right again, Roger. I feel stiff, myself, though pretty well accustomed to horse exercise. However, when we present ourselves at the hold, dusty and footsore, we shall look our characters thoroughly."

Neither were sorry when they arrived at a small village, a quarter of a mile from the Bairds' hold. They went in together to the little ale house, and vigorously attacked the rough fare set before them.

"Hast thou travelled far?" their host asked, as he watched them eating.

"Indifferently far," the monk said: "'tis five-and-twenty miles hence to Moffat, and it would have seemed farther to me, had not this good fellow overtaken me, and fell in with my pace. He is good company, though monkish gowns have but little in common with steel pot and broadsword; but his talk, and his songs, lightened the way."

"Whither are you going, father?"

"I am making my way to Carlisle," he said. "I have a brother who is prior in a small monastery, there, and it is long since I have seen him. Who lives at the stronghold I saw on the hills, but a short distance away?"

"It is the hold of William Baird, the head of that family; of whom, doubtless, you may have heard."

"I have heard his name, as that of a noted raider across the border," the monk said; "a fierce man, and a bold one. Has he regard for the church? If so, I would gladly take up my abode there, for a day or two; for in truth I am wearied out, it being some years since my feet have carried me so long a journey."

"As to that, I say nothing," the host said. "It would depend on his humour whether he took you in, or shut the gates in your face without ceremony; but methinks, at present, the latter were more likely than the former; for his hold is full of armed men, and I should say it were wisest to leave him alone, even if you had but the bare moor to sleep upon."

"Nevertheless, I can but try," the monk said. "He may be in one of those good tempers you spoke of. And I suppose he has also a priest, in his fortalice?"

"Ay, the Bairds are not--but I would rather not talk of them. They are near neighbours, and among my very best customers."

As he spoke, four armed men came in at the door.

"Good day, Wilson! Whom have you here? An ill-assorted couple, surely. A monk, though a somewhat rough one, and a man-at-arms."

"Fellow travellers of a day," Roger said calmly. "We met on the road, and as I love not solitude, having enough and to spare of it, I accosted him. He turned out a good companion."

"You are a man of sinew yourself, monk, and methinks that you would have made a better soldier than a shaveling."

"I thought so sometime, myself," the monk said; "but my parents thought otherwise, and it is too late to take up another vocation, now."

"Is that staff yours?" the soldier asked, taking it up, and handling it.

"Yes, my son. In these days even a quiet religious man, like myself, may meet with rough fellows by the way; and while that staff gives support to my feet, it is an aid to command decent behaviour from those I fall in with. I have not much to lose, having with me but sufficient to buy me victuals for my journey to Carlisle; where, as I have just told our host, I am journeying to see a brother, who is prior at a convent there."

"This fellow--where did you fall in with him?"

"He overtook me some twenty miles north, on the road to Glasgow."

"And are you travelling to Carlisle, too?" the man said to Oswald.

"Nay," he said, "I purpose not going beyond the border. I have lost my employment, and have tried, in vain, to find another as much to my liking. I have come south to seek service, with one who will welcome a strong arm to wield a sword."

"Hast tried the Douglas?"

"No," he said, "the Douglas has men enough of his own, and methinks I should not care to be mewed up in one of his castles. I have had enough of that already, seeing that I was a man-at-arms with George Dunbar, till he turned traitor and went over to the English."

"You look a likely fellow; but, you know, we do not pay men, here, to do our fighting for us. 'Tis all very well for great nobles, like Dunbar and Douglas, to keep men always in arms, and ready to ride, at a moment's notice, to carry fire and sword where they will. War is not our business, save when there is trouble in the air, or mayhap we run short of cattle or horses, and have to go and fetch them from across the border. It is true that there are always a score or two of us up there, for somehow the Bairds have enemies, but most of the followers of the house live on their holdings, raise cattle and mountain sheep, grow oats, and live as best they can."

"For myself, I would rather live with others," Oswald said. "I am used to it, and to live in a hut on the moors would in no way be to my fancy; and if I cannot get a place where I have comrades to talk to, and crack a joke with, I would rather cross the seas, take service with an Irish chieftain, or travel to Wales, where I hear men say there is fighting."

"You need not go very far, if it is fighting that you want," the man said. "Those who ride with the Bairds have their share, and more, of it. If you like to stop here a day or two, I will take an opportunity to talk to William Baird, or to one of his sons, if I find a chance; but I cannot take you up there, now. At the best of times they are not fond of visitors, and would be less so than usual, now."

Other armed men had come in, while the conversation was going on. No further attention was paid to the travellers. The others, sitting down at a table across the room, talked among themselves.

"I care not for the work," one said presently, raising his voice to a higher pitch than that in which the others had spoken. "Across the border, I am as ready for work as another; but when it comes to Scot against Scot, I like it not."

"Why, man," another said, "what qualms are these? Isn't Scot always fighting against Scot? Ay, and has been so, as far back as one has ever heard. It does not take much for a Douglas or a Dunbar to get to loggerheads; and as to the wild clans of the north, they are always fighting among themselves."

"Yes, that is all very well," the other said, "and there is no reason why neighbours should not quarrel, here; but I would rather that they each summoned their friends, and met in fair fight and had it out, than that one should pounce upon the other when not expected, and slay and burn unopposed."

"Ay, ay," two or three others of the men agreed. "It were doubtless better so, when it is Scot against Scot."

"'Tis border fashion," another put in. "There is no law on the border, and we fight in our own fashion. Today it is our turn, tomorrow it may be someone else's. We follow our chiefs, just as the northern clansmen do; and whether it is a Musgrave or a Baird, a Fenwick or an Armstrong, he is chief in his own hold, and cares neither for king nor earl, but fights out his quarrel as it may please him. I am one of William Baird's men, and his quarrel is mine; and whether we ride against the King of Scotland or the King of England, against a Douglas or a Percy, an Armstrong or a Musgrave, it matters not the value of a stoup of ale."

"That is so, Nigel, and so say we all. But methinks that one may have a preference for one sort of fighting over another; and I, myself, would rather fight a matter out, man against man, than fall suddenly on a hold, where none are ready to encounter us."

Roger, during a pause in the conversation at the other table, got up from his seat and stretched himself.

"Well, friend," he said to Oswald, "I will go up and see if they will make me welcome, at the hold. If they do, I may see you no more. If not, I shall return here to sleep. Therefore I bid you good day, and hope that you may find such service as will suit you. Benedicite!"

And, paying for his refreshment, Roger took his staff from the corner, and went out.

"A hearty fellow, and a stalwart one," the man who had spoken to him said. "I should not care to have a crack over the crown, with that staff of his. You met him coming down from the north, comrade?"

"Yes, some twenty miles away. It was near Moffat that I overtook him. I would rather drink with him than fight with him. Seldom have I seen a stronger-looking man."

"I am of your opinion, comrade; and some of these monks are not bad fighters, either. There have been bishops who have led the monks to battle, before now, and they proved themselves stout men-at-arms."

After the others had gone out, Oswald strolled through the village, and then mounted an eminence whence he could take a view across the valley, and of some of the hilltops to the northeast. On one of these, two miles away, he could make out a man standing by a horse. He watched him for some little time, but beyond taking a few steps backwards and forwards, the man did not move.

"He is a lookout," he said to himself, "and is no doubt watching some road from Kelso and Jedburgh. Baird will hardly think that the Armstrongs can have so soon gathered a force sufficient to attack him, but he may have thought it as well to place one of his men on the watch.

"I wonder how Roger is getting on! I think they must have taken him in, or he would have been back before this."

Roger had walked quietly up the hill on which the Bairds' hold was perched. A man stepped forward from the gate, as he neared it.

"None enter here," he said, "without permission from the master."

"Will you tell him that a poor monk, of the order of Saint Benedict, on his way from his convent at Dunbar to one near Carlisle, of which his brother is prior, prays hospitality for a day or two, seeing that he is worn out by long travel?"

The sentry spoke to a man behind him, and the latter took the message to William Baird. The latter was in a good humour. He himself had not taken part in the raid on the Armstrongs, which had been led by Thomas Baird, a cousin; but the fact that the latter had been entirely successful, and had burned down Armstrong's house, and brought back his daughters, had given him the greatest satisfaction. There was a long-standing feud between the two families, and the fact that the Armstrongs were on good terms with their English neighbours, and still more that one of them had married the sister-in-law of a Forster of Yardhope, had greatly embittered the feeling, on his side. He had long meditated striking a blow at them, and the present time had been exceptionally favourable.

Douglas had his hands full. He was on ill terms with Rothesay, whose conduct to his daughter had deeply offended him. The newly-acquired land of the Earl of March gave him much trouble. He was jealous of the great influence of Albany, at court; and was, moreover, making preparations for a serious raid into England. It was not likely, then, that he would pay any attention to the complaints the Armstrongs might make, of any attack upon them; especially as their aid was of small use to him, while the Bairds could, at any moment, join him, in an invasion across the border, with three hundred good fighting men.

William Baird had not, as yet, even considered what he should do with his captives. He might give them in marriage to some of the younger men of his family, or he might hold them as hostages. As to injuring them personally, he did not think of it. Slaughter in a raid was lightly regarded, but to ill-treat female prisoners would arouse a general feeling of dissatisfaction along the border. Reprisals might be made by the Armstrongs and their friends, and in any case, there would be such widespread reprobation excited, as William Baird, reckless as he was, could hardly afford to despise.

Therefore, when Roger's request was brought to him, he said at once:

"Take him up to Father Kenelm. Tell him to look after the monk's comfort. This evening he can bring him down to the hall, and I will question him as to his journey."

Roger followed the man through the courtyard. He paid, apparently, no attention to what was going on there, but a quick glance enabled him to perceive that the hold was full of men. He followed his guide up a winding stair, to a turret on the wall, the lower story of which was inhabited by the priest.

The soldier knocked at the door, and on its being opened by the priest, he gave Baird's message to him. He was a tall man, spare and bony. He himself was a Baird, and report said that, in his youth, he had ridden on many a foray in England. But fighting men were common in the family, and it had been thought well that one should enter the church, as it was always good to have a friend who could represent them there and, should any complaint be made, explain matters, and show that the family were in no wise to blame. And moreover, as it was necessary to have a priest at the chief fortalice of the family, it was best that it should be one who would not be too strict in his penances, and could be conveniently silent as to the doings within its walls.

The priest had accepted the role not unwillingly. He was an ambitious man, and saw that, as one of the fighting Bairds, there was but small opportunity of rising to aught beyond the command of one of the holds. Douglas regarded them with no friendly eye, for their breaches of the truces brought upon him constant complaints from the English wardens, who might, some day or other, lead a force to punish the family, which had been one of the few exempted from the general pardon, at the last truce. As a priest he would have better opportunities, for the Bairds had much influence along the border; and might, some day or other, exert it in his favour.

So far, no such opportunity had occurred. It had been a disappointment to him that Henry, in his last invasion, had kept along the eastern coast; and he hoped that the war, which assuredly would, ere long, break out violently, would give him the chance he longed for; and he might be sent by his uncle to Douglas, with offers of service, or might even go north, and have an interview with Albany.

Once fairly away from Liddesdale, he was resolved that it would be a long time, indeed, before he returned. He was now some thirty years of age, with a hard, keen face.

"Well, brother," he said, "it is not often that any of your order sojourn here. I am glad to have one with whom I can converse, of other matters than arms and armour, forays and wars."

"These matters are, indeed, too much in men's mouths," Roger said; "though I own that I, myself, in some degree am interested in them; for, had I had the choice of a vocation, I would rather have been a man-at-arms than a monk."

"I wonder not at that," the other said, "seeing that nature has been bountiful to you, in the matter of height and strength; and I doubt not that you could, in case of need, use that staff you carry with good effect."

"Methinks that I might do so, but happily none have molested me on my way, seeing perhaps that my wallet was not likely to be a full one; and that, mayhap, it was hardly worthwhile to meddle with me, with so small a prospect of plunder."

"But come in, and sit down," the priest said. "My uncle has consigned you to my care. We shall sup in half an hour."

"I shall not be sorry," Roger replied, "for though I broke my fast on black bread and small beer, down in the village, 'tis but poor nourishment for a man who has travelled far, and who has a large frame to support."

"But how come you to be here?"

Roger again repeated his story.

"It would have been shorter for you to have travelled down through Berwick, brother."

"The difference was not great," Roger replied; "and I had to carry a message to Edinburgh, and from there it was shorter to keep west of the Pentlands, and come down to Lanark, and thence through Moffat."

"Yes, I suppose it is as short. And you had no trouble on your way?"

Roger shook his head.

"No; I generally join some traveller or other, and that makes the journey pass all the quicker. I came down here today with a stout young fellow, who overtook me this side of Moffat. He was somewhat out at elbow, and I looked askance at him at first; but he turned out a blithe companion, and we got on well together. He could troll a good song, and my own voice is not wanting in power. It was curious that he also was from Dunbar, though not immediately; having, it would seem, wandered for some time, on the lookout for service."

"What was he, a cattle drover?"

"No, he had been a man-at-arms, of George of Dunbar--at least, so I understood--and when the earl fled, and Douglas took possession of Dunbar, he lost his living. He told me that he had made his way down here in hopes of finding employment on the border, where blows were common, and a good blade was of more use than it was farther north. I said that he might have found employment under Albany, or under some other great lord; but he said that he had seen the Earl of March a fugitive, and that he cared not to enter the service of another noble, who might, in turn, be ousted from his place and lose his life; but as for Albany, he thought, from what he heard, that he would rather serve him than any other master.

"I said, 'Why not Rothesay, who would be King of Scotland?'

"He laughed lightly, and said as Rothesay had managed to get upon ill friendship, not only with the Earl of March but with Douglas, and, as he heard, with Albany, he thought that his chances of becoming King of Scotland were not worth considering."

"He must be a bold varlet, thus to speak irreverently of great ones."

"I think not that he was bold," Roger said, "but only a merry, thoughtless young fellow, who in such company as mine let his tongue loose, and said what first came into his head. As to the matter, methought he spoke not without warrant."

"And he came from the north, now?"

"I know not whence he came last, but I think that he was at Edinburgh, and had taken service there, when the English king sat down before it; but, as you know, nought came of the siege."

At this moment a horn blew.

"There is supper," the priest said. "We will go down."

The meal was laid in the hall; which, however, was not large enough to contain more than the ordinary retainers of the hold. These, and the men who had come in at the summons of Baird, were provided for in the courtyard, the table being occupied entirely by members of the Baird family, and others who always acted with them. These had not yet taken their seats, when the priest entered with his companion, whom he at once took up to Sir William Baird.

"By Saint Andrew! Monk, I have seen no finer figure, for many a day. A pity that a monk's gown should clothe such limbs as yours."

"That has always been mine own opinion," Roger said, with a heartiness that raised a smile on the hard faces of the men standing round.

"You look as if you had carried arms."

"I did so, in my wild youth," Roger said, "and had no thought of ever donning monk's hood; but I was grievously wounded, in a foray in Northumberland, and when I reached my home at Lauder, I well nigh died of the fever of the wound; and I swore that, if my life was saved, I would become a monk. I got well, and I kept my vow; but methinks, had I but known how dull the life was, I would rather have died of the fever."

As this story was perfectly true, save the name of his birthplace, Roger spoke so heartily that no one doubted his story.

"And your monastery is at Dunbar?

"You have been at Dunbar, Rotherglen. Ask him where the convent stood."

As Roger had stayed there, when with Oswald he was at Dunbar, he was able to answer this, and other questions, satisfactorily. The party then took their places at table, the priest and Roger sitting at the bottom of it. The conversation at the upper end naturally turned on the foray, and a general disbelief was expressed, as to the chance of the Armstrongs retaliating.

"'Tis out of the question," one of the Bairds said, "they could not raise fifty men. Doubtless they will send a complaint to Douglas, but he has his hands well full; and is not likely to quarrel with us about such a trifle, when he may want our aid, at any moment, either against Albany or against the English."

"What do you intend to do with the girls?"

"I have not settled yet," William Baird said, shortly. "At any rate, for the present I shall hold them as hostages. I don't think that anything is likely to come of the affair; but if we should hear of any force approaching, likely to give us trouble, we could send word to them that, if an arrow is loosened at our walls, we will hang the girls out as marks for their archers. I fancy that will send them trooping off again, at once."

As soon as the meal was over, and the carousal began, the priest rose and, accompanied by Roger, retired to his chamber.

Chapter 13: Escape.

Oswald, who was thoroughly fatigued with the events of the last thirty-six hours, slept soundly, on an armful of rushes that his host threw down in a corner of the room for him. At eight o'clock, the man who had spoken to him on the previous evening came in.

"I have spoken to William Baird," he said. "I told him that you seemed a likely fellow. He called down the monk, and asked him several questions about you; and he told me, at last, that I could bring you up to see him. So come along, at once."

"Thanks, comrade," Oswald said, as he slung his long two-handed sword from his shoulder.

"A likely-looking young fellow, indeed," Baird said to Rotherglen, whom he had sent for to be present; "over six feet and, I should fancy, has not attained his full width.

"So you would fain take service with me?" he said.

"I want a master," Oswald replied, "and from what I hear, I am more likely to see fighting, under you, than under any other on the border."

"And you were with George Dunbar?"

"I was," Oswald replied. "But indeed, the service was not altogether to my taste, for we were always pent up in Dunbar; and, save in a street broil, there was no need to draw a sword. I was glad enough to leave his service, though in truth, I have fared but badly, since."

"Now do you question him, Rotherglen."

A number of questions were put to Oswald, concerning the names of the streets, the direction, the name of the principal inns, and the approaches to the castle. All these were satisfactorily replied to.

"He knows Dunbar, there is no question about that.

"And you can use your arms?"

"I think so."

"We will have a trial," Baird said. "A man is no use to me, who cannot use his weapon. Send Robert here."

In a minute, one of the young Bairds entered. He was a man of about twenty-five, tall and sinewy, and was accounted the best swordsman of his family.

"Cousin Robert," William Baird said, "this young fellow would enter our service; but before I take him, I must see that he knows his business. Do you take a turn with the sword with him.

"No, no, not a two-handed sword; I don't want him to be slain. Take a couple of swords from the wall. Give him another steel cap, and full body armour. That of his own would not keep out a good, downright stroke."

By the time that Oswald was armed, a number of the Bairds and their friends had assembled in the hall, hearing of what was going to take place.

"A fine young fellow, truly," Rotherglen said. "In height and width, he matches Robert well, though of course your cousin must be the more powerful, seeing that he is some four or five years older than this young fellow; who, when he reaches his age, bids fair to be well-nigh as strong a man as that monk."

Roger had just entered, with the priest.

"Well, monk," Baird said, "we are going to try the mettle of your companion of yesterday."

"I answer not for his mettle," Roger said; "but if he fights as well as he talks, he will not do discredit to himself."

As they took their places, facing each other, the lookers on, men well qualified to judge of strength and sinew, murmured to each other that it would be difficult to find a better-matched pair. They were about the same height, both stood lightly on their feet, and their figures seemed full of life and activity. Both were smiling, Robert Baird with a smile of confidence, and of assurance in his skill; while Oswald's face expressed only good temper and, as the others took it, a belief that he would, at any rate, be able to make such a defence as would assure his being taken into the Bairds' service.

The first rally, indeed, proved more than this. Robert Baird had at once taken the offensive, and showered his blows heavily down, while springing backwards and forwards with wonderful quickness and activity; but Oswald's blade ever met his, and he did not give way an inch, even when Baird most fiercely attacked him. Then suddenly he adopted the same tactics as his opponent, and pressed him so hotly that he was, several times, obliged to give ground. Oswald could twice have got in a heavy blow, but he abstained from doing so. He could see that his antagonist was a favourite among his kinsmen, and felt that, were he to discomfit him, he would excite a feeling of hostility against himself. Both, panting from their exertions, drew a step backwards and lowered their swords.

"Enough!" William Baird said, "The matter need be pushed no further. 'Tis long since I have seen so good a bout of swordplay. This young fellow has learned his business, and if, in other respects, he does as well, he will make a good recruit, indeed.

"What say you, lad? Will you join us for a month, till you see whether you like our service, and we can judge how your service will suit us? For that time you will have your living here, and drink money. After that, if we agree, you can either be a retainer here, or we will give you a holding on the moor, build you a shelter, give you a horse, and, after our next foray, a clump of cattle."

"That will suit me well," Oswald said; "and I like well the month of trial you propose."

"I will take him, if you will let me, Uncle, as my own man," Robert Baird said. "If, at the end of the month, he chooses service with us, and likes better to follow a master, with half a dozen men, than to live alone on the moors. Methinks he would make a cheery companion, and one I could take to, heartily; and indeed, during the long winters, 'tis no slight thing to have one merry fellow, who can keep one alive, and of whose mettle and skill you are well assured."

"So let it be, then, Robert. You have tried him, and yours should be the advantage. But for the month he shall remain here, under Malcolm's eye."

Oswald went down with the man, who was Baird's right hand in the hold.

"What will be my duties?" he asked.

"To keep your arms and armour ready for service."

"That will be an easy task, methinks; for I see that instead of being polished and bright, as were ours at Dunbar, the others keep their steel caps and back pieces painted a sombre colour."

The other nodded.

"Yes, our arms are for use and not for show; and when we ride by moonlight, we care not to have our presence shown, miles away, by the glint of the moon on our armour.

"You will do your turn of keeping watch and ward. Just at present there will be a good deal of that, for we have been stirring up a wasps' nest, and mayhap they may come and try to sting. When you are off duty, you will be your own master, save that you had best be within sound of the warder's horn.

"I will hand over a horse to you. For the present, it is at that croft on the opposite hill. Each of the tenants keeps two or three at our service. We have only the Bairds' own horses kept in the hold. It would be too much trouble to gather forage for those of the twenty men who always live here, and indeed, we have no room for such number.

"Mind that you drink not too much, over in the village there; for though the Bairds care not, on feast days, if the whole garrison gets drunk, so that there are enough sober to keep watch and ward, they set their faces against it at other times, seeing that it leads to broils and quarrels."

"I will take care. I like my cup, occasionally; and can drink with others, without my head getting addled, but as a rule I care not overmuch for it."

After being roughly introduced to several of the retainers as a new comrade, Oswald was left to follow his own devices. Presently, Roger came out into the courtyard.

"So you have got service, comrade," he said, in a voice that could be heard by any of those standing near. "You had better fortune than I had expected."

"That have I," he replied. "Still, I thought that it would be hard, if one who could use his sword indifferently well, and puts no great value on his life, could not find service on the border. How long do you stay here?"

This was a question that had been arranged, for had they been seen speaking privately together, it might have aroused suspicion.

"Methinks I shall stay here two days, to get rid of my leg weariness. I am not so accustomed to long marching as you are."

The real meaning of the question, as arranged, was, "Have you found out where the prisoners are kept?"

The answer meant "Yes, and it will not be difficult to get at them."

The evening before, indeed, when he returned with the priest to his chamber, they had broached a bottle together. The priest, on his part, had asked many questions as to the state of things in Edinburgh, and Dunbar; what were the opinions of people with regard to the Duke of Albany, and the Prince; and what would probably come of the coldness that was said to exist between them.

Roger was able to conceal his ignorance of these matters by saying that he knew little of what was passing, for that he had been the cellarer in the convent, and went out but little. Nevertheless, he had kept his ears open; as they rode north to Jedburgh, he had heard a good deal of talk and speculation, and was able to give various pieces of news that had not before reached the ears of the priest. He was not long in discovering that the latter was ill satisfied with his present position, and was ambitious to take part in more important affairs, and he presently said:

"I wonder, father, that a man of your ability should be content to remain as chaplain in a border hold, when there are so many opportunities beyond, for one like you, to make his way in the church."

"In truth," the priest said, "I have had such thoughts myself; and hope, some day, to see a little more of the world.

"By the way, can you read and write, brother?" he asked suddenly.

"Assuredly," Roger replied.

He guessed, at once, that the question had been put at the instigation of William Baird; who perhaps still had some doubts whether he was really a monk, and an affirmative answer would be an almost conclusive proof that he was so, for very few outside the walls of the convents, even among the nobles and knights, possessed any knowledge of letters.

"I have a missal here," the priest said carelessly, "that has somewhat troubled me, being written in a cramped hand. Perhaps you could read it for me," and, getting up, he took a roll from a closet.

Roger smiled quietly, as he turned it over. By a private mark upon it, he knew that it had been written at Alnwick, and was doubtless the proceed of some foray upon a monastery across the border. He ran his eye over it; and then, in a sonorous voice, proceeded to read it aloud.

"I thank you," the priest said, when he had finished. "Truly you are an admirable reader, and well skilled in deciphering. I wonder that you held not some more important post than that of cellarer."

Roger laughed.

"I might have done so," he said, "but in truth, I am not strict enough in matters of discipline to suit our prior, and am somewhat over fond of the wine cup. More than once, when it seemed that I might have been chosen as reader to the monastery, I fell into disgrace, and lost my chance; and indeed, I was far better pleased with my post, there, than if they had appointed me sub-prior."

Any vestige of doubt there might have been in the priest's mind had vanished, as Roger read; for he was conscious that he, himself, could not have picked up a manuscript and have deciphered it so easily and fluently.

"It must be trying to you, good father," Roger went on, "to be among men who, if reports speak truly, are somewhat lawless, and hold even the church in but slight respect. Surely, among them there can be but little scope for your abilities?"

"'Tis true, brother; but they are, you know, kinsmen of mine. They have many foes across the border, and some on this side, and are forced to hold their own as they may. It was but two days ago that they were obliged to punish a family that have long been at feud with them, and who might well have fallen upon their holds, if they marched into England with Douglas. However, they have brought off two hostages for the good behaviour of these people."

"Yes, I heard a chance word, in the village, that a party had just returned from a foray, and had brought back a number of prisoners."

"Not a number, brother, but two girls."

"I have seen no women in the castle," Roger said.

"No. William Baird lost his wife years ago, and cares not to have women in the hold. There is not a married man among the garrison. If a man takes him a wife, he must go and settle on the lands.

"The women are in a safe place of keeping. They are overhead. There are wild young fellows among the Bairds, and the girls are good looking; therefore he thought it best to place them in my charge, and that is why you see two sentries marching on the battlements, one on each side of this turret. He himself keeps the key of their chamber, handing it over to me every morning, and receiving it again at night--a precaution wholly unnecessary, methinks."

"Surely, surely," Roger said. "I wonder that you are not offended."

"I told him that it was strange he could not trust me, a priest, with the charge of them; but he laughed and said, 'As a priest you are well enough, Father Kenelm, but remember also that you are a Baird. Though a priest, I would trust you to ride with me on a foray across the border; but as a Baird, I would not entrust you with the custody of women. You may take it as a compliment that I have trusted you as far as I do.'"

Roger's answer to Oswald had been eminently satisfactory to the latter. Still more pleased was he when, later on in the day, Roger repeated, as he passed him, "They are lodged in the turret, over my chamber."

Oswald was scarcely surprised, for he had noticed that two sentries were on the wall on that side, although it was the one farthest removed from the direction in which any foes were likely to appear. He had, moreover, just before dinner, observed one of the kitchen men go up, with two dishes in his hand, by the steps leading to the top of the wall, on that side. There was no hindrance to the men going freely in and out of the hold, and as no duty had been assigned to him that evening, he strolled out of the gate when it became dusk, soon after six o'clock, for it was now the beginning of April, 1401, and walked down through the village; and then, taking off his armour and steel cap, and laying them down under a bush by the roadside, set off at the top of his speed in the direction of Parton. He did the ten miles in under an hour, and nearly ran against a man who was standing in the middle of the road, a short distance from the little town.

"Is that you, Fergus?"

"No, I am John, master. Fergus will take the watch tomorrow evening."

"Good. Keep the horses saddled at this time, every evening; and hold them in readiness all night. Things are going on well, and I may be here any night. Which is the house?"

"That is it, master, where you see the light, a quarter of a mile farther up the hill."

"Where are you sleeping?"

"In the stables, with the horses. It is some ten yards off the right of the house."

"Then you must keep watch through the night, by turns, and get your sleep in the daytime. I hope we shall get them away without waiting for a force to come. The hold is a very strong one, and a strict watch is kept at night; and, before we could carry it, we should have all the Bairds on the countryside down upon us.

"Can you get me a rope? I want a long and a strong one."

"There are some ropes in the stable, master, but they are in use, and would be missed."

"Then run, at the top of your speed, down to the town; and buy a rope strong enough to hold the weight of half a dozen men. I shall want a hundred feet of it. Here is money."

The man shot away into the darkness and, in a little over a quarter of an hour, was back again with the rope. Oswald took off his doublet.

"Wind it round and round me," he said. "Begin under the arms. Wind it neatly, and closely, so that it will make no more show than necessary."

This was soon done, and then Oswald started on his way; and an hour later entered the tavern, and took his seat with three or four of the men from the hold, and called for wine for the party. He sat there for some time, and then one said:

"It is half-past eight; we had best be going. At seven o'clock the gates are shut; but they are opened, for those who belong to the hold, till nine, after which none are admitted till morning, and any who come in then are reported to Baird, and they are lucky if they get off with half a dozen extra goes of sentry duty. Baird is a good master in many things, but he is a bad man to deal with, when he is angry; and if anyone was to be out a second time, and he did it too soon after the first offence, he would have his skin nearly flayed off his back, with a stirrup leather. There is no fooling with the Bairds."

Oswald arranged with Roger that, if the latter remained in the castle, he should always come down half an hour before the garrison were moving, as they might then exchange a word or two unseen; and accordingly, he took his place at an angle of a building, where he could keep his eye on the steps leading up to the battlements, on the north side.

Presently he saw Roger descending. He waved his hand, and caught his follower's eye; and the latter, on reaching the courtyard, at once joined him.

"I have a rope, Roger," Oswald began, "that will reach from the turret to the foot of the craig. I took it off during the night, and have just hidden it away behind a pile of rubbish, in the stable. Are the girls locked up?"

"Yes."

"Is there any getting the key?"

"No, William Baird himself keeps it."

"Then we must have something to force the door open, or to saw round the lock."

"The door is studded with iron."

"Are the windows barred?"

"No; but they are mere loopholes, and there is no getting through them."

"I suppose there are steps from their room on to the platform above?"

"No doubt. In fact, there are sure to be."

"I suppose that you will have no difficulty in silencing the priest?"

Roger smiled.

"No; I think I can answer for him."

"Could you speak to the girls through the keyhole, Roger?"

"There would be no difficulty about that, master. I have but to choose a time when the priest is out."

"Then tell them that we are here, Roger, and they are to be ready to escape, whenever we give the signal. Ask them if the trapdoor leading on to the platform is fastened, and whether they can unfasten it. If not, we must break it in, from above. We can get on to the top of the turret, easily enough, by throwing the rope up with a hook attached.

"Of course, the two sentries must be first silenced. I would wait till I, myself, should be on sentry there; but that might not occur for a week, and you cannot prolong your stay here more than another day; therefore, we will try it tonight. I have given the men with the horses notice.

"Do you get the priest bound and gagged, by ten o'clock; everything will be quiet by that time. I will come noiselessly up the steps. At that hour, do you be at the door, and on the lookout for me. The sentries will have to be silenced--that is the most difficult part of the business."

"We can manage that," Roger said, confidently. "One blow with my quarter-staff, on the back of the head under the steel cap, will do that noiselessly enough."

"That would not do, Roger. The man would go down with such a crash, that the fall of his armour on the flags would be heard all over the castle. He must be gripped by the throat, so that he cannot holloa; and then bound tightly, and gagged before he has time to get breath."

"I suppose that would be the best way," Roger said regretfully; "but I should like to have struck two good blows; one for the sake of Dame Armstrong, and one for Allan. However, your plan is the best. The only difficulty will be the trapdoor."

"Well, we must look about today, and get a couple of bits of iron that we can use as a prise. Still, I hope that it will not be needed. I saw a bit of iron, in the stables, that I think I can bend into a hook for the rope; and if I can't, I have no doubt that you can.

"That is all. You had better move away now. People will be stirring, directly."

That night, at ten o'clock, when all in the hold had been asleep half an hour, Oswald rose quietly from the rushes, on which he and a dozen of his comrades were sleeping, and made his way noiselessly out of the room; went into the stables and fetched the piece of iron, which he had, during the day, placed so that he could feel it in the dark; took the coil of rope in his hands, and ascended the steps. The top was but some ten feet from the turret. He stood quiet, until he heard the sentry moving away from him, then he mounted the last steps, and in a moment reached the foot of the turret stairs. Roger was standing there.

"All right, master!" he whispered. "I took the priest by surprise, and he was gagged before he knew what was happening. I tore the blanket up into strips, and tied him down onto his pallet with them. He is safe enough.

"Now for the sentries. I will take the one to the right, first. I will go out and stand in the angle. It is a dark night, and there is no chance of his seeing me. When you hear his walk cease, you will know that I have got him. I have managed to bring up a rope, that I have cut into handy lengths. Here are two of them.

"There, he has just turned, so I will go at once."

"How about the trapdoor?"

"It is all right, master. It is bolted on the inside. They have tried the bolts, and find they can move them;" and with these words, he at once stepped noiselessly out.

Oswald stood listening. Presently he heard the returning steps of the sentry. They came close up to the turret, and then suddenly ceased.

He at once hurried round. The sentry hung limp in Roger's grasp. Oswald bound his hands tightly, and twisted the rope three or four times round his body, and securely knotted it. Then he tied the ankles tightly together.

"I will lay him down," Roger whispered, when he had done so.

Oswald bent the man's legs and, trussing him up, fastened the rope from the ankles to that which bound the wrists. Roger now relaxed his grip of the man's throat, thrust a piece of wood between his teeth, and fastened it, by a string going round the back of the head. He then took off his steel cap, and laid it some distance away.

"That will do for him, master. I reckon that he will be an hour or two, before he will get breath enough to holloa, even without that gag."

The other man was captured as silently as the former had been. When he was bound, Roger said:

"Now for the hook, master."

"Here is the iron. It was too strong for me to bend."

Roger took it and, exerting his great strength, bent it across his knee. Then he took the coil of rope, and tied a knot at the end, and with some smaller cord lashed it securely along the whole length of the hook.

"Now, Master, do you get on to my shoulders, and I think you will be able to hook it to the battlements. It is not above twelve feet. If you find that you cannot, step on my head."

"I am sure I can reach it without that, Roger."

And indeed, he found that he could do so easily; and having fixed it firmly, he got hold of the rope, and hoisted himself to the top of the turret. In a minute, Roger was beside him.

Feeling about, they soon discovered the trapdoor, on which Roger knocked three times. Then they heard a grating sound below and, shortly, one end of the heavy trapdoor was slightly raised. The two men got their fingers under it, and pulled it up, and Janet and Jessie ran out, both crying with joy and excitement.

"Hush!" Oswald whispered. "Do not utter a sound. There are sentries on other parts of the walls, and the slightest noise might be heard.

"Now, we will knot this rope."

He and Roger set to work, and before long knots were tied, a foot apart, along the whole length of the rope.

"I will take you down first, Jessie, for you are the lightest," Oswald said.

"Now, Roger, tie us together."

One of the pieces of rope Roger had brought was passed round and round them, tying them firmly, face to face.

"Now, Jessie, you had best take hold of the rope, too, and take as much of your weight off me as you can. It is a long way down; and, though I think that I could carry your weight that distance, it is best that you should help me as much as you are able."

The rope was shifted to the outside of the turret. Roger, after fixing it firmly, helped them over the battlements, holding Oswald by the collar, until he had a firm grasp of the rope in his hands, and obtained a hold with his feet.

"That is right, Jessie," he whispered, as the girl also took a firm hold of the rope. "You are no weight, like that. Now, let the rope pass gradually through your hands and, when I tell you, hold tight by one of the knots."

After lowering himself forty feet, Oswald found that he was standing on a ledge of rock, three inches wide, at the foot of the wall.

"Now, dear, it will be more difficult," he said. "You must use one of your hands, to push yourself off from any rugged points. There are not many of them. I had a look at the rock today, and its face is almost smooth. I will do the best I can to keep you from it."

In another three minutes, they stood at the foot of the craig. Oswald shook the rope violently, to let those above know that they were down. Then he untied the cord that bound him to his cousin, who at once sat down, sobbing hysterically. Oswald put his hand upon her shoulder.

"Steady, Jessie, steady. You have been brave and quiet, coming down. The danger is over now, but we have a long walk and a longer ride before us, and you will need all your strength."

In a very short time, Roger and Janet joined them. As soon as she was untied, Janet threw her arms round Oswald's neck, and spoke for the first time.

"Oh, Oswald, from what have you saved us! How brave and good of you to risk so much!"

"Tut, tut, Janet, as if we should leave you here, in the hands of the Bairds, without making an effort to free you! Now, come along, dear. Be very careful how you walk, till we get down to the bottom. It is pretty steep and, if you were to set a stone rolling, we might have them after us, in no time. As it is, we shall only have an hour and a half start, for the sentries will be relieved at midnight. However, by that time we shall be on horseback, and of course they won't know which road we have taken."

As soon as they came to level ground, they set off at a run. They were but a mile from the village when they heard, on the still night air, distant shouts, followed half a minute later by the winding of a horn; then, almost immediately, a glimmering light appeared on the highest turret of the hold, and this rapidly broadened out into a sheet of flame.

"They have discovered our escape, by some misfortune or other," Oswald exclaimed, "and they will be after us, before many minutes have passed. You must run in earnest now, girls."

"Do you run on, Oswald," Janet said, "you and Roger. We will turn and walk back. They will do us no harm."

Oswald thought of the murder of the girls' mother, and knew that, in their fury at having been tricked, the Bairds were capable of anything.

"It is not to be thought of," he said. "Such a watch would henceforth be kept that there would be no possibility, whatever, of effecting your rescue. We must take our chance together.

"What think you had best be done, Roger?"

"In sooth, I know not. I am ready to do whatever you think best."

"We cannot hope to reach Parton, before they overtake us," Oswald said. "Besides, the Bairds are sure to have many friends there, and the lighted beacon will warn all the countryside that something unusual has happened. No, we cannot think of going there."

"But you said that there were horses," Janet said.

"They are but a short distance on this side of the town. We could not hope to get there before the Bairds; and, even if we did, it would be a quarter of an hour before we could mount and be off."

"Could we not hide and get the horses after they have passed, master?" Roger suggested.

"It would be useless, Roger. The road leads up and down this valley, and there would be no possibility of riding the horses across the hills, at night; so that we should have either to ride down through Parton, or up past the Bairds' hold. No, the horses must be given up, for the present. The only thing that I can see is to cross the Esk, and to take refuge in the hills. I know not if there are any fords, or where they are; but, were we to turn to the right, we should be getting farther and farther away. The Esk is no great width, and we can carry them across it, easily enough."

"The water will be dreadfully cold," Jessie said, with a shiver, for it was now the beginning of April.

"Hush, Jessie!" her sister said. "What matters a little cold, when our lives are at stake?"

"No, that is our only hope," Oswald said. "Quick, girls, there is no time to lose."

The river was but some fifty yards from the road, and they ran down to it.

"Now, girls," Oswald said when they reached it, "you must take off your cloaks, and all upper garments. Were you to get these wet you would, before morning, die of cold. Don't lose a moment. Undress under the shelter of these bushes.

"Now, Roger, let us move a few yards away, and then take off our doublets and shirts, and swim across, holding them above the water. By the time that we are back, the girls will be ready."

"I will carry them across, master. It is of no use two of us going, with so light a burden. I shall make nothing of it."

Oswald made no opposition and, a minute later, the shirts and doublets were made into a bundle, and bound on Roger's head. He waded into the water until it reached his chin, and then swam out. The distance to be traversed was but some fifteen yards, and a few strokes of his brawny arms brought him to the opposite bank. Having laid down his bundle there, he swam quickly back again.

"Are you ready, girls?" Oswald asked.

"Yes," Janet replied, and two white figures came out from the bushes, each carrying a bundle.

"Do you go into the bushes again, for a minute. We cannot take you and the bundles over together; and it is better that you should stand here, in dry things, than wait in wet ones, over there."

A minute sufficed to tie the bundles on the heads of the two men. They soon swam across to the other side, left them there, and returned.

"The water is bitterly cold for the girls," Oswald said, as they swam across together.

"It is, master, but they will only be in it for a minute, and they will soon be warm again."

"Now, girls."

"We have just heard the sound of horses in the distance, Oswald," Janet said.

He listened.

"Sound travels far, this still night," he said; "they can only just have started. We shall be across long before they come along.

"Now, Jessie, we will take you first. The stream runs strongly, and it were best that you went over separately. All you have to do is to put a hand on a shoulder of each of us. Come along."

"I will carry her till we get into deep water," Roger said, catching the girl up in his arms, and running into the stream.

Jessie gasped, as the water reached her.

"It will be over in a minute," Oswald said encouragingly. "Now, we are going to swim. Put your hands upon our shoulders. That is right."

Striking out strongly, they easily carried her until she was in her depth.

"Now, dear, get ashore, and stand behind those bushes, and take off your wet things and put on your dry ones. We will have Janet across, in no time."

The girl was carried across as easily as her sister had been.

"Here is your bundle, dear. Jessie has taken hers. Dress as quickly as you can. Stoop down, as soon as you reach the bushes. They will be here, directly."

Janet ran to the thicket, and Oswald and Roger threw themselves down behind a great stone. Two minutes later, they could hear the thunder of hoofs go along the road opposite, but could not make out the figures.

"How many are there of them, do you think, Roger?"

"A dozen or so, master."

"Yes, I should think you are right. However, it makes no difference; were there ten times as many, they would not catch us, tonight."

Chapter 14: In Hiding.

The moment the horsemen had gone by, Oswald and Roger hastily dressed again. It was three or four minutes before the girls joined them.

"We have been a long time, Oswald, but our fingers are so cold that we could not tie the strings."

"You will soon be warm. Climbing the hill will set your blood in motion."

There was no hurry now. They were safe until the morning.

"We will make up the hill until you are thoroughly warm, and then we will discuss matters."

Before they were very far up the ascent, both girls declared that they were comfortably warm again.

"Well, Roger, what do you think our best course will be? The Bairds have, of course, sent horsemen along the other road. They will have heard, from the priest, that we have but a few minutes' start; and will know that we cannot have gone far. The party who passed us will doubtless stop at Parton, the other at the next village higher up; and they will be sure that either we concealed ourselves as they passed, or have taken to the hills on one side or other of the valley. They will naturally suppose that it is this side, as it would be madness for us to plunge farther into the country to the west; and you may be sure there will be scores of men out on these hills, tomorrow, searching for us; and some of them may ride nearly to Hiniltie, to cut us off there in case we escape the searchers on the hills.

"I think that the only plan will be to hide up for a couple of days, or so; then to make our way down again to where the horses are, and then make a dash through Parton."

"That would certainly be far the best way," Roger said; "but how are we to manage for food for the ladies?"

"We will go on until we get to the top of the hill, Roger, and then find a sheltered spot, where they can stop. It is of no use trying to go on much farther, for the night is cloudy, and there are no stars to be seen, and we should lose our way directly, for there is no wind that would serve as a guide as to which way we were travelling. When we find a good shelter, we must stop with them; and I will make my way down to the place where the horses are, and warn the men as to what has happened, and tell them to lie quiet till I come again. I will bring back whatever food they may have with them, a big jug of water, and the four horse cloths."

"I will go, master."

"I would rather go myself, Roger. I am accustomed to traverse the moors at night, and am sure that I can find this place again, without difficulty."

On nearing the top of the hill, they came upon a number of rough stones.

"We cannot do better than stop here," Oswald said. "It will be bare on the top of the hill. Now, Roger, help me to pile a few of these stones together, so as to make a sort of shelter."

They set to work at once, Roger's strength enabling him to lift stones that ordinary men could scarcely have moved. In a quarter of an hour a little inclosure, six feet long by four wide and three high, had been constructed. An armful of dry heather was then pulled up, and laid on the ground.

"There, girls, I think you will be able to manage to keep yourselves warm, by lying close together."

"What are you going to do, Oswald?"

"We shall be all right; and we can, if we like, make another shelter; and, if we feel cold, can walk about to warm ourselves. Now, Roger, get half a dozen sticks and lay across the top."

While Roger was away getting the sticks, Oswald helped the girls over the wall, for no entrance had been left.

"Now, Janet, give me those two wet smocks; I see that you have brought them with you."

"What do you want them for, Oswald?"

"I want them for the roof, Janet. It is beginning to freeze hard, and it is of no use having walls, if you have not a roof."

"Won't you take my cloak, instead?"

"Certainly not, Janet, you will want your cloak for a covering. Don't be silly, but hand them over."

By this time, Roger had returned with the sticks. They were laid across the top, and the girls' smocks spread over them.

"Now, go to sleep," Oswald said; "we must be on foot, an hour before dawn."

Oswald then started down the hill for Parton. When he got within a mile of the town, he could see lights moving about on the road; and guessed that the Bairds had got torches, and were making sure that the fugitives had not hidden themselves anywhere close to the road; for they must have felt certain that they could not have reached the town, before being overtaken. When the lights had gone along the road, he descended to the river, took off his doublet and shirt, as before, and swam over; crossed the road, and was not long in finding the trees that marked the spot where he was to turn off to the farmhouse.

He made his way to the stable, raised the latch, and entered. A lamp was burning, and the two men sitting and talking together. They leapt up, with an exclamation of pleasure, as Oswald entered.

"We were afraid that something might have gone wrong; for, as I was waiting for you in the road, I heard a body of horsemen coming along, and hid behind the trees. As they went by, one of them said, 'We must have passed them long ago, if they came by this road. They had not more than a quarter of an hour's start.'

"I heard no more, but it suggested that, maybe, you had managed to escape with the ladies, and that the Bairds were in pursuit of you."

"That was exactly the case. We have got them out of the hold, and methought that we should have got two hours' start, at least, in which case they would not have overtaken us before we had crossed the Liddel, at the ford, six miles above the junction of the Esk with it, and were well on our road towards Longtown; but by some accident, I know not what, the matter was discovered before we have been gone ten minutes. As it was certain that they would overtake us, long before we got to Parton, we swam the Esk, and I have left the ladies on the hill over there, in charge of Roger, while I came here. We know that, by morning, the countryside will be up and searching the hills; and that, with the two lasses, it would be hopeless for us to try and make our way on to Hiniltie.

"Therefore, we decided to hide up for two or three days, then to make our way down here at night, mount, and ride through. By that time the search down in the valley here will have slackened, and we shall get through Parton all right, and our only danger will be at the ford across the Liddel; where, possibly, the Bairds may set a guard, lest we find our way down there. I had intended that we should take the four horses, and that you should make your way to Hiniltie across the hills; but as there will now be no great occasion for speed, one of you had best ride with us, while the other bears the news to Hiniltie that we have carried off the girls.

"You had better settle between yourselves which shall go with us. You may take it that there is about equal danger, both ways, for the one that goes to Hiniltie must travel cautiously, as it will be a week before the Bairds give up the search among the hills."

"We had best decide by lot."

Oswald picked up a piece of straw, and broke off two fragments, one an inch longer than the other; and, closing his hand on them, he held the two ends out.

"Do you draw," he said, holding it out to Fergus. "The longest straw goes to Hiniltie, and shortest with us."

The man drew.

"I have the longest," he said, "and perhaps it were best that it should be so, for I know the way thoroughly, having often been over the hills in search of missing cattle."

"You will both remain here, till we come. Now, what food have you?"

"We bought a supply in Parton, yesterday evening, and have enough for a week; for we thought that some might be needed by the whole party, on our way; and moreover, we care not to go down often to the town, as we might attract attention."

"That is good. Keep enough for tomorrow, for yourselves; I will take the rest."

"There is no need for that. We can get what we want from the house and, tomorrow evening, one of us will go down into Parton again."

"Or better still," Oswald said, "give the money to the hind here. I suppose there is one."

"Yes; he sleeps in the house."

"Give him money, then, and a present for himself, and get him to fetch it for you. Some of the Bairds may remain there, and you may be sure that every stranger will be strictly questioned. I want also the four horse cloths, which please make into a bundle. Is your water skin full?"

"We filled it this afternoon, thinking it possible that we might make a hasty start tonight."

"How much does it hold?"

"About two gallons."

"It would have been better had it been four. However, we must manage with it. Now, do you know of any ford across the river? for I certainly could not swim across, with this load."

"There is one half a mile farther up. We were asking the hind about it, the other day, thinking that it might be useful should we have to fly suddenly. I will go down with you; and indeed, I shall be glad to go the whole way with you, for the provisions and those blankets and the skin will be no light weight; and, as I am going to Hiniltie, it will cheer Armstrong if I could tell him that I saw his daughters."

"It would be a good plan, Fergus, though in truth the weight would be no great burden; but certainly, Armstrong would be pleased to know that you had seen his daughters."

A few minutes later they set out, forded the river breast high, carrying the loads on their heads; and then, climbing the hill, made their way to the shelter, whose exact position Oswald had marked, on starting, by a huge boulder that stood on the crest of the hill, some fifty feet above it.

Roger was on the lookout. Seeing two figures approaching, when he expected but one, he grasped his staff firmly.

"Who comes there?" he asked.

"It is I, Roger. I have brought one of the men with me, to help carry the things. He is going to Hiniltie, and thought that Armstrong would be pleased to know he had seen his daughters. I have got plenty of food, and a skin of water."

"That is capital," Roger said cheerfully. "I was fearing that, having so many things to think of, you might forget water."

Oswald went to the shelter.

"Are you awake, Janet?"

"Yes," she replied. "I have been anxious, while you were away."

"Are you cold?"

"I am not very warm," she answered; "but do not trouble about it, we shall do very well."

"I have two blankets here," he said, as he removed the covering. "One of these I will put over you both, and tuck it well in, each side, to keep out the wind that comes in between the stones. Then I will lay your smocks over that. I wrung them well, before putting them on the sticks; and although I cannot say they are dry, yet they are not damp enough to matter, and will help keep you warm. The other blanket I will put over the sticks."

"Thank you indeed, Oswald," the girl said, gratefully. "That feels very much more comfortable."

"Now, Roger, there is a blanket for you, and one for me, to wrap round us, plaid fashion."

"I do not need one, master. In faith, I have more respect for this gown than I ever had before--it is wondrously warm and, with the hood over my head, I want nothing more."

"That is all very well, Roger. If you don't need it for your shoulders, you need it for your legs; for being without hose, and with nought but those sandals, you must be freezing. We will walk up and down here, for a bit, and do you wrap it round your legs, like a Highlander's petticoat. When we have tired ourselves, we will lie down and try to get a sleep, for an hour or two."

As they walked, they talked over their plans; and Oswald decided that, before daybreak, he would set out on the search for a place of concealment.

"I will leave my helmet and breast and back piece behind me," he said, "and will take your staff. Then, if I am caught sight of by any party in the distance, I shall look like a shepherd; while, had I on my iron harness, they would at once suspect me of being of the party, even though I were alone. As for you, your monk's robe would be detected, miles off."

"I could leave it behind me," Roger said.

"You have not much on underneath, Roger; and your bareness, in such weather as this, would be as noticeable as your gown. Mind, before it gets light, get the ladies up, and carry our bag of victuals and the water skin over the crest. You may be sure that, as soon as it is light, there will be many sharp eyes watching the hillside, all along here."

The man who had come up with them had already wrapped himself in the blanket he had brought with him, had crawled in among the bushes, and was, as they could hear by his heavy breathing, already sound asleep. After a time Oswald said that, as they had nothing more to settle, he would try and get a few hours' rest. There was not the slightest fear of surprise, and Roger and he were not long before they were both sound asleep. Oswald woke two or three times and, at first sign of dawn, shook Roger.

"You had better wake the ladies, in a few minutes, Roger, and get them over the crest. Let their man, as soon as he has seen them, start at once, keeping along behind the ridge, and warn him not to go down into the valley until he is fully a mile beyond Parton. Tell him to look carefully along the road, before he begins to descend, and to see that it is clear. Even then, let him hide as much as may be, behind brushwood and rock, until he gets down. When he has swum the river, let him make a wide detour round Parton, so as to come down to the stables without being noticed.

"I shall not be very long away. 'Tis scarce likely, among these hills, that I shall find any place that we can crawl into; and I think we shall have to content ourselves with lying down among the heather. I must find a spot where no one, on any hill above, can look down on us. We shall be quite safe from any party moving along on the same level as ourselves."

Oswald had gone but a little distance, when he determined that no better place could be found than the plateau itself. This extended, for two or three hundred yards from the edge, looking down into the valley. Beyond, the ground sloped sharply down again into a deep hollow; and beyond, it was broken into rounded swells, rising one above another. A party lying among the heather, where he was standing, could not be seen by watchers from any other point. Moreover, it was most important that all should be in shelter before it was fairly daylight. He therefore, as soon as it was light enough to take in the principal features of the scene, hurried back to his companions.

"We can do no better, girls, than to lie down together, two hundred yards away. Pick your way through the bushes where they are thinnest, so as not to disturb them. Please be off at once, and choose a spot close to where the ground falls away, on the other side. Roger and I must tumble this shelter down, and scatter the sticks; for if anyone searching the hillside came along, he would guess that we had slept here, and there would be a hue and cry at once."

The man had left, sometime before, for the valley; having gone off as soon as he had spoken to the girls. Oswald and Roger ran down to the shelter, speedily threw the stones into a heap, and scattered the sticks; then, after glancing round to see that nothing had been left, they collected the blankets, provisions, and water skin; and, taking up these and Oswald's armour, ran in the direction that Oswald had pointed out to the girls.

The ground was thickly covered with heather, and they had to step carefully to avoid pressing it down. They reached the edge of the plateau without seeing the girls and, after looking round for a minute or two, Oswald called aloud.

He was answered by a merry laugh, and Jessie's head rose above the heather. They had, indeed, passed within five or six yards of the girls.

"That is good, indeed," Oswald said, as he lay down beside them. "If I could not see you, when I was sure that you were quite near, there is no fear of any searchers lighting upon you.

"The sun has just risen, and a mist still hangs on the top of the hills," he went on; "and I am convinced that we cannot have been seen, for men placed on the watch are sure to be high up on the hills, and it will be some time yet before the sun rises high enough to drive away the mist."

Although it was freezing sharply, they felt by no means cold as they lay, wrapped in their blankets, with the heather rising well above them, and sheltering them from a light breeze that had sprung up at sunrise. After chatting with the girls for a time, Roger and Oswald left them and, crawling along on their stomachs, got to the edge of the descent.

By this time the sun was well above the hills, the mist had cleared off, and they had an extensive view. From time to time they caught sight of groups of three or four mounted men moving about, searching the valleys; while single men, on foot, rambled over the hills.

"They are keeping up an active search, Roger. 'Tis well that we went no farther. They will scarce suspect us of lying close to the valley we left. I expect the main body has gone much farther. I have no doubt the Bairds have a couple of hundred men and boys out. They would call out every man and boy from their holdings, and most likely get a couple of score of men from their village, and perhaps twice as many from Parton. No doubt they will think that, if we came in this direction, we should, last night, have found our way to one of the tracks across the hills, and it is near these that their search will be the keenest. Fortunately, they cannot know that I am here, nor guess that it is to Yardhope that we intend to take them, and not to Hiniltie. Still, they may expect that we shall try to cross the border, and I fancy we shall scarcely get through without a fight."

"All the better," Roger grumbled. "My fingers tingle to bring down this staff on the head of some of the Bairds, after all the trouble they have given us."

They remained watching until it became dusk, except that, twice during the day, they crawled back and partook of a meal with the girls. The last time they joined them, Oswald said:

"Now, in half an hour it will be quite dark, and then we can safely get up and walk about for a bit. I am sure you must feel stiff, lying still so long."

"I have never kept quiet for so long a time, since I can remember," Jessie said, laughing.

"That shows that you have had no illnesses, Jessie. However, I shall be glad to get up and stretch my limbs, myself. Half an hour will be enough, and then we will have a good, long night. Another day of it, and I think it will be safe to start."

The next afternoon they saw a number of parties searching the hills, in all directions.

"I expect they have become convinced that we have not tried to get straight through, Roger, and are hunting back for us. It is as well that it will be dark in another half hour, and they will then have to give up their search, for the night. If there were a couple of hours more light, I should feel very uneasy."

"So should I, master. You and I would have little chance of mercy, if we fell into their hands. It might well be that, in their anger, they might slay the ladies, also."

"That would be like enough, Roger. However, there can be no chance of their coming here, before it is dark."

At nine o'clock they started, and made their way down, with some difficulty and many slips and falls, into the valley. Then they kept along near the river, till Oswald was sure they were close to the ford. He bade them halt here, and went forward alone. Before he had gone fifty yards, he nearly stumbled against a man.

"Is it you, John?"

"Yes, it is I."

"Is all well?"

"It is all well, but I had a fright, yesterday morning. The Bairds searched every cottage and hut over the hills, on this side, and they say their men rode almost as far as Galloway; but they gave up the search before they got here, feeling assured that they must have passed you, very soon after you left the hold, and you could never have got as far down as this."

"'Tis well they did not search, indeed," Oswald said. "Your story about the horses might do well enough, for those who have no interest in the matter, but it would never have done for the Bairds. All has been quiet today?"

"They seem to have given up searching on this side. I hear that they feel sure, now, the ladies have made for Hiniltie; and they have had great forces out among the hills, and feel confident that they must catch them soon."

"Have you got the horses saddled?"

"They are saddled, and brought down close to the road. Fergus is with them."

"Then bring them across, at once. The sooner we are off now, the better. Are there any of the Bairds' men in the town?"

"There are a few of them, but as no one has any idea that you are like to pass through there, they will not be on the lookout. Besides, all will have been among the hills, from daybreak this morning; and I expect, by this time, there is scarce a soul awake in Parton."

Oswald returned to the girls, and they went out together to the ford. In a couple of minutes the men were seen making their way across, riding two horses, and leading the others.

"We thank you heartily," Janet said, "for having so risked your lives for us; for, had you been caught with the four horses, they would at once have connected you with us, and it would have gone hard with you."

"We have been keeping away from the horses, yesterday and today, just going to a distance and lying down where, without being seen ourselves, we could watch anyone who went up to the farm. We could have done no good, and thought that it was better that we should be able to warn you, if they had come and taken the horses away."

After crossing the river, Fergus at once started, on foot, for Hiniltie.

They had already discussed how they should ride, and it had been settled that, at starting, Janet should ride the fourth horse; and that Jessie should ride behind the others, by turns. If an attack was threatened, Jessie was to mount behind her sister, and they were to take their place between Oswald and Roger, while their own man rode close behind them.

It was just ten o'clock as they rode through Parton. Not a light was to be seen. The whole place appeared wrapt in sleep. They went through at a walk, so that, if any heard them, they would suppose that it was a belated party of the searchers, and would give the matter no further thought.

After riding for a short distance, they put the horses into a trot. Four hours later they halted, at the point where the road down the Esk valley divided, one going to the ferry a few hundred yards farther on, while the other turned to the left, and followed the bank of the Liddel.

John had inquired about the ferry, and learned that the ferryboat no longer plied, as, since the troubles began, there was so little traffic that it did not pay the ferryman to remain there. As they had already decided to cross by the ford, four miles higher up, this did not matter. As none of them was aware of its exact position, they decided to wait where they were, until daylight.

Searching about, they found a deserted hut, with a shed adjoining it. The horses were led into this, and the party then gathered in the hut, and John struck a light, while Oswald and Roger broke up a fallen gate, and the fire was soon blazing. Although there was not the slightest chance of anyone travelling the road, at this hour, they hung one of the thick blankets across the window, thus keeping out the cold air, as well as preventing the light from being seen. Then the party lay down, the men taking it by turns to stand guard outside, being relieved every two hours.

As soon as day dawned they again mounted. It was about four miles' ride to the point where the road divided, one branch going towards the river, some seventy or eighty yards away. Here stood a square building of some size, used as a refuge by travellers who arrived when the Liddel was swollen, and the ford impracticable.

When the riders had come within a few yards of this building, two men, hearing the sound of horses' hoofs, came out. As their eye fell upon the party they gave a shout, ran out into the road, and drew their swords.

Roger and Oswald rode at them. Parrying a thrust of one of the men, Oswald cut him down; while Roger, with a tremendous blow from his staff, stretched the other man on the road.

"Ride on, girls! We will follow you," Oswald shouted.

Jessie was sitting behind John, and they and Janet dashed forward, and rode into the water. Oswald and Roger followed, as six men, armed with spear and sword, ran out from the house. Seeing that they were too late, the leader shouted to the others: "Fetch out the horses, and chase them!" and, before the party had gained the opposite bank, their pursuers dashed into the water.

"Don't press your horses too hardly," Oswald said, as they galloped along. "They are too close behind us for us to get help from any of the small villages, but they dare not follow us into Longtown, and we have barely a ten miles' ride."

They had some two hundred yards' start, and for the first four miles held their own; then their pursuers began to gain upon them. One of the horses was carrying double, and Roger and Oswald were both heavier than any of the moss troopers.

"We shall have a fight for it, Roger."

"That is just what I was thinking, master. Well, there are three of us; and, as there are only six of them, we ought not to have much trouble. John will be a match for one. Methinks you and I can each make short work of a man when they first come up; and with but three of them against two, it will be mere child's play."

The road was a narrow one, and little used; and, when they came to the foot of a sharp rise, Oswald called to those ahead to stop.

"Jump down, Jessie, and mount behind Janet, and ride on ahead. We will soon get rid of these fellows. Be quick!"

The moss troopers were now but seventy or eighty yards behind.

"I shall fight on foot," Roger said, as he leapt off his horse. "I want both hands, for this staff."

Turning his horse, and bidding John to do the same, Oswald reined back his animal three or four lengths; and when the Bairds' party were within twenty yards, touched it with his spur and dashed at them, meeting them just abreast of Roger. The first man he met thrust at him with his spear, but Oswald parried with his sword, and with a back-handed blow smote the man just under the chin, and he fell with a crash from his horse. At the same moment he heard a blow like that of a smith's hammer, as Roger's staff fell upon the steel cap of the first who attacked him.

John was less fortunate, for his opponent's spear struck him in the throat, and he fell heavily from his saddle.

"Well stricken, Jock!" one of them shouted. "Ride on after the women. We will settle with these fellows."

But before the moss trooper could obey the order, Oswald, with a touch of the spur and the bridle, caused his horse to curvet round, and smote the man so mighty a blow on the shoulder as well-nigh to sever his arm from his body. As he wheeled his horse again he was nigh unseated, by a spear thrust that struck him on the breast piece; but, upon recovering, he struck his opponent, as he passed, so heavy a blow in the face, with the pommel of his sword, that he sent him senseless to the ground.

The other two men had furiously attacked Roger, but, whirling his staff round his head, he had kept them both at bay; then the staff descended between the ears of one of the horses, which fell headlong; and before the rider could get his foot from the stirrup, the staff struck him below the steel cap, just in front of the ear, and without a cry he fell dead beside his horse. At that the last of the moss troopers turned his horse, and galloped off at full speed.

"We have not taken long over that, master," Roger said, with a grim smile. "Five men in a minute is not so bad."

"I am afraid John is killed, Roger. See to him."

"Ay, he is sped," Roger replied, as he turned the body over. "The spear struck him full in the throat. That is what comes of not learning to use your weapons. What shall we do with him?"

"He was a faithful fellow, Roger, and as there is no need for haste now, we will give him some sort of burial, and not let him lie here in the road."

"We have nought to dig a grave with," Roger remarked.

"No, but there are plenty of stones about."

He dismounted, and with Roger's help carried the dead man a short distance away, laid him down by the side of a great boulder, and then piled stones around and over him.

"That will do, Roger. 'Tis not like that anyone will disturb those stones, for years to come. He will rest as well there as if he lay in a grave. Now, let us look to the others."

The man he had struck across the throat, and the last Roger had hit, were both dead. Two of the others were but stunned, while the one upon whose shoulder Roger's blow had fallen was lying insensible, and evidently was fast bleeding to death.

"We can do naught for him," Oswald said. "Even had we the king's leech here, we could not save him. Now let us be off."

"Shall we take the horses, master?"

"No, they will be but an encumbrance; and now that poor fellow has gone, we have one apiece. Bring his horse along with you."

Mounting, they rode quickly on, and at the top of the hill came up with the girls; who, having seen the result of the combat, had waited for them.

"Now we are safe and free, thanks to you both," Janet said. "Jessie looked back, and saw the fight as we rode. How quickly it was over! But I am grieved, indeed, that John has fallen. We saw you carrying off his body, and covering it. Jessie had noticed him fall, and we feared 'twas all over with him. He was an old retainer of our father's, and a faithful one."

"I am sorry, indeed, that he has been slain, Janet; but we could hardly expect to come out altogether scatheless."

"Are all the others killed?" Jessie asked.

"No. Two of them are but stunned; and will, ere long, be able to mount and ride off again."

"Master Oswald has gained the most honours in the fight. I killed one, and stunned another. He has stunned one also, but has slain two."

"I had a better arm, Roger."

"I know not that," Roger replied. "A quarterstaff, of that weight, is a fine weapon. I say not that it is to be compared to a mace but, when on foot, I would as lief have it as a sword."

"Now, Jessie, do you mount John's horse. We can ride quietly, for Longtown is but some three miles ahead."

They rested there for a couple of hours, then mounted again, and crossed the Pentlands by a horse track between Cristindury and Gele Craigs. Coming down into Tynedale, they put up for the night at the first place they came to. At daybreak they set off northwards, crossed Reddesdale, and came down, in the afternoon, into the valley of the Coquet, within two miles of Yardhope.

Great indeed was the surprise and joy of John Forster and his wife, when they made out the two girls riding, with Oswald, towards the hold.

"What miracle is this, lad?" the former said, while his wife was embracing her nieces. "We heard, but two days since, of the raid on the Armstrongs, and how the girls were carried off by the Bairds."

Here Oswald put his finger to his lips, to stop him from saying aught of Jane Armstrong's death. He had, after dismounting, whispered in his mother's ear, before she had time to speak to the girls, that as yet they knew nought of their mother's death, and that he had left it to her to break it to them.

"I have been, since, scouring the country," his father went on, "to try to get my friends to take the matter up; but in truth, they were not over willing to do so. All know that it is no slight enterprise to attack the Bairds in their stronghold. We fared but badly, last time we went there, though that was but a blow and a retreat; but all know that the Bairds' hold is not to be taken like a country tower. 'Tis greatly bigger and stronger than ours, and scarce to be attempted save by a royal army; especially as the whole countryside would be swarming round us, in a few hours after we crossed the border. This time, too, it is no quarrel of my people; and, as they say, the risk would be indeed great, and the loss very heavy.

"I sent off a messenger this morning to Armstrong, to tell him that I feared I could not raise more than sixty spears; but with these I would ride to Hiniltie, and join any force he could collect, and try with him to surprise the Bairds' hold and rescue the girls, though it seemed to be a mighty dangerous enterprise."

"He will have learnt, yesterday morning, Father, that we have carried them off. We could have brought you the news last night, but to do so we must have ridden fast and, the girls being with us, we thought it were better to take two days over the journey. So we slept in Tynedale last night."

"And how did you manage it? For unless you and Roger flew into the Bairds' hold, and carried them off on your backs, I see not how it could be managed. Why, the place is so strong that even the Douglases have not cared to carry out the terms of the treaty, for the arrest of William Baird as a notorious breaker of the truce between the two countries."

"It was because I knew Armstrong deemed that it was scarce likely a force could be gathered, by you and his friends, strong enough to undertake such an enterprise, that we decided to rescue them by strategy. The affair turned out to be easy enough."

And he then related, in detail, the manner in which he and Roger had obtained entry into the hold, and had succeeded in rescuing his cousins.

"By the bones of Saint Oswald, from whom you got your name, lad," John Forster exclaimed, when he had finished his story, "you have carried out the matter marvellously well! Hotspur himself could not have contrived it better; and I own that I was wrong, and that that fancy of yours, to be able to read and write, has not done you the damage that I feared it would. Henceforth I will maintain, with all my might, that these things in no way tend to soften a man; but on the contrary, in some way sharpen his wits, and enable him to carry out matters with plans, and contrivances, such as would scarce be conceived by men who had not such advantage.

"But why do we not go inside?"

"I have been keeping you here, Father, because I doubt not that my mother has been breaking the news to the girls, of their mother's slaughter. I said nought to them about it. They knew the hold was burnt, and I told them that Allan was wounded; but I thought that, if I gave them the worst part of the news, it would throw them into such deep grief as to unfit them for the journey. It might not have been discovered till two hours after we had started that they had escaped, and in that case we should have been mounted before the Bairds overtook us, and it would have been a ride for life, and the girls would have needed all their strength and courage to keep them up."

"It was as well so, Oswald, and doubtless your mother will break it more easily to them than you could have done. Women are better at such things than men, who are given to speak, bluntly and straight, what has to be told."

Chapter 15: Another Mission To Ludlow.

While Oswald was talking with his father, Roger had taken the four horses round to the long shed, that ran along one side of the wall; and had there been telling the moss troopers the same story Oswald had been relating to his father, whom he now joined.

"Well, friend Roger," John Forster said as he came up, shaking him heartily by the hand; "by my faith, my son is fortunate in having so stout a fellow as his henchman."

"'Tis rather that I am fortunate in having him as a master," Roger replied. "I have but to strike as he bids me, and there is no need for me to think, for my brain bears no proportion to my bulk; and indeed, even in the matter of strength he bids fair to equal me, for he seems to me to grow taller and stronger every month; which is not surprising, seeing that you are, yourself, much beyond the common. In all this matter there is no credit due to me, save that I have, as faithfully as I could, carried out his orders."

"All men can try to carry out orders, Roger, but it is not all who can do it with intelligence. Doubtless, it has something to do with the book learning that you have, and in which you were his instructor."

"I think not that it is so, in any way, Master Forster," Roger replied quickly, for he liked not the thought that he had gained any advantage, whatever, from his stay in the convent. "It might likely be useful to a man of small stature, whose thoughts would naturally turn to being a scribe, and to making his living by such finicking ways instead of by bearing himself as a man should; but for one like myself, 'tis but time thrown away. Yet I say not that it may not be useful to Master Oswald, who will some day be a knight, and go to court, and have occasion to write letters, when he has no scribe at hand to do it for him; but a good downright blow is more advantage, to the man that strikes it, than all the book learning that he can get."

"I have done well enough without it, Roger; but I think that it must be of some use, else why is it that Oswald is so good at devising plans? Had I been in his place, when he heard the news of the harrying of Hiniltie, and the carrying off of Armstrong's daughters, I should never have thought of starting on such an adventure as he did."

"It may be that it may improve the mind, Master Forster, just as wielding a mace strengthens the muscles of the arm. I only speak from my own experience; and, so far as I can see, all the hours I spent on these matters have been as good as wasted."

"Nay, Roger," Oswald, who had been an amused listener to the conversation, broke in, "you have had evidence, but lately, that it is not so. Had you not been able to read the priest's missal, he would have seen, at once, that you were not a monk; but the fact that you did so, and that much better and more fluently than he could, himself, have read a strange manuscript, was to him a confirmation of your story; which not only enabled us to rescue my cousins, but probably saved your own skin, to say nothing of mine; for had Baird learned that you were deceiving him, he would as likely as not have hung us both over the gateway of his hold, as spies."

Roger scratched his head, in some embarrassment.

"I cannot gainsay it, Master Oswald, though I did not think of it before; and it is certainly a proof that the time I spent in learning was not thrown away; for, as you say, had I not been able to read that missal, doubtless it would have gone hard with both of us. I am not ashamed to own when I am wrong. It would not be English, or honest, not to do so. Reading certainly came in mightily useful, there."

"And you must also remember, Roger," Oswald said with a smile, "that if it had not been that you read and wrote, better than most of the other monks, the abbot would not have picked you out as my instructor, I should not have asked for you to come with me to Scotland, and Sir Henry Percy would never have begged the abbot to allow you to go forth into the world."

"Say no more, Master Oswald--never again will I say a word against reading and writing--I see that they are excellent things, and it never entered my thick head how greatly I have benefited by acquiring them--but will maintain, against all who say the contrary, that they are of great value; and that they in no way tend to soften a man, as I can prove in my own person, and also in yours."

At this moment, Mary Forster appeared at the top of the steps.

"Supper is ready," she said. "I have broken the news to the girls. They are quite broken hearted, poor things, and I have sent them to bed.

"I suppose you are not leaving us, tomorrow morning, Oswald?"

"No, I shall be off at daybreak, the next day. I must not stay longer, for I ought to have been back three days ago, and Sir Henry will be wondering what has befallen me."

Talking the matter over, that evening, as to what had best be done with the girls, Mary Forster said that they had expressed great anxiety to get back, as soon as they could, in order that they might try and comfort their father, and nurse Allan; and John Forster said that he would ride with them, with four of his men, to Hiniltie, in a day or two. The next evening, however, there was a knock at the outside gate; and on its being opened, Adam Armstrong himself entered.

"I could not rest, for thinking of the girls," he said, as he entered the house. "The man arrived safely, yesterday morning, after having, with great difficulty, made his way unobserved through the Bairds, who had some fifty or sixty men scattered, all over the hills."

"Do you go to them, Wife, and tell them that their father has arrived.

"They have been terribly upset," John went on, as his wife left the room. "They were only told of the loss of their mother after they arrived, yesterday. Oswald thought that they would need all their strength for the journey, and that it were better that Mary should break the news to them, when they got here. We have all felt for you sorely, Adam, since your messenger brought the news."

Armstrong pressed his hand, silently.

"She was a good wife to me, John, a right good wife. We buried what seemed to be her remains, yesterday morning. It was that, that kept me from starting the moment the man came in with the news that Oswald had got the girls out of the hands of the Bairds."

"And how is Allan?"

"I trust he will get right, now. He has come partly to his senses, though he is still dazed. We had him carried, in a litter, to the monastery where I obtained the monk's robe for your man; for I feared to leave him in the village, lest the Bairds, furious at the escape of the girls, might return to finish their work."

He was about to speak to Oswald, when the door opened, and the girls ran in, and it was some time before Adam Armstrong again turned to him.

"Now, lad," he said, "do not think, because I am a long time coming to the point, that I think lightly of the service you have rendered me. Ah, lad! I could scarce believe my ears, when Fergus told me that you and your henchman had got the lasses out of the Bairds' hands, and had gone off on horseback with them. I had to put the question, again and again, as to whether he was sure that it was really the girls you had with you. It seemed to me to be altogether impossible; but I had to believe him, at last, though how it came about he could not tell me."

"We had no time for talking," Oswald said. "Every moment was of importance. But the matter was simple enough, and worth but a few words' telling."

And he then related the manner in which he and Roger had obtained entrance to the hold, and had succeeded in getting the girls away.

"It sounds simple enough, in the telling," Armstrong said; "but it needed stout hearts, and good nerves, to enter the Bairds' den on such an errand. You carried your lives in your hands, and well must you have borne out your story, to have passed without suspicion. It was well thought of, indeed, and well carried out, and would have done credit to the boldest and craftiest leader on the border.

"What say you, John?"

"I am proud of him, Adam. As for myself, I should never have thought of such a plan. If I had had the matter in hand, I might have taken twenty stout fellows, and tried to scale the walls unseen, and to fall upon them with spear and sword, and in the confusion carry the girls off; but it would have been a desperate plan, with but small hope of success."

"Small indeed, John, small indeed," Armstrong said, shaking his head. "With prisoners in the hold, the Bairds were not likely to be caught sleeping; and had they been, accustomed to surprises as they are, the whole garrison would have been afoot in a minute, and not a man of ye would have lived to tell the story. Some such mad thought passed through my brain, when I first heard the news, but it was not for long. Even with your spears, and others you might gather, and all my friends in Tweeddale, we should have had but a small chance of capturing the Bairds' hold. We should have had all Annandale and Nithsdale down on us, before we could have done it. At any rate, we should have had to bide our time, and wait until the Bairds were away to England with all their dalesmen; and by that time, none could say what would have become of the girls. In fact, there was but one way of doing it, and that is the way Oswald hit upon.

"Well, lad, I fear I shall never have an opportunity of repaying the debt I owe you; but after this, there is not an Armstrong on the border, on our side or yours-- for we are half English and half Scotch--but will hold you as among our closest of kin, and will give you welcome and aid, whensoever you may need it. And where is your man Roger?"

"I will call him," Oswald said and, stepping to the door, he shouted to his follower; who came out, at once, from one of the outhouses occupied by the retainers of the hold.

"Come up, Roger!" Oswald said; "Master Armstrong wishes to see you."

Roger came up and, as he entered, Adam grasped him by the hand.

"Whenever your time for fighting is over, my brave fellow, remember that there is a home for you at Hiniltie, so long as an Armstrong dwells there. I thought, when I fetched that monk's gown for you, that you and my nephew Oswald might be able to gather some news; and let me know, possibly, how the girls were faring; but little did I think that, alone and unaided, you would rescue them from the hands of the Bairds."

"It was a merry business, Master Armstrong, and pleased me hugely, save that it went against my heart to have this bald patch on my head again, just when the hair had so well grown and covered it; but it was well nigh as good as fighting, to trick the Bairds in their own hold, when they, as they thought, were so mightily sure that I was but a harmless brother of a monastery. For the rest, it was an easy business, and scarce worth talking of."

"It was done easily because it was done well, Roger. It was well planned, and well carried out."

"I had nought to do with the planning, and the carrying out was simple enough. There were those there who tested me, as to my knowledge of Dunbar, and of the monastery I came from, and who further tested my knowledge of reading. Once assured that my story was true, they paid no further attention to me, believing that I should stay but a day or two, to rest myself on my way south."

"You had occasion, however, to use that heavy staff you carried."

"Some slight occasion, but I would that I had had the chance to have used it on the heads of some of the Bairds. For what little I did, master Armstrong, your daughters thanked me very prettily, and more than enough; and therefore, I pray thee, say no more of it.

"And how is your son?"

"He is going on well, and both Meg Margetson and the monks, in whose hands I have put him, say that they hope he is out of danger."

The next morning Oswald and Roger mounted, soon after daybreak, and rode to Alnwick. It had, the night before, been arranged that the girls should, for the present, remain at Yardhope; until the hold at Hiniltie was repaired, and put in a state of stronger defence. It was agreed, too, that it was as well that no word should be said by Armstrong, on his return, as to the whereabouts of his daughters, as the Bairds might then, in their anger, make an attack on Yardhope; whereas, at present, they could have no reason whatever for suspecting that they were there, and, if they obtained news that they were not with their father at Hiniltie, would suppose that they had been lodged with some of the family elsewhere, or perhaps placed for safety in Jedburgh.

"I had wondered what had become of you," Hotspur said, when Oswald entered his apartments, to report his return. "I expected you two or three days since, and I indeed wanted you, for other business."

"I am sorry, my lord; but after having fulfilled the orders you gave me, to the governors of Roxburgh and Jedburgh, I became engaged in an affair of my uncle, Adam Armstrong, of so pressing a character that I deemed you would excuse me, when you heard its nature."

And he then briefly related how he had been occupied, since leaving Jedburgh.

"'Tis a good excuse, indeed," Hotspur said, "and you must tell me more of it this evening, when the earl and my wife can also hear it. As to the business I spoke of, it is of no consequence at all; it was but to carry a message to the Earl of Westmoreland. This I have now sent, by another hand."

The winter passed quietly. Oswald's work was light. He more than once rode home for a few days, and once paid a visit to Hiniltie.

Here a number of men were at work. The exterior walls had in no way suffered, and the shell of the central building had so far resisted the fire, that it was not necessary to rebuild it. The roof and floors had been replaced, and the defences considerably strengthened. A portcullis had been placed above the door; so that, in case of the outer wall being carried, or the gate forced, it could at once be lowered. A projecting battlement had been thrown out over this, with openings below, through which boiling lead and pitch could be poured on an enemy trying to break in. Flanking turrets, for archers, had been built at each corner of the house; and the exterior walls had been strengthened by towers, in the centre of each face, and on either side of the gateway.

"We shall be safe now, I think, Oswald," said Allan, who had almost recovered. "The place can hardly be taken by a sudden attack, even by all the forces the Bairds could bring against it; and we could get help from Jedburgh, long before they could gain even the outside wall. My father and I are going, in a fortnight, to fetch the girls. I rode over there a week or two since, and found them looking very well and happy, with your people; but of course they are anxious to get back again, especially as you are so seldom at home."

"If you will fix the day before I go, I will try to be there to meet you. I suppose, as soon as spring sets in fairly, we shall be having troubles again, and it is certainly as well that Janet and Jessie should be at home again before they begin; for although Yardhope is strong enough to resist any attack by the Bairds, or any other border rangers, it can scarcely hold out against a regular invasion."

Four days after his return to Alnwick, Oswald was sent for by Percy.

"The Scots do not seem to be moving yet," the latter said, "but Glendower is ever increasing in strength, and boldness. I have received startling news this morning. A party of Welshmen were seen near Ruthyn, and Earl Grey, with a body of mounted men, rode out against them. They retired at once, and he, briskly pursuing, fell into an ambush and was captured.

"'Twould have been thought that Glendower would have put his chief enemy to death, at once, but it was not so, and it is said he holds the earl to ransom. Glendower has plenty of men, but no doubt needs money sorely. He can draw no revenue from his estates in Denbigh, and those in South Wales cannot suffice for the expenses of feeding the body of men, always under arms. Doubtless he will ask for a great sum, and 'tis like that he will get it. Grey is a favourite of the king, and the latter will doubtless aid him, for he needs his services to hold Flint and Denbighshire against the Welsh.

"Moreover, methinks that the king would, for another reason, make every effort to buy Lord Grey's freedom; for it is no secret that he has no great love for Mortimer; for although he holds the young Earl of March a prisoner, at Windsor, he cannot forget that the lad is the rightful heir to the throne, and that the friends of Richard would place him there, had they the opportunity. Mortimer is the boy's uncle and, not only from his own estates, but as guardian of the young earl's wide possessions in Hereford and in Shropshire, is a very powerful noble.

"The king has no real reason for doubting him, for I know that Mortimer has no thought of supporting the Earl of March's claim to the throne; having held, with the rest of the kingdom, that Henry, who is wise and politic, is a far fitter ruler than the lad could be. Doubtless, Henry is well aware of this, but he sees that when the young earl grows to manhood he might become dangerous; and might supplant him, as he supplanted Richard. Thus, then, I have no doubt the king will use every effort to obtain the release of Lord Grey, in order that he may act as a counterpoise, in the Welsh marches, to the influence of Mortimer.

"However, that is not now the question. It is evident, by this daring deed of Glendower, that he will be busy this year; and the success of his first attempt will assuredly add to his following. Therefore, as the Scots are, at present, quiet, I would that you ride again to Ludlow, and sojourn there a while.

"Sir Edmund sends me but scant news, and I would fain know more closely how matters are going there, and how great this insurrection is like to grow. It may well be that the Scots, seeing how powerful Glendower is becoming, will enter into agreement with him, that while he invades the west country, they shall pour across the border with all their forces; in which case we should be hard pressed, for the king's power in the south might be fully engaged against the Welsh, and we should have to battle with the whole strength of Scotland, alone. Therefore, write at length, giving me full reports of the talk of the country as to the bearing of the Welsh, not only beyond the border, but those settled in the west counties.

"You will, of course, take the fighting monk with you; and he can aid you in this matter, being a good scholar, though a bad monk; so, when you are weary of holding the pen, you can dictate the matter to him. I will send two well-mounted couriers with you, and will have relays of horses placed on the road, so that you can despatch me a letter once a week; and they will also, of course, carry any letters Sir Edmund Mortimer may wish to send."

"Very well, Sir Henry. Shall I start today?"

"Nay, the matter is not so urgent as all that."

"Then I will ride tomorrow morning."

"Good.

"I am well pleased with you, Oswald. That affair, in which you rescued your cousins, showed that you have discretion and ability, as well as skill and courage; and you see, the knowledge that you gained at the monastery is coming in useful to you, now. As a mark of my approbation, I will order that one of my warhorses shall be saddled, and be in readiness for you, in the morning. The steed that Mortimer gave you is a good one, but you have need of another; for one may fall lame, or be killed or wounded, and 'tis well to have a second string to the bow. Moreover, riding as you do in my service, 'tis but meet that I should provide you with horseflesh.

"I marked you on your horse today, the one you rode when you came here; and in truth, you have outgrown it altogether; and though I doubt not that the sturdy little beast would, even yet, carry you for a long day's journey, 'tis scarce in accordance with your position as our representative."

Oswald thanked Hotspur heartily for the gift, for he, himself, had felt that he needed a second charger, but had been reluctant to ask his father for the money required to buy one; for the expenses of repairing the hold, after the last Scotch invasion, had been heavy, and gold was a scarce commodity at Yardhope.

He started at daybreak the next morning, riding the fine horse Hotspur had given him. Roger rode behind him, and was followed by the two lightly-armed men, who were to act as messengers. One of these led Oswald's second horse. As soon as they had left the castle, Oswald called Roger up to his side.

"Well, Roger, I dare say you are as pleased as I am, that we are on the move again. 'Tis nigh five months since we returned from Ludlow and, save for our adventure with the Bairds, we have had a quiet time, since."

"Think you there will be work with the Welsh again, master?"

"I think so, indeed, Roger. They say that Glendower's forces are greatly increasing, and he has captured Lord Grey, and holds him to ransom. The king must regret, now, that Parliament refused to listen to Glendower's complaints, because he had been one of Richard's men, and had perhaps spoken more hotly than was prudent, touching the king's murder."

"But they say that Richard is still alive, and that he is with the Scots."

"They may say so, Roger, but think you that it is likely? The king's figure was well known to hundreds of men. Why does he not show himself? Even in Scotland there are many nobles who, during the truces between the kingdoms, have been to London, and have known King Richard; and had this man been he, they would have recognized him, at once. Besides, think you that when the king had Richard caged, in Pomfret, there was any chance of his getting free again? It may suit Albany, at present, to set up some puppet or other, in order to cause uneasiness to Henry, and to render Richard's friends here unwilling to obey the orders of the king, and to take the field against the Scots; but had he been Richard, 'tis not in Scotland that he would have shown himself, but in France, where he would gladly have been received, as Anne of Bohemia's husband, and would have had aid and support to urge his claims."

"Well, master, I care not what takes us to Wales. At any rate, I am glad to journey thither; for it seems, at present, as if there, only, is there a chance of giving and taking hard knocks. How is it that you do not take a party of men-at-arms, as you did last time?"

"Mortimer has plenty of men, without them, and the handful that Percy can spare would be of little use. I am going principally because Hotspur is anxious to be kept well informed of what happens in the west, for he feels sure that, if Glendower's power increases, it will be needful to send a strong English army there. The Scots will make a great invasion, and it will behove all the northern counties, and lords, to hold themselves in readiness."

They travelled fast and, in five days after leaving Alnwick, arrived at Ludlow.

"Welcome back again, Master Oswald!" Sir Edmund said, when he arrived. "I thought that maybe Sir Henry Percy would send you hither. Matters here are becoming serious, and 'tis said that there have been Scotch emissaries with Glendower, though for the truth of this I cannot answer; but Percy will certainly wish to know, well, what passes in the west; and I am but a poor hand with the pen, and moreover, too much busied to write often. He knows that right well, and I doubt not you are instructed to inform him of all that passes."

"You are right, Sir Edmund. It is for that purpose that he has sent me hither, charging me to write to him, frequently, as to the situation and the power of Glendower; which must needs be on the increase, since nought has been done to bring him to reason. And I have also his commands, to place myself at your service, and to obey you, in all respects, as if I had been your squire."

"I shall be glad for you to ride with my knights," Sir Edmund replied, courteously. "I have not forgotten that you did good service, last year, and trust that you may find opportunity for winning your spurs."

"I shall be glad, indeed, to do so, Sir Edmund. May I ask where Glendower is supposed to be, at present?"

"He has his headquarters on the summit of Plinlimmon, a great hill on the borders of Montgomery; and thence ravages and plunders all the country round him, slaying all who are supposed to be attached to the English cause. Unfortunately, he meets with but little resistance, for the castles have, for the most part, been suffered to get into a bad state; since, for a hundred years, it has seemed that they would no longer be required against the Welsh, who appeared to have become as peaceful as the people in our own counties. Many of the knights have built themselves more convenient houses, and have let the castles become almost ruins.

"Then, too, the garrisons, where garrisons are kept, are for the most part composed of Welshmen. These can be no longer trusted, and it is no easy matter to obtain Englishmen in their places, for so great is the terror caused by the slaughter, by Glendower, of those who fall into his hands, that few even of adventurous spirit would, at present, care to leave their homes beyond the Severn, to take up such desperate service. Glendower's movements are so rapid that there is no notice of his coming, and it is not until he and his band suddenly appear, burning and slaughtering, that any know of his approach."

"Surely it must be difficult to victual so large a force, on the summit of a mountain?"

"It would assuredly be so, only he keeps but a hundred and fifty chosen men with him. But, were his beacon fires to be lighted, there would in a few hours be ten thousand men on the mountain. Then again, as the whole population are with him, were I to start with five hundred men from here, the news would reach him, by means of smokes on the hills, before I had marched five miles away. 'Tis a warfare in which there is no credit to be gained, and much loss to be sustained; and I see not that, with anything less than an army large enough to march through Wales from end to end, burning the towns and villages, and putting to the sword all who resist, the affair can be brought to an end.

"It was only thus that Harold brought Wales to reason, and that so strongly that it was two generations ere they ventured again to cross the border. It was so that Edward finally stamped out their rebellions, and methinks that the work will have to be done again, in the same manner. So far from doing good, the king's invasion last autumn has but encouraged them; for, though so numerous, his army effected nothing, and showed the Welsh how powerless the troops were to enter the mountains, or to take the offensive anywhere save on level ground."

Oswald's life, at Ludlow, differed in no way from that at Alnwick. He took his meals at the high table, sitting below the knights, with Sir Edmund's squires. He practised arms with them; tilted in the courtyard of the castle; occasionally rode out, hunting and hawking, with a party of knights and ladies; helped to drill the bodies of tenants who, a hundred at a time, came in to swell the garrison. Sometimes he carried Mortimer's orders to the governors of the castles, or rode with a strong party into Hereford or Radnor.

A short time after his arrival, Montgomery was taken by storm by Glendower; and all Englishmen, and Welshmen suspected of friendship for the English, slain. Shortly afterwards, the suburbs of Welshpool were burnt by him, to the great loss of the Earl of Powys; whose annoyance was all the greater, since most of his own tenants were under arms, with Glendower. Following hard upon these pieces of bad news came word that he had fallen upon the Abbey of Cwmhir, six miles from Rhayader, in Radnorshire, which he entirely destroyed. The news caused great indignation, and the reason for this sacrilegious act was warmly discussed at the castle.

"The reason, methinks," Sir Edmund said, after he had listened to the knights for some time, "is twofold. In the first place the ecclesiastics, for the most part, and the monks of all the orders save the Franciscans, favoured King Henry against Richard; but the chief reason is the long animosity between the Church and the Bards, of whom Glendower is a great patron; and who have done him great service, by stirring up the people with their songs. The bards have ever been foremost in instigating insurrections in Wales. Edward the First attempted to suppress them altogether, and his edict for executing them, by martial law, is still unrepealed; and they dare not venture to show themselves, in any castle or town held by us. But they have, to a man, rallied round Glendower. His house was always open to them, and he was even distinguished by some Welsh name, meaning the protector of the bards. Now, after being hunted fugitives for so many years, they have, no doubt, used their influence with him to stir him up against the religious houses."

But a heavier blow still was struck by Glendower, and the feeling at Ludlow was nothing short of consternation, when a fugitive arrived from the town of New Radnor, saying that the strong castle there had been carried by assault, the garrison of three-score men all beheaded, and the town laid in ashes. This was the heaviest blow yet struck by Glendower. The castle was of great strength, and the town had been walled by the Lords of the Marches. That such a place should have been carried by Welsh kerns seemed well-nigh incredible, and the execution of the whole of the garrison aroused the most lively indignation.

"This is war to the knife, indeed," Sir Edmund Mortimer said; "and yet, abhorrent as is this wholesale murder of the garrison, I cannot but own that it is a politic step, on the part of Glendower. The news will spread throughout Wales, and if so strong a place as New Radnor could not defend itself, how can lesser castles hope to do so? Nor, indeed, will garrisons care to man the walls, since resistance means death. Doubtless there were many Welsh among these men who were murdered, and you may be sure that their compatriots, in other castles, will hasten to desert and join Glendower."

This, indeed, proved to be the case, the garrisons of the castles dwindled away, and hold after hold fell without resistance. Even in Ludlow, every precaution was taken; all Welshmen were expelled from the town, and the garrison was also purged of them, although some of the men-at-arms had served for many years. These men were told that, after the troubles were over, they should again be taken into the service if they chose; but that, in the present state of things, one traitor might endanger the safety of the castle and town; and that, as it was impossible to tell who were true men and who had been corrupted by Glendower's agents, it was necessary that all should suffer, even if innocent.

Among the tenants of Mortimer's estate, and those of the young earl, were many Welsh. Against them no measures were taken. They and their fathers, sometimes indeed three generations of them, had lived peaceably; and had rendered military service, when required, in the troubles of England; and Mortimer was reluctant to treat them harshly, especially as all declared their readiness to serve, and prove their devotion to their English lord.

"They are not sufficiently numerous," he said, "to be a source of any danger. Were Glendower to invade England in great force doubtless they would join him, to save their lives and those of their families; but being but one to four or five of the English tenants, I see not that they can be a source of danger to us."

Chapter 16: A Letter For The King.

large number of Flemings had settled in Wales, having left their own country in consequence of the constant troubles there; and many of these had set up cloth mills, at Welshpool and other places. Having suffered great destruction of property at the hands of Glendower, and seeing no hope of the insurrection being put down by the English, they resolved to take the matter into their own hands. Fifteen hundred of them gathered, secretly, and surrounded Glendower in one of his mountain intrenchments.

He repulsed their attacks, but the situation was desperate. Provisions ran short. He was unable to summon help, and at last determined, with his little body of followers, to endeavour to cut his way out through the besiegers. The attack was sudden and fierce. The Flemings, who, knowing the smallness of his force, had made no preparations to repel an attack, were seized with a panic at the fierce appearance and the wild cries of the Welsh, who fell upon them with such fury that two hundred of the Flemings were slain, and the Welsh cut their way through the beleaguering line.

The news of this feat was received with immense enthusiasm, throughout the principality. Great numbers flocked to Glendower's standard; the bards sung songs of his victory, at every village in Wales; and so formidable did his position become that the Lords of the Marches wrote to the king, saying that the matter had gone altogether beyond them, and that his presence, with an army, was urgently needed.

Even in Ludlow, extra sentries were placed upon the walls, the garrison was kept in a constant state of vigilance, and mounted men were stationed, miles out, to bring in the news of the approach of any hostile force.

"'Tis a thousand pities," Sir Edmund said, when the news of the defeat of the Flemings reached him, "that these fellows did not send news to me, a day or two before they undertook this business; for in that case I would have myself headed a force of a couple of hundred of my best men-at-arms, and joined them at some spot in the mountains; and had we been there, you may be sure that Glendower would never have fought his way out. The Flemings are doubtless stout fighters, as they have proved over and over again, in their own country; but they are all unused to mountain warfare, or to fight with wild men, and were doubtless scared by the shrill cries with which the Welsh always advance to battle. Doubtless, too, these men Glendower keeps with him are his best fighters, and they knew that, if they did not succeed in making their way out, no mercy would be shown to them, seeing that they have shown none themselves. Had the battle been on a plain, I doubt not that the Flemings would have stood against many times the number of Welshmen that Owen had with him; but this hill warfare was altogether strange to them, and of course they had not the habit of quickly rallying, and meeting the attack, that is second nature with our men-at-arms. The affair is serious, and unless the king comes hither with an army, Glendower is likely to have it all his own way on his side of the border; and, ere long, there won't be an Englishman left west of the Severn."

However Henry, when informed of the danger, lost no time in assembling another great army; and in the beginning of June advanced into Wales, and ravaged a wide extent of country, carrying his arms into Cardiganshire, and destroying the Abbey of Strata Florida, one of the most venerable and famous abbeys in Wales. Founded in 1164, it was burnt down in 1294, during the wars of King Edward the First with the Welsh, but was soon rebuilt. Here Llewellyn, in 1237, convened all the chieftains of Wales to take the oath of allegiance. There were two copies of the national records, one of which was kept at this abbey, and the other at that of Conway.

The abbey having fallen, Henry's army met with scarcely any resistance, Glendower knowing that his wild followers were no match for the royal troops. He therefore contented himself with harassing them continually, and the army suffered greatly by this continued annoyance, as well as from fatigue and famine. Thus the king returned across the border without having achieved any success, whatever.

The Lords of the Marches were not now ordered to contribute any troops, but were to hold their castles strongly; lest, when the army was fairly entangled among the mountains, Glendower should make a great incursion into England. The only advantage gained by the English invasion was that the king, by promises of pardon and rewards, drew away a number of the leading men who had hitherto acted with Glendower. Their defection, however, was more than made up by the enthusiasm excited by the spectacle of the second retirement of a great English army, without having effected anything of importance.

So evident was this, that in October Henry again advanced, with the contingents of no fewer than twenty-two counties. The season, however, was already unfavourable for operations and, after enduring great hardships and suffering, the army again fell back, having effected even less than the two which had preceded it.

Things, however, turned out fortunately for Oswald. The army had advanced a week across the border when a messenger arrived at Ludlow, with a letter from London for the king.

"It will be no easy matter to forward it," Sir Edmund said, as the despatch was handed to him. "Indeed, I see not how it is to be done. Beyond the fact that the king intended to march west, I know nothing whatever of his intentions, or of the exact road he was likely to take. His orders were strict, that we were to keep our forces well in hand; and to send the letter forward would need two hundred men, at least, as an escort. It places me in an awkward position, indeed."

"If it so please you, Sir Edmund," said Oswald, who was one of the group standing round, when the messenger handed the letter to Mortimer; "I will endeavour to carry the despatch for you. Methinks that, while fifty men would not succeed in getting through to the army, two might, perchance, manage to do so. I shall, of course, ride first to Shrewsbury, through which the king passed; and so follow up the course he took. There should be no great difficulty in doing that, for the march of so great a body of men must have left many traces behind. They will, doubtless, have harried the country, for some distance each side of the line they followed; and it is not likely that I should meet any of the Welsh, until I was near the army. Then, of course, great caution would have to be used; for it is like enough that there are parties of Glendower's men hanging on its skirts, to cut off stragglers, and plunder any waggons whose horses may have fallen by the way."

"'Tis a terribly dangerous service," Sir Edmund said, gravely; "but in truth, I see no other way of forwarding this letter; which, for aught I know, may be of high importance. But if this is a desperate enterprise, it is also one that will bring you great credit, if safely carried through. I will myself, if you go, give you a letter to the king, saying that you have volunteered for this desperate undertaking, from your loyalty to his person, and because it is possible that the letter may contain matter of the highest importance, to him and the realm in general. I shall add that you have already greatly distinguished yourself, in service against the Welsh, and are the trusty esquire of my brother-in-law, Sir Henry Percy."

"I quite feel, Sir Edmund, that the enterprise is a dangerous one; but I am nevertheless determined, with your permission, to undertake it. My henchman and myself have, together, gone through dangers as great; and may pass through this, as well."

"I will give you my answer in half an hour, Master Oswald, when I have talked it over with my knights, and heard their opinions as to whether any better plan can be devised."

Oswald bowed and retired and, seeking out Roger, told him of the offer that he had made.

"Well, master, if you are bent upon this enterprise, you will not find me backward; and indeed, I am so sick of this six months of idleness, and of seeing others marching to Wales to fight, while we do nothing here; that, by Saint Bride, were you to ask me to go into Glendower's stronghold, and pluck him by the beard, I would willingly go with you."

Oswald laughed.

"'Tis not so bad as that, Roger, and yet 'tis a service of great danger. How think you that we had best set about it, on horse or on foot?"

Roger looked surprised at the question.

"It would surely be better to go on horseback, master; for if we met too many Welshmen to fight, we might at least ride away from them."

"There is truth in that, Roger; but, on the other hand, our feet will carry us up and down mountains, and fells, where our horses could not go. If mounted, we must travel by beaten tracks, and might be seized by parties of Welsh, lurking in the woods, before we knew of their presence. Without horses, we could ourselves keep within shelter of the trees, and could so evade the observation of any who might be stationed on lofty hills, to watch if any body of troops were following the track of the army. Moreover, we should have no trouble about forage and water for our steeds."

"Enough, master, I see which way your inclinations lie; and as my legs have had a long holiday, it is but right that they should carry me for a bit; and assuredly, 'tis easier for footmen to hide than it is for horsemen."

"I should say, Roger, that it would be best to leave armour, as well as horses behind. If we are attacked by numbers, our armour will serve us but little; while if without it, we may be able, even if chased, to avoid the hands of these Welshmen. They say that they are swift of foot; but, as we can hold our own with the Northumbrian border men, we ought to be able to do so against these Welsh, especially as our legs are nigh a foot longer than those of the greater part of them."

"Very well, master. I myself have no great love for travelling in armour, and would almost as soon march in a monk's gown, again, as in breastplate and back piece."

"Very well, so we will arrange it. We shall have to carry our provisions, for you may be sure that we shall get nothing, whatever, while we are following the army. They will strip the country clean. You know how terribly they have suffered by famine, on the two previous expeditions; and it will assuredly be no better, now. Food, however, we can procure at Shrewsbury, from which point we shall take our start."

A retainer, at this moment, came out from the hall, and informed Oswald that Sir Edmund would speak with him. When he entered, Mortimer said:

"My knights and I agree that this letter ought to be sent forward to the king; for if it contains matters of importance, great harm might result from delay, and the king's anger be excited against us, for not having sent it to him. His orders to me were strict, that neither I nor any of my force should join him; therefore I accept your offer, with thanks. Have you formed any plan for your proceeding?"

Oswald repeated the substance of what he had said to Roger.

"I think, perhaps, you are right," Mortimer said, "and that you may have more chance of getting safely through, on foot, than if you rode with but a small force to escort you. When you are ready to start, I will speak to you in private, touching some things connected with your journey."

When Oswald returned, Mortimer said to him:

"You see, Master Oswald, the position is by no means simple. There can be no doubt that the king regards me with no favourable eye. He holds my nephews in his keeping, and doubtless imagines that I bear him ill will. As their uncle, he supposes that, should at any time a party be formed to place the Earl of March on the throne, I should be the leader in the matter; though assuredly I have never given him any reason to doubt my loyalty.

"I say not that I approved of the deposition of King Richard; and indeed I have not, like Lord Grey and many other nobles, among them the Percys, been a warm supporter of King Henry's cause. I hold myself altogether neutral, in that matter. I saw that nothing would be more ruinous, for the country, than that a boy like my nephew should mount the throne; and had a party been formed to make him king, instead of Henry, I would have taken no share in it. Nevertheless, there is no getting over the fact that, by right, the Earl of March is King of England, and there is no saying what may come about in the future; but assuredly, at the present time, I am as ready to do my duty towards King Henry as are those who are louder in their expressions of attachment to him.

"Nevertheless, I am well aware that the king distrusts me. As you see, he has not, these three times that he has invaded Wales, come near Ludlow. He has not summoned me to join his banner; nay, more, has strictly ordered me not to send a man-at-arms to join him.

"I own that this letter troubles me, somewhat. Why should it not have been carried to Shrewsbury, instead of being brought hither? It has, indeed, come from London, and those who sent it may not know that the king would move by Shrewsbury, and not by this line; which would, indeed, be more direct for him in advancing into Montgomery and Cardiganshire. On the other hand, it may be a snare. If I send it not forward, he might blame me greatly for holding it back. If I send it forward, and perchance it falls, on the way, into the hands of the Welsh, he might harbour the thought, even if he did not accuse me openly, of conniving with Glendower. One pretext is as good as another, however unlikely it may be, when a king desires to make a quarrel with one of his vassals. Your offer to carry it is, then, a very seasonable one, and goes far to get me out of the difficulty.

"In the first place, by sending it by you, I afford no ground for him to say that

I have disobeyed his orders, to send no one of my following to his army; and in the next place, whatever suspicion he may have of me, assuredly he can have none of the Percys, to whom he so largely owes his crown; and that a trusted squire of Hotspur should be the bearer of the letter, is sufficient proof that all that could be done, was done, for its safe carriage. Should you fail to deliver it, he can, at least, not put it down to any fault of mine.

"Sir James Burgon and Sir Philip Haverstone both offered to carry it, urging that the danger should fall on them; and not upon you, who are still an esquire, and have no duty towards me in the affair; and that it were a shame that they should remain here, idle, while you rode, perhaps, to your death.

"Assuredly, my feelings were with them and, were it not for the circumstances in which I am placed, I should certainly intrust the enterprise to them; but on my laying the whole matter before them, and pointing out that the coming of two of my knights to him would be a breach of the king's orders, they saw that, since you were willing to undertake it, it were best that it should be so.

"I doubt not that Henry would, not unwillingly, fasten some quarrel on me. He has his army at hand and, did he march hither, he could seize my lands, and those of my nephew, and partition them out among his friends; for I am in no condition to strike a single blow in my defence. We know, well enough, that when a king wishes to get rid of one of his nobles, there is never any great difficulty in finding a pretext for his arrest, and execution."

"I quite understand, Sir Edmund; and for my part, I will assuredly do my best to place this letter in the hands of the king. I shall say that, being of Sir Henry Percy's household, and knowing that my lord would be glad that I should have the opportunity of striking a blow under the king's leading, I volunteered at once, when the letter arrived, to bear it to him; and that, seeing his majesty had laid his orders on you, to keep all your force in readiness to repel Glendower, should he issue out in this quarter, you granted my request that I should be its bearer."

"That will do well, Oswald. I know that the danger is by no means small, but I trust that you may surmount it. I shall send off a letter, today, to Hotspur. Doubtless you will, yourself, be writing to him, and explain to him why I have suffered you to undertake so dangerous an enterprise."

Two hours later, Oswald, having despatched the messenger to Hotspur with his own letter, and that of Mortimer, mounted, and with Roger rode to Shrewsbury. Here he was able to gather but little news, as to the present position of the army. For four days no messengers had arrived from the king.

The last news was to the effect that the army was marching forward, through Montgomeryshire. On first starting, they had made a long march to Welshpool, and thence had proceeded to Newtown. On the way, the Welsh had rushed down from the hills, and had fallen on the baggage, slain many of the drivers, and killed so many horses that it had been necessary to leave some of the waggons behind.

At Newtown they halted, and parties had been sent out in all directions to harry the country, while a part of the force left at Welshpool marched upon Llanfair. This was the last news that had come through from the king.

But from Welshpool they heard, next day, that there had been several skirmishes with the Welsh, and that heavy rains had made the roads all but impassable. No more messages had come. This was not surprising, as it was certain that the Welsh would close in behind the army, as it advanced; and as there would be no great occasion to send news back, the king would not care to weaken himself, by detaching escorts of sufficient strength to make their way down.

"If we could have been sure which way the king had been going, Roger, it would have been much shorter for us to have made direct for Llanidloes."

"Certainly it would, Master Oswald; but you see, he might have turned more to the north, in which case we should have, perhaps, been unable to gather news of his whereabouts, while we should have run no small risk of getting our throats cut."

"It is evident, Roger, that the king is marching, at present, in the direction of Plinlimmon. No doubt he hopes that Glendower will come down and give him battle, but methinks he will not be foolish enough to do so. The weather, and the hills, will fight far better for him than the Welsh, themselves, can do; and he has but to leave the army to wander about through the mountains and forests, as he did last time, to ensure that they must, ere long, fall back."

At daybreak the next morning, they set out and rode to Welshpool. This being a walled town, and the population almost entirely English, they could leave their horses here, in safety. They first went to the governor's, and upon Oswald's explaining that they were the bearers of a letter for the king, and asking whether he could give them any information as to the direction they had best take, he shook his head.

"No news has come hither, for the last five days," he said. "A herd of bullocks arrived here, three days since, and were to have been forwarded on to the army; but the Welsh are out in force, and every road beset. Parties have come down from the hills overlooking us, and have fired several houses, that escaped when they last attacked us. My force is sufficient to hold the town against any attacks, but I cannot spare so many men as would be required to convoy the cattle. I told the king so, before he went on; but he said that no Welshman would dare show himself, when the army had once passed on; and that every Welsh house and village would be destroyed, and all within them put to the sword, so that I should have no difficulty in sending forward cattle, and other supplies.

"That the villages have been destroyed I have no doubt, for the messengers who came in from Llanfair told me that, as they passed over the hills, they could see smoke rising from the forests in all directions; but whether the inhabitants remained, quietly awaiting the arrival of the troops, is more than doubtful. There were beacon fires on all the hills, the night before the army left Shrewsbury, and again on the next night. Since then, we have seen no more from here, but those who came from Llanfair told us that they were burning, on every hill, the night they got there; so I have no doubt that the old men, women, and children were at once sent off, probably to shelter in the Plinlimmon district, or mayhap in the forests of Cader Idris. At any rate, we may be sure that very few will be found at their villages. It was so the last time the king's army marched along, and the same when he made his way through Denbigh to Anglesey.

"The Welsh care little for the burning of their houses. It takes but two or three days' work to rebuild them. The harrying of the villages will not bring the matter a day nearer to a conclusion. It is by destroying the castles and houses of the better class that an effect will be produced. The peasants have little to lose. The Welsh gentry have houses and estates, and the fear of losing these may drive them to abandon Glendower, and to come over to us. Many did so, after the king's last invasion. Methinks the best policy would be to spare the villagers, and give the peasants no cause for complaint, and to war only against their leaders.

"But as to yourself, sir, there is not the most remote chance of your getting through; and you had best wait here until the army returns, or some levies, who may have arrived late at Shrewsbury, come up on their way to join the king."

"I inquired at Shrewsbury, last night, sir; but I heard that no more parties were expected, the contingents from all the counties having joined the king, at Worcester, on the day ordered. My intention is that I and my man-at-arms will leave our horses here, and go forward on foot. In that way we can travel, for the most part, through the forests; and may escape being seen. We have already left our armour behind us, at Ludlow, so as to be able to move more rapidly. We are both Northumbrians, and are accustomed to traverse moors and fells; and, even should we be seen by any straggling party of the enemy, we shall have a fair chance of outrunning them, and throwing them off our track. At any rate, it is my duty to endeavour to carry the letter to the king."

"Is it a matter of life and death?"

"That I know not, sir. A royal messenger brought it, from London, to Ludlow. He had ridden with relays of horses, but had no means of getting farther, and begged Sir Edmund Mortimer to forward it. I myself, an esquire of Sir Henry Percy, was staying as a guest with Sir Edmund--who is, as you know, my lord's brother-in-law--and I volunteered to carry it, being anxious to have an opportunity of doing service to the king."

"It was a bold offer, young man, and doubtless, when you made it, you were scarce aware how dangerous was the business that you undertook. Did I think that it would be of any use, I would furnish you with twenty men-at-arms to ride with you; but I know that such a force would, in no way, add to your safety. You might get as far as Llanidloes, or Llanfair, whichever route you might choose, though I think not that you would do so; but beyond that, it would be hopeless for any force, of less than five hundred good fighting men, to attempt to make their way through.

"From what I hear, there are at least fifteen thousand Welshmen in arms. Many, doubtless, are with Glendower himself. The rest will be scattered among the hills, ready to pounce upon any party who may be moving up the valleys to join the king; and there are plenty of places where a couple of hundred men could check the advance of an army."

"Then it is all the more necessary, sir, that we should trust to good fortune, and to making our way unseen. May I pray you to take care of our horses, till we return to claim them? Should we never do so, there are doubtless many upon whom you could bestow them; and they are both rarely good animals, for one was presented to me by Sir Henry Percy, and the other by Sir Edmund Mortimer."

"I will take care of them, willingly. If you do not return, before the king marches back; and I find, when he comes, that you did not reach him; I will use the horses myself, holding them always as your property should you, at any time, return to claim them. Is there aught else that I can do to help you?"

"No, sir; what would, of all other things, be most valuable to us would be a guide; but, from what I have seen and heard of the Welsh, I fear that no reliance, whatever, can be placed on one of them."

"Certainly not at present. Did you take one, he would but slip away at the first opportunity; and there is no Englishman, so far as I know, who could guide you through the mountains."

"In that case, sir, we must perforce travel close to the roads, so as to be sure that we do not wander from the track, but keeping in the shelter of the forest."

"That is the only possible course," the governor agreed; "to be lost, among those hills, would be certain death. If you failed to fall in with anyone, you would die of hunger. If you did meet anyone, you would be killed. Glendower spares no Englishman who falls into his hands."

"I don't know that he can be greatly blamed for that, sir," Oswald said with a smile, "seeing that the Welsh meet with such scant mercy, from us."

"'Tis a savage war," the governor said, shrugging his shoulders, "and it seems to me that it will continue, until the last Welshman is exterminated."

"That will be a difficult thing, indeed, to effect," Oswald laughed; "as difficult as was the extermination of wolves in England; but I hope that matters will arrange themselves, long before that. Surely, in time, the Welsh leaders will see that the struggle is a hopeless one; and that they will lose their homes, and their possessions, and their lives, if they continue it.

"Brave as the Welsh may be, they cannot withstand the whole strength of England. They may exist in the forests, for a time; but, with all the valleys and fertile lands in English hands, they will at last be forced to submit."

"It would seem so; but Edward said the same thing, of Scotland. He carried fire and sword through it, time after time; and yet Scotland has still its king, and holds its own on the border."

"That is so, sir; but Scotland is a large country, whereas Wales is a small one; and the towns and castles are English, as are all the ports; and the people themselves, although brave, are wholly without discipline, and are able to fight only in the mountains; while the Scots are strong enough to give battle to us on level ground, and have defeated us, more than once."

"My advice to you is to leave the town at night," the governor said, as Oswald rose to leave. "There may be many of the Welsh lying round us now; and doubtless they learn, from their countrymen here, all that is doing. I will give you a scroll, ordering that you are allowed to pass out at any time, by night or day."

"Thank you, sir. I had intended to start tomorrow morning, two hours before daybreak, so as to get well into the forest before sunrise. I shall, of course, go first to Llanidloes; where, doubtless, a strong guard will have been left. As far as that I cannot well miss my way, as I shall have but to keep along the side of the valley."

"That is so. Beyond that, the river is a mere streamlet, and you will have to make across the hills."

"Do you know, sir, whether the force that went to Llanfair was to effect a junction with the king?"

"No, I believe not; at any rate, not for the present. The party was to march west; the king's force was to move south of Plinlimmon; Lord Talbot's to cross the range of hills, and come down upon the river Dovey and, if possible, prevent Glendower, if he is still on Plinlimmon, from making his way to Dinas Mowddwy, or Cader Idris, or up to Snowdon again. The plan is doubtless as good as another, but I doubt whether Talbot's force, if ten times as numerous as it is, could prevent Glendower from slipping away."

That evening Oswald bought a supply of bread and meat, sufficient to last Roger and himself for three days. This was divided in halves and placed in bags, which would be slung over their shoulders. The horses had already been sent up to the castle and, after sleeping for a few hours, the two left the town and, turning to the right, ascended the hill.

Oswald carried his sword and dagger. Roger, in addition to these, had a heavy oaken quarterstaff.

"This," he said, "may be of service in mountain work, and may suffice to crack the skulls of any half-dozen Welshmen we may fall in with."

Both had put on plain leather jerkins and cloth caps, and wore, underneath, their own suits with the Percy cognizance embroidered on them, in order that they might present themselves in proper attire, should they arrive at the king's camp. The weather was already becoming cold, and the double suit was therefore not uncomfortable. As the dress of the Welsh, in the towns and valleys, was very similar to that worn by English villagers; they would attract but little attention, should they have cause to take to the road, for any short distance.

Keeping within the edge of the belt of trees, they followed the valley down past the ruins of Montgomery, and passed Newtown without entering it. Many times during the morning they heard loud shouts, from the woods in which they were, answered by similar cries from the other side of the valley; and were obliged to move with great caution, for it was evident that a considerable number of Welsh were in ambush in the woods, in readiness to attack any party who might be proceeding up or down the valley.

Towards noon, they were obliged to leave the edge of the forest, and to ascend to the brow of the hills; as it was certain that any parties of the enemy, who might be in the forest, would be assembled near its edge, in readiness to pour suddenly down.

More than once they heard voices, but a short distance away; and paused, for a time, to allow parties of men to cross ahead of them. Their greatest danger lay in crossing the side valleys, but as the Welsh would be expecting no one to come down these, they succeeded in crossing without being observed.

They were well content when, just as night was falling, they came down upon Llanidloes. Crossing the wooden bridge over the stream, they entered the town boldly; for, looking down upon it, they had seen many men in armour in the streets, and knew that the place was occupied by the English.

At the gate at the end of the bridge they were asked their business, but they replied that they could only answer that to the officer commanding, and were taken before him.

"Whence come you, friends?" the latter said. "Surely you must be English, by your height; but what you are doing here, in times like the present, I know not. Come you from the king's army, or from the north?"

"We left Welshpool before daybreak," Oswald said, "and have travelled through the forest."

"Then you must be as bold as you are tall, sirs, for the woods are full of these wild Welsh."

"Of that we are aware, sir, and we had some difficulty in making our way through them, unobserved. I would not answer the guard, when we entered; for we are going farther, and had it been mentioned, in the hearing of a Welshman, news might have been sent on ahead."

"I think not that you can reach the king. When we last heard, his foremost divisions were marching forward, and devastating the country on both sides of their line of march. We have heard reports that some of the parties have been attacked, and well-nigh destroyed; and certain it is that Glendower's men are scattered all over the country.

"We were three days without news, but this morning a strong party came, in escorting sick and wounded. They had to fight hard, but beat off their opponents, and got in with the loss of a third of their number. They had started at night, and fortunately arrived within five miles of here, before they were attacked."

"And where is the king now, sir?"

"The king himself is at Capel Bangor, and the army lies between that place and Yspetty Cynfyn."

"Then 'tis but a day's march from here!"

"It would be but a short day's march, could you follow the road; but it would be impossible to do so, for 'tis beset everywhere, and 'tis so rough and hilly that, in places, the men-at-arms had to dismount. You will have to wait here till a large force sets out, with provisions; for those who came in declare that they will not attempt to return, so great is the number of Welshmen along there, and so fierce and reckless are they.

"But you have not yet told me who you are, and why you would push on to the army thus rashly."

Oswald opened his jerkin, and showed the handsome attire beneath it, embroidered with the Percy cognizance.

"I am an esquire of Sir Henry Percy," he said, "and have been staying for a while with Sir Edmund Mortimer, whose sister is my lord's wife. A royal messenger arrived at Ludlow, with a letter for the king; and as there was no other way of bringing it forward, I volunteered to carry it, with my man-at-arms, here."

"It was a brave offer, young sir, but I fear that you will scarce be able to carry it into effect. The men who came here report that it is unsafe to stir a yard from the camp; for those who wander away, for however short a distance, are sure to be slain by the lurking Welshmen. No resistance is offered when strong parties go out, but less than two hundred men-at-arms cannot hope to move, unattacked."

"'Tis for that reason that I have come on foot," Oswald said. "I saw that it would be hopeless for two horsemen to get through, but on foot we may travel through the woods without being discovered; while if we are seen, methinks it would need speedy feet to catch us."

"Well, since you bear a royal letter I cannot stop you; but it seems to me that your chance of getting through is small, indeed."

Chapter 17: Knighted.

Rain was coming down in torrents, when Oswald and Roger started the next morning. On leaving the town they turned to the left, with the intention of making a considerable detour; keeping well away from the road, as it was near this that the Welsh would be most likely watching. They chose this side because, to the right of the road, the country was more broken, rising swell after swell towards Plinlimmon; and it was likely that the largest portion of the Welsh would be on that side, so that they could, at any time, retire to their fastnesses.

They were soon in the woods. The streams they met with were turbid, and full to the brim.

"We shall have trouble with this water, Roger," Oswald said, as they waded across one, waist deep. "This is but a little stream, but if there are larger ones, as is like enough, we shall have to swim before we are done. There is one advantage; in such weather as this, even the Welsh will scarce be active."

"They have not got much clothing to wet," Roger said. "Their dress is better suited than ours for such weather."

The way was a rough one. Hills, although of no great height, had to be crossed, and many streams to be waded. Fortunately, they met with few larger than that they had first crossed; for the water from that side of the hills made its way, for the most part, direct into the Severn; while that which came down from the slopes of Plinlimmon, towards the road, fell into a stream; dry in fine weather, but now a raging torrent, which ran past Llandulas and into the Severn, at Llanidloes.

"Do you think that we are going right, Roger?" Oswald said, after they had been walking for six or seven hours; "for, what with these ups and downs, and turnings and windings, there is no saying which is east and which is west. If the sun were shining we should be sure of our direction, but with these dull leaden clouds there is no saying."

"I have no idea, master. If we were out on a moor we should be able to judge, and to make a fairly straight course, keeping the wind and rain on one side of us; but in this thick forest, though most of the leaves have fallen, those that remain on the branches break up the rain, and it seems to come straight down upon us."

Presently they came to another watercourse.

"Why, Roger, the water is going in the other direction!"

"So it is, master. How can that be?"

"It is just possible that we have crossed some dividing point, and the water is making its way towards the south, and will fall into some other river; but I am very much afraid that the real explanation is, that we have entirely lost our way, and are going in the opposite direction to that in which we started. The question is, shall we cross it or shall we follow it down?"

"Just as you like," Roger said. "For myself, I think that the best way would be to find some place where we could shelter. Tomorrow the sun may be out again, and that will tell us which way to go. If we start at daybreak, and keep it to our back, we can't go far wrong."

"Except that we may pass the army altogether, Roger. They told us that the rearmost division was not more than ten miles ahead."

"We must have walked double that already, I should say, master."

"Not so much as that. We have been a long time over it, but it is slow travelling over this broken ground, and thick wood. I am sure I hope that we have not gone twenty miles, or anything like it; for in that case, if we have been keeping fairly in the right direction, we must have passed the army. If we have been going in the wrong direction, there is no saying where we may be.

"Still, I think that your suggestion is a good one. It is of no use our going on, when we may be getting farther away at every step. It is lucky that we bought these thick cloaks, at Welshpool; for without them we should have been soaked to the skin, hours ago."

"Well, as we have been wetted to the waist a score of times, in the streams, I don't see that it would have mattered much, if the rest of us had been wet through."

"Well, now let us look for a shelter."

After searching for half an hour, they found a spot where a wall of shaly rock barred their way. At one spot some of this had fallen in, forming a sort of shallow cave, some three feet deep.

"This is not a bad beginning, Roger, but we must try and make it a great deal more snug."

They first cut down some young fir poles, and placed them so as to form a sort of penthouse against the wall. On these they piled a number of branches, of the same trees, until it was over a foot in thickness.

"So far, so good," Oswald said. "Now, Roger, look about for a fallen tree. We have passed scores on our way. You must get a thoroughly rotten one, and cut away a portion of the under side; it will be dry enough, there."

"You might get a little of that to start with," Roger said; "but the ground is covered everywhere with fir cones, and there is no better stuff for fires."

Taking off his cloak he laid it down, and they both piled the fir cones on this, until a great heap was collected. This they carried into their shelter, through an opening they had left in the penthouse.

"We must have something dry to start it with. These cones are a great deal too wet to burn, without a good heat to start them. There is nothing better than the fir needles, master, if we can find some dry ones."

After some searching, a considerable number of these needles were collected; some lying under fallen trees, and others swept by the wind into rocky corners, where the rain had not reached them.

"Now I think that we shall do, Roger."

As soon as they were inside, Roger produced a large lump of dry fungus he had found, on the other side of the Severn; and, by the aid of his flint and steel, soon succeeded in striking sparks upon it. As soon as these began to spread, he put a little pile of fir needles on it; and, blowing gently, bright flames soon darted up. A few more handfuls of fuel were added, and fir cones placed at the top; and in a quarter of an hour, a clear, bright fire was burning.

The dripping cloaks were hung up to the fir poles, to dry; and the jerkins, which were also damp, although the water had not penetrated through them, were spread near the fire.

"It was well that I bought this little skin of wine, last night," Roger said. "You thought it was better to be without such a burden, but the weight of a gallon of wine doesn't count for much, and it makes all the difference in our comfort, here."

The rain had soaked through their provision bags, but the bread and meat in the centre were dry; and of these they made a hearty meal and, laying the wetted food round the fire to dry, they wound up the repast with a long draught of wine.

"Now, as soon as our breeches are dry, Master Oswald, we shall be thoroughly comfortable."

"Yes, one can wish for nothing better. But we must not forget that some Welshmen may come along, and if so, will be sure to want to know what is inside."

"Then, unless there happen to be more than a dozen of them, their curiosity may cost them dear," Roger said grimly. "I don't think there is much fear of it. We have neither seen nor heard of any, since we started; and it would be evil fortune, indeed, if a party happened to come along just at this spot."

"The fact that we have heard no one is a bad sign, Roger; for it would seem to show that we must have gone a long way out of our course."

The rain continued to fall heavily, all that afternoon and throughout the night, and no change of the weather was discernible the next morning.

"We had best stop here for another day, Roger, unless the sky clears; we are not likely to find so good a place for shelter, and it is of no use to wander about, when every step may be taking us farther away. However, we can climb up to the top of this hill, at whose foot we are, and endeavour to get a view over the country."

Roger shook his head.

"In this heavy mist we should not see a quarter of a mile away. We have got all our clothes dry, now, and it would be a pity to get them wet again, without need or profit. Anyhow, we will find some more of those fir cones. Our supply is nearly gone."

In half an hour they had got sufficient to last them all day. There was nothing for them then to do but sleep, one or other keeping watch, so as to prevent the chance of their being surprised.

Before lying down for the night, Roger looked out.

"Methinks that the rain has stopped, though it would be difficult to say, for the drops keep pattering down from the trees. Well, I mightily hope that it will be a fine morning."

Oswald was first upon his feet and, on going out, uttered an exclamation of satisfaction. The morning was breaking and, though light clouds were moving across the sky, glimpses of the blue were visible, here and there. Already the light showed where the sun would presently rise.

Food was hastily eaten, and they then started on their way again. There could be no mistake, now, as to the general direction; and, keeping the sun on their right hand, they made their way north. From the top of a hill, somewhat higher than the others, they caught a view of Plinlimmon.

"If we make straight for it," Oswald said, "we ought to come down on the road near the camp. We can go on fearlessly for some time, for the Welsh were hardly likely to be moving about, yesterday or the day before; and I have no doubt they sheltered themselves, as best they could, in arbours like ours."

After walking for another two hours, they heard the distant sound of a trumpet.

"That cannot be more than two or three miles away, Roger. Now, we shall have to be careful."

They had walked a mile when, as they descended into a glen, they came suddenly on a party of twenty Welshmen, sitting round a fire. These had been concealed from them by the thick undergrowth, and were not twenty yards away, when they first saw them. The Welsh had evidently heard them coming, by the rustle of leaves and the breaking of twigs; and two or three were standing up, looking in their direction, when they caught sight of them. These gave a loud yell, which brought the rest to their feet.

"Run, Roger, run. It is a question of legs, now;" and, turning, they darted up the hill they had just descended.

Looking back for a moment as, after running for about a mile, they reached the crest of a swell; Oswald saw that five of their pursuers had distanced their comrades, but were no nearer than when they started.

"I think we can hold them, Roger. Take it a little more easily now. We are all right as far as speed goes. It is simply a question of bottom."

Their pursuers, however, still stuck to them and, after running for another half-mile, the five men were still but some thirty yards behind; while their comrades' shouts could be heard through the forests and, from time to time, the men close behind them joined in a loud quavering cry.

"We must stand and rid ourselves of these fellows, Roger; or we shall have half the Welsh nation down on us."

"So I have been thinking, for some time."

"Don't stop suddenly. We will slacken our pace, and they will think that our strength is failing, and will redouble their efforts. Then, when they are close to us, we will turn suddenly."

They heard a yell of exultation, as their pursuers found that they were gaining upon them.

"Choose a clear space, Roger, with room to swing our weapons."

The Welsh were running in a close body, but ten yards behind them, when they arrived at a spot clear of trees.

"Now, Roger!"

As he spoke, Oswald drew his sword and swung round, facing his pursuers, while Roger did the same. The Welsh, taken by surprise, endeavoured to check themselves; but before they could do so, Roger's staff fell upon the head of one of them, while Oswald cleft another to the chin. With the quickness of an adroit player with the quarterstaff, Roger followed up his blow by almost instantaneously driving the other end of the staff, with all his force, against the chest of another, who was at the point of leaping upon him; and the man fell, as if struck with a thunderbolt. So swift had been the movements that the remaining two men were paralysed, by the sudden fall of their companions; but before they could turn to fly, the weapons descended again, with as fatal result as before.

"To the right!" Oswald exclaimed, and he dashed off into the forest again, at a right angle to the line that they had before taken. A minute later they heard an outburst of yells of fury, from the spot they had quitted.

"I don't think they will be quite so ready to follow, now," Roger said. "They are like to be some time, before they take up our track again."

"We will break into a walk, in a few minutes, Roger; and then go along quietly, and keep our ears open. Their yells will be bringing others down, from all directions, and we might run right into the middle of another party, if we kept on at this rate."

In another five minutes they dashed down a steep descent, at whose foot a streamlet, swelled now into a rushing stream, five or six feet wide, was running.

"We will follow this down," Oswald said, as he stepped into it.

It was a little over two feet deep, and they waded along it for a couple of hundred yards, and then stepped out, where some rock cropped out by the side of the stream. It had not yet dried after the rain, and their feet therefore left no marks on it.

"That was a sharp run, Roger," Oswald said as, with rapid but stealthy steps, they strode along.

"Ay, it was. My breath was coming short, when you gave the word to stop. Another half mile would have finished me. Those Welshmen run well."

"I have no doubt we should have beaten them, easily enough, on the open ground, Roger; but they are more accustomed to this forest work than we are.

"Mind where you tread, and don't put your foot on fallen sticks. There must be scores of them in the forest behind, yet, though I don't think that they have struck our track. The nearest must be a quarter of a mile away. I am not afraid of their overtaking us. It is the risk of falling in with other parties that I am afraid of."

They now bore away to the right again. More than once they heard parties moving near them, and stood quiet until their voices died away; which they quickly did, as all were hurrying towards the spot whence the shouting still continued.

For an hour they kept straight onward, and then the trees thinned; and as they stepped out from the edge of the forest they saw, to their delight, a few tents in front of them, and a large number of soldiers scattered about. As they were seen, some of the soldiers caught up their arms; but when they saw that but two men were approaching, they laid them down again, and proceeded with the work on which most of them were engaged; in polishing up their arms and armour, whose brightness had been grievously dimmed by the rain. A sub-officer with four men came up to them, as they reached the line.

"Who are you, sirs?" he asked.

"I am an esquire of Sir Henry Percy, and have brought hither a letter for the king."

The man looked doubtfully at him, and Oswald continued, "I know not whether the Earl of Talbot is in the camp, but if so he will, I think, recognize me."

"The earl arrived, with five hundred of his men, yesterday," the officer said, with a tone of more respect than he had before used. "I will take you to his tent;" and he led the way to a tent, pitched a short distance away from that before which the royal standard waved.

Oswald took off his cloak, which was rolled up over his shoulder, and handed it to Roger, and then opened his jerkin. As they came up to the tent the front opened, and the earl himself came out.

"Whom have we here?" he asked the officer.

"They have just come out of the forest, my lord, and this gentleman asked to be taken to you, saying that you would recognize him."

The earl looked scrutinizingly at Oswald.

"I seem to know your face, sir," he said, "but I cannot recall where I have seen it."

"My name is Oswald Forster, an esquire of Sir Henry Percy. I joined you at Chester, my Lord Talbot, with a band of his men; and some of Sir Edmund Mortimer's, led by one of his knights."

"I remember now," the earl said. "Yes, I see you wear the Percy badge; but how have you got here, and why have you come?"

"I come as a simple messenger, my lord. A royal courier arrived at Ludlow, with a letter from London for the king. His majesty had laid his commands on Sir Edmund Mortimer, that he was not to weaken his force by a single lance; and as, for aught Sir Edmund knew, the letter might be of great importance, I volunteered to endeavour to carry it through; taking with me only this man-at-arms, on whom I could wholly rely, whatever might happen, he having accompanied me on more than one dangerous expedition.

"Sir Edmund consented. We rode first to Shrewsbury, to obtain information as to the course the king had taken. At Welshpool we left our horses behind us, thinking it easier to make our way through the woods on foot, seeing that the roads were said to be beset by the Welsh. So we reached Llanidloes; and then, hearing where the king was then posted, from a convoy of wounded that had been brought in that day, and who had been attacked and very hardly treated as they came along, we thought to make a detour through the woods, so as to get behind any Welshmen who might be watching the road.

"Unfortunately, in the storm of rain, having no guide, we lost our way; and were so detained, near two days, in the forest. This morning, the weather having changed and the sun come out, we learned the direction that we must take. On the way we fell in with a party of some twenty Welshmen, who pursued us hotly. We outran all but five. As their shouts would have brought large numbers upon us, we stopped and slew them; and though search was hot for us, we succeeded in making our way through, without adventure, until we came out from the forest, close by."

"Truly it was an adventure of great peril," the earl said, "for the Welsh are swarming round us; though we see nought of them, when we are once in the saddle. Assuredly you would never have got through, even as far as Llanidloes, if you had followed the road on horseback; for the last party that came along brought word that the Welsh had felled trees across it, in many places, and had broken down the bridges.

"It was a gallant exploit, sir. I will, myself, take you in to the king."

Oswald took off his jerkin.

"I am but in poor plight to show myself before his majesty," he said, as he handed it to Roger.

"Ah! I remember this good fellow," the earl said. "He is not one easily forgotten, for 'tis seldom one sees so stout a man-at-arms.

"As to your dress, 'tis nought; and indeed, it is in better order than most in camp, for the soldiers have no tents, and have, for the last forty-eight hours, been over their ankles in mud and water.

"Have you been with Mortimer ever since we harried Glendower's valley?"

"No, my lord. I returned after that to the north, and was at Alnwick for nine months. Then Sir Henry sent me back again to Ludlow, in order that I might keep him well informed of the extent of this rebellion, concerning which but few tidings came to him." They had, by this time, arrived at the entrance of the king's tent. The two sentries on duty there stood back and saluted, as the earl entered, followed by Oswald.

"This, sire, is a messenger, one Master Oswald Forster, an esquire of Sir Henry Percy's. He had been sent by his lord to Ludlow, to keep him acquainted with the extent of this rebellion. Some few days since, a royal messenger reached the town, with a letter for you; as doubtless, in London, they cannot have known which way you were marching, and directed it there, so that it might be forwarded to you thence. Sir Edmund, having your royal order not to send any force away, would have been at a loss how to forward it; deeming that it would need a strong body of men-at-arms to penetrate to you, as he knew, from what had happened on the two last expeditions, that the Welsh, being unable to oppose your advance, would swarm behind you, so as to prevent reinforcements or convoys of provisions from reaching you. He was, therefore, doubtful as to what course to adopt, when this gentleman volunteered to carry it to you; and this he has accomplished, attended by but a single follower. Knowing that he could only hope to reach you on foot, he and his man-at-arms left their horses at Welshpool; and have made their way through the woods on foot, not without adventure, having lost their way in the storm, and having slept in the wood for two days, and killed five Welshmen, scarcely escaping a crowd of others as they came in."

"A very gallant deed, sir," the king said to Oswald, as the latter bent upon one knee and handed the letter to him. "By Our Lady, it was no slight thing to venture through the woods, swarming with these wild Welshmen. How long have you been an esquire to Percy?"

"Over three years, sire."

"I met Master Forster at Chester," the earl said. "He commanded a score of Percy's men, and rode with us when we captured Glendower's house. The knights with him told me that he and his little band had done excellent service, in the fight when the Welsh made their first irruption; and that Sir Henry Percy had written in the warmest terms to Mortimer, saying that the gentleman stood high in his regard, and that he had the most perfect confidence in him, and had selected him for the service since he was able to write well, and could, therefore, communicate freely with him as to the troubles on the Welsh border."

"And have you been at Mortimer's ever since that time?" the king asked.

Oswald noticed that each time Mortimer's name was mentioned, the king's brow was somewhat clouded.

"Not so, your majesty. I returned to the north, with Percy's men, a few days after the capture of Glendower's house. I came back to Ludlow in the spring."

"Why did Sir Henry Percy despatch you there again?" the king asked, sharply.

"From what he said, sire, it was because he was anxious to know whether the rebellion was growing, fearing that there might be some correspondence between

Glendower and the Scots; and that, if it should come to a point when you might have to lead the whole force of the south to put the Welsh down, the Scots might make a great irruption into the northern counties, and it would be needful for him to keep a larger body of men than usual under arms; as the earl, his father, and the Earl of Westmoreland, would have to stand the whole brunt of the matter, for a time, without aid from the south."

The king's brow cleared.

"It was a thoughtful act of Sir Henry," he said; "and 'tis like enough that the Scots will, as you say, take advantage of our troubles here; and it is well, therefore, that the Lords of the Northern Marches should hold themselves in readiness.

"What think you, Talbot? It seems to me that the bold service this esquire has performed merits reward."

"I think so, indeed," the earl said. "It was a singular act of courage."

The king drew his sword from his scabbard.

"Kneel, sir," he said.

And, as Oswald knelt, the king laid the sword across his shoulder, and said, "Rise, Sir Oswald Forster."

Oswald rose.

"I thank you, my Lord King," he said, "and trust that I may live for many years to do worthy knightly service to my liege, who has so highly honoured me."

"My lord," the king said to Talbot, "I leave it to you to see that this young knight is provided with horse and armour. Unfortunately there is more than one suit without an owner, at present. You will do well to wait with me while I open this letter; which, maybe, contains matter of moment."

Feeling that his audience was over, Oswald bowed deeply, and left the tent to rejoin Roger.

"What said the king, master?"

"He spoke much more highly of what we had done, Roger, than it deserved; and as a reward for the service, he has just knighted me."

"I think that he has done well, master!" Roger exclaimed, joyously. "I had hoped that Hotspur would have done it, after that adventure with the Bairds; of which, as Alwyn told me, he spoke to him in tones of wondrous praise."

"That was a private business, Roger, and he would know that I would much rather that, when knighthood came, I should receive it for service in the field. The king regards our coming here as a service to himself, and therefore rewarded me; but I would rather that it should have been for service in the field, against the enemy, than for tramping through the forest."

"Yes, but a forest full of Welshmen," Roger said, "who are more to be feared, in that way, than when met in open fight."

"Earl Talbot spoke very kindly of me, and said that he had heard that, with Percy's men, I had done good service in that fight with the Welsh, near Knighton."

"That was certainly pretty hot work, master--I shall get to say Sir Oswald, in time; but at present my tongue is not used to it. What are we to do now?"

"The king asked Lord Talbot to provide me with armour, and a horse; so we must wait until he comes this way."

It was half an hour before the earl came out.

"The letter was of importance," he said, "and it is well that it was brought on.

"Now, Sir Oswald, let us see to your matter. Two days ago Sir William Baxter was killed, by a sudden attack of the Welsh, while he was burning a village. His men rallied, beat off the Welsh, and brought his body in; and methinks his armour will fit you, though he was shorter, by two or three inches, than yourself."

He accompanied Oswald to one of a small group of tents, standing a quarter of a mile farther down the road.

"Is Sir William Baxter's squire here?"

A young man at once came up.

"I was his esquire, my lord."

"I have the king's orders," the earl said, "that his arms, armour, and horses are to be handed over, forthwith, to Sir Oswald Forster here, who will take command of his troop. He will take over all the other belongings of the knight."

The young squire bowed.

"I will hand them over to you, sir."

"You will, of course, take possession of the tent also, Sir Oswald. Sir William was one of my knights. He was unwedded, and has no male kin; therefore, you need have no hesitation in taking his belongings; which indeed we should, in any case, have little chance of taking back with us, for our waggons are but few, and will daily become fewer: for on such roads as these, both waggons and horses break down, and it will be as much as we can do to carry even necessities with us.

"Come to my tent at noon, it lacks but an hour of it, and I will present you at dinner to some of my knights; among whom, for the present, I shall rank you."

So saying, he turned away. The young squire held open the entrance of the tent, for Oswald to enter, and followed him in.

"It seems a strange thing to be thus possessed of another man's goods," he said.

"It is often so," the squire said, "and sometimes even his estates go with them, also. As the earl said, Sir William Baxter had none to whom these things could have been given; seeing that he had, so far as I know, only one sister, to whom armour and horses could be of no use. She is one of the Countess of Talbot's ladies."

"And what are you going to do, yourself?"

"For the present, I know not," the squire said. "I had been with Sir William Baxter but three years. The knight I served with, before, was thrown from his horse and killed; and Sir William, who had been just knighted, took me into his service."

"How long have you been a squire?"

"Six years, and I hoped that, in this campaign, I might have done something to win my spurs."

"I am but a poor knight, Master--" and he paused.

"Henry Pemberton," the squire said.

"And being but knighted today, and having no lands to keep up my knighthood, it may be that the earl will appoint you to another of his knights; but should he not do so, I shall be glad if, for the rest of this campaign, you will ride with me; and trust that you, too, may have an opportunity of gaining knighthood, before it is over. But whether or no, as soon as we cross the border again, I doubt not that you will be able to find some lord under whom you may gain advancement."

"I will gladly do so, Sir Oswald. 'Tis strange that I should not have seen your face before; for, since we left Worcester, I have come to know the greater part of the esquires here."

"I arrived but an hour ago," Oswald replied, "having made my way through the Welsh, on foot, with that tall fellow you saw without."

"That was a dangerous deed, truly," Pemberton said, in tones of surprise. "May I ask why you essayed so perilous a feat?"

"I was the bearer of a despatch for the king. I was an esquire to Sir Henry

Percy, but have for some time been staying with his brother-in-law, Sir Edmund Mortimer.

"Had Sir William a man-at-arms, who served as his servant? For I shall make my man-at-arms, who has gone through many adventures with me, has fought by my side, and saved my life, my second squire."

"Yes, a very good and trusty fellow."

"Then of course I shall keep him on. Now, will you tell my man to come in?

"Roger," he said, "You doubtless heard the earl's words, and I am now master of this tent, together with the armour, horses, and clothes of Sir William Baxter. Master Henry Pemberton will act as my squire, during the campaign. You will be my second squire."

"Well, master, I never looked so high as to become an esquire; and would rather remain a simple man-at-arms, were it not that it will keep me near you."

"You will find Roger a good comrade, Master Pemberton. He has been a man-at-arms at his own choice; for, as he can read and write as well as any clerk, he might have done better for himself."

Pemberton looked, with some surprise, at Roger. He himself had not these accomplishments, and he was surprised at finding a man-at-arms so well endowed.

"As you may tell by his speech," Oswald went on, "he is, like myself, a Northumbrian; and has done good service in the wars with the Scots."

"That I can well imagine," the squire said, with a smile. "I would certainly wish for no stouter comrade."

"We must see about arms and armour for you, Roger," Oswald said.

"There will be no difficulty about that. None whatever, Sir Oswald. We have lost fully three hundred men, since we crossed the border, and a hundred and fifty since we came here, four days since. There is a pile of harness and arms, lying by the roadside; and there, methinks, it is likely it will lie. You have but to go with him, when you have attired yourself and buckled on spurs, and you can pick and choose among it. Assuredly, no one will gainsay you."

Oswald now changed his attire. The clothes were handsome, and fitted him well. Then he buckled on the golden spurs, put on the knightly armour--for he had observed that the earl, and the knights that he had seen in the camp, all kept on full armour, being ever in expectation of sudden attack.

"Truly you make a handsome figure, Sir Oswald," said Roger, who had been assisting him. "Little did I think, when I used to rail at you at your books, that you would grow into so stalwart a man; and that I should follow you in the field, as your squire. Your armour fits you as if made for you, save that these cuishes scarce meet your body armour. In truth, though bad for him, it was lucky for you that the master of this tent came to his death when he did."

"I like a steel cap better than this helmet, though I say not that it looks so well."

"Not by a long way," Roger said. "Nought could become you better. What cognizance do you mean to take?"

"I have not thought about it, yet. There will be time enough for that, after the war is over."

"Well, at any rate, master, I will today set about getting Sir William Baxter's off the shield. Methinks that, with some sand from the river bed, I shall be able to manage it with an hour's rubbing."

"Now, come along, Roger. There is no time to be lost, for I dine at midday with the Earl of Talbot. Master Pemberton will show us where the armour is lying."

There was, indeed, a large pile.

Oswald then said, "As you are known, Master Pemberton, you had better stop here; for it will take some picking before Roger is suited. As it is but two minutes to twelve, I must hurry back to Lord Talbot's tent."

Some seven or eight knights were already there. Lord Talbot introduced him to them and, as they dined, Oswald related, at their request, more particularly how he had got through the Welsh--a task that seemed to them well-nigh impossible, since the soldiers dared not venture even to the edge of the forest, so thickly were the Welsh posted there.

"That man-at-arms must be a stalwart fellow, indeed," said one, "to kill three Welshmen with nought but a quarterstaff."

"If you had seen the man, and the staff, Sir Victor, you would not be surprised," Lord Talbot said. "He stands some six feet four, and has shoulders that might rival Samson's. As to his quarterstaff, I marked it. It was of oak, and full two inches across; and a blow with it, from such arms, would crack an iron casque, to say nothing of a Welsh skull."

Chapter 18: Glendower.

For the next ten days the weather was so bad that no operations could be carried on. Every little stream was swollen to a raging torrent. Horses, carrying men in full armour, could scarce keep their feet on the slippery moor; and even the footmen had the greatest difficulty in getting about; and all excursions were given up, for the Welsh, barefooted and unweighted with armour, would have been able to fall upon them to great advantage, and could then evade pursuit, with ease.

The number of sick increased rapidly, and it became necessary to send another convoy back to Llanidloes; where the guard were to join the force that had gone there, ten days before, and to escort some waggons of flour and a number of cattle, that had been brought there from Welshpool by a strong levy from Shropshire.

Ten knights, a hundred mounted men-at-arms, as many on foot, and fifty archers were considered sufficient to escort the sick; who, to the number of two hundred, were closely packed in the ten waggons that were to return with flour. Three of Lord Talbot's knights were to form part of the escort, and among these Oswald was chosen by the earl.

It was hoped that the convoy would reach the town without being attacked, for great pains had been taken to prevent the news of its approaching departure getting about; for there were many Welshmen in the camp, employed in looking after the baggage animals, and in other offices. They had all been hired for the service on the other side of the border; but it was believed that some of them, at least, must be in communication with the enemy; who were thereby enabled to gather in force, to oppose any parties who sallied out from the camp.

The consequence was that, until half an hour before it left, none save a few of the leaders were aware of the starting of the convoy. Then orders were rapidly issued. The knights and men-at-arms who had been selected for the service had but a few minutes to prepare themselves. The horses were harnessed to the waggons, and the sick and wounded carried out and placed in them, with the greatest expedition, and the party set out in less than half an hour after the first order had been given. It had gone but a quarter of a mile when the shouts among the woods, on either side, showed that the Welsh were vigilant. Horns were blown in all directions, the sound growing fainter and fainter, in the hills.

"We shall not get through undisturbed," one of the knights said to Oswald, who was riding next to him.

"No, I think we shall have fighting. It would have been better had we and the men-at-arms been told to leave our horses behind. In this deep soil they will be of little use in a fight, and we should do better on foot."

"It would be terrible, marching in our heavy armour."

"Doubtless it would have been so, but I should not have minded that. The distance is but six miles; and although, in this slippery plain, the toil would have been great, methinks that we could have made a better fight than on horseback; and as these waggons travel but slowly, we could have kept up with them."

"We can dismount, if necessary," the knight said; "but, for my part, I would rather ride than tramp through this deep mud."

Their progress was indeed slow, the waggons frequently sank almost up to their axles in the mud, and it needed all the efforts of the dismounted men to get them out. A deep silence had succeeded the outcry in the woods.

"I like not this silence, Sir Oswald," the knight said; when, after an hour's hard work, they were still but two miles from the camp.

"Nor do I," Oswald said. "It seems unnatural. Do you not think, Sir William, that it would be well if all were to take the picket ropes from their horses' necks, and knot them two and two, fastening one end to a waggon and the other to a horse's girth. In that way fifty men-at-arms might be roped on to the waggons, and would aid those drawing them, greatly."

"The idea is a very good one," the knight said.

He rode forward to Sir Eustace de Bohun, who was in command, and informed him of Oswald's suggestion, which was at once adopted. As soon as it was carried out, the dismounted men were ordered to push behind the waggons, which now proceeded at a much faster rate than before.

They were just half-way to the town, and beginning to entertain hopes that they should get through without being attacked, when a horn sounded; and from the forest on both sides, a crowd of men rushed out, and poured a volley of arrows into the convoy. Hasty orders were shouted by Sir Eustace, the ropes were thrown off, and the troops formed up in a double line on each side of the waggons.

The knights and mounted men formed the outside line, and the footmen stood a pace or two behind them; so as to cover them from attack, should the Welsh break through. Oswald's esquire was on one side of him, Roger on the other.

The waggons continued to move forward, for at this point the road was better, running across a bare rock, and the horses were therefore able to draw them along without any assistance. Sir Eustace therefore gave the order for the escort to continue their way, marching on each side of the train.

"We must fight our way through, men," he shouted; "every minute will doubtless add to their numbers."

For a short time the arrows flew fast. But the Welsh bows were not to be compared, in point of strength, with those used by the English archers; and the arrows fell harmlessly upon the armour of the men-at-arms, while on the other hand, the English archers shot so strongly and truly that, after a short time, the Welsh bowmen fell back. As they did so, however, a crowd of footmen poured out from the forest; and, with loud shouts and yells, rushed forward.

"Halt the waggons!" Sir Eustace cried. "Keep good order, men, and we shall soon drive this rabble off."

The archers had time but to send three flights of arrows among their assailants, when these threw themselves upon the line. They were armed with short axes, heavy clubs, and other rough weapons; and for a time, the horsemen kept their order and beat them back; but as the horns continued to sound, the Welsh swarmed down in such numbers that they broke in between their mounted foes; some trying to tear them from their saddles, while others crept beneath the horses and drove their long knives into their stomachs, or tried to hamstring them with their axes.

Then the dismounted men-at-arms joined in the fight, and drove the enemy back beyond the line. Many of the horsemen were, however, dismounted. These joined their mounted comrades when Sir Eustace gave the word to charge the multitude, before they could rally for a fresh attack.

The Welsh went down in numbers before their lances, but so close was the throng that the horsemen were brought to a stand and, slinging their spears behind them, betook themselves to sword and mace. Great was the slaughter of their opponents, but these pursued their former tactics. Horse after horse rolled over in mortal agony and, as they fell, the riders were stabbed before they could recover their feet. Soon they were broken up into knots; and their dismounted companions, with one accord, left the waggons and rushed into the fray, for a time beating back the Welsh.

"It were best to dismount," Oswald cried, and he swung himself from the saddle, just as one of the enemy hamstrung his horse. Roger and the squire did the same, and joined the ranks of the footmen.

"Keep together!" Oswald shouted, to those within hearing; "we can cut ourselves a passage through, in that way, while separately we shall perish."

Ten or twelve men followed his orders and, gathering in a ring, for a time beat off every attack. Looking round, Oswald saw that scarce a man remained mounted. The shouts of the English, and the wild war cries of the Welsh, rang through the air. In a dozen places fierce contests were raging--swords and axes rose and fell, on helmet and steel cap.

In obedience to the shouts of Sir Eustace, who, with three or four men-at-arms around him, was still mounted, the English bands tried to join each other, and in several cases succeeded. Oswald had been near the rear of the convoy when the fight began, and the party with whom he fought were separated by some distance from the others, and the prospect became more and more hopeless. His squire had fallen, and fully half the men who had joined him; and although the loss of the Welsh had been many times as great, the number of their assailants had in no way diminished.

He and Roger strove, in vain, to cut a way through; and their height and strength enabled them to maintain a forward movement, their opponents shrinking from the terrible blows of Roger's mace, and the no less destructive fall of Oswald's sword; but the men-at-arms behind them fared worse, having to retreat with their face to the foe; and more than one, falling over the bodies of those slain by their leaders, were stabbed before they could rise. Several times the two men turned and covered the rear, but at last they stood alone.

"Now, make one effort to break through, Roger;" and they flung themselves with such fury upon the Welsh that, for some twenty yards, they cut their way through them.

Then Roger exclaimed, "I am done for, master," and fell.

Oswald stood over him and, for a time, kept a clear circle; then he received a tremendous blow on the back of his helmet, with a heavy club, and fell prostrate over Roger.

When he recovered his senses, the din of battle had moved far away. The other groups had gathered together and, moving down, had joined those who still resisted on the other side of the road; and, keeping in a close body, were fighting their way steadily along.

A number of the Welsh were going over the battlefield, stabbing all whom they found to be still living. The sick men in the waggons had already been murdered.

A Welshman, whose appearance denoted a higher rank than the others, approached Oswald, as soon as he sat up, and called to four or five of his countrymen. Oswald, with difficulty, rose to his feet. He still wore, round his wrist, the chain that Glendower's daughter had given him; and he now pulled this off and held it up, loudly calling out the name of Glendower, several times. The Welsh leader waved his followers back.

Oswald was unarmed, and evidently incapable of defending himself. He came up to him. Oswald held out the chain:

"Glendower, Glendower," he repeated.

The man took the chain, and examined it carefully. Some Welsh words were engraved upon the clasp. Oswald was unaware what they were, but the words were, "Jane Glendower, from her father."

The Welshman looked much surprised, and presently called to another, some distance away. The man came up, and he spoke to him in Welsh.

"How did you obtain this?" the man asked Oswald, in English.

"It was given in token of service, rendered by me and my squire here, to Glendower's daughter. She told me that it would be of service if, at any time, I were taken prisoner by her father's followers."

This was translated to the Welshman, who said:

"These men must be taken to Glendower. The story may be true, or not. The chain may have been stolen. At any rate, the prince must decide as to their fate."

He now bade the men round him take off Oswald's armour. As soon as this was done, the latter knelt down by Roger's side, and removed his helmet.

An arrow, shot from behind, had struck Roger just above the back piece--which, being short for him, did not reach to his helmet--and had gone through the fleshy part of his neck; while, at the same moment, a blow with an axe had cleft the helmet in sunder, and inflicted a deep gash on the back of the head.

At a word from their leader, the men at once aided Oswald, who drew out the arrow. The wound bled but slightly, and one of the Welshmen, tearing off a portion of his garment, bandaged it up. Water was fetched from the stream below, and a pad of wet cloth laid on the wound at the back of the head, and kept in its place by bandages. As this was done Roger gave a faint groan and, a minute after, opened his eyes.

"Do not try to move, Roger," Oswald said. "You are wounded; but not, I trust, to death. We are prisoners in the hands of the Welsh, but that chain Glendower's daughter gave me has saved our lives."

A rough litter was constructed of boughs. On this Roger, after his armour had been taken off, was laid. At their leader's orders six Welshmen took it up, while two placed themselves, one on each side of Oswald. Then the leader took the head of the party, and moved away into the forest.

Oswald's head still swam from the effects of the blow, but as they went on the feeling gradually ceased, and he was able to keep up with his captors. Their course was ever uphill, and after an hour's walking they arrived at a farmhouse, situated just at the upper edge of the forest.

The litter was laid down outside the house. The Welshman went in, saying something to his men, who at once sat down on the ground; for the journey, with Roger's weight, had been a toilsome one. He made signs for Oswald to seat himself by the side of Roger. The latter was now perfectly sensible.

"What has happened, master?" he asked.

"We have been badly beaten, Roger; but when I last saw them our men had got together, and were fighting their way along the road. I fancy more than half have been killed; but, as far as I could see of the field, I should say that three or four times as many Welsh had fallen."

"That was a lucky thought of yours, Sir Oswald, about that chain."

"I had always an idea that it might be found useful; and it at once occurred to me, as soon as I recovered my senses."

"Are you wounded, too?" Roger asked anxiously.

"No. I was beaten down by a heavy club, and my head still rings from the blow. Otherwise, I am uninjured."

"What has happened to me, master?"

"You had an arrow through your neck, Roger; but fortunately it was on one side. An inch to the right, and it would have struck your spine, or perhaps gone through your windpipe. As it is, it does not seem to have done much harm. Very little blood flowed when I pulled the arrow out. You have got a bad gash on the back of the head, but your head piece broke the force of the blow. It has laid your skull bare, but has not, so far as I can see, penetrated it."

"Then we need think no more about it," Roger said.

"Well, that was a fight! The one we had at Knighton was as nothing to it."

"Yes, I think that even you could not want a harder one, Roger."

"No; this was quite enough for one day's work. I should like a drink of water, if I could get one."

Oswald made signs to one of the men, who went into the house and returned with a large jug of water, of which Roger took a deep draught; and Oswald then finished the contents, for he, too, was parched with thirst.

Half an hour later a tall man, in full armour, followed by a number of Welsh chiefs, issued from the forest. He was some five-and-forty years old, and of noble presence. The leader of the party who had brought Oswald up advanced to meet him; and, saluting him most respectfully, spoke to him for a moment, and then produced the chain. Glendower--for it was the prince--examined it, and then at once walked up to Oswald, who had risen to his feet.

"How became you possessed of this, Sir Knight?"

"It was given me by one of your daughters, sir. I and my squire, here, were on guard round your house, on the night after the Earl of Talbot took it. We were at some distance from the other guards, when two figures rose from the bushes near us. We pursued them and, coming up to them, found they were two ladies; and they at once avowed that they were your daughters. My instructions were to watch and see that no Welshmen approached the house; and nought had been said to me of arresting any leaving it, seeing that it was not supposed that any were there.

"I war not with women. Being myself from Northumbria, I have no enmity with your people. Therefore I let them proceed on their way--a breach of duty for which, doubtless, I should have suffered, had it been known. Happily, none but my follower here, who was then but a man-at-arms, and I a squire, knew of it; and to this moment I have spoken of it to no one. As they left us, one of the ladies gave me this chain, saying that some day it might be of use to me, should I ever fall into the hands of their people. I have carried it on my wrist, ever since; and when your follower came up, and I saw the necessity had arisen, I showed it to him."

"I have heard the story from my daughters," Glendower said warmly, holding out his hand. "They told me how courteously you had treated them, and that you had refused to accept the jewels they offered you. They said that you had also declined to tell them your name, as it might do you injury, should it become known; and I have often regretted that I did not know the name of the gentleman who had behaved so nobly to them, and had saved them from an English prison. Had they been captured, it would have been a sore blow to me, not only in my affections but to my cause; for, had he held them in his power, Henry could have put a heavy pressure upon me. May I ask, now, what is your name, Sir Knight?"

"Sir Oswald Forster. I was, at that time, a squire of Sir Henry Percy's."

"Of Hotspur!" Glendower said, in surprise. "I did not know that we had levies from the north fighting against us."

"You have not, sir. I had simply been sent, with twenty men-at-arms, by Sir Henry to Sir Edmund Mortimer--who is, as you are doubtless aware, of kin to Sir Henry, who had married his sister--and was sent by Sir Edmund to join the Earl of Talbot and Lord Grey, when they made that foray upon your house. After that I returned to the north; but was, some months since, again sent to Ludlow, to keep Sir Henry informed of the doings on this border."

"But I had heard that Mortimer had sent no troops to Henry's army."

"That is so, sir. I am here by an accident. A despatch came from London to Ludlow for the king, and as there was no other way of forwarding it, I volunteered to carry it here, and succeeded in doing so: for which service the king conferred knighthood upon me, upon my arrival, ten days since."

"Ah, then, it was you that I heard of! I was told that two great men had been seen in the woods, some distance south of the camp; and that they had succeeded in making their escape, after slaying five of my followers; and that, though none knew for certain, it was supposed they had reached Henry's camp."

"You are right, sir. The two men were my companion, here, and myself."

"It was a notable feat. I think not that any other messenger has got through my scouts, since the king left Welshpool. You must be swift of foot, as well as brave and courteous; for I heard that you had outrun the greatest part of those who followed you."

"We in the north have to be swift of foot," Oswald said, with a smile, "for the Scots keep us in practice; either in escaping them, when they come in too great a force to be resisted; or in following them, when it is our turn to pursue.

"I trust, sir, that you will put myself and my squire to ransom, and will take my word for the payment; for, until I go north, I have no means of satisfying it."

"That will I not," Glendower said. "Or rather, I will take a ransom; since, were I to release you without one, it might cause surprise and inquiry; and it were well that your noble conduct to my daughters should not be known, for Henry would not be likely to regard it favourably. Therefore we will put you to ransom at the sum of a crown for yourself, and a penny for your squire."

"I thank you, indeed, sir, and shall ever feel beholden to you; and I will, moreover, give you my knightly word that, whatever service I may have to perform, I will never again war with the Welsh.

"May I ask if any of our party succeeded in reaching Llanidloes?"

"Yes, some sixty or seventy of them got in. They fought very well; and indeed, in close combat my Welshmen cannot, at present, hold their own against your armour-clad men. Still, though it would have pleased me better had we annihilated the force, our success has been sufficient to give Henry another lesson that, though he may march through Wales, he holds only the ground on which he has encamped.

"Now, Sir Oswald, I pray you to enter my abode. 'Tis a poor place, indeed, after my house in the Vale of the Bards; but it suffices for my needs."

Before entering, he gave orders that Roger should be carried to an upper room, and despatched a messenger to order his own leech, as soon as he had done with the wounded, to come up and attend to him. Then he led the way into a room, where a meal was prepared. In a few words in Welsh he explained to his chiefs, who had been much surprised at the manner in which he had received Oswald, that the young knight had, at one time, rendered a great service to his daughters, Jane and Margaret; but without mentioning its precise nature. His experience had taught him that even those most attached to his cause might yet turn against him; and were they to relate the story, it might do serious injury to Oswald.

"You must, on your way back," he said presently to the young knight, "call and see my daughters; who are at present staying with their sister, who is married to Adda ap Iorwerth Ddu. They would be aggrieved, indeed, if they heard that you had been here, and that I had not given them the opportunity of thanking you, in person."

Oswald remained for a fortnight with Glendower, while Roger's wound was healing. At the end of that time he learned that Henry, having marched into Cardigan and ravaged the country there, was already retiring; his army having suffered terribly from the effects of the weather, the impossibility of obtaining supplies, and the constant and harassing attacks by the Welsh.

Glendower was often absent, but when at the house he conversed freely with Oswald, who was no longer surprised at the influence that he had obtained over his countrymen. His manners were courteous in the extreme, and his authority over his followers absolute. They not only reverenced him as their prince, the representative of their ancient kings, and their leader in war, but as one endowed with supernatural power.

The bards had fanned this feeling to the utmost, by their songs of marvels and portents at his birth, and by attributing to him a control even over the elements. This belief was not only of great importance to him, as binding his adherents closer to him; but it undoubtedly contributed to his success, from the fact of its being fully shared in by the English soldiery; who assigned it as the cause of the exceptionally bad weather that had been experienced, in each of the three expeditions into the country, and of the failure to accomplish anything of importance against him.

This side of the character of Glendower puzzled Oswald. Several times, when talking to him, he distinctly claimed supernatural powers; and from the tone in which he spoke, and the strange expression his face at this time assumed, Oswald was convinced that he sincerely believed that he did possess these powers. Whether he originally did so; or whether it had arisen from the adulation of the bards, the general belief in it, and the successes he had gained; Oswald could not determine. Later, when Glendower sullied his fair fame by the most atrocious massacres, similar to that which had already taken place at the storming of New Radnor--atrocities that seemed not only purposeless, but at utter variance with the courtesy and gentleness of his bearing--Oswald came to believe that his brain had, to some extent, become unhinged by excitement, flattery, and superstition.

At the end of the fortnight Roger's wound, although not completely healed, was in such a state that it permitted his sitting on horseback, and Oswald became anxious to be off. Glendower, who was about to set out to harass the rear of the army, as it retired from Cardiganshire, at once offered to send a strong escort with him; as it would have been dangerous, in the extreme, to have attempted to traverse the country without such a protection. Two excellent horses, that had been captured in the engagement with the English, were handed over to him, for his own use and that of Roger. Oswald's own armour was returned to him, and he was pleased to find that it had been carefully attended to, and was as brightly burnished as when it came into his possession.

When Glendower bid them adieu, he presented each of them with rings, similar to those he himself wore.

"You have promised that you will not fight against me again; but it may be that, on some errand or other, you may ride into Wales; or that you may be staying, as you did before, at some castle or town near the border, when we attack it. You have but to show these rings to any Welshman you may come across, and you may be sure of being well treated, as one of my friends.

"I trust that, when we meet again, the war will be over; and that my title to the kingdom of Wales may be recognized, by your king and people, as it is on this side of the border."

"Well, Sir Oswald," Roger said, as they rode away, accompanied by twenty of Glendower's followers, under the orders of an officer; "we have got out of that scrape better than could have been expected. When you and I were alone, in the midst of that crowd of Welshmen, I thought that it was all over with us."

"So did I, Roger. You see, that matter of our getting Glendower's daughters away, uninjured, has borne good fruit."

"It has indeed," Roger agreed. "I thought it much more likely, too, that it would have gone the other way."

"Be sure you keep a silent tongue as to that, Roger; and remember that our story is, that I have been put at knightly ransom, and on the condition that I will never serve in Wales again. When we once get across the border we will ride straight for Northumberland, without going near Ludlow. I observed that the king much doubted the Mortimers, and were we to return there, and the news came to his ears, he might take it as a proof that there was an understanding between Glendower and Mortimer; and that it was to this that leniency, such as had been shown to no other prisoners, was due; whereas, if we go straight to Percy, 'tis not likely that the matter will ever come to his hearing, and at any rate, if it did so, he would scarce connect Mortimer with our escape."

"I understand, Sir Oswald; and will, you may be sure, keep silent as to aught beyond what you have bade me say."

Two days' journey brought them to the house of Glendower's married daughter. On the officer stating that the knight with him had been sent, under his escort, by Glendower himself, she requested that he should be shown in. Her husband was away.

"What is the knight's name?" she asked.

"Sir Oswald Forster, Lady."

"I have never, so far as I know, heard it before. Methought that he might be one whom I may have met, in the houses of my two sisters married to Englishmen, in Hereford; but I have no memory of the name. Show him in, sir."

Roger had removed Oswald's helmet, while the officer was away.

"Come with me, Roger," he said, "since we were both concerned in this affair."

He bowed deeply to the Lady Isabel; who, as she returned his salute, saw with surprise that his face was quite strange to her.

"It seems, Sir Oswald," she said, "from the tenor of the message given me by the officer, that you have come to me as a visitor; and that 'tis as an escort, only, that he has been sent with you?"

"That is so, Lady; but 'tis as a visitor rather to your sisters, the Ladies Jane and Margaret, that I am here. I had, once, the pleasure of meeting them."

Glendower's daughter at once told a maid, who was working with her when the officer had entered, to request her sisters to come to her; and these entered the room a minute later.

Isabel, seeing that they did not appear to recognize the young knight, said:

"Our father has sent this gentleman, Sir Oswald Forster, whom you know, to visit you."

The two girls looked with surprise at Oswald.

"Do you not know this gentleman?" their sister asked, in equal surprise.

"He is not known to us," Jane replied. "I have never seen him before--at least, that I can remember."

"We have met before, nevertheless, Lady," Oswald said, with a smile; "though it may well be that you do not remember my face, or that of my squire there; seeing that we were together but a few minutes, and that in the moonlight."

The girls looked up at him puzzled, and then their eyes fell upon Roger.

"Now I know!" Margaret exclaimed. "Look at the squire's height. Surely, Jane, these are the two soldiers who allowed us to pass them, that night when we fled from Sycharth."

"That is so," Oswald said. "I thought that you were more likely to recognize my squire than myself, seeing that I have grown several inches since then, and have but lately assumed this knightly armour in which you see me."

"Oh, sir," Jane said, going swiftly up to him and holding out her hand, which he raised to his lips; as he did that of Margaret, as she followed her sister; "we have thought of you so often, and have prayed that you should both be rewarded for your kindness to us! How glad I am to see you again, and have an opportunity of thanking you!

"You have heard, Isabel, of our adventure, and how we escaped, by the kindness of two Englishmen on guard near the edge of the forest, from being carried as prisoners to London; where, but for them, we should now be lodged in some dungeon of the usurper; but till now, I have never known the name of our preserver."

"Thanks also to you, good squire," she said, turning to Roger.

"I but carried out the orders of my master," Roger said, colouring like a boy, as she held out her hand to him. "There is no credit due to me."

"But how came you here?" Lady Isabel asked Oswald.

"Your sisters have, although they know it not, more than repaid their obligations to me; for while they may perhaps owe their liberty to me, I owe my life to them.

"See, ladies," and he turned to Jane, "there is the chain you gave me. I have worn it, always, on my wrist. I and my squire were beaten down by, your father's followers; my squire grievously wounded and insensible, while I had been left for dead, though but stunned from a blow. I luckily recovered my senses, just as those employed in despatching the wounded came up; and, happily remembering your bracelet, I took it off and held it up, calling out your father's name.

"Struck, I suppose, by the action and words, an officer examined the bracelet closely; and, making out the inscription on the clasp, had my squire and myself taken to the house where your father lodged, so that the manner of my being possessed of the trinket might be explained. On your father's return he recognized it; and, having heard from you the circumstances of our meeting, treated us with the greatest kindness and hospitality; and freed us without ransom, save a nominal one in order that, on my return, I could say that I had been put to ransom. On the recovery of my squire from his wounds, he restored our armour to us, presented us with horses, and sent us here under escort, deeming that you might be glad to see us."

"There he was indeed right," Jane said. "We have oft regretted that you would not accept a more valuable jewel than that little chain, which was given to me by my father, when I was but a child. But 'tis well, indeed, that you so withstood us; for had it been any other of our jewels but this, it would not have been recognized."

"That is so, Lady and, since my capture, I often thought that it was strange it so happened."

After staying a day there, Oswald continued his journey; to the regret of the ladies, who were glad to hear that he would never again fight against the Welsh. His escort accompanied him, as near the border as it was safe for them to go. The next day they rode into Chester, and then, by easy stages, up to Alnwick.

Oswald went to Hotspur's apartments, as soon as he entered the castle.

"I congratulate you heartily," Hotspur said, as he entered. "I see that you have won your spurs. I said to myself, when I received your letter, saying that you were starting to carry a letter to the king, that your enterprise would bring you either death or a pair of gold spurs. I am glad, indeed, to see that it was the latter.

"I hear that the king's army is falling back. A messenger brought me news from my kinsman. He said that it was but a rumour that had reached him; but that it seemed likely enough, for it was said that they had suffered terribly, both from the weather and the attacks of the Welsh."

"That rumour is true, Sir Henry, and also that the army is retiring."

"And they have done no more than they did before?"

"No more, indeed, Sir Henry. They have burnt many villages, and slain many Welshmen; but they have done nothing, whatever, towards subduing Glendower."

Chapter 19: The Battle Of Homildon Hill.

But how have you made your way back, ahead of the army?" Hotspur asked, after Oswald had given him full information as to the military operations.

"Roger and I were left for dead, in that fight I have told you of, near Llanidloes; and we fell into the hands of the Welsh, and were taken before Glendower, who treated us well, and put me to ransom, with the engagement that I was not again to bear arms, in Wales."

"That was a strange leniency, on his part," Hotspur exclaimed; "for I hear he puts to the sword all who fall into his hands, without any regard for the rules of civilized war."

"He is a strange man, Sir Henry, and subject, I fancy, to changeable moods. When I was brought before him he was in a happy one, over the success he had gained; and it may be that he took a liking for me. At any rate, he fixed my ransom at a very small sum."

"Which I will, of course, pay," Hotspur said, "since you were my squire, and were at Ludlow on my service."

"I thank you much, Sir Henry, but 'tis so small a sum that I myself discharged it, without difficulty."

"'Tis strange, most strange, that you should have gone into the lion's den, and have come out unscathed. Strange, indeed, that Glendower, who, as we know, is greatly in want of money, should have fixed your ransom at a low sum. How much was it, Sir Oswald?"

"I will tell you the story, Sir Henry, though I would tell no one else; for my freedom is due to something that happened, nigh two years ago, when I was first with Sir Edmund Mortimer. I failed in what was my strict duty, although I disobeyed no orders that I had received, and my conscience altogether acquits me of wrong."

"You may be sure, Sir Oswald, that the matter will go no further; and knowing you as I do, I feel sure that, whatever the matter was, it was not to your discredit."

"So I trust, myself, my lord; but it might have cost me my head, had the king come to know it. I will first tell you that my ransom was fixed at a crown, and that of Roger at a penny."

Hotspur, who had been looking a little grave, laughed.

"Surely never before was so much bone and sinew appraised at so small a sum."

"It was so put, simply that I might, with truth, avow that I was put to ransom. However, I paid the crown and the penny, and have so discharged my obligations.

"This was how the matter came about;" and he related the whole circumstances to Sir Henry; and the manner in which the little chain, given to him by Glendower's daughter, had been the means of saving his life.

"I blame you in no way, Sir Oswald," Hotspur said cordially, when he had heard the story; "though I say not that the king would have viewed the matter in the same light. Still, you held to the letter of your orders. You were placed there to give warning of the approach of any hostile body, and naught was said to you as to letting any man, still less any women, depart from the place. But indeed, how could I blame you? Since heaven itself has assoiled you. For assuredly it was not chance that placed on your arm the little trinket that, alone, could have saved your life from the Welsh.

"Now to yourself, Sir Oswald. You will, I hope, continue my knight, as you have been my squire."

"Assuredly, Sir Henry, I have never thought of anything else."

"Very well, then; I will, as soon as may be, appoint to you a double knight's feu. I say a double feu, because I should like to have you as one of the castle knights, and so have much larger service from you, than that which a knight can be called upon to render, for an ordinary feu. I will bid Father Ernulf look through the rolls, and see what feus are vacant. One of these I will make an hereditary feu, to pass down from you to your heirs, irrevocably; the other will be a service feu, to support the expenses caused by your extra services, and revocable under the usual conditions."

A week later there was a formal ceremonial at the castle, and in the presence of the earl, Hotspur, and the knights and gentlemen of their service, Oswald took the oath of allegiance to Sir Henry Percy; and afterwards, as required by law, to the king; and received from Hotspur deeds appointing him to two knight's feus, including the villages of Stoubes and Rochester, in Reddesdale. There were, at the time, six knight's feus vacant; and as Percy had left it to him to choose which he liked, he had selected these, as they lay but a twelve miles' ride, over the hills, from his father's place in Coquetdale.

The oath of allegiance to the king, as well as to the feudal lord, was enacted by Henry the Second; with the intention of curbing, to some extent, the power of the great vassals; but although taken by all knights, on being presented with a feu, it was deemed of no effect in the case of the immediate lord being at war with the king; and whenever troubles arose, the lord's vassals always sided with him, it being universally understood that the oath to him, from whom they had received their land, was paramount over that to the king.

There having been several formalities to be observed, and matters to be discussed, Oswald was unable to ride home until after this ceremony had taken place; but upon the following morning he and Roger started early, and arrived, that evening, at Yardhope. His welcome was a warm one, and the satisfaction of his father, and the delight of his mother, at seeing him in knightly armour was great, indeed; and it increased when he told them that he had received knighthood at the hands of the king himself, and that Hotspur had granted him the feus of Stoubes and Rochester.

"Then we shall have you within a ride of us," his mother exclaimed. "That will be pleasant, indeed."

"The feus have always gone together," John Forster said, "and Stoubes castle, although small, is a strong one. How many tenants will you have?"

"Twenty-three. That, at least, was the number of names set down in the parchments."

"That is not bad, as a beginning. Of course, you will keep some ten or twelve retainers in the castle; and with such men as will come in from the villages, at the approach of danger, you will be able to muster fifty or sixty in all for the defence."

"I shall live chiefly at Alnwick, Father. Rochester is given to me as an hereditary feu, but I shall hold Stoubes for extra service at the castle; and I have little doubt that Percy will, if I do him good service, make it also hereditary. He as much as said so."

"It will make a good portion, lad. Yardhope is a knight's feu, though I have never taken up the knighthood; and the Percys know that I should fight just as stoutly, as John Forster, as if I wore knightly armour; but though the lands are wide they are poor, while yours are fertile, lying down by the river. Moreover, Coquetdale is more liable to Scotch incursions than Reddesdale, as the road into Scotland runs along it. If needs be we can lend a hand to each other; though, both together, we could not hold either your place or mine against a strong invasion.

"Now, tell us how it was that you won your spurs; and how it was that the king, himself, knighted you."

"After I have eaten and drank I will do so, Father; for indeed, Roger and I are well-nigh famishing."

After the meal, he related the whole story of his adventures.

"Well, lad, you were in luck," his father said, when he had finished. "The help you gave those maidens might have brought your head to the block; but it turned out well, and was the saving of your life, so I will say nought against the deed; especially as you owed no allegiance either to Mortimer or to Talbot, and were, save for the orders that Hotspur had given you, your own master."

Two days later, having sent over, on the morning after his arrival, a message to the tenants to present themselves at Stoubes to take their oaths to him, Oswald, accompanied by his father, rode into Reddesdale. He found the castle a much stronger place than Yardhope, which was but a fortified house; while this was a moated building, with strong walls and flanking towers, and a keep that could be held successfully, even if the walls were captured by a sudden assault.

At twelve o'clock the tenants assembled. Oswald read to them the two parchments, and they then took the oaths to him. They were well satisfied to have a young knight as their lord; for the feus had been held by a minor, who had died two years before; and had not been at the castle since he was taken away, as a child, to be brought up at the town of Alnwick, where he had remained under the eye of the Percys. It had long been understood, however, that the feu would not be granted to him; for he was weakly from his birth, and wholly unfitted for the charge of a castle, so near the Scottish border.

According to feudal usage, each tenant expected that he would be called upon to pay a heavy sum, under the name of a relief, as was customary in the case of a new lord taking possession; and they were greatly relieved when Oswald told them that, as he already possessed armour and horses, he would quit them for a fourth part of the usual amount; although he should, of course, require their services to enable him to repair such dilapidations as the castle had suffered, during the long term that it had stood empty.

For the next three months, he stayed in Stoubes. Roger had been sent off at once, with two men-at-arms, to bring the horses and armour that had been left at Welshpool; bearing a letter to the governor from Oswald, thanking him much for having taken care of them, and saying briefly that he had been left on the field for dead, after the fight near Llanidloes; but had recovered, and been well treated by Glendower, who had put him to ransom. He took money with him, to pay the expenses for the keep of the horses; and returned, with them and the armour, after an absence of three weeks.

Passing through Worcester on his way back, he had, at Oswald's order, purchased for himself clothes suitable for his position as an esquire. As for armour, it had been arranged that he should have it made for him at Alnwick, as it would be difficult to obtain a suit sufficiently large for him.

At the end of the three months the necessary repairs to the castle were finished. The gates had been greatly strengthened with thick bands of iron, the moat cleared out, and at various points the defences had been strengthened. The small amount of furniture then deemed necessary still remained there and, where needful, had been repaired and put in good order. Eight men-at-arms had been taken by Oswald into his service, and a trusty man appointed as seneschal.

Then, after paying another visit to Yardhope, Oswald rode, with Roger and two well-mounted men-at-arms, to Alnwick.

It was now April, and bad news had just arrived. Glendower had commenced the campaign with great vigour, as the appearance of a comet had been interpreted, by the bards, as an omen most favourable to him, and his force had greatly increased during the winter. He had destroyed the houses and strong places of all Welshmen who had not taken up arms at his orders, and had closely blockaded Carnarvon. He marched to Bangor, levelled the cathedral, and that of Saint Asaph, by fire, burnt the episcopal palaces and canons' houses. So formidable did he become that the king issued writs, to the lieutenants of no fewer than thirty-four counties, to assemble their forces at Lichfield, to crush Glendower.

The latter had now taken the offensive, and advanced towards Hereford, and carried fire and sword through Mortimer's lands. Sir Edmund gathered his own and his nephew's tenants and retainers, from Herefordshire and Radnorshire, and advanced against Glendower. The armies met on the 22nd of June, 1402, at a short distance from Knighton. The battle was obstinately fought, but was decided by the desertion of the Welsh tenants, and by the Welsh bowmen in Mortimer's service turning their bows against his men-at-arms; and, finally, the English were defeated, with the loss of eleven hundred men, Sir Edmund himself being made a prisoner.

After the battle the Welsh behaved with the greatest savagery; killing all the wounded, stripping the fallen, and horribly mutilating their bodies. The news created great excitement at Alnwick and, had not the situation in the north been critical, Percy would have gathered his forces and marched, with all speed, to avenge the defeat and capture of his brother-in-law.

The Earl of Dunbar, with many of the tenants of his former estates, and numbers of the English borderers, had entered Scotland and carried out considerable raids. In revenge for this, Douglas despatched Thomas Halliburton and Patrick Hepburn, each with a considerable force, to invade Northumberland. Halliburton ravaged the country as far as Bamborough, collected great spoils, and returned with them. Hepburn, who had a still larger force, penetrated farther into England, carried his ravages to within a few miles of Alnwick; and then retired north, with an enormous amount of booty.

When, however, he had crossed the border into the country known as the Merse, north of Berwick, the Earl of Dunbar fell upon him at West Nesbit, and completely defeated him. Hepburn himself, with a large number of his men, fell in the battle; and many important prisoners were captured. This battle was fought on the same day that Glendower defeated Mortimer.

The victory caused great exultation on the border; but Alwyn said to his nephew:

"Although this is good, as far as it goes, Oswald, you may be sure that Douglas will not brook this disaster with patience, but will gather the Scottish forces; and we may expect him, ere long, at the head of twenty thousand men, and we shall have a fight as stiff as that of Otterburn. We shall have Northumberland ablaze, and you will see that the earl and Hotspur will soon be preparing to meet the storm.

"These last forays took them by surprise; and, as lords of the marches, they have suffered serious humiliation, for this victory was not theirs, but the work of Dunbar; and had he not intercepted the Scots, on their own side of the border, they would have returned, scatheless, with the spoils of our northern districts. This disgrace will spur them on to make great efforts, and these will be needed, or we shall see Northumberland, Cumberland, and Durham in flames."

Alwyn was not mistaken. Messengers were sent off to all those holding knights' feus, throughout the county, bidding them to prepare to answer to the Percy's call; and to hold themselves, and their tenants, in readiness to march to any point fixed upon for a general rendezvous. They were to warn all the countryside that, directly news arrived that the Scots were in motion, they were to drive their cattle and horses to the nearest fortified town, or to take them to hiding places among the hills. Everything of value was to be taken away, or hidden, so that the enemy should find but empty houses.

Oswald rode to Yardhope, with the message to his father.

"I know, Father," he said, "that it needed not to warn you; but as it was but a short distance out of my way to come round here, I thought that I would pay you a day's visit."

"No, lad; directly I heard of the victory of Dunbar, I said to myself, this will bring the Scots upon us in force. Douglas will never put up with the defeat, and will make every effort to turn the tables. I shall send all there is worth taking away, to a shepherd's hut among the fells; and shall, as soon as I hear that Douglas's preparations are well-nigh complete, journey with your mother to Alnwick, and leave her there. I shall return, and with my men will drive the cattle and horses to places where there is little chance of the Scots finding them; and will then, after leaving three or four men to look after them, come back to Alnwick.

"What do you propose to do?"

"I shall do much the same, Father. Stoubes is strong enough to hold out against any ordinary raid, but not against an army led by Douglas. I shall remove the furnishing and tapestry, and shall send the most valuable into Alnwick, and have the rest of them hidden in the woods. These are the orders that have been sent, all along the border. Any whose places are so strong that they may well defend themselves, for some time, are to gather all their neighbours there. The rest are to repair to Alnwick, to join Percy's force.

"You see, there is no knowing where the storm may break. The Scots may cross the Cheviots anywhere between Berwick and Carlisle; and, until their movements are known, the earl and Hotspur must keep their forces at Alnwick, in readiness to march wheresoever required.

"Hotspur has sent messengers down to the Midlands, to engage as many archers as he can get. Of course, we have many here; but the borderers are spearmen rather than archers, and it were well to strengthen our force. Still, however large a force he may raise, we cannot hope to check their first incursion. The whole country is open to them and, if they enter near Carlisle, they may be in the heart of Cumberland, or Durham, before we are fairly in motion. We may count, however, on meeting them as they retire, if not before."

Oswald then rode to his own place, bade all the tenants prepare to ride with him to Alnwick, at an hour's notice; and either to send their women and children on there, as soon as it was known that the Scotch army was gathering strongly on the border; or else to gather stores of provisions, up in the hills, and to send the women and children there, the moment word came that the Scots were on the move.

The news of Mortimer's defeat and capture had been received, by the time Oswald returned to Alnwick.

"'Tis bad news, indeed," Percy said to him, "and I know that, as you have been staying so long at Ludlow, you will be deeply grieved at the misfortune that has befallen Mortimer. However, I doubt not that he will soon be ransomed. I know that the king appointed a commission of knights, to treat at once with Glendower for Lord Grey's ransom, and has given orders for the raising of the great sum demanded. It is to be gathered from a tax on church properties, and in other ways; and doubtless he will do the same for Mortimer, whose lands have been so harried, by the Welsh, that it will be impossible to raise any large sum from the tenants."

"I fear, Sir Henry," Oswald said, "that the king will be lukewarm on the subject. During his three invasions, he has never once summoned Sir Edmund to join him;

nor has he passed through Ludlow, as he might well have done, seeing that it is a central position, and the nearest way for an army marching towards Plinlimmon. I remarked, too, that when I mentioned Mortimer's name in my discourse with him, the king's brow clouded, as if ill pleased at the name."

"Then he acts wrongly," Hotspur said angrily. "Mortimer has given no cause for offence. He has never, in any way, upheld the cause of the young Earl of March; and knows, well enough, that it would be madness to set up his claim to the throne, when Henry has given no cause for complaint, and that the boy's existence seems to be well-nigh forgotten by the country.

"However, as soon as this business is over I will, myself, to London; and will beg the king to exercise the same benevolence, in the case of Mortimer, as he has shown on behalf of Lord Grey. Why, he might as well suspect us, to whom he largely owes his kingdom, as Mortimer, seeing that my wife is aunt to the young earl."

Early in August it became known that preparations were being made, upon a great scale, by Douglas for the invasion of England; and that, as Military Governor of Scotland, he had summoned all the great nobles to join, with their forces; and it was even said that numbers of French knights were, on account of the long friendship between France and Scotland, crossing the seas, to fight under Douglas against their old enemies.

"Methinks," Hotspur said to his knights, "there can be little doubt that there is an agreement between Scotland and Glendower; and this would account for the fury the Welshmen have been showing, and the manner in which they have destroyed the cathedrals, churches, and castles alike; and so forced Henry to march against them, with the forces of the greater part of England, just when Douglas is preparing to assail us here.

"The forces of Westmoreland, Cumberland, Durham, and Northumberland, if together, might hope to make a stout resistance, even against so large a force as Douglas is collecting; but we cannot so gather. The Earl of Westmoreland, who commands the forces of his own county and Cumberland, must needs hold them together; lest the Scots pour down, besiege Carlisle, and carry fire and sword through those counties.

"From here up to Berwick the country has been so plundered, and devastated, that it is almost a desert; and I can draw no strength from there. As to Durham, they urge, and with some truth that, as the Scots have, before now, laid portions of their county waste, they cannot send their forces so far north as this place; as it would leave them unprotected, should the enemy march through Tynedale into their county.

"The king has entered Wales with the fighting men of thirty-four counties, so from him no aid can be expected; and it seems to me that we shall be quite unable to make head against the invasion; though assuredly, when we have gathered our forces, and are joined by those Dunbar will bring us, we will meet them as they return, spoil laden, to the border."

Well-mounted messengers had been placed on every road by which the Scots could cross the border; and on the 18th of August, one came with the news that, twelve hours before, they had crossed into Cumberland at Kirksop Foot; that they were reported to be ten thousand strong; and that a dozen villages were already in flames. Another portion of their army had crossed near Tynehead, and were pouring into Tynedale.

John Forster and his wife had arrived, some days before. Oswald had found comfortable lodgings for his mother in the town, which was already crowded with women and children from the border. His father had left again, at once; but returned, with twenty spears, twelve hours after the messenger had brought the news.

"I had two or three of my men out," he said to Oswald, as he rode in and dismounted in the castle yard; "but as soon as I heard that the Scots had entered Tynedale, I knew that it was time to be off, for they are sure to send over strong parties to ravage Coquetdale. The road was well-nigh blocked, in some places, with fugitives. In spite of the warnings that have been issued, most of the people seem to have thought that the Scots could never come in their direction, and the news has caused a panic.

"However, near the border the Scots will find but little plunder. We have had so many invasions that no man is foolish enough to spend money on aught that he cannot easily carry away, and the raiders will, there, find but empty houses. They may sweep in some of the cattle from the hills, to supply them with food on their march; but more than this they will not take, as they go south, as it would be but an encumbrance."

In a few days a strong force was collected at Alnwick; but, though chafing at the news of the terrible devastations, that were being made by the Scots in Cumberland and Durham, the Earl and Hotspur could, at present, do nothing. The invasion was, indeed, one of the most disastrous that had ever taken place; and after having almost devastated the two counties, Douglas, with the united force, and an enormous train of waggons laden with plunder, great quantities of cattle, and other spoil, turned north again, at the end of the second week of September.

In the meanwhile, Percy's force had been steadily growing. He had early resolved that upon the return of the Scots the battle must be fought, and contented himself with sending small bodies, of well-mounted knights and horsemen, to hover in the neighbourhood of the Scotch army; and to keep him informed of their intentions, and the route they seemed disposed to take.

Douglas had carried his devastations up to the walls of Newcastle, but had not attempted to attack that strongly-defended town. He had, indeed, gathered as much spoil as could possibly be taken along; and he moved north in a quiet and leisurely way, being greatly hampered by the enormous train of loaded waggons.

As soon as the Earl of Northumberland and his son saw that he intended to march up through Northumberland, instead of returning by the line that he had come through Tynedale, they set their force in motion and marched out; leaving a sufficient strength to hold Alnwick, should Douglas attack it. Being joined, two days later, by the Earl of Dunbar, they posted themselves in a position whence they could march to intercept the Scots, upon any road they might follow on their way north.

On the 12th, they learned for certain that the Scots were following the road that would take them through Wooler. Moving instantly, the Earl with his forces came up to them, posted on a hill, a mile to the northwest of Homildon. He at once seized a hill facing it, and disposed his knights, men-at-arms, and spearmen along the crest.

Hotspur would straightway have charged down, and attacked the Scots in their position; but Dunbar put his hand on his bridle, and urged him, strongly, to await the assault; and to provoke the Scots into taking the offensive by galling them with his archers, in which he was far superior to them; while, on the other hand, they were much stronger in spears and horsemen.

Hotspur, seeing the goodness of the advice, assented to it; and ordered the archers to descend, at once, into the valley between the two hills; and to launch their arrows against the Scots. On descending, it was found that the Scottish bowmen were already in the valley. These they speedily drove up the hill, and then sent their arrows thick and fast among the Scottish men-at-arms.

Douglas had, like the Earl of Dunbar, perceived at what disadvantage the party who took the offensive would have to fight; and had determined to stand on the defensive, especially as, if he moved forward, the English could detach bodies of horsemen to work round the hill, and fall upon his immense train of waggons.

For a time, he refused to accede to the earnest entreaties of his knights to advance. But as man after man fell under the English arrows, their impatience increased; until one of his best knights, Sir John Swinton, rode a few paces out of the ranks, and in a loud voice said:

"My brave comrades, what fascinates you today, that you stand like deer and fawns in a park to be shot; instead of showing your ancient valour, and meeting your foes hand to hand? Let those who will descend with me and, in the name of God, we will break that host and conquer; or if not, we will at least die with honour, like soldiers."

A mighty shout followed his words, and the whole Scottish host dashed down the hill. The English archers fell back a little, still shooting as they did so; but halted a short way up the hill, and shot so hotly and strongly that they pierced helmet and armour with their arrows.

Nothing could withstand these missiles, shot by the finest and strongest bowmen in the world. The Scots rolled over in heaps. Douglas, although clad in the most perfect steel armour, was wounded in five places, one arrow destroying the sight of one of his eyes. He fell from his horse, and utter confusion reigned in the Scottish ranks.

Swinging their bows behind them, the archers drew their axes and rushed into the crowd, effecting a terrible slaughter. Douglas was made prisoner, as was the Earl of Fife, a son of the Regent Albany, the Earls of Moray and Angus and Orkney. Two barons, eighty knights, among whom were several Frenchmen, and several other persons of rank were also captured; while Swinton, Gordon, and many other knights and gentlemen were slain, together with seven hundred of the commonalty. With the exception only of Flodden, no battle on the Border was so fatal to the

Scottish nobility, whose defeat was effected by the archers only.

The confusion was so terrible that the Earl of Northumberland refused to allow his knights and men-at-arms to charge, seeing that they must trample down both friend and foe; therefore they stood as passive spectators of the desperate fight, not a lance being couched nor a blow struck by any of them. When all was over they took up the pursuit of the fugitives; many of these were overtaken and killed, and the pursuit was continued to the Tweed, where, not knowing the fords, many of the fugitives were drowned while endeavouring to swim the river.

"Roger, what say you to that?" Oswald asked, as he and his squire drew rein, after pursuing the enemy for some distance.

Roger's face expressed the strongest disgust.

"Well, Sir Oswald, I don't call it a battle, at all. Who ever heard of a battle where neither knight nor man-at-arms drew sword? 'Tis out of all reason to fight in that manner."

"Nevertheless, Roger, as we have won a great victory, what matter is it whether we or the archers bore the chief hand in it? The last battle we fought in was a different matter. We had plenty of fighting, but no victory."

"It was more to my taste, nevertheless," Roger grumbled, "even though the Welsh well nigh made an end of me; and, for myself, I could not help hoping that the archers would be beaten, and leave it to us to take our part in the fighting. They had done more than their share when they had broken the Scottish ranks, and slain I know not how many; and it would have been fair of them, after that, to draw back, and leave it to us to finish the business."

"'Tis well as it is, Roger, and for one I am well satisfied. We have given the Scots a lesson that will keep them quiet for a long time. We have recovered all the spoil they were carrying off, and we could have won nothing more, had we been in the thick of the melee, and come out of it, perhaps, sorely wounded again."

Roger, however, was by no means satisfied; and, to the end of his life, always fell into a bad temper when the battle of Homildon was spoken of.

All the prisoners of consequence were taken to Alnwick, where the army fell back; much to the disgust of some of the more eager spirits, who would fain have crossed the frontier, and made reprisals for the woes the Scots had inflicted. Northumberland, however, was well satisfied with what had been won, and did not wish to provoke the Scots to extremities; feeling that with so many of their leaders in his hands, he might be able to arrange terms that would ensure peace, for a considerable time, on the border.

The prisoners were all treated with great kindness and consideration. They were lodged in the castle, and were treated as guests rather than as prisoners.

Oswald and his father were both pleased to hear, two days after the battle, that when the Scottish dead were examined, the bodies of William Baird and ten of his kinsmen were found, lying together. They had resisted desperately to the last, refusing to surrender themselves; well knowing that their misdeeds and many depredations, in England, would bring them to the gallows, if taken alive.

"Well, Father, we shall be able to live in peace for a time, now. No doubt the Bairds have brought with them every spear they could muster, for none would willingly have stayed at home, when there was a promise of gathering so much booty; therefore their strength must be altogether broken, and it will be long, indeed, before the Bairds ride in a raid into Northumberland."

His father nodded.

"'Tis a good thing, Oswald, assuredly; though I would rather that we had had the attacking of them in their own hold. Still, at any rate, there is an end of the feud for years to come; and I shall be able to lie down to sleep, without wondering whether they will be knocking at the gate, before morning."

Chapter 20: The Percys' Discontent.

During the time that had elapsed, between his receiving the news of Mortimer's capture by Glendower, and the battle of Homildon Hill, Percy had written several times to the king, with reference to his taking the same steps to ransom Mortimer that he had taken on behalf of Lord Grey. The king, however, answered very coldly; and one of his letters more than hinted that he believed that Mortimer had voluntarily placed himself in Glendower's hands, and that an agreement existed between them. Not only was Hotspur furious at such an accusation, but the earl, himself, was deeply angered.

"'Tis past all belief," Hotspur said, "that such a charge should be made. Had Mortimer wished to join Glendower, he could have gone to him, not as a prisoner, but at the head of three thousand good fighting men. Why should he have thrown away the lives of twelve hundred of his own vassals, and those of his nephew? Nay, more, had Mortimer intended treachery, he might have marched and fallen on the rear of the king's army, entangled among the Welsh mountains and forests, while Glendower fell upon him from in front. 'Tis a lie, and bears its mark on its face; 'tis but an excuse for refusing to ransom Mortimer, who he hopes will be kept a prisoner for years, and whose estates he will thus be able to appropriate. 'Tis an insult not only to Mortimer but to us, to whom he owes his crown.

"But let him beware! Those who built up, can pull down."

The knights standing round put their hands on their sword hilts, significantly. The king was, to the followers of great barons, a person of but small consequence in comparison with their lord; and they would draw their swords, at the latter's order, as willingly against a king as against a foreign foe. That it was their duty to do so was so fully recognized that, in the troubles between the king and his nobles, while the latter were, if defeated, executed for treason, their vassals were permitted to return home unmolested; and it was not until the battle of Barnet that Edward, enraged at the humiliation that he had suffered, when he had been obliged to fly to France, gave orders that no quarter was to be shown to Warwick's vassals and retainers.

Northumberland and Hotspur were still smarting under this treatment of Mortimer when, eight days after the battle, the messenger they had despatched to the king, in Wales, with the report of their great victory, and the capture of Douglas and other important nobles, returned with an order from the king that these prisoners were not to be ransomed.

This order was received with passionate indignation by the earl and Hotspur. Although not altogether contrary to the usages of the age, since similar orders had, more than once been, issued by Edward the Third; the ransom of prisoners taken in battle was regarded as one of the most important sources of revenue, and as the means of defraying the expenses that nobles and knights were put to in aiding, with their vassals, the king in his wars. Occasionally, however, in the case of prisoners of importance, monarchs deemed it necessary, for political reasons, to forbid the ransom of prisoners.

The Scottish nobles were as indignant as the Percys. They had regarded it as a matter of course that they would be shortly liberated. Their ransom, however heavy, would be soon forthcoming; for it was one of the conditions on which land was held that, in case of the lord being taken prisoner, each of his tenants must contribute largely, in proportion to his holding, towards the payment of his ransom.

The order of the king clearly meant that they were to be taken to London and held there as hostages, perhaps for years; and so not only to ensure England against another invasion, but to further any designs of conquest that the king might entertain. With three of the great earls of Scotland--one of them the son of the Regent--and Douglas, the military leader of the Scots, in his hands; and with the Earl of Dunbar as his ally, Scotland would be practically at his mercy.

An important meeting was held at Alnwick, at which the Scottish nobles, the Earl of Northumberland, and Hotspur were alone present, and here matters of vital interest to the kingdom were arranged.

For six months things remained in the same state. The king's fourth expedition into Wales had effected no more than the preceding. Glendower was still virtually master of Wales. Cardiff had been burned by him, with its numerous priories and convents, with the exception of that of the Franciscans; the castle of Penmarc, and the town and castle of Abergavenny had been burned, and other strong places captured.

The Percys remained, during this time, sullen and inactive; although somewhat mollified by the thanks voted them by Parliament. The king, as a reward for their services, bestowed upon them the estates of Douglas. This, however, they treated with scorn, for as well might he have presented to them the city of Naples or Paris; since, unless all Scotland was conquered, they could not come into peaceful mastership of the Douglas estates. Nor, indeed, could the king have intended it in earnest; for he was far too politic to think of adding so great an increase of territory to the estates of the Percys, who had already shown their power by placing him on the throne, and who might some day take back what they had given him, by declaring in favour of the Earl of March.

One day in February, 1403, Oswald was summoned from Stoubes to Alnwick and, on his arrival there, was requested to go to the earl's chamber. Such a summons was extremely unusual. Hotspur had his own estates, and his own retinue and following; and was, jointly with his father, warden of the marches; and though he dwelt, generally, with him at Alnwick, he had his own portion of the castle. Thus it was seldom that the earl had any communication with Hotspur's knights.

Hastening to obey, Oswald found Hotspur with his father.

"I have a mission for you, Sir Oswald," Hotspur said, "on the part of the earl and myself. You know that, for a long time, there has been a disputation between my father and the Earl of Westmoreland, respecting the Scottish prisoners. The earl sent a small force to fight under me at Homildon, but it was a mere handful; and on the strength of this he advanced a claim to a considerable share of the ransoms of the prisoners; or, since they could not be ransomed, to the custody of the persons of the Earls of Moray and Angus. The king has now, contrary to all reason, inflicted upon us the indignity of appointing four commissioners, two of whom are but knights and the other two men of no consequence, to inquire into the question between my father and my uncle, the Earl of Westmoreland.

"Does he think that two of his earls are going to submit themselves to so gross an indignity?--we, who are as much masters in the north of England as he is in the south--and even that he owes to us. I have ridden over and seen Westmoreland, who is as indignant as we are, and we at once arranged the little matter in which we are at variance, and agreed upon common measures.

"But this is not all. Seeing that the king absolutely refused to do to Mortimer the same service that he did to Lord Grey, whose ransom he has now paid--and who, by the way, has married Glendower's daughter, Jane--Mortimer's vassals, with some aid from ourselves, have raised the money required to free Mortimer. Now the king has interfered, and has given orders that such ransom shall not be paid. 'Tis evident that he determines to drive us to extremities.

"I tell you these things, in order that you may see how intolerable the condition of affairs has become. My father and myself believe that it is the judgment of heaven upon us, for having helped to dethrone King Richard, the lawful sovereign of this country, and to place this usurper on the throne. Even had Richard's conduct rendered his deposition necessary, we did wrong in passing over the lawful heir, the young Earl of March. 'Tis true he was but a child, at that time; but he is older now, and we feel shame that he should be kept as a prisoner, by Henry. Had not the king perjured himself, we should not have been led into this error; for, before we assisted him, he swore a great oath that he had no intention of gaining the throne, but only to regain his own dukedom of Lancaster. It was on that ground that we lent him our aid; and now, forsooth, this perjured usurper treats us, who made him, as dirt under his feet!

"We are resolved to suffer it no longer; and since we may not ransom Mortimer, we will secure his freedom in other ways, and for this you may give us your aid."

"Assuredly, Sir Henry, and my Lord Earl," Oswald, who was deeply indignant at the unworthy treatment of his lords, replied hotly. "My life is at your service."

"I expected nothing else," Hotspur said, warmly. "The matter stands thus. Owen Glendower was a warm partisan of King Richard, and was one of the few who remained faithful to the end; thereby incurring the deep hostility of Henry, and of his adherent Lord Grey. It was for this his lands were unjustly seized, for this that Henry's parliament refused to accede to his complaints, and so drove him to take up arms. Thus, then, in an enterprise against Henry, Glendower is our natural ally; and we intend to propose to him that alliance, undertaking that, if he will give us aid, his claim to the crown of Wales shall be acknowledged, and that he shall govern his country without interference from England.

"There is none who could carry out this negotiation so well as yourself, since you can, by virtue of that ring he gave you, pass unarmed to him; while any other knight would be assuredly slain. You will bear a letter, signed by the earl and myself, offering him our friendship and alliance, on those terms; and explain to him, more fully, the manner in which we have been driven to throw off Henry's authority. You can tell him that we shall proclaim the Earl of March lawful king; and if he agrees to join in our project, which would be clearly both to his liking and advantage, it would be as well that he should, as soon as we move, which may not be for some time yet, release Sir Edmund Mortimer; who, as the boy's uncle, will assuredly raise his vassals on his behalf, now that Henry has shown such animosity against him."

"I will gladly undertake the mission, my lord; and all the more gladly, since it may lead to the liberation of Sir Edmund Mortimer, who treated me with the greatest kindness and condescension, during my stay at Ludlow."

"Prepare to start tomorrow, then," the earl said. "The letter shall be ready for you tonight; and beyond what my son has told you, you can tell Glendower that we have good hopes of large help from Scotland; with whom, it is said, he is already in alliance."

The next morning Oswald started, taking no one but Roger with him. He had, the evening before, told his squire only that he was starting on a journey; promising to tell him more, as they rode. Accordingly, when well away from Alnwick, he beckoned to Roger to bring up his horse alongside of him.

"Where think you that we are going, Roger? I will give you fifty guesses, and would warrant that you would not come at the truth."

"It matters nothing to me, master; so that I ride with you, I am content."

"You know, Roger, how grievously the king has treated the Percys; how he has prevented their taking ransom for their prisoners, and has refused to ransom Sir Edmund Mortimer; how he, in bitter jest, offered the earl the estates of Douglas; and how he has put upon them the indignity of sending four men, of no import, to decide upon their difference with Westmoreland?"

"Ay, ay, Sir Oswald, everyone knows this, and not a few have wondered that the Percys have suffered these things, in quietness."

"A fresh thing has happened, Roger. The tenants of Mortimer, with aid from the earl and Hotspur, have raised the sum that Glendower demanded as ransom; and now the king has laid on them his order, that this money is not to be paid."

"By our Lady," Roger exclaimed wrathfully, "this is too much! Sir Edmund is a noble gentleman, and that the king should refuse to allow his friends to ransom him passes all bounds."

"So the earl and Hotspur consider," Oswald said, "and, ere long, you will see that they will hoist the banner of the young Earl of March, and proclaim him King of England."

"'Tis good," Roger exclaimed, slapping his hand on his leg. "To me it matters nought who is King of England, but I always held that it was hard that King Richard should be deposed, and murdered, by one who was not even his lawful successor. I am not one to question the conduct of my lord, but I always thought that the Percys were wrong in bringing this usurper over."

"They feel that themselves, Roger, and consider the ingratitude of the king to be a punishment upon them, for having aided him to the throne."

"But what has this to do with your journey, master?"

"It has much to do with it, Roger, seeing that I am on my way to Glendower, to offer him alliance with the Percys."

"A good step!" Roger exclaimed. "We know that these Welsh can fight."

"Moreover, Roger, it may bring about the freeing of Mortimer; for the evil feeling the king has shown against him will surely drive him to raise all his vassals, and those of the young earl, in Herefordshire and elsewhere; and thus the Percys will gain two powerful allies, Glendower and Mortimer; and as they advance from the north, the Welsh and Mortimer will join them from the west. When victory is gained, there will be peace on the Welsh marches. Owen will be recognized for what he is, the King of Wales; and doubtless he will then suffer the English to live quietly there, just as the Welsh have lived quietly in England.

"Then, too, all the western counties will see that it is their interest to side with Mortimer and Glendower. Four times, during the last three years, have they been called out, and forced to leave their homes to follow the king into Wales; and as often have had to return, leaving behind them many of their number. They will see that, if Glendower is acknowledged King of Wales, this hard and grievous service will no longer be required of them."

"That is so, Sir Oswald, and in truth I like the project well. It matters not a straw to me who is king; but if a king treats my lords scurvily, I am ready to shout 'Down with him!' and to do my best to put another up in his place; though, indeed, 'tis a salve to my conscience to know that the man I am fighting against is a usurper, and one who has set himself up in the place of the lawful king."

"My conscience in no way pricks me, Roger. I fight at my lord's order, against his foes. That is the duty I have sworn to. As between him and the king, 'tis a matter for him alone. At the same time, I am glad that the business is likely to end in the rescue of a knight who has been very kind to me. Between Henry and the young Earl of March I have no opinion; but it seems to me that, since Henry ascended to the throne by might, and by the popular voice, he has no cause to complain, if he is put out of it by the same means."

"But, should the war go against the Percys, master?"

"That, again, is a matter for the earl and Hotspur. They know what force they and the Earl of Westmoreland can put in the field. They know that Glendower can aid with ten thousand Welshmen, and that Mortimer can raise three or four thousand men from his vassals. They should know what help they can count on from Scotland; and doubtless, during the last six months, have made themselves acquainted with the general feeling respecting the king. It is upon them that the risk chiefly falls. We knights and men-at-arms may fall in the field of battle; but that is a risk that we know we have to face, when we take to the calling of arms. If our cause is lost, and we escape from the battlefield, we have but to depart to our holds or our villages, and we shall hear nought more of the affair; while our lords, if taken, would lose their heads. It will be a grief for us to lose masters we love, and to have to pay our quittance with money or service to a new lord; but beyond that, we risk nought save our lives in battle. Therefore I trouble myself, in no way, as to the matter between the Percys and the king, which I take it in no way concerns me; and am content to do my duty, and to render my service, as I have sworn to do."

"It is well, Sir Oswald," Roger said, after a long pause, "that Glendower gave us those rings; for from all accounts he and his Welshmen are more furious than ever, and there would be small chance of our ever reaching him, without them. The chain did its work, last time. 'Tis not every Welshman who would stop to examine it before striking, and few who could read the inscription, if they did so; while 'tis like that most of them are well acquainted with Glendower's signet."

"That is so; but nevertheless, Roger, it will be better, when we have once crossed the border, that you should ride behind me with a white flag displayed; as a token that we come, not for war, but on a peaceful mission. 'Tis probable, at any rate, that any band of Welshmen who may meet us will, in that case, before attacking, stop to inquire on what errand we come."

They rode fast, for the earl had said that he needed to have the news of Glendower's decision, before proceeding further in the matter, and in four days arrived on the border. At Shrewsbury Oswald inquired, carelessly, of the host of the inn where he put up, where Glendower was now thought to be; as he intended to journey south to Hereford, and would fain know whether there was any risk of falling in with bands of the marauders.

"Methinks, Sir Knight, that you may travel without uneasiness; seeing that the country between this and Hereford has been so harassed, by them, that there is nought to tempt them to cross the border, save with so large a force that they can invade Gloucester or Worcestershire. Men say, moreover, that Glendower is, at present, in Cardiganshire. There are still a few Welsh inhabitants here. They declare that they are loyal to the king, and love not their wild countrymen. Whether it is so, or not, I cannot say; but they certainly manage to keep up communications with the Welsh. This may be for a treacherous purpose, or it may be as they say; that, knowing that they and all belonging to them would be slain, should Glendower capture the town; they, for their own safety, try to learn his intentions and movements, in order to warn us, should a surprise be intended."

Starting early the next morning, Oswald crossed into Montgomeryshire, by a road through Worktree Forest, so as to avoid both Ludlow and Welshpool; and kept along by a country track, near the border of Radnor, so passing south of Llanidloes. As soon as they had left Radnorshire, Roger fastened to his spear a white cloth they had brought from Shrewsbury; then they continued their journey west.

It was not until they had crossed the Wye, here an insignificant stream, that they came upon a native of the country. They were following a track, between two rough hills covered with brushwood, when a man, evidently of the better class, stepped out before them.

"Sir Knight," he said in English, "'tis a strange sight to see an Englishman, with one esquire, travelling alone by so wild and lonely a road as this; and strange, indeed, that he should bear a flag of truce; for were you here on your king's business, you would surely be attended with a braver show. I had notice, two hours ago, brought by one who had seen you cross the Wye; and in the bushes round lie fifty men who, did I raise my hand, would let fly their arrows against you. But if you have reason for your coming this way, assuredly we should not hinder you."

Oswald held out his hand.

"This signet ring, sir, was given me by Glendower, who said that any Welshman to whom I might show it would act as my guide and escort to him. I come on an important mission, not from the king, but from one from whom Glendower may be glad to hear; therefore I pray you take me to him, or at least send a party of your men; for I might, peradventure, fall in with some who would shoot before they questioned."

"'Tis assuredly the prince's signet," the man said, after carefully examining it, "and right gladly will I escort you to him. He is, at present, at Aberystwith."

"Thanks for your courtesy, sir. To whom am I speaking?"

"My name is Howel ap Ryddyn. You passed my abode, which cannot be seen from the road; and I would, were you not pressed for time, gladly entertain you; but if we push forward, we may reach Aberystwith before nightfall, and I make no question that would better suit your wishes."

"Thanks, sir. My business is somewhat urgent, and I shall be glad to meet the prince, as soon as possible. Indeed, I should not be sorry to reach a spot where we can sup and sleep, seeing that we have twice slept in the woods, since we left Shrewsbury."

The man called out an order, in Welsh. Four men at once issued from the bushes, and under their guidance the horsemen soon reached Aberystwith.

"I had scarce expected this pleasure, Sir Oswald," Glendower said warmly, as the young knight entered. "To what good fortune do I owe your visit?"

"But no, 'tis but poor hospitality questioning thus, when it will be time enough to talk of such things, later."

"And 'tis a matter that is best discussed in private," Oswald replied, in an undertone.

"And how have you fared since we parted?"

"Since I saw you, over a year ago, the time has passed quietly, save for the battle with the Scots; where, although we beat them, there was no credit gained by the knights and men-at-arms; seeing that the archers, alone, did the fighting."

"So I heard. On our side, we have been busy ever since."

"And successful, too, as I have heard."

"Yes, fortune has been in our favour. Lord Grey's ransom has been of much use to us and, having married my daughter Jane, he can no longer be considered a foe. Yet, to do him justice, he would not promise even to stand neutral; though, unless under special orders from the king, he will not draw his sword again. I love a stanch man; and though Grey has taken, as I consider, the wrong side, he stands to it faithfully. I offered him freedom, without ransom, if he would promise neutrality, and that, when I had put down all other opposition, he would hold his Welsh lands from me; but he refused, and said that he would rather remain in chains, all his life, than be false to his vows to Henry.

"That was good, and I would that all Welshmen were as faithful. They take the oath to me one week, and make their peace with Henry the next. Nay, some, to please him, would go so far as to try to assassinate me. Two such plots have there been this year, and it was only that I wore a good mail shirt under my garments, that my life was saved from a bow shot, and from one who professed to be my warm friend, and who had taken bread with me, half an hour before.

"It is destiny, Sir Oswald. The powers watch over me, and keep me from harm; and these will, I know, protect me to the end, against the stroke of English foes, or of Welsh traitors."

After supper was over, Glendower led Oswald to his private chamber.

"Now, Sir Oswald, you can speak freely. I have placed a guard outside the door, and there is no fear of interruption. Do you come on your own account, or from another?"

"I come from the Earl of Northumberland, and his son Sir Henry Percy; and am charged, in the first place, to deliver this letter to you; and then to give you such further intelligence, as to the matter, as it may be needful for you to know."

"From the Percys!" Glendower said, in surprise, as he cut the silk that held the roll together.

His countenance expressed great surprise, as he read the contents.

"There is no snare in this?" he said suddenly, after reading it through two or three times, and looking sharply at Oswald. "'Tis not from the Percys, who, more than any other, assisted the usurper to the throne, that I should have looked for such an offer."

"I should be the last to bring such a letter to you, Glendower, were there aught behind what is written. The earl and Hotspur spoke of the matter at length to me. They regret, now, the part they took in enthroning Henry; at whose hands they have now received such indignities that they are resolved, if it may be, to undo their work, and to place the lawful king, the young Earl of March, on the throne."

He then related the various complaints that the Percys had against the king, and told Glendower that the matter had been brought to a head by Henry's refusal to allow them to pay the ransom that had been collected for Sir Edmund Mortimer.

"Whom have they with them?" Glendower asked, after listening in silence.

"They have the Earl of Westmoreland, who, like themselves, is greatly offended at the appointment of four commissioners, men of no standing or position, to judge between two of the great barons of England; blood relations, too, whose difference is on a matter of but small importance. No other name was mentioned before me, but the earl stated that he looked for much assistance from Scotland."

"Ay, ay! As they hold in their hands Douglas, and the Regent's son, Moray, and Angus, they may well make terms with Scotland. Yes, it is a very great plot, and since I can get no ransom for Mortimer, and he can raise some three or four thousand men, he would be of more value to us free than as a prisoner."

"It is not only that," Oswald said. "The fact that he, as young March's uncle, should head his following and raise his banner, will show that the Percys and you are not using young March's name as a mere pretext for taking up arms. If Mortimer, the head of his house during his minority, and guardian of his estates, were with them, men would see that 'tis really a struggle to place the lawful king on the throne; and many would join who, did they think it was but an affair between the Percys, of whom they know but little in the south, and you, whom they have been taught to consider a rebel, would stand aloof."

"'Tis well thought of, and the project pleases me. Even without such allies, I may hold my mountains and continue my warfare, but there could be neither peace nor prosperity for years; but with the overthrow of the usurper, and my acknowledgment as King of Wales, and of the entire independence of the country, from the Dee to the Severn, the freedom of my country might be permanently secured.

"But I will give no certain answer, tonight. 'Tis a matter to be turned over in my mind, as it seems to me that I may gain much good by the alliance; and that, even if the Percys fail in their enterprise, I can be no worse off than I am, at present."

It was not until the following evening that Glendower gave a decided answer.

"I accept Percy's offer," he said. "I have thought it over in every way; even putting aside the benefits, to my country and myself, I would enter upon it; were it but for the satisfaction of seeing the usurper, and murderer of my dear master, King Richard, have the same measure meted out to him that he gave to his sovereign. Tonight I will write an answer to the Percys, for you to bear to them. Tomorrow morning I will ride, with you, to the stronghold where Mortimer is at present held in durance; and if he consents to join us, I will give him his freedom, without ransom."

They started the next morning, early; and at noon arrived at a strong house, lying in the heart of the hills.

"It were best that you should see him first, Sir Oswald, and explain the matter to him. After that, I will meet him with you."

Great was the astonishment of Sir Edmund, when Oswald was ushered into the little room in which he was confined. It was some ten feet square, furnished with a pallet, chair, and small table. The window was very strongly barred, and Oswald observed, with pain, that his ten months' imprisonment had told very heavily upon Mortimer.

"Why, Oswald! Ah! I see I should say Sir Oswald. What brings you here? Some good news, I trust. Has my ransom been collected?"

"It has been collected, Sir Edmund," Oswald said, as they shook hands, "but the king, who refused altogether to pay your ransom, as he did Lord Grey's, has forbidden the money, raised partly by your tenants and partly by the tenants of your nephew, to be handed over. 'Tis clear that he views you as an enemy; and has, indeed, ventured to declare his belief that your capture by Glendower was a thing arranged, beforehand."

"He lies!" Sir Edmund exclaimed angrily. "We fought stoutly and, had it not been for the treachery of the Welsh bowmen, should have won the day.

"Then how stands the matter, Sir Oswald, and how is it that you are here?"

Oswald then related the purport of his mission, and gave Mortimer some messages with which Hotspur had charged him, on the evening before he started.

"Assuredly I will join," Sir Edmund exclaimed, when Oswald brought his story to a conclusion. "Have I not suffered enough by keeping a force on foot, by having my lands harried and my vassals slain, in order to support Henry's claims to the kingdom of Wales, only to be suspected of treachery? Had I intended to join Glendower, I should have done so a year before; and with my force and his, we could have kept Henry at bay. Why should I have kept up the pretext of loyalty, when there was nought to have prevented my joining Glendower? Why should I have fought him, at the cost of the lives of some twelve hundred of my men, when I could have marched them into his camp, as friends? Why should I suffer nine months of close imprisonment, at the hands of an ally?

"Henry lied, and knew that he lied, when he brought such a charge against me. He wished to be able to work his will on the young earl, and maybe to murder him as he murdered Richard, without there being one powerful enough to lift his voice to condemn the murder. All is at an end between us, and henceforth I am his open enemy, as he is mine; and would be heart and soul with the Percys in the overthrow of Henry, even if my nephew were not concerned, and did the earl purpose, himself, to grasp the crown."

"Glendower is below, Sir Edmund, and will himself speak to you; but he thought that it were best that I should first open the matter to you."

A quarter of an hour later the keeper of the hold came up, and said that the prince bade Sir Edmund to descend and speak with him. As they entered the room where Glendower was waiting, the latter glanced at Oswald, inquiringly.

"The matter is settled," the latter said. "Sir Edmund will join us, with heart and hand."

"I am indeed glad to hear it, Sir Oswald.

"Sir Edmund Mortimer," he went on, courteously, "hitherto we have regarded each other as enemies; henceforth we are friends, and you are my guest and not my prisoner. I have thought it over, and methinks that you must tarry here, till we have certain news of the day on which the Percys will set on foot their enterprise. It would not be safe for you to return to your estates, until you are in a position to call your vassals to arms at once; for the king, were he to hear that you were at Ludlow, might call on the lieutenants of the western counties, and the owners of all the castles, to attack you at once. Therefore, until it is time to strike, it were best that you should remain with me.

"I do not propose that you should accompany me on my expeditions, for to do so might do harm across the border. I will, therefore, assign you a suitable house at Aberystwith, with such attendance and furnishing as are due to a guest of your quality.

"The prospect seems to be a fair one. The northern lords, aided by the Scots, should by themselves be a match for any gathering Henry could collect at short notice; and, joined by my forces and yours, should surely be able to overthrow all opposition."

"So it appears to me," Sir Edmund said. "'Tis indeed a powerful confederation and, if all goes well, ought to leave no option to the usurper but to die in battle, or to fly to France."

"Will you return with us to Aberystwith, Sir Oswald?" Glendower presently asked the young knight.

"I will ride straight for England, with your permission," Oswald said. "I am already thirty miles on my way, and the Percys urged me to return as soon as possible."

"So be it. As soon as we have dined, an officer and four horsemen will be in readiness to ride with you, as an escort."

A week later Oswald reached Alnwick. He was the bearer of letters from Glendower and Mortimer, and was able to report the complete success of his mission. As a mark of his satisfaction, the earl ordered a deed of gift to be made to him, of a large strip of land extending over the hills between Stoubes and Yardhope.

"Some day," he said, as he handed the document to him, "you will be master of Yardhope, and by thus joining that feu to that of Stoubes, you will have an estate that will make you a power in the upper glades of Reddesdale and Coquetdale; and will support the dignity of a knight banneret, which I now bestow upon you, and also appoint you a deputy warden of the marches, with power of life and death over all marauders, reivers, and outlaws. I have long felt that it would be well that there should be one who, in case of necessity, could raise a hundred spears; and so prevent bodies of marauders, from the other side of the border, making sudden irruptions into the dales; and from what I have heard of you, from Sir Henry, I am sure that you will carry out the charge most worthily."

The new acquisition would not very largely increase Oswald's revenues, for the greater portion of the grant was hill and moor. Nevertheless, there were a good many houses and small villages scattered in the dales, and it was these that raised the tract of land to the value of a knight's feu.

In point of position, however, it was a large addition. As a knight banneret, with the castle of Stoubes at one end of his holding, and the hold of Yardhope at the other, he would occupy an important position on the border; and could raise at least a hundred spears among his tenants, in addition to the men-at-arms of the two strongholds.

Three days later Hotspur released the whole of his Scottish prisoners; and sent them, under escort, to the border. The Percys now began, in earnest, their preparations for war. For greater convenience Hotspur went down to Morpeth, while the earl betook himself to Berwick-on-Tweed, where he could confer more easily with his Scottish allies; who, on their part, were carrying out the condition on which they had been released without ransom; namely, that they would join their forces to those of the Percys.

Oswald made another journey to Wales, this time by ship from Carlisle to Aberystwith, and there acquainted Glendower and Mortimer with the preparations that had been made, assuring them that the rising would take place at the end of May. He also asked Glendower to raise as large an army as possible, without delay; and Sir Edmund Mortimer to betake himself at once to Hereford, there to raise his banner and summon his vassals, and those of the Earl of March, to join him--the king having, on his return from his last expedition, entered Ludlow, seized Mortimer's plate and other property, and appointed to the governorship of Ludlow a knight on whose devotion he could rely.

Chapter 21: Shrewsbury.

The Percys' preparations could not be carried on without exciting attention; and in March the king, seeing that the open defiance of his authority, by the release of the Scottish prisoners, would assuredly be followed by armed rebellion, which the Douglas would probably have pledged himself to aid as the condition of his release, began, on his side, to make similar preparations. Levies were called out, and the Prince of Wales was appointed to the command of the Welsh marches, and the governorship of Wales.

Towards the end of June Douglas, faithful to his agreement, crossed the frontier; and was at once joined by Hotspur, with the force he had gathered. Hotspur's father was lying sick at Berwick, but was to follow, as speedily as possible, with the army collected in the north of the county, and from Dunbar's estates.

It had been arranged that Glendower should meet the allies at Lichfield; and on his being joined by his uncle, the Earl of Westmoreland, with his following, Hotspur marched south. His intention was, after effecting a junction with Glendower, to march and give battle to the army with which Henry and the Prince of Wales were advancing against him. At Lichfield, however, he learned that Glendower had not completed his preparations in sufficient time to join him. He therefore changed his direction, and made for Shrewsbury, towards which place Glendower was marching.

Percy's array had swollen as he went south. He had been joined by a number of archers, from Cheshire, and by other adherents of the late king; these regarding the war as an attempt, not to place the Earl of March upon the throne, but to overthrow the usurper who had dethroned their king.

Oswald rode with sixty spearmen from his own estate; while his father, with thirty men from Yardhope, rode in his company. Both regarded the failure of Glendower to come to the place appointed as a serious misfortune.

"Of course," Oswald said, "if he joins us at Shrewsbury, before the king comes up, it will not matter much; and indeed would be, in one respect, the better. Mortimer with his force will be coming on; and though he is scarce likely to arrive at Shrewsbury in time for the battle, for he could not leave Wales, to summon his levies to the field, until the Prince of Wales had drawn off his force and marched to join his father; his reinforcement, afterwards, will fill up the gaps in our ranks, and be a great assistance, should Henry be able to rally another army in the Midlands. He cannot hope to do so before we reach London."

"That sounds fairly, Oswald, but 'tis always better to carry out the plans you have made; and this absence of Glendower, at the point arranged, to my mind augurs ill."

Henry was an able general. Believing that the Percys would make for the Welsh border, he had posted himself at Burton-on-Trent; but as soon as he heard that they had changed their course he started for Shrewsbury, and marched so quickly that he arrived there before Hotspur, thus throwing himself between the Percys and the Welsh.

Hotspur, on arriving near the town, was enraged at hearing that Glendower had not arrived, according to his promise. The king's army was encamped on the eastern side of the town, and the northern forces took post a short distance away. That night Hotspur sent a document into the royal camp, declaring Henry to be forsworn and perjured: in the first place because he had sworn, under Holy Gospel, that he would claim nothing but his own proper inheritance, and that Richard should reign to the end of his life; secondly, because he had raised taxes and other impositions, contrary to his oath, and by his own arbitrary power; thirdly, because he had caused King Richard to be kept in the castle of Pontefract, without meat, drink, or fire, whereof he perished of hunger, thirst, and cold. There were other clauses, some of them regarding his conduct to Sir Edmund Mortimer. The claims of the young Earl of March to the throne were also set forward, and the document ended with a defiance.

Henry simply sent, as reply, that he had no time to lose in writing; but that he would, in the morning, prove in battle whose claims were false and feigned.

Nevertheless, in the morning, when the two armies were arrayed in the order of battle, the king sent the Abbot of Shrewsbury to propose an amicable arrangement. Hotspur and Douglas, however, rejected the offer. The trumpets then blew on either side, and the armies joined battle.

Their numbers were about equal. Each consisted of some fourteen thousand men. Douglas and Hotspur had taken their place in the centre of their line, having behind them a party of their best knights. These charged with fury down upon the king's standard, which stood in the centre of his array. Hotspur and Douglas, his former rival, were accounted two of the best knights in Christendom, and the fury of their charge was irresistible. The centre of the royal line was cleft in sunder, the king's guards were at once dispersed; and, had not Henry taken the precaution of arraying himself in plain armour, while two of his knights had put on royal surcoats, the battle would at once have been decided.

As it was, the two knights were both killed, as were the Earl of Stafford and Sir Walter Blount. The royal standard was overthrown, and the young Prince of Wales sorely wounded in the face.

He had already shown signs of great military talent; and, in spite of his wound, now showed a courage and presence of mind that justified the confidence his father had shown, in giving him important commands. He rode hither and thither among the disorganized troops, saw that the gap in the centre was again closed up, and was ever to be met where the fight was hottest.

The impetuous charge of Hotspur and Douglas was the ruin of themselves, and their army. Had they paused until their troops had advanced close to the enemy, and the mounted men-at-arms were all ranged closely behind them, and in a position to support them, the fight would assuredly have speedily terminated in their favour; but before these arrived the royal army had closed its ranks, and the rebel leaders, with all their principal knights, were cut off from the main body. In vain the men of the north tried to cut their way through the southern ranks, and to come to the assistance of their chiefs; who, surrounded now by the English knights and men-at-arms, were fighting desperately against overwhelming numbers.

An hour after the battle began, many parties of Welshmen came up and joined in the conflict; but the absence of leaders, and the loss of their respective captains, Hotspur and Douglas, paralysed the efforts of the Northumbrians and the Scottish contingent. Yet both fought stoutly, and suffered very heavy losses.

For upwards of two hours Hotspur maintained the unequal fight; but at length an arrow pierced Hotspur's visor, and he fell dead from his horse. Further resistance was useless, and the survivors of the group, which had been reduced to a mere handful, surrendered. For another half hour the main battle raged; then came the news that Hotspur was killed, and Douglas and Westmoreland prisoners; the English horsemen dashed down on the flanks of the northern line, the spearmen pressed forward, and the Scotch and Northumbrians broke and fled.

When the knights first charged, Oswald had been with his own following, and a hundred other horsemen, on the left flank. As soon as he saw what had happened, he endeavoured to ride round the right flank of the royal army; but was met by a much larger force of men-at-arms and, after hard fighting, driven back. Oswald himself, with Roger on one hand and his father on the other, had several times hewed his way deep into the enemy's squadron; and would have been cut off, had not the Yardhope moss troopers spurred furiously in to the rescue, and brought them all off again.

Several times the charge was renewed, but ineffectually. Half the rebel army had been killed; and when, at last, the infantry broke, and it was clear that there was no more to be done, Oswald, who was wounded in half a dozen places, called the survivors of his troop to follow him; and, with his party, rode off in good order.

A mile from the field they halted for a few minutes. Not one of them but had been more or less severely wounded in the desperate melee. They now took off their armour, and bandaged each other's wounds; and then, mounting again, they rode off.

"What do you say, Father," Oswald asked; "shall we circle round, and join Glendower? We know that his army is close at hand and, were they to attack tonight, they should win an easy victory; for the king's men have suffered well nigh as sorely as we have."

"No, Oswald; we have done enough. We have not been fighting for the Earl of March. We have been simply following our feudal lord, as we were bound to do. He is dead, and we have nought to do with this quarrel. What is it to us whether March or Henry is king?"

They were not pursued. The greater part of the English cavalry were exhausted by their exertions against Hotspur and Douglas. Their loss was extremely heavy, and those in a condition to pursue took up the comparatively easy work of cutting down the flying footmen.

The battle had been a disastrous one, for both sides. Their losses were about even, the number who fell altogether being put at ten thousand men. With Douglas, the Earl of Westmoreland, Baron of Kinderton, Sir Richard Vernon, and other knights were captured. Westmoreland, Kinderton, and Vernon were at once executed on the field of battle, as rebels; but Douglas, as a foreign knight, was simply viewed as a prisoner of war, and was kindly treated.

Glendower took no advantage of the opportunity for striking a blow at the royal army; and instead of attacking it, when spent by fatigue and encumbered with wounds, retired at once to Wales. Had he, instead of doing this, marched to meet Sir Edmund Mortimer, who was hurrying forward with a powerful array, the united force would have been fully double the strength of the English army; and a great commander would, at once, have fought a battle that would probably have altered the whole course of events in England. Glendower's conduct here showed that, although an able partisan leader in an irregular warfare, he had no claim whatever to be considered a great general.

Travelling rapidly, Oswald and his party crossed the Tyne; and hearing that the earl, now recovered from his illness, was marching down with his army to join his son, they rode to meet him. It was a painful duty that Oswald had to discharge, and the old earl, when he heard of the defeat of the army, the death of the son to whom he was deeply attached, and the capture of his brother, the Earl of Westmoreland, gave way to despair, dismissed his army to their homes at once, and retired, completely broken down in body and spirit, to his castle at Warkworth.

So depressed was he that when royal messengers arrived, summoning him in the king's name to surrender, and journey with him to London, he instantly obeyed. When questioned by the king why he had displayed the banner of revolt against him, he said he had done so on the urging of Hotspur; and the king, who was always inclined to leniency, when leniency was safe, pardoned him, and permitted him to retain his dignity and estates.

Oswald speedily recovered from his wounds, but his father suffered much.

"I have fought my last fight, Oswald," he said, when his son rode over to see him, a few days after their return from the south. "I say not that I am about to die, but only that methinks I shall never be able to wield sword manfully again. I have talked the matter over with your mother, and she agrees with me that it were well that I handed over Yardhope to you. I do not mean that I should leave the old place--for generations my fathers have lived and died here, and I would fain do the same--but that I should hand over to you the feu, and you should take oath for it to Northumberland, and lead its retainers in the field. Were it that there was a chance of another raid by the Bairds, I would still maintain my hold myself; but their power was altogether broken, at Homildon.

"Moreover, the border Scots and we are at peace now, as we have not been so long as memories run; seeing that we have fought side by side against the King of England, and have suffered the same misfortune in defeat; therefore, I can hang up my sword.

"But for you there may be more fighting. From what I know of the old earl, I am sure that he will never forgive Hotspur's death; and although, at present, he is reinstated in his estates, there can be no doubt that the king will strike further blows against the power of the Percys. Northumberland is a valiant soldier, tenacious in his purposes, and lasting in his hatreds. Had it not been that he was utterly broken by the news that we brought him, he would assuredly have marched down with his army, and tried to join Glendower and Mortimer; and at least have died fighting, the end that he would best like. I doubt not that we shall see his banner raised again, ere long."

"I hope not, Father. The undertaking would be desperate."

"However that may be, Oswald, as I can no longer render service for the feu, I wish to hand it over to you. 'Tis but a nominal change, but I should like to see the estate yours. I and my fathers have held our own, and were content to do so, adding somewhat to our means by such plunder as we could carry off from Scotland; but you have greatly advanced the family, and as a deputy warden of the marches, it is as well that Yardhope should be added to your holding. I should be glad, too, to have you known as Sir Oswald Forster of Yardhope, and not as Sir Oswald Forster of Stoubes; and in time, if things go well with you, I charge you to build a castle here, in place of this hold; which has been good enough for plain men like myself and my father, but which is no fit residence for the estate you now hold.

"I don't mean to say that I wish you always to live here, for, maybe, Stoubes is a more pleasant abode, standing in a fair country, and with the climate somewhat less hard than this; but I should like you to come up here, at times, and to be known as Forster of Yardhope."

"I will carry out your wishes, Father; but it would please me more for things to remain as they have been."

"My plan is best, lad. I shall be seneschal here for you, and little will be changed; save that you will ride at the head of the retainers, instead of myself. 'Tis not meet that I should hold the feu, when I can no longer render due service.

"Your mother is wholly of opinion that I have done enough of fighting for my life, and should trouble myself no longer with raidings and wars. Your mother has shown sound judgment, and her advice has generally been good; though I never fully recognized this, till I saw what great good had come of her wishing you to learn to read and write; for it is to that, to no small extent, that you owe your rapid rise and present dignity."

Accordingly, a few days later, Oswald rode with his father to Warkworth, to which castle the earl had returned after his visit to England. At the request of John Forster he received back the feu from him, and appointed his son to it. This done, Oswald rode to pay a visit to his cousins; while his father returned to Yardhope, with two retainers he had brought with him.

Oswald had not seen Adam Armstrong, since the latter had come to Yardhope after the rescue of his daughters; and he was received by him with the greatest warmth, as also by Allan, who, although now nearly recovered from his wounds, had, fortunately for himself, not gained sufficient strength to be able to accompany Douglas, either to Homildon or in his march into England to join Percy.

The girls were out when he rode up; but, upon their return, both showed the greatest pleasure, Jessie being the most demonstrative in her welcome.

"It has always been a sore subject with me, Oswald," Allan said, "that you should have ridden away in that gallant enterprise to rescue my sisters, while I was lying here helpless; and knew, indeed, nought of it, until after you had taken them safely to Yardhope.

"Ah! Roger, I am glad to see you again; and to thank you, too, for the share you took in it."

"In faith, Master Allan, there are no great thanks due. It was but a poor affair, and I had but one opportunity, and that not worth naming, of striking a hearty blow. It seems to me that these things are never fairly divided. Both in that adventure, and at Homildon, I scarce struck a blow; while in that affair in Wales, and at Shrewsbury, there was even more fighting than I cared for. I had to be nursed like a child after the first, and I am still stiff from the wounds that I got in the second.

"There should be reason in such matters. It vexed me sorely that we had to ride away from the Bairds, without striking a few good blows in part payment of their raid here."

"I am very glad that you did not have to do so," Janet said. "I think there was quite enough excitement in it, and especially as we went down that rope; though indeed, you are so strong that I felt that I was quite safe with you."

Roger laughed.

"I could have carried two of you; and sooth, you did not show your confidence at the time, for you held on so tightly to the rope that I began to think that we should never get to the bottom."

"You told me to hold tight," Janet said, indignantly.

"Yes, yes, that was natural enough. The difficulty was, that you would not let go, and at each knot it was as much as I could do to get you to let it slide through your fingers."

"Very well, Master Roger. Then I shall take care not to let you lower me down a rope again."

"I trust there will never be the need," Roger laughed; "but indeed, although your weight was as nothing, I felt uneasy myself as we went down; for I feared that I might grip you too tightly, seeing that I am altogether unaccustomed to the handling of girls."

"Well, I suppose, Roger," Jessie said, "that now the wars are over, you will be marrying and settling down."

"I don't know how that might be," Roger replied, slowly. "I do not say that the matter has never entered my mind; and seeing that I am now seven-and-thirty, 'tis one that should not be much longer delayed. I mean not that I have ever thought as to who should be the woman, but I have thought whether, when the time comes that Sir Oswald takes him a wife, it would not be well that I should do the same.

"But I know not how I stand. The abbot of Alnwick has, so far, allowed me to go out into the world, to unfrock myself, and to become a man-at-arms instead of a peaceful monk; but I have not been dispensed from my vows of celibacy and, were I to marry, the matter might be taken up by the Church, and I might be put to many and sore penances, and punishments, for the breach of them."

The others all laughed at the seriousness with which Roger had answered the girl's jesting remark.

"It is a matter that I have never thought of before, Roger," Oswald said; "but assuredly it would, as you say, be fitting and right that, when I take a mistress, you should do so also--like master like man, you know. Since your thoughts have been turned that way, I will see the abbot, next time I go to Alnwick, and lay the case before him. Of a truth you have made a most excellent man-at-arms, and 'tis equally certain that you were an exceedingly bad monk. It would doubtless be well that you should obtain a complete absolution from your vows; for although I am sure that the good abbot regards you, now, as altogether beyond his control, and would take no steps against you were he to hear of your marriage, it might not be so in the case of his successor. He is an old man, and the next abbot may be of a very different character; and, looking through the books of the convent, he might say, 'What has become of Brother Roger? I see no record of his death.'

"Then, pushing matters further, he might discover your backsliding, and might summon you before him, and there is no saying what pains and penalties he might inflict upon you."

Roger moved uneasily in his seat.

"Do not speak of such a thing, I pray you, master--imprisonment in a cell, flagellation, nay, even worse might befall me at the hands of a rigorous abbot; for in truth, nought could well be more serious than the offences that I have already committed; and he might hold that, even though the present abbot had been back-ward in taking notice of the matter, this in no way would absolve him from doing his duty.

"And indeed, as it is, it was to Hotspur that he gave permission for me to go out into the world. Hotspur is dead, and there is nought but my own word in the matter."

"That, at any rate, I can put right, Roger, by going myself to the abbot; and learning, from his lips, that he did give that permission to Hotspur. Moreover, I received it from Hotspur's own lips. Still, it would be useful for me to obtain, from the abbot, a letter giving full absolution for all offences committed, up to the present time."

"That would be a great thing," Roger said eagerly. "'Tis a matter that I have often turned over in my mind, when on a long day's ride, and I have thought of what might happen were a new man to become abbot of Alnwick; but such an absolution would assuredly go for much. No one can doubt, more especially an abbot, that absolution by an abbot is most effectual; and that the offences committed before it are wholly wiped out, and cannot be revived."

"It would be best to obtain total absolution from your vows. Can the abbot grant that, Roger?"

"'Tis a moot question," Roger replied. "Many affirm that he can do so, and assuredly many abbots have exercised that power; others again hold that, although abbots cannot lawfully do so, bishops can; while a few maintain that even these are incapable, and that nothing short of the absolution by the Holy Father himself is of avail. Still, whatever be the true state of things, I should be well satisfied with an abbot's absolution, and still more so by a bishop's; for though, were a great prince concerned, someone interested might contest the matter, none would be likely to do so in the case of a man-at-arms or an esquire."

"Very well, Roger. Then I will endeavour to obtain a full absolution from your vows, by the abbot; and should he decline to give them I will, when I next see the earl, pray him, in consideration of the good services that you have rendered, to obtain it for you from the bishop."

"And you have not yourself thought of marrying, Oswald?" Adam Armstrong said.

"Nay, Uncle. I came of age but a few days since, and it will be time to think of taking me a wife four or five years hence. So, until these troubles have wholly ceased, it were better, methinks, for a knight to remain unwed than to take a wife, with the risk of leaving her a young widow."

"In that case, Oswald, methinks there would be little marrying in Northumberland; for, saving short truces, and these but ill observed, there is ever trouble on the border."

"I speak not of that," Oswald replied. "Doubtless we shall always be subject to border raids, on both sides, and even to serious wars between the two countries; but I speak not of that, but of troubles in England. 'Tis natural to fight when English-men and Scotchmen meet, arrayed in battle; but when Englishmen meet English-men, 'tis terrible indeed; and though the slaughter at Shrewsbury was great beyond measure, who yet can say that the fire is extinguished? As long as one may be called to arms again, by the earl, it is, in good sooth, better to remain single than to have to ride to the wars, leaving the young wife behind."

"Spoken very wisely and well, Oswald," Adam Armstrong laughed. "'Tis well to argue as to policy; but such arguments go for nought, as soon as a man's heart is fixed on any particular woman."

"It may be so, Uncle; but as I have never thought of marriage, I am able to look at the matter dispassionately."

"Ah! Well, the time will come, Oswald, and you will then speedily come to consider that there are other things than the reasonableness of waiting to be con-sidered.

"By the way, I trust that, should England invade Scotland again by the valley of the Esk, you will not forget our debt to the Bairds. Though I lamented the disaster at Homildon, where many of my friends and acquaintances fell; I could not but feel that the death of William Baird, and so many of his kin, was a relief, indeed, to me. I have strengthened my hold, as you see, but I should have been ever obliged to re-main on guard. The Bairds never forgive nor forget, and the manner in which they were tricked out of their captives must have discomposed them sorely, and rankled in their minds; and, sooner or later, they would have tried to wipe out the memory in blood. I wonder that they had not done it before Homildon, but doubtless they had other matters in hand.

"Now I can live in peace; but I, too, have not forgotten the injuries I have suf-fered at their hands, and should rejoice, greatly, did I hear that their stronghold had been levelled to the ground."

"I hope that it will be long before our kings march against Scotland again. The ill success of all our efforts should have taught them that, do what they will, they will never conquer Scotland; and Henry is not likely to court another failure, such as he met with two years since. 'Tis not like the wars with the Welsh. They are a different people, speaking in a different language, while we and the lowland Scots are of one blood and one language--scarce a noble in Scotland who is not of Norman descent--and a quarrel between us seems, to me, almost as bad as a civil war."

"I hope that all will come to think so, some day, Oswald; but as long as the two kingdoms stand apart, with various interests and different alliances, it will hardly be likely that there will be a permanent peace between them."

"That is so," Oswald agreed. "'Tis the part that Scotland plays by her alliance with France, and the aid she gives her by always choosing the time when we are fighting there to fall upon us, that keeps the trouble afoot. If Scotland would hold herself aloof from France, I see no reason why we should interfere with her in any way."

"No good has ever come to us from such alliance. No French army has ever gone to Scotland, to aid her when pressed by Englishmen. France uses Scotland but as a cat's paw, with which to annoy and weaken England."

"That may be so; but you must remember that France does aid Scotland, when she keeps the main army of England busily occupied."

"Yes; but she does not fight England with that intent. She simply fights to gain back the provinces she has lost, and is ready to make peace when it suits, wholly regardless of the interest of Scotland."

"France is never to be trusted," Oswald said. "Glendower made a treaty with her, a few years ago, and what good has it done to him? Why, when he needed her aid the most, she had made a truce with England. 'Tis whispered that she made a treaty with the Percys, and what good came of it? She is ever ready to make treaties, but never observes them, unless it is to her plain interest to do so."

"I suppose it is with nations as it is with individuals, Oswald. Selfishness has a large share in the management of affairs. France, being a powerful country, is glad enough, when pressed by the English, to have diversions made for her, whether in Scotland or Ireland; but she has no idea of putting herself out, for the sake of her allies, when she desires peace with England."

France had indeed been quick to take advantage of the trouble caused to Henry by the rising in the north. While he was gathering his army, although there was a truce with England, a French expedition, in which many of the royal princes took part, had invaded Guienne, captured several castles held by the English adherents, made frequent descents on our coast, plundered every ship they met with, captured a whole fleet of merchantmen, taken the islands of Guernsey and Jersey and, while Henry was fighting at Shrewsbury, landed near Plymouth and plundered the whole country round. On the news reaching them of the result of the battle of Shrewsbury, they at once burned Plymouth to the ground, and then, re-embarking, sailed for France. All remonstrances on the part of Henry were met by declarations that these raids were carried on without the knowledge of the French king, and were greatly against his inclinations, which were wholly for the strictest observance of the truce.

Nevertheless, a few months later, the Count of Saint Pol landed a force in the Isle of Wight; but the people of the island rose in arms, and defeated the invaders, who sailed hastily away.

Although, having other matters in hand, Henry professed to believe the French king's assurances; the sailors and ship masters were in no way content to suffer unresistingly, and the men of the seaports of the east coast, and of Plymouth and Fowey, banded themselves together, and carried on war on their own account; capturing several fleets of ships, loaded with wine and other valuable commodities; burning the coast towns; and making several raids into the interior of France, and carrying off much plunder.

Enraged at this retaliation, the French incited the Flemings, Dutch, and Hollanders to cruise against the English; and these, sailing in great ships, executed so many atrocities upon English crews and ships that, later, Henry himself sent out a fleet, under his second son, who executed his commission, effectually destroying ships, burning towns, and putting the people to the sword without mercy.

Thus the breaches of the peace by the French recoiled terribly upon themselves, and they suffered vastly greater loss than they had inflicted upon the English.

From the time when he let slip the opportunities, both of joining Hotspur and of falling on the royal army after their victory, Glendower's power declined. For a time he continued to capture castles, and to carry out raids across the border, but gradually he was driven back to his mountain strongholds. His followers lost heart. He became a fugitive, and died on the 20th of September, 1415, in the sixty-first year of his age, at the house of one of his married daughters, whether at Scudamore or Mornington is unknown.

Mortimer died in Harlech Castle, during the time it was besieged by the English. It is said that his death was caused by depression and grief at the misfortunes that had befallen him.

The Earl of Northumberland, as John Forster had anticipated, raised the standard of revolt in 1405, in concert with the Archbishop of York and some other nobles; but before he could join these with his forces, they had been forced to surrender to the king, who had marched north with a great army. The archbishop and some of his associates were executed, and the earl, finding himself unable to oppose so great a force, fled into Scotland. Alnwick surrendered without resistance, and Warkworth after a siege of eight days. Berwick was captured, and its governor and several knights executed.

Escaping from Scotland, where he feared that he might be seized and surrendered to England, the earl sailed to Wales, and for some little time stayed with Glendower; then he crossed to the Continent, and in 1408 landed in Yorkshire and again raised his standard. The sheriff of the county called out the levies, and attacked him at Branham Moor, where the old earl was killed and his followers defeated.

In 1415 the king, being on the eve of war with France, and anxious to obtain the goodwill and support of the Northumbrians, restored Hotspur's son, who had been for years a fugitive in Scotland, to the estates and honours of his father and grandfather.

Fortunate it was, for Oswald, that the capture of his fellow conspirators caused the earl to retreat, in 1405, without giving battle. The young knight had, at his summons, called out his tenants, and with them and his retainers had joined Percy. As soon as the latter decided to fly to Scotland, his force scattered, and Oswald returned home with his following.

He took no part in the final rising. Before this took place he had married his cousin, Janet. His father lived to be present at the wedding, but died the following year; and, in accordance with his wishes, Oswald took up his abode at Yardhope, which he largely added to, and strongly fortified. Here his mother lived with him until her death, ten years later.

Oswald offered to Roger the command of his castle at Stoubes, but the burly squire preferred staying at Yardhope, with his master. He himself had taken a wife, the daughter of one of the principal tenants on the estate, on the same day that Oswald married Janet.

His uncle, after the surrender of Alnwick, lived at Yardhope until, at the return of Hotspur's son as Earl of Northumberland, he resumed his old position as captain of the garrison, and maintained it until his death.

The Codes Of Hammurabi And Moses
W. W. Davies

QTY

The discovery of the Hammurabi Code is one of the greatest achievements of archaeology, and is of paramount interest, not only to the student of the Bible, but also to all those interested in ancient history...

Religion   ISBN: *1-59462-338-4*   Pages:132
                                              MSRP $12.95

The Theory of Moral Sentiments
Adam Smith

QTY

This work from 1749. contains original theories of conscience amd moral judgment and it is the foundation for systemof morals.

Philosophy ISBN: *1-59462-777-0*   Pages:536
                                              MSRP $19.95

Jessica's First Prayer
Hesba Stretton

QTY

In a screened and secluded corner of one of the many railway-bridges which span the streets of London there could be seen a few years ago, from five o'clock every morning until half past eight, a tidily set-out coffee-stall, consisting of a trestle and board, upon which stood two large tin cans, with a small fire of charcoal burning under each so as to keep the coffee boiling during the early hours of the morning when the work-people were thronging into the city on their way to their daily toil...

                                              Pages:84
Childrens   ISBN: *1-59462-373-2*   *MSRP $9.95*

My Life and Work
Henry Ford

QTY

Henry Ford revolutionized the world with his implementation of mass production for the Model T automobile. Gain valuable business insight into his life and work with his own auto-biography... "We have only started on our development of our country we have not as yet, with all our talk of wonderful progress, done more than scratch the surface. The progress has been wonderful enough but..."

                                              Pages:300
Biographies/ ISBN: *1-59462-198-5*   *MSRP $21.95*

The Art of Cross-Examination
Francis Wellman

QTY

I presume it is the experience of every author, after his first book is published upon an important subject, to be almost overwhelmed with a wealth of ideas and illustrations which could readily have been included in his book, and which to his own mind, at least, seem to make a second edition inevitable. Such certainly was the case with me; and when the first edition had reached its sixth impression in five months, I rejoiced to learn that it seemed to my publishers that the book had met with a sufficiently favorable reception to justify a second and considerably enlarged edition. ...

Reference   **ISBN: *1-59462-647-2***

Pages:412
MSRP $19.95

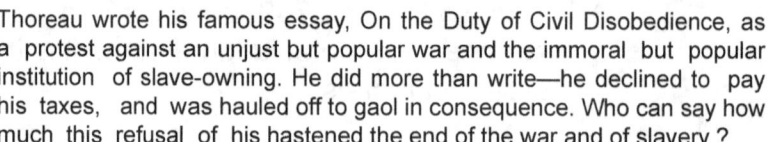

On the Duty of Civil Disobedience
Henry David Thoreau

QTY

Thoreau wrote his famous essay, On the Duty of Civil Disobedience, as a protest against an unjust but popular war and the immoral but popular institution of slave-owning. He did more than write—he declined to pay his taxes, and was hauled off to gaol in consequence. Who can say how much this refusal of his hastened the end of the war and of slavery ?

Law   **ISBN: *1-59462-747-9***

Pages:48
MSRP $7.45

Dream Psychology Psychoanalysis for Beginners
Sigmund Freud

QTY

Sigmund Freud, born Sigismund Schlomo Freud (May 6, 1856 - September 23, 1939), was a Jewish-Austrian neurologist and psychiatrist who co-founded the psychoanalytic school of psychology. Freud is best known for his theories of the unconscious mind, especially involving the mechanism of repression; his redefinition of sexual desire as mobile and directed towards a wide variety of objects; and his therapeutic techniques, especially his understanding of transference in the therapeutic relationship and the presumed value of dreams as sources of insight into unconscious desires.

Psychology   **ISBN: *1-59462-905-6***

Pages:196
MSRP $15.45

The Miracle of Right Thought
Orison Swett Marden

QTY

Believe with all of your heart that you will do what you were made to do. When the mind has once formed the habit of holding cheerful, happy, prosperous pictures, it will not be easy to form the opposite habit. It does not matter how improbable or how far away this realization may see, or how dark the prospects may be, if we visualize them as best we can, as vividly as possible, hold tenaciously to them and vigorously struggle to attain them, they will gradually become actualized, realized in the life. But a desire, a longing without endeavor, a yearning abandoned or held indifferently will vanish without realization.

Self Help   **ISBN: *1-59462-644-8***

Pages:360
MSRP $25.45

QTY

The Rosicrucian Cosmo-Conception Mystic Christianity by *Max Heindel* ISBN: *1-59462-188-8* **$38.95**
The Rosicrucian Cosmo-conception is not dogmatic, neither does it appeal to any other authority than the reason of the student. It is: not controversial, but is: sent forth in the, hope that it may help to clear... New Age/Religion Pages 646

Abandonment To Divine Providence by *Jean-Pierre de Caussade* ISBN: *1-59462-228-0* **$25.95**
"The Rev. Jean Pierre de Caussade was one of the most remarkable spiritual writers of the Society of Jesus in France in the 18th Century. His death took place at Toulouse in 1751. His works have gone through many editions and have been republished... Inspirational/Religion Pages 400

Mental Chemistry by *Charles Haanel* ISBN: *1-59462-192-6* **$23.95**
Mental Chemistry allows the change of material conditions by combining and appropriately utilizing the power of the mind. Much like applied chemistry creates something new and unique out of careful combinations of chemicals the mastery of mental chemistry... New Age Pages 354

The Letters of Robert Browning and Elizabeth Barret Barrett 1845-1846 vol II ISBN: *1-59462-193-4* **$35.95**
by *Robert Browning* and *Elizabeth Barrett* Biographies Pages 596

Gleanings In Genesis (volume I) by *Arthur W. Pink* ISBN: *1-59462-130-6* **$27.45**
Appropriately has Genesis been termed "the seed plot of the Bible" for in it we have, in germ form, almost all of the great doctrines which are afterwards fully developed in the books of Scripture which follow... Religion/Inspirational Pages 420

The Master Key by *L. W. de Laurence* ISBN: *1-59462-001-6* **$30.95**
In no branch of human knowledge has there been a more lively increase of the spirit of research during the past few years than in the study of Psychology, Concentration and Mental Discipline. The requests for authentic lessons in Thought Control, Mental Discipline and... New Age/Business Pages 422

The Lesser Key Of Solomon Goetia by *L. W. de Laurence* ISBN: *1-59462-092-X* **$9.95**
This translation of the first book of the "Lernegton" which is now for the first time made accessible to students of Talismanic Magic was done, after careful collation and edition, from numerous Ancient Manuscripts in Hebrew, Latin, and French... New Age/Occult Pages 92

Rubaiyat Of Omar Khayyam by *Edward Fitzgerald* ISBN:*1-59462-332-5* **$13.95**
Edward Fitzgerald, whom the world has already learned, in spite of his own efforts to remain within the shadow of anonymity, to look upon as one of the rarest poets of the century, was born at Bredfield, in Suffolk, on the 31st of March, 1809. He was the third son of John Purcell... Music Pages 172

Ancient Law by *Henry Maine* ISBN: *1-59462-128-4* **$29.95**
The chief object of the following pages is to indicate some of the earliest ideas of mankind, as they are reflected in Ancient Law, and to point out the relation of those ideas to modern thought. Religion/History Pages 452

Far-Away Stories by *William J. Locke* ISBN: *1-59462-129-2* **$19.45**
"Good wine needs no bush," but a collection of mixed vintages does. And this book is just such a collection. Some of the stories I do not want to remain buried for ever in the museum files of dead magazine-numbers an author's not unpardonable vanity..." Fiction Pages 272

Life of David Crockett by *David Crockett* ISBN: *1-59462-250-7* **$27.45**
"Colonel David Crockett was one of the most remarkable men of the times in which he lived. Born in humble life, but gifted with a strong will, an indomitable courage, and unremitting perseverance... Biographies/New Age Pages 424

Lip-Reading by *Edward Nitchie* ISBN: *1-59462-206-X* **$25.95**
Edward B. Nitchie, founder of the New York School for the Hard of Hearing, now the Nitchie School of Lip-Reading, Inc, wrote "LIP-READING Principles and Practice". The development and perfecting of this meritorious work on lip-reading was an undertaking... How-to Pages 400

A Handbook of Suggestive Therapeutics, Applied Hypnotism, Psychic Science ISBN: *1-59462-214-0* **$24.95**
by *Henry Munro* Health/New Age/Health/Self-help Pages 376

A Doll's House: and Two Other Plays by *Henrik Ibsen* ISBN: *1-59462-112-8* **$19.95**
Henrik Ibsen created this classic when in revolutionary 1848 Rome. Introducing some striking concepts in playwriting for the realist genre, this play has been studied the world over. Fiction/Classics/Plays 308

The Light of Asia by *sir Edwin Arnold* ISBN: *1-59462-204-3* **$13.95**
In this poetic masterpiece, Edwin Arnold describes the life and teachings of Buddha. The man who was to become known as Buddha to the world was born as Prince Gautama of India but he rejected the worldly riches and abandoned the reigns of power when... Religion/History/Biographies Pages 170

The Complete Works of Guy de Maupassant by *Guy de Maupassant* ISBN: *1-59462-157-8* **$16.95**
"For days and days, nights and nights, I had dreamed of that first kiss which was to consecrate our engagement, and I knew not on what spot I should put my lips..." Fiction/Classics Pages 240

The Art of Cross-Examination by *Francis L. Wellman* ISBN: *1-59462-309-0* **$26.95**
Written by a renowned trial lawyer, Wellman imparts his experience and uses case studies to explain how to use psychology to extract desired information through questioning. How-to/Science/Reference Pages 408

Answered or Unanswered? by *Louisa Vaughan* ISBN: *1-59462-248-5* **$10.95**
Miracles of Faith in China Religion Pages 112

The Edinburgh Lectures on Mental Science (1909) by *Thomas* ISBN: *1-59462-008-3* **$11.95**
This book contains the substance of a course of lectures recently given by the writer in the Queen Street Hall, Edinburgh. Its purpose is to indicate the Natural Principles governing the relation between Mental Action and Material Conditions... New Age/Psychology Pages 148

Ayesha by *H. Rider Haggard* ISBN: *1-59462-301-5* **$24.95**
Verily and indeed it is the unexpected that happens! Probably if there was one person upon the earth from whom the Editor of this, and of a certain previous history, did not expect to hear again... Classics Pages 380

Ayala's Angel by *Anthony Trollope* ISBN: *1-59462-352-X* **$29.95**
The two girls were both pretty, but Lucy who was twenty-one who supposed to be simple and comparatively unattractive, whereas Ayala was credited, as her Bombwhat romantic name might show, with poetic charm and a taste for romance. Ayala when her father died was nineteen... Fiction Pages 484

The American Commonwealth by *James Bryce* ISBN: *1-59462-286-8* **$34.45**
An interpretation of American democratic political theory. It examines political mechanics and society from the perspective of Scotsman James Bryce Politics Pages 572

Stories of the Pilgrims by *Margaret P. Pumphrey* ISBN: *1-59462-116-0* **$17.95**
This book explores pilgrims religious oppression in England as well as their escape to Holland and eventual crossing to America on the Mayflower, and their early days in New England... History Pages 268